GLYPH 2

GLYPH

JOHNS HOPKINS TEXTUAL STUDIES

2

THE JOHNS HOPKINS UNIVERSITY PRESS

Baltimore and London

The Johns Hopkins University Press, Baltimore, Maryland 21218
The Johns Hopkins Press Ltd., London
Library of Congress Catalog Card Number 77–4536
ISBN 0–8018–1993–8 (hardcover)   ISBN 0–8018–1994–6 (paperback)

STATEMENT TO CONTRIBUTORS

The Editors of *Glyph* welcome submissions concerned with the problems of representation and textuality, and contributing to the confrontation between American and Continental critical scenes. Contributors should send *two* copies of their manuscripts, accompanied by return postage, to Samuel Weber, Editor, *Glyph*, Humanities Center, The Johns Hopkins University, Baltimore, Maryland 21218. In preparing manuscripts, please refer to *A Manual of Style*, published by the University of Chicago Press, and *The Random House Dictionary*. The entire text, including extended citations and notes, should be double-spaced.

Copies of *Glyph*, both hardbound and paperback, may be ordered from The Johns Hopkins University Press, Baltimore, Maryland 21218.

The illustration on the cover and title page, an Egyptian crocodile from the Ptolemaic period, is reproduced through the courtesy of the Walters Art Gallery, Baltimore.

CONTENTS

ACKNOWLEDGMENTS

The editors would like to express their sincere gratitude to the following individuals for their assistance in the preparation of the first two volumes of *Glyph*.

To Harry Woolf for his material and spiritual generosity, particularly in the crucial planning stages.

To Timothy Murray for his first-rate technical work and his unflagging commitment in assisting in all other phases of operation.

To Richard Macksey, Jeffrey Mehlman, and Walter Michaels for monitoring both the accuracy and eloquence of our translations.

To Maria Brewer for her timely help in manuscript preparation and translation for *Glyph* 2.

GLYPH 2

ONE
THE IDIOMS OF THE *TEXT:* NOTES ON THE LANGUAGE OF PHILOSOPHY AND THE FICTIONS OF LITERATURE
Eugenio Donato

Il n'y a pas de symbole et de signe
mais un devenir signe du symbole.
Derrida

THE QUESTION of the relationship between philosophical texts and literary ones has always been uncomfortable and problematical. The problem, in fact, from Plato's expulsion of the poet from the ideal city-state to a "text" like *Glas*, has a long history. It would not be exaggerated to say that the history of the question coincides with a certain history of philosophical discourse at least as we know it within a certain Western tradition.

Having started with such a generalization, let me hasten to add that in my remarks I shall have neither the pretentions to address myself to the history of the problem nor the audacity to offer a solution. I should like simply to suggest by a quick and partial reading of a number of texts a possible form that the question might take today for a literary critic.

If the problem of the relationship between the idiom of philosophy and the idiom of literature is a perennial problem for philosophy, it

This text consists of a lecture given at a symposium held at SUNY-Stonybrook in the fall of 1976 on the subject "Language and Literature."

Eugenio Donato

remains nevertheless true that at particular times the problem becomes particularly exasperating. Such is the case now in what is commonly referred to as "Continental criticism" and more specifically with the analysis of Derrida and his disciples, in particular with those of Philippe Lacoue-Labarthe and Jean-Luc Nancy.

Let us schematically—that is to say with an inevitable distortion— summarize the issues.

A. Can philosophy or more exactly the idiom of philosophy master its own tropology? The common denominator of all of Derrida's writings, more explicitly stated in "La mythologie blanche" and "Le Puits et la pyramide" is to answer no to the question. For Derrida, philosophical language cannot, any more than literary or ordinary language, master the tropes or the oppositions with which it constitutes its idiom. The specificity of its idiom resides precisely in an attempt to erase the play, the residue, the displacements introduced by its passage through language. For Derrida, philosophical concepts are the artifacts of linguistic machines whose purpose is to generate identity, adequation, propriety, etc. . . . by minimizing the effects of irrecuperability, non-presence, negativity inherent in all language. To quote an example, after analysing Hegel's view of language Derrida concludes:

Considering the machine together with the entire system of equivalencies . . . we can venture the following proposition: what *could never be thought* by Hegel, the interpreter who rises out of the whole history of philosophy, is a machine that would function. One that would function without being governed by a reappropriative order. Such a functioning would be unthinkable inasmuch as it inscribes within itself an effect of pure loss. It would be unthinkable as a non-thought that no thought could recover [*relever*] by constituting this non-thought as its opposite proper, as *its* other. Philosophy would doubtless see in this a non-functioning, a non-working, thereby missing that which nevertheless in such a machine, works. By itself. Outside.

Of course, this entire logic, this syntax, these propositions, these concepts, these words, Hegel's language—and to a certain extent, this one—are engaged within *the system of this impuissance*, of the structural incapacity of thinking without recovery.[1]

B. As Lacoue-Labarthe, after Derrida, has systematically shown, at the beginning of the nineteenth century the linguistic, literary presentation of philosophy, its form, in a word its *Darstellung*, again became a philosophical problem, the task of philosophy becoming then in part, to either attempt to master the *Darstellung* of philosophy, claiming that philosophy does have a specific, privileged *Darstellung*, or to try to erase the recognized effects of the *Darstellung* or the "presentation" of the concepts. Not the least extraordinary result of Lacoue-Labarthe's reading is that the effective project of the reading of Heidegger of Plato and Nietzsche is precisely to erase the play of *Darstellung*. In Lacoue-Labarthe's words:

But we see that fiction-making has nothing to do finally with *Darstellung*, exposition, or *mise-en-scène*. The myth of the *Phaedrus* no more either contains, according to Heidegger, its own *mise-en-abyme* or is implicated in that of which it is the "interpretation" (namely, as "fiction"), than does the "gestaltist" onto-typo-logy of *Zarathustra* engage the nevertheless specific *Darstellung* of this "song," "poem," "dithyramb," non-"sacred book," etc.—*Fiction-making does not ground or figure itself* [*Le fictionnement ne s'abyme pas*]. In any case, nowhere in Heidegger is it at all a question of this. It is in the very lack of ground, paradoxically (?) that something is lost. Something in other words, it goes without saying, which the *mise-en-abyme* must necessarily always reflect so as to guarantee its (re)presentation (the *Darstellung*), namely reflection itself as (re)presentation.[2]

C. The "text" that uniquely exasperates the problem of the philosophical *Darstellung* is of course Nietzsche's, which in its deconstructive strategy makes it impossible to separate a "conceptual" moment from its linguistic substratum or from the "literary form" in which it expresses itself. Of all the converging readings of Nietzsche to have come forth in recent years we might single out two articles of Paul de Man that summarize the problems admirably.

De Man quotes Nietzsche as saying: "No such thing as an unrhetorical 'natural' language exists that could be used as a point of reference: language is itself the result of rhetorical tricks and devices. . . . Language is rhetoric, for it only intends to convey a *doxa* (opinion) not an *episteme* (truth). . . . Tropes are not something that can be added or subtracted from language at will; they are its truest nature. There is no such thing as a proper meaning that can be communicated only in certain particular cases." De Man comments, "the trope is not a derived, marginal or aberrant form of language but the linguistic paradigm par excellence. The figurative structure is not one linguistic mode among others but it characterizes language as such."[3] Rhetoric itself cannot be mastered, cannot be said to be an ultimate proper language for "rhetoric is a *text* in that it allows for two incompatible, mutually self-destructive points of view and therefore puts an insurmountable obstacle in the way of any reading or understanding."[4] De Man then quotes Nietzsche as saying, "Truth kills, indeed kills itself (insofar that it realizes its own foundations in error)" and adds, "Philosophy turns out to be an endless reflection on its own destruction at the hands of literature." Philosophy is thus an endless narrative, a specific type of literary discourse. ". . . This self-destruction infinitely displaces in a series of successive rhetorical reversals which, by endless repetition of the same figure, keep it suspended between truth and the death of truth. A threat of immediate destruction, stating itself as a figure of speech, thus becomes the permanent repetition of this threat. Since this repetition is a temporal event, it can be narrated sequentially, but what it narrates, the subject matter of the story, is itself a mere figure. A non-referential, repetitive text narrates the story of a literally destructive but non-tragic linguistic event. We could call this rhetorical mode, which is that of the 'Conte philosophique' *On Truth and Lie* and, by extension, of all philosophical discourse an ironic allegory."[5]

D. The collapsing of philosophical discourse upon literary discourse, that is to say between on the one hand texts that postulate an adequation of their idiom to Another Language, to a Concept, to Being, to Truth, etc. . . . and on the other texts that move unreflectively in the medium of ungrounded representation or avowed fiction, is, curiously, not as disquieting for the philosopher or the producer of fictions as it is for the literary critic. For what is the status of *his* discourse? Is he simply writing another "ironic allegory"? And in that case why does the critic always systematically need the "pre-text" of another text that has mastery and authority over his?

It has often been argued—Hartman's "Crossing Over: Literary Commentary as Literature" being one of the more recent and lucid examples—that the distinction between literary discourse and critical discourse is untenable. The position has its merits for it recognizes that critical discourse could have a distinct status only in as much as the oppositions between literary and philosophical discourse could be maintained. With that opposition it is easy for critical discourse to pretend that it philosophically determines the textual, psychological, historical *ground* of a literary representation or fiction. Should the distinction collapse, the space in which criticism traditionally places itself collapses. Nevertheless, even within a unified "theory" of the *text* the question as to whether one can triangulate the space of the text in such a way as to maintain within it distinct philosophical and literary *moments* is worth asking, for if such an enterprise were possible then the critical text would have a space into which to move—even if it were its very movement that obliterated the original opposition and made the contradictory concept of a unified text possible.

The following remarks have no other pretention than to hint at the possibility of such a question.

Heidegger in his *Holzwege*, commenting upon a fragment of Anaximander, writes:

Only in thoughtful dialogue [*Zwiesprache*] with what it says can this fragment of thinking be translated [*übersetzen*]. However, thinking [*Denken*] is poetizing [*Dichtung*], more than poetry and song. Thinking of Being is the original way of poetizing. Language first comes to language, i.e. into its essence, in thinking. Thinking says what the truth of Being dictates; it is the original *dictare*. Thinking is primordial poetry [*Urdichtung*], prior to all poesy, but also prior to the poetics of art, since art shapes its work within the realm of language. All poetizing in the broader sense, and in the narrow sense of the poetic, is this narrower sense of the poetic, is in its ground of thinking. The poetizing essence of thinking preserves the sway of the truth of Being. Because it poetizes as it thinks, the translation that wishes to let the oldest fragment of thinking be said, itself necessarily appears violent.[6]

Heidegger wishes, then, to say again the oldest saying that speaks of the truth of Being. Yet Heidegger's comment cannot, from the start, in a simple and unequivocal way, say the saying of Anaximander. To be able to say the oldest saying, Heidegger's discourse has to submit itself to the form of a *Zwiesprache*, a dialogue, a dramatization, that is to say a literary form par excellence.

According to Heidegger, this presentation, this *Darstellung* belongs to the discourse of Philosophy. The dialogue as necessary to the expression of thought properly belongs to the *Dichtung* of Philosophy. Never does Heidegger question the possibility that the passage of the "saying" through a specific form could contaminate the *Dichtung* of philosophy. For Heidegger Philosophy can recuperate without residue the linguistic and poetic machinery that it sets in motion. At any rate, without this passage through a presentation, the saying will not say. The saying will only come forth through a properly literary form belonging to that "poesy" that Heidegger would like to think of as secondary with respect to an original form of thought or poetry (*Urdichtung*).

Yet what the *Zwiesprache* imposes is far from innocent, for the most cursory glance at say Grimm's *Deutsches Wörterbuch* will remind us that *Zwiesprache* besides meaning "discussions," "conversations" can also mean "arguments," "verbal duels," but also figuratively "communication with the dead" and poetically "communication or exchange with natural things and powers." What the dialogue then imposes is a violent division of the voice into two voices and reduces one of the voices to the status of "natural ghost." What the saying of Heidegger will then eventually translate is a dead origin assumed as "nature," an original nature assumed dead or death at the origin as "nature." Heidegger thus recognizes the necessity of a form added to an original saying, yet glosses over it, allowing for the possibility of the dialogue and of poesy to remain silent while the saying is brought forward. One of the voices, the belated one that establishes the dialogue, activates another voice while at the same time it silences itself. The function of the dialogue of the play of two voices of two sayings will be to give voice to an original privileged silent voice through the interventions of another secondary voice that somehow succeeds in silencing itself in its presentation. What this presentation through a dialogue will bring forth, however, is not the original voice *qua* original voice. The recovery of the original voice *as is* would seem to be an impossible feat even for the *Dichtung* of philosophy. The second voice will solicit the original voice but what will come forth is something other, something different. The function of the dialogue will be to make an *Übersetzung*, a translation, possible.

What this presentation through a dialogue will bring forth is not the original voice of the original thought but a translation, a saying in a different voice, a different tongue, a different language. In a word, if the original saying can only come forth as an *Übersetzung*, it can only come forth as a translation. *Übersetzen* has as diffuse and extensive a semantic field as the word *translatio* has in Latin or "translation" has in English. Again, according to Grimm, among its meanings we find "to transport from one place to another," "to transform," "to metamorphose," "to use a stronger or exaggerated expression hyperbole," "to jump over or above something." And, incidentally, here Grimm significantly gives the example *"den Abgrund übersetzen,"* hence to jump over an abyss or a groundless space. If we are to look for the abyss in Heidegger we would find it easily, nevertheless, as Lacoue-Labarthe suggests: it is always bridged, covered, or erased. In his essay "Identity and Difference," for example, Heidegger writes, "Where does the spring go that springs away from the ground? Into an abyss? Yes, as long as we only represent the spring in the horizon of metaphysical thinking. Not insofar as we spring and let go. Where to? To where we already have access: the belonging to Being. Being itself, however, belongs to us; for only with us can Being be present as Being, that is, become present." But let us return to the *Zwiesprache* which makes the *übersetzen* possible. The function of the dialogue will be to displace the original voice, to mix it with another voice, to tropologize the original voice, in short, to metaphorize the original voice.

The presentation of an original thought gives us an original metaphor, a metaphor at the origin and hence Heidegger's text constitutes itself as a metaphor for an origin but also places at the origin an abyss. The name of the original voice will then be indistinctly the abyss of metaphor or the metaphor of the abyss.

Let us continue. Heidegger tells us that "thinking is poetizing," *Denken* is a *Dichten*. How are we to read this *Dichten*? If we turn again to Grimm—or, for that matter, to any dictionary—the difficulty is obvious. If *Dichten* can mean poetizing it can also mean "thinking," "reflecting," "composing," "writing," but more importantly, "imagining" or fictionalizing. We would soon reach the conclusion that the original philosophical thinking in the form of an original metaphor is oscillating between a tautological metaphor—thinking is thinking—and the fictional play of representation.

Let us, however, proceed more systematically. Since Heidegger will associate *Dichtung* with *dictatio*, let us again turn to Grimm's *Deutsches Wörterbuch* which from the start also associates *Dichtung* with *dictatio* —"*in das französische und englische ist das Wort nicht aufgenommen, man umschreibt* s'addoner a la poèsie, faire des vers: to compose a poem, to make verses, to versify, *doch hier auch* to poetize dichten *ist das latein* dictore." *Dichten* at first is, then, a poetizing, a creating "filled with a higher spirit." Heidegger's gesture in identifying thinking with poetizing is not very original and has a long tradition behind it. What is interesting to note at this point is his distinction between two poetizings, an original one and a derived one, the first being nothing but language coming to itself. *Dichten* however is also a thinking—*sinnen, nachdenken*—poetizing there is also thinking. If *Denken* is *Dichten*, then *Denken* is also *denken*. In other words, the original poetizing, language's first coming to itself is also a first metaphor. This metaphor in the form of A is A allows within the original difference of the original metaphor the appearance of a first identity which will make denomination possible but will also always subordinate it to an original metaphoricity. *Dichten*, however, is also a fictioning, an inventing of "that which is not real or true," a "fingere," a "confingere." *Dichten* then is also a creation of representation that does not coincide with any outward reality. *Dichtung*, in at least Grimm's presentation, will be, to use Derrida's expression, a perfect linguistic *pharmakon* for, if on the one hand it will come to mean "the exhaltation of reality into a higher truth, in a spiritual existence," on the other it will also mean "a fiction in opposition to reality, in both a good and a bad sense."

It should be obvious by now how difficult the reading of Heidegger's *Denken ist Dichten* is. Thought at the origin gives itself as the original fusion of metaphor and representation. It must be added, however, that this original metaphor as representation, representation as metaphor, is primarily linguistic. The propositions are in fact interchangeable. Thought is poetizing, poetizing is language coming to itself, language coming to itself is discovering its own original metaphoricity and representational quality—"Language first comes to language, i.e., into its essence in thinking." But also language first comes to language in fictional representation.

This *Dichtung*, according to Heidegger, is a *dictare*. Not a *dicere* but a *dictare*. The word *dictare* is not easy to interpret. Minimally, however, *dictare* is a "frequenter *dicit*," a "frequently said," a "repetition of words uttered by another," "the utterance of words uttered by another." In short the repetition by another which in repeating tells of repetition.

Heidegger's strategy is easy to detect. At the origin thought is a linguistic utterance, the repeated linguistic utterance of another, of a "truth of being," of a "Wahrheit des Seins." Nevertheless, what stands at the origin is also language as original translation, as original *übersetzen*, as an original abysmal metaphor.

Heidegger, then, postulates a beyond of language and yet allows it to be apprehended through the linguistic displacement of an original metaphor. And in this way his gesture is similar to Nietzsche's, who in the often commented text "Truth and Illusion in an Extra Moral Sense" dooms perception and language and hence cognition to the play of metaphor at the origin. Thinking at the origin as "primordial poetry," *Denken* as *Urdichtung*, "shapes its work within the realm of language." It is not surprising, then, that what we should be left with at the origin is a displacement, an *Übersetzung*, a metaphoricity, and a violence inherent to the representational play of language. To repeat Heidegger's injunction, "the translation that wishes to let the oldest fragment of thinking itself speak necessarily appears violent."

It is thus this primary representational metaphoricity of language, Heidegger's *Urdichtung*, Nietzsche's first metaphor, that in a derivative way makes various types of discourses, philosophy and literature, philosophy as metaphysics, and literature as fictional play of language possible. It is obvious, though, that the two activities as derived from language are really inseparable, that *Dichtung* as "thought" and *Dichtung* as fictional representation are the inseparable by-products of the original metaphorical play of language.

Flaubert often compared the act of writing to that of building pyramids: "a book is not made like a child, but like the pyramids, with a premeditated design, by laying large blocks one upon the other, by dint of toil, time and sweat, and it's good for nothing! and it remains in the desert!"[7] One may pay little attention to such a text and dismiss it as a banal comparison illustrating Flaubert's esthetics regarding the composition of his novels and their utility. This passage cannot be so easily dismissed, however, for besides the anti-genealogical stance it proclaims regarding literary works, the pyramid is not an indifferent term. The metaphor "a book is a pyramid" offers a certain resistance to the very metaphoric play of substitution. A pyramid is not any building and indeed one would fall into banality if one displaced the metaphor *a book is a pyramid* into *a book is an edifice*. What if the pyramid in itself were a metaphor of language? Then the metaphor *a book is a pyramid* would be a metaphor stating the ultimate metaphoricity of language. The inevitability of such a reading is forced upon us by, in fact, a text of Hegel. Regarding the Egyptian pyramids Hegel in his Esthetics—a text that incidentally Flaubert must have known—writes:

On the purpose and meaning of the Pyramids all sorts of hypotheses have been tried for centuries, yet it now seems beyond doubt that they are enclosures for the graves of kings or sacred animals. . . . In this way the Pyramids put before our eyes the simple prototype of symbolic art itself; they are prodigious crystals concealing in themselves an inner meaning in such a manner that it is obvious that they are there for this inner meaning separated from pure nature and only in relation to this meaning. . . . The Pyramids are such an external environment in which an inner meaning rests concealed.[8]

In his discussions of Hegel's semiology, Derrida has already given us a reading of this passage. Derrida's strategy, however, in commenting on this passage is to go along with Hegel's critique of what the latter takes to be the semiology of the Egyptians in the name of another more arbitrary sign system. Derrida thus undertakes the more considerable task of showing how Hegel's dialectical mastery is not sufficient to completely contain the play of metaphor of which his privileged semiology was only one instance.

My purpose in this context is more modest as I should like simply to underscore the play of metaphor in the context of what Hegel calls symbolical art and which is best exemplified by Egyptian art.

For Hegel Egyptian art is symbolical art par excellence and what characterizes symbolical art is its representational mode. Symbolical art expresses itself in symbols and not in signs. For Hegel a sign is constituted by the arbitrary associations of two distinct elements: "Now the symbol is *prima facie* a *sign*. But in a *mere sign* the connection which meaning and its expression have with one another is only a purely arbitrary linkage." On the other hand "the symbol is no purely arbitrary sign, but a sign which in its externality comprises in itself at the same time the content of the idea which it brings into appearance. Yet nevertheless it is not to bring itself before our minds as this concrete individual thing but in itself only that universal quality of meaning [which it signifies]."[9]

A symbol, then, more obviously than a sign, is a metaphor. It brings together two distinct elements, a representation and a meaning, but does so in such a way that the representation partakes of the meaning it conveys. A symbol is a metaphor where the element of identity is strong enough to hide the distinct nature of the two elements brought together in the symbol/metaphor. In a different terminology we would say that for Hegel a symbol is a metaphor based upon synecdoche. Let us return to the passage upon the pyramids, "the pyramids put before our eyes the simple prototype of symbolical art itself," in other words, the pyramids are the symbol or the emblem of symbolical art itself or if you prefer the pyramids are a metaphor whose signification is the process of metaphor in the act of signification itself. What the pyramids in fact signify is the fact that signification is metaphorical. But the process does not stop there, for if the pyramids signify symbolic art itself *qua* signs they also signify death. Those "prodigious crystals . . . conceal in themselves an inner meaning," and such an "inner meaning" is nothing but the "realm of death and the invisible." The pyramids are thus second degree metaphors pointing to the complicity of metaphor and death. Read from the perspective of Hegel, that which translated itself in the original metaphor of Heidegger, of the *Denken des Seins* which spoke through an original *übersetzen*, is nothing but death itself.

If I began by quoting Flaubert it is because Flaubert clearly echoes Hegel the way Nietzsche will later echo Flaubert.

In contrast to Hegel, Flaubert does not shy away in front of the constructed nature of the pyramid. The pyramid is not a natural crystal but a cultural construct, with Flaubert we are so to speak doomed to language and hence to the pyramid, that is to say, to the indefinite play of language against the absolute negativity inscribed within it.

In another remarkable passage relating tomb and language, Flaubert writes:

I, too, was constructed like that. I was like the cathedrals of the fifteenth century, lanceolate, flashing . . . Between the world and me there existed some sort of stained-glass window, painted yellow, with streaks of fire and gold arabesques, so that everything was reflected on my soul as on the slabs of a sanctuary, embellished, transfigured, and melancholic, however, where nothing but the beautiful passed. These were dreams more majestic and more adorned than cardinals' robes. Ah! what trembling from the organ! what hymns! and what sweet incense rising up from a thousand open censers! When I am old, to write all that will give me warmth. I shall do as those, who before leaving for a long voyage, go to bid farewell to cherished tombs. Before dying, I will revisit my dreams.[10]

Writing, then, for Flaubert is a belated act. To write is to turn back towards an irrecoverable past, not so much to recover that past to try to give it presence, and permanence, but on the contrary, to bid it a farewell. The moment of writing is caught in between a dead past and a dead future. This past remains prior to being revisited by language, a dream that is pure representation. The content of the dream is the absent figures written on a gravestone and then erased. Literary writing in this case revisits a lost past in the face of a beingless future. Flaubert's text can be taken then as emblematic of a certain ontology of language. What makes language possible in the first place erases itself, yet condemns language to the quest for the absent traces it may have left in the very act in which it erases itself. *Language is the metaphor of an absence*, and has to move forward in an impossible quest by an equally absent future. Flaubert's ontology for language is an ontology of nostalgia similar in some ways to Heidegger's. Flaubert's cathedral will be echoed by Nietzsche when the madman after proclaiming the death of God has to revisit its grave to repeat the death of the ever absent transcendental origin.[11] The difference between a Flaubert and a Nietzsche is, of course, the latter's refusal to dwell on the nostalgic moment, to read the murder of the forever-absent privileged origin of language as a liberating movement that will permit a liberating laughter during the free fall in the infinite well of the fourth part of *Zarathustra*.

It is in the proclamation of the death of an original God—and we should remember that for Nietzsche one of the names of God is Grammar: "I fear we are not getting rid of God because we still believe in grammar"[12]—that Nietzsche finds the necessary liberation to permit the linguistic excesses of Zarathustra where the nostalgia of philosophy spills over into the mindless dance of a literary discourse.

Within language, then, or rather to return to Heidegger's expression, with language's first coming to language, we of necessity encounter the original violent play of an original displacement, of an original metaphor; *translatio*, translation, *übersetzen*. This original tear or wound —which could also be read as the original complicity of language and negativity, of language and death as the necessary inscription of death in language—cannot be closed or healed. Because of it language will be in a constant drift that will always mark and define a space which separates it from any possible resting place in any object or intention. The law to which metaphor subordinates language is the law of the same as different and the order of language is not one of identity and presence but of absence and difference. To speak, then, within the play of language of a literary discourse or a philosophical discourse is at best trite and at worse the symptom of an impossible desire for a mastery, doomed to failure, over the constant play of language. A mastery which would permit the comforting coming to rest of language over the objects it is supposed to represent or the possibility of allowing language to identify with an originating intention and hence to permit a subject the presumed satisfaction of self-identity. The two qualifications of literary discourse and philosophical discourse need nevertheless not be useless if they are used to qualify two possible strategies with respect to the primacy of the representational metaphoricity in language.

As we suggested, language is never adequate to the identities that it inscribes within its play of differences, and in its representational metaphoricity language somehow exceeds the "objects" or "meanings" that it displays. Rather than define two distinct languages, one capable of mastering its own metaphoricity and the other blindly erring in its representational phantasmagoria, we may instead—after having recognized an original loss in language that triggers the open-ended play of its representational metaphoricity—view language as it assumes mutually-negating attitudes. On the one hand, language nostalgically seeks an "original object," a transcendental signifier, the "truth of Being" the loss of which constitutes its origin as primary metaphor. But on the other hand, there is a pronounced refusal to take up such a quest. Language thus sheds the burden of nostalgia and on the contrary accentuates its own playfulness, proclaiming unashamedly its incapacity to control its tropology.

For the sake of simplicity, we may of course label these contradictory injunctions "philosophical" and "literary." We may recognize in the first our Heideggerian inheritance and in the latter a Nietzschean temptation and detect for example in as great a philosopher and literary figure as Derrida a joint fascination, a double project of allowing language the possibility of both retelling an unrecoverable original loss yet to answer Zarathustra's demand for an active forgetfulness, to become the light-footed dancer falling forever in the infinite well. Of course, the important thing, for us, is to recognize that our own project has to insert itself in the excess of language. No matter what we call *our* project, whether we name it "philosophical" or "literary" we may not escape language's contradictory injunction to recover the memory of an irrecoverable past yet to quest after an impossible future. This simultaneous contradictory demand constitutes the impossible present of language.

NOTES

    1. Jacques Derrida, "Le Puits et la pyramide" in *Marges de la Philosophie* (Paris: Editions de Minuit, 1972), p. 126.
    2. Philippe Lacoue-Labarthe, "Typographie" in *Mimesis des Articulations* (Paris: Aubier-Flammarian, 1975), pp. 199–200.
    3. Paul de Man, "Nietzsche's Theory of Rhetoric," *Symposium* 28, no. 1, 35.

4. Paul de Man, "Action and Identity in Nietzsche" in *Nuova Corrente*, 68–69 (1975–76): 584.

5. Paul de Man, "Nietzsche's Theory of Rhetoric," p. 43.

6. Martin Heidegger, "Der Spruch des Anaximander," in *Holzwege* (Frankfurt am Main: Klostermann, 1972), pp. 302–3.

7. Gustave Flaubert, *Correspondence* (Paris: Louis Conard, 1926–1953), 4: 239–40.

8. G. W. F. Hegel, *Aesthetics. Lectures on Fine Art*, trans. by T. M. Knox (Oxford: Clarendon Press, 1975), p. 356.

9. Ibid., p. 304.

10. Gustave Flaubert, *Correspondence*, 3: 130.

11. See Friedrich Nietzsche, *The Joyful Wisdom*.

12. See Nietzsche, *Twilight of the Idols*.

TWO

LARVATUS PRO DEO
Jean-Luc Nancy

for Francine

Vision . . . comes precisely to the point where it itself sees itself . . . between and behind two eyes invisible in principle to itself, at the very moment that it sees two eyes, other, like the visible mask or front of an invisible eye that nevertheless casts hereupon a 'visible' look in that it reverses the vision that prevails here in the visible.

BENE LATUIT

CERTAIN reputations shine with such brilliance that they produce a lengthy blindness in those who contemplate them—or who believe themselves to do so. Doubtless nothing is more famous within what might be called the ornamental history of modern philosophy than the saying of Descartes, *"masked I go forward."* But nothing is more constant than the effects produced by this illustrious mask. Dazzled by such a declaration, commentators rush forward confidently, some to remove the mask—failing to see that after all they know not how to grasp it,

This study is part of a work in progress concerning what I call the *structure fictice* of the truth of the *cogito*, such as it is presented through the function of *fable* given by Descartes to his *Discours*. But the assignation of the fable is itself preceded by that of the painting, which I attempt to develop here. The epigraph comes from Marc Richir, *La vision et son imaginaire*, in *Textures* nos. 10–11 (1975).

others to locate it—thereby bound to contrive either this or that "hidden Descartes." More precisely, they are bound *to feign* the *real* Descartes, that is, to engage Descartes' most admitted, most established process, that which involves Descartes himself and "truth." And hence they entrap themselves anew in the mask.[1]

No one can claim after all to go further in this or to be better at it, and I do not propose to overcome such a necessary blindness. At the very most, we can propose to accept for a moment the singular encounter between a reader who can make out nothing and the empty gaze of a mask. Let us read for the first time the famous text:

In order that the blush of their faces does not show, actors on the stage put on a mask. Like them, when I go out into this theater of a world, where hitherto I have been but a spectator, masked I go forward [*larvatus prodeo*].[2]

A few lines later Descartes will of course write, "mathematical thesaurus of Polybius the Cosmopolitan." Here we have the mask, the pseudonym intended for this first treatise that never saw the light. And for us knowing readers, the trick is exposed. Going by the name of Polybius, the author of this text of the 1620's is Descartes. But just who is Descartes? And what if subsequently Descartes had never ceased to go forward masked? He had taken as his motto Ovid's saying, *"bene vixit, bene qui latuit."*[3] We must take the mask on its own terms according to its maxim. We will finally have to reread the pseudonymous text, *Les Préambules*.

To do so, a digression is necessary. We must first consider an anonymous text of 1637 entitled *Discours de la méthode*.

UT PICTURA

Descartes "devised a method" for his "search for the truth," and he "ventures to believe" it to be the only human occupation that is "substantially good and important." Yet such a statement is not self-evident. On the contrary, what is self-evident, by virtue of the very principles of Cartesian reform, is that this method cannot be cloaked in an argument from authority. It can be presented only according to what might be called an *authorial argument*: that of which *I* alone am the author can impose itself only upon the judgment that each *I* will be able to pass upon it. This formulation sums up the Cartesian mode and model of the communication of truth—communication essentially dependent upon the very process whereby this truth is constituted as *certitude*. (Unless, in far more complex fashion, this constitution is dependent in turn upon the project itself of communicating truth. In a sense we must concern ourselves here with this as well—with the Cartesian inauguration of the modern obsession with the subject of communication, with the communication of truth, and with communication *as* truth.)

The truth/certitude of the method accordingly imposes a certain organization upon its presentation. Beyond the order of authority, beyond that of demonstration, there must be produced the presentment of the author, or more exactly, of the "becoming-oneself-author" (of the method).[4] This is why Descartes, scarcely having stated his invention of method, immediately adds the following, which is to provide the rule of the *Discours*.

Nevertheless, it may be that I am wrong, and that what I take for gold and diamonds is but a bit of copper or glass. . . . But I shall be pleased indeed to show in this discourse the paths that I have followed, and to represent my life here as in a painting, in order that each may pass judgment thereupon, and by learning from the general reports the opinion that will be formed thereupon, that this become for me a new means of instruction, which I shall add to those that I am in the habit of using.[5]

Taking glass to be diamonds is the act of a blind man. Descartes had written this to Beeckman:[6] "Imagine before your eyes a blind man so crazed by greed that he spent days on end searching for precious stones among the refuse from his neighbor's house, and that as soon as his hand came across some pebble or small piece of glass, he straightaway believed he had found a stone of great value. . . ." We have here all of Descartes' preoccupations—all the obsessions with the *improper* (a *false* treasure, taken from *another's refuse*)—and brought together within the supreme obsession—blindness. The inability to see is an immersion in impurity and alienation. If Descartes errs, then, it cannot be a question of a partial error. It is all or nothing, clear-sightedness or blindness.

We shall not pause to consider the obviously rhetorical character of this "nevertheless. . . ." It is clear that this hesitation is *feigned*. Yet it is precisely the status and the function of the feint that must be examined —a philosophical status and function that over-determine rhetoric here, indeed that reverse or pervert it to the point of making it a *feigned rhetoric*. . . . Hence, let us consider that Descartes must assure himself that he is not blind, that he sees what he touches, and that what he touches is not filth, but in truth gold.

To this end he exhibits his painting. "Representation" here does not denote a secondary, imitated copy, one that consequently is always more or less factitious, but rather presentation itself, presentation of the thing itself. Descartes will show himself, and the comparison with a painting allows him to summon up all the values of exactitude, of authenticity and of living presence that one can expect from a faithful portrait. Descartes presents this portrait, and the portrait is faithfulness itself, in other words that which makes one see. What is at stake in the *Discours* is to have Descartes see/be seen, *to show the author of the method* [*faire voir l'auteur de la méthode*]. However, it turns out that this expression must be understood in all its possible meanings. I need not force the argument to show this.

It is in fact sufficient—as well as inevitable—to refer to Descartes' stated intentions concerning the exhibition of his painting. He wrote of them to Mersenne in a letter informing him of the first draft of the *Météores*. "Moreover, I ask that you speak of this to no one, for I have resolved to exhibit it publicly as a sample of my Philosophy, and to be hidden behind the painting so as to hear what shall be said of it."[7]

The painting, the faithful painting and even the painting's faithfulness itself are in reality charged with dissimulating from the public the painting's author (and by the same token, its original). The Philosophy referred to here is not founded in the act of its exhibition—it manifests itself only so as to allow the author, remaining hidden, to learn what is said of it.

The *Discours* assigns to the painting the same function—to apprise Descartes of the judgment of others, to instruct him in his hiding place. Since the *Discours* is anonymous, the reader of 1637 knows that the author stands on the other side of the painting. The dissimulation is not dissimulated, the feint is admitted. However, it remains a feint—among Descartes' feints there is always a plus feint and a minus feint—for what is said in the letter and not in the *Discours* is that Descartes does not believe in the frankness of others. Hence, from his hiding place he wishes to take this frankness by surprise.[8]

The dissimulation of the author, the feint of his absence thus provides him with the means to know by surprise what he is—blind or clear-sighted. Could it be that Descartes counts upon this verification by the judgment of others? But how is it possible to verify [*véri-fier*] by this means that which is constituted only in and by the exclusive certitude of the author? The *Discours* repeatedly denies its author external access to a "new means of instructing oneself." Whatever comes to me from others is by principle situated on the same gnoseological level as everything against which the method sets itself: examples, customs, stories, fables. Thus in the sixth section Descartes will write, in superb contradiction with his prefatory statement: "It has rarely happened that an objection has been raised that I failed entirely to foresee . . . so that I have almost never encountered a critic of my opinions who did not appear to me either less rigorous or less equitable than myself."[9] From behind his painting Descartes can expect nothing and can hear nothing that might amend his certitude.

And yet, perhaps there is instruction to be gained from this exhibition. Perhaps in fact it is solely by means of such an arrangement that Descartes is able to assure himself of his certitude—and consequently, at once of the *cogito*. Perhaps the *cogito* can hear and comprehend itself only by listening to those who behold the painting in which it is portrayed. If the truth of the portrait resides then in its conformity with the original, the dissimulation of the latter implies that this conformity is not that upon which viewers are to pass judgment. Confronted with a resemblance that is unassigned, unverifiable, the viewer should pass judgment upon a conformity contained entirely within the painting or created by it. The viewer would have to repeat the famous *ut pictura poesis*, understanding it in the following way: creation, the *poiesia* of truth, here assumes the form of the painting through the subject of his own authenticity. Nothing is less realist or naturalist than the pictorial esthetics that could be derived from the *Discours*. But nothing is less "esthetic" than this painting whose representational function is from the outset indistinguishable from the presentation of its author. The author of the method can present himself only in painting—and this painting is at once its own original as well as the mask of the original, which is concealed at two removes behind the portrait. Standing before the portrait, engaged in commentary upon it, the viewer would perhaps verify not the resemblance (insofar as the painting is a copy, its faithfulness is guaranteed *by principle*, by reason of the frankness, the veracity of its author); rather he would verify the very existence, the *sum* of the original. I am this thinking being that the other sees, or thinks he sees.

The resulting situation is a familiar one. It is homologous in Cartesian doctrine to the recognition of the existence of God by seeing his idea (a faithful copy) in myself. The viewer of the painting sees Descartes as Descartes sees God (just as well, therefore just as badly). This is the function to be performed by the portrait in the position of mask. Thus the phrase should read *larvatus pro Deo*—I am masked in order to occupy the position of God.

VIDERE VIDEOR

One begins to suspect that this complex and artful arrangement is not there for mere pleasure. Or rather, its sole purpose is precisely to guarantee an enjoyment related to the voyeuristic, in other words to theory. Here the voyeur listens to people—a kind of perverse refinement of voyeurism—the viewers of his portrait. Thus the voyeur is also an exhibitionist. And it is through this perverse positioning that he obtains the desired vision of himself—theory. Neither rhetoric nor painting serves here to please or embellish; we must admit the strictest necessity of the perversion that is set working by the subject of the theory of the subject. That this perversion is not accidental but rather stems from the constitution of this subject is what we shall have to confirm. Like others, the subject of the theory of the subject is perverse from birth. Better still, his birth is his perversion. I mask myself only in order to appear to myself, to see myself.

Yet this requires taking into account henceforth all the operations and all the positions prescribed along the perverse path of the gaze.

Just who is watching here? The viewer of course, and the painting. The sightless eyes of the portrait watch whomever looks at them. As for Descartes, he sees nothing, except the obscure other side of the canvas. But it is precisely in order to see, to see himself, and thus to see whether he is blind or clear-sighted that Descartes must remain hidden from others and from his own portrait.

The model taken from optics is not self-evident; it does not function within its own transparency as is customarily believed (not without reason) concerning Cartesian doctrine. Indeed, optics possesses the privilege of privileges for this *theory*. The *Dioptrique*, which is introduced by the *Discours*, begins with the following: "The entire conduct of our lives is dependent upon our senses, among which sight, the most universal and noble. . . ."[10] But in the *Dioptrique* itself, access to vision —and to the light—is possible only by way of a deviation, a deviation through blindness. The famous comparison of the transmission of light to that of the movement of a stick includes not only a mechanist analogy, it refers at the same time to the stick of blind men, about whom "one could almost say that they see with their hands."[11] Contrary to what a tradition consecrated by Auguste Comte led one to believe, Descartes never lays claim to self-vision—a speculation—of the eye. The eye, light and vision can see and be seen only through a blindness that constitutes their indispensable condition of possibility. The eye sees the eye—sees the theory of the seeing eye—through a dead eye, as is proposed by the experimental arrangement of the *Dioptrique*.

taking the eye of a man recently expired, or, lacking that, of an ox or some other large animal, you carefully cut away the three membranes that enclose it . . . then . . . if you set this eye in a specially made window space . . . if you look . . . you will see there, perhaps not without admiration and pleasure a

Jean-Luc Nancy

picture representing in naïve perspective all objects that are on the other side.[12]

The living eye glued to the back of the dead eye—with a disquieting curiosity, as if at the key-hole behind which truth unveils herself—sees what seeing is, which is to see the painting of the world—in perspective, (which should be borne in mind, for we shall return to it). A naïve painting, in other words one that is natural, original—a first painting in which objects accede to the authenticity of theoretical existence.

But in order to reach the *Dioptrique*, to see sight and its painting, it is necessary first to have gone through the method and its exhibition. If the author hidden behind the painting can learn nothing from what he hears, it is because he is there to see: hidden by this strained ear is the eye that is glued to the back of the blind eye of the painting. Descartes learns nothing through hearing—except that since he hears voices, someone is watching, looking at the lifeless gaze of the portrait. And in this way he sees—without seeing—and he sees his own gaze—at the very moment that he blinds it by gluing it to the dark and formless other side of the canvas that represents his eye.

I repeat—the gaze sees nothing. Neither the one painted on the canvas nor that of the painter behind the canvas can see. They only appear to see. But to appear to see, or *to appear to oneself to see* is the necessary and sufficient condition upon which may be established the luminous evidence of the *cogito*. The second *Méditation* states this precisely.

however, at the very least, it is highly certain that it appears to me that I see (*videre videor*), that I hear and that I feel heat . . . and this . . . is none other than thinking.

. . . it cannot be that when I see or (I make no distinction here) when I believe I see, that I who think am not something.[13]

Videor: I seem, I appear, I am seen. I appear to myself in that I am seen—and I am seen as appearing to see. The *videor* guarantees the *cogito*, for it attests to the only presence into which even the most radical doubt cannot make a breach: *videor* endures, even at the height of phantasmagoria and illusion. To appear is to create an illusion. The *videor* is that illusion which, through an unheard-of twist or perversion, anchors certitude in the utmost depths of illusion. The space of the *videor* is indeed the painting, the portrait, at once the most factitious and the most faithful of faces, the blindest and the most clear-sighted eye.

It is not because of its faithfulness of reproduction that Descartes' portrait is authentic, but because as a portrait he only appears to see. Or rather, the truth function of the painting is at work at this strange intersection, which brings about—in the same space, on the canvas—an endless exchange of representational values (if he seems to see, it is because he is admirably painted) and their counter-values of factitiousness (if it is a painting he only seems to see).

INTEGUMENTA

This is not all. In hiding himself thus behind his painting, in telling a friend that he is hiding and dissimulating from others that he has said he was hiding, Descartes imitates someone else. The hidden Descartes is himself a portrait, one made moreover in the likeness of a painter. Or perhaps we should say in the likeness of *the* painter par excellence. In a letter to Mersenne, Descartes in fact makes use of a trait attributed to Apelles. (Consequently, by not naming himself Apelles, and even if Mersenne might already be familiar with the anecdote, Descartes dissimulates that he is guided by a model: the admission of dissimulation thus carries with it in turn its own feint.)

What then is this model? It is precisely the model of painters. It is in these terms that Apelles was celebrated by all antiquity. He was the master of the portrait, as well as—the inversion is unavoidable—the portraitist of the master, since he had the exclusive privilege to execute the official portraits of Alexander.[14] Of course he owed this privilege and this mastery to his highly accomplished art of resemblance. The lifelike faithfulness (as language would have it) of Apelles' portraits was such (as legend would have it) that soothsayers (*métoposkopoi*, those who "see upon the forehead," physiognomists, as the viewers of Descartes' portrait must be in order to be philosophers) were able from these portraits to predict how many years were left to their originals. This astonishing resemblance is called *indiscreet* resemblance, (perhaps) in the mathematical sense of the indiscrete, that is, a resemblance in which no distance from the model remains. The indiscretion of resemblance—that which will allow the viewer to know everything about Descartes, as unveiled as his truth—is thus the perfection of illusion. Ultimately, as is proven by the *métoposkopoi*, it is even the strictly indiscernible illusion of reality. It could be argued that failing to be as *true* as truth, this illusion nevertheless is infinitely more than apparently true (*vrai-semblable*) in that it is as *operative* as truth. Perhaps it is precisely this operativity that founds or forms Cartesian truth. In any case the perfect illusion is the *trompe l'oeil*, in which Apelles indeed excelled, for when people viewed his portrait of Alexander as Zeus (as God), they thought they saw a hand armed with thunder (with light) springing from the painting towards them.* Having lived a long while at Ephesus, Apelles is both the fellow countryman and successor of Parrhasios, creator of the celebrated absolute *trompe l'oeil*, a painted veil that covered a painting, which consequently existed only as the fiction of the visible this side of the irremovable veil. The non-unveilable painting of Parrhasios governs all of pictorial mimetics: perfect resemblance is that which cannot be set aside, raised up or taken off so as to expose the truth of its model, since resemblance *is* itself this truth—even though (or perhaps because) *at the same time* the expectation of this truth is deluded, the desire for it deceived. Such as the case with the *Discours*, whose author places it in a highly secretive manner under the authority of glaringly truthful resemblance.

What then is seen by the viewers of the *Discours*? Alternately, simultaneously, the paintings of Apelles and Parrhasios. They see the portrait of Descartes (of Descartes' model, of the model Descartes), and they see a veil that they are told conceals a portrait, whereas in reality this painted veil covers nothing. The actual portrait is the veil itself: or the veil already represents the portrait of which it appears to be the covering. Thus the viewer simultaneously sees Descartes and does not see him; he will never see the true Descartes beneath a veil that cannot be removed.

But just who is "Descartes"? Not René Descartes, the French nobleman who withdrew to Holland, and who provides precisely in his *Discours* a sufficient number of details to be recognized or at the very least suspected. (As we shall see later in his text one of the constitutive elements of the *fable of the* DISCOURS is to hide nothing of the life that is depicted therein.) In this sense, for a contemporary of the salons or schools of Paris, the anonymity of the *Discours* is not a very difficult "portrait game." "Descartes" then is he who says *I* in this discourse, I insofar as I therein acquire the certitude of the *I* of my thinking being. It is probably this *I* that must be shown in painting, for it is perhaps his countenance that I cannot see without seeing the portrait. Descartes, the *subject* of the *Discours* in which he does not see, would obtain his vision by listening to viewers who in turn see only a veil—a veil painted on a gaze-feigned-to-be-painted, or a gaze painted upon a model feigned-to-be-true. Ultimately the "true" model always will be the example of a very ancient master of illusion.

The curious structure of this anoptic labyrinth corresponds to a

* In art a *trompe l'oeil* is a painting or part of a painting that makes use of perspective so as to create the illusion of relief. The term may refer as well to any deceptive appearance or illusion. Literally *trompe l'oeil* means to "deceive the eye." As shall become evident, this structure or process of deception (of the viewer, the reader) is as essential to the exposition of Cartesian philosophy as to J.-L. Nancy's view or reading of that exposition.—Trans.

necessity of Cartesian science. The veil or the painting (which may now be understood as undecidably the same) is absolutely necessary. The *Regulae* set forth that the *mathesis universalis* was dissimulated by the ancients (Cartesian authority is always ancient, and its ancientness always serves to dissimulate), so as to be discovered anew by Descartes, and to be covered up once again by him. Without the coverings beneath which Descartes presents it, indeed without the *integumenta* that "common mathematics" constitutes, the *mathesis* would not be accessible—at least not readily—to human intelligence. "If I have spoken of covering (*integumentum*), it is not because I wish to envelop this doctrine nor to veil it so as to keep it from the masses. It is rather that I intend to clothe and adorn it so as to be able to adapt it best to human intelligence" (*Regulae*, IV).

We must of course comprehend as well as *not* comprehend the denial here; we must grasp the truth of the feint along with the feint of the truth. We must ask just to what extent clothing differs from a veil (or a mask . . .), and whether or not the relation between them is precisely one of indiscrete resemblance. Adorning and dissimulating are perhaps accomplished by the same gesture, and if the thing or the person can be better shown by means of adornment, one can imagine the kind of artful necessity required for the presentation of *mathesis*. As if Mathesis could be seen only in the guise of Mimesis.

We must bear in mind as well that one of the sources of Apelles' talent was his involvement in the art based on arithmetic and geometry, the mathematics upon which perspective is based, and without which there can be no pictorial illusion. Like perspective, the Cartesian *integumenta* are indispensable for making comprehensible the incomprehensible depth of science—the science that nevertheless at the same time they cover. The *mathesis* is neither presented nor apprehended directly; it can be reached only by means of an intermediary veil, but this veil is the mathetic ornamentation itself. The colors of the guise of Mimesis are authentic, the genuine flesh tones of Mathesis. Or vice versa.

Perspective, brought into play without reserve by the *trompe l'oeil*, is the procedure whereby three dimensions may be simulated upon a surface. It thus constitutes the procedure of exhibition of Descartes himself. In the fifth section of the *Discours* he explains that this is the manner in which he composed *Le Monde* (the treatise that the *Discours* at once conceals and reveals, dissimulates and supplements by way of a theological-political conjuncture).[15]

My design was to include in it all I thought I knew concerning material things, before setting to writing. However, in the same manner as painters, who, unable to represent all the various sides of a solid body equally well in a flat

Jean-Luc Nancy

painting, select one of the principle sides that alone they highlight, shading the others, and have them appear only as they may be seen when we look upon the former, thus, fearing I would be unable to put in my discourse all that I had in mind, I undertook to exhibit at length only that which I understood of light.[16]

Perspective is thus a necessary procedure because of a plane or flat character of discourse (planeness? or flatness? is it depth or poetry that is missing?) and because of what runs counter to it, namely, an excess of relief and of depth of thought. As it must, this traditional arrangement refers to a flaw of writing. Perspective supplements the impoverishment of writing, and is thus a palliative. Yet this palliative is remarkably successful, to the point that it does more than perhaps simply dissimulate a flaw. What Descartes sets up in the foreground, what he thus paints "towards the light" is light itself. Perspective paints the relief of the light that allows perspective itself to be seen. The painting paints its own exteriority, thereby getting around or diverting in magisterial fashion its own flatness. The painter here shows the act of showing [*fait voir ce qui fait voir*] (but has the painter ever painted anything else?). By deceiving the eye of the viewer, the painter offers him the element of his vision: the relief of light. Between the living eye and the painted eye, one no longer knows which illuminates [*éclaire*] the other, or keeps an eye on it, for the verb *éclairer* may be understood here in the sense that it possessed in the seventeenth century—to oversee, to spy, from behind a painting for example.

The portrait of Descartes is thus the portrait—striking in its resemblance—of light.

SIBI SIMILE SIGNUM

This would thus be the self-portrait par excellence, the painting prior to all painting of light that poses—on what obscure canvas if not on the black reverse side of light, on this blind foil of light, far more obscure and older than at night—the stroke of its resemblance, the stroke that renders it visible.

Apelles, to whom an autobiography was attributed as well, is the author of the oldest self-portrait in the annals of painting. Descartes will invoke Apelles—this time by name—when he explains the origin in the self of the idea of God, which is the second cornerstone of his doctrine. As stated in the second *Méditation*, this idea is "like the mark of the workman imprinted upon his work," with Descartes adding that "this mark need not necessarily be something other than this same work." The mark of God can thus be myself, thinking matter as such. It is enough to establish that this indeed is the case: "Given only that God created me, it is highly believable that he in some way produced me in his image and resemblance, and that I conceive of this resemblance (in which is contained the idea of God) by the same faculty as that whereby I conceive. of myself."[17] Proof, which is very curiously limited to a high degree of credibility, rests then upon the act of creating. Moreover, this can be argued in at least two ways, neither one of which excludes the other: creation would mark the fall of the creator if it were not his reproduction; or creation leads necessarily to the order of secondary reality, of the image, yet the first image can have no other model than the creator. Thus the creator does his self-portrait. This is what Descartes will describe in his commentary of this passage in the Fifth Reply, invoking Apelles. "It is as if, recognizing in some painting such a high degree of art, I were to judge it impossible for such a work to be by another hand than that of Apelles."[18] Descartes continues, concluding the argument in which the operation of God with the painter's work and "the generation of a father" were simultaneously compared: "Nor is it true that there is never a relation between a craftsman and his work, as appears when a painter produces a painting that resembles him (sibi simile signum)."[19]

Descartes' model is thus double, and hence doubly hidden. It is both Apelles, in whose image Descartes with a consummate art paints the image (the idea) of God (Alexander or Zeus), as well as the self-portrait, in the image of which Descartes composes his Discours, which means that he proceeds or that he creates in the image of God himself. Once again, in exhibiting sibi simile signum, Descartes states (dissimulates that he states) larvatus (as painter) pro Deo.

But it is not certain that the divine—or pseudo-divine—author and model of the Discours is simply the thinking "I" who in Descartes' soul reproduces the semblance of God. What is uncertain is not whether the portrait is that of the subject of the Discours, but whether this subject himself is—or is but—his cogito's luminous presence unto itself. The painting of light perhaps in turn creates an illusion.

The Discours holds yet another feint. When in the fifth section Descartes sets down the essential points of the treatise Le Monde, which the Discours conceals and supplants, he indicates that in this treatise he proceeded not only according to the rules of perspective, but also out of cautiousness, according to a fiction (which Le Monde names "fable"). "In order to shade all these things somewhat . . . I resolve . . . to speak only of what would happen in a new [world], if God were now to create somewhere in imaginary space enough matter . . . to form from it a chaos as disordered as any that poets might simulate."[20]

An initial feint is uncovered here, that of Le Monde itself: the fable of creation of another world is but a protective rhetoric with respect to "the erudite." For it is indeed the truth of this world's laws that Descartes intends to make manifest. He admits as much here by presenting his fable as a technique of painting ("in order to shade . . .").[21] Yet this admission deceives the eye as far as the dissimulation that follows is concerned. Descartes continues, "Thus, I firstly described this matter and strove to represent it such that there is nothing in the world, it seems to me, clearer or more intelligible, save what was said previously of God and the soul. . . ." But it is exactly at this point that *Le Monde* is most camouflaged by the *Discours*—for in the former it is not a question of "what was said previously of God and the soul." In *Le Monde*—in the feigned world of mathetic truth—the matter (in other words extension) of original chaos, similar to that of poets, is the *only* thing that is most easily conceived, and whose conception is at the same time the condition of all other conceptions: "And its idea is included to such an extent in all those that our imagination can form that necessarily either you must have a conception of it, or you never imagine anything."[22] Here the matter of chaos is the outer limit of the feint of the "new World": this is the point where one can no longer feign, for the feint authenticates itself in truth. The matter of poetic chaos turns out to be the same thing (the thing itself) as the primary matter of divine creation. It thus occupies the structural position of the *cogito*, and in the coming into being of Descartes' thought it is this matter that furnishes the *cogito* with its matrix. To the full measure that the *cogito* is equal to and functions as the ultimate point of a verified feint or fiction [*véri-fiée*], at least its equivalent and at most its origin are situated in this matter of chaos. Now this measure—that which affirms the *cogito* as operation rather than as content—is far from negligible, for it doubtless constitutes the very nature and function of the *cogito*. I shall not undertake to analyze it here.[23] For the moment I ask only that faced with the painting of Descartes we not forget that the *cogito* is preceded, and as if doubled or lined (in the sense that lining gives material resistance and holding, but also one might say in the theatrical sense of the actor's "double") by the position of elementary chaos.

Light itself proceeds from chaos, both in the order of divine operations and in that of Descartes' fiction-making operations (which are the same). "I shall tell you that I am engaged in separating chaos in order to bring forth from it light. . . ."[24] The radical, even original nature of the Cartesian enterprise requires that it begin with chaos—indissociably, indiscernably with chaos and with the subject. The minimal condition is at once the creation of a chaos by a subject and the conception of a subject attested to by the matter of chaos. One precedes the other, the other precedes the one, at the same time. Henceforth, one cannot avoid the suspicion that the *cogito* itself, the *luminous cogito*, still serves as mask for something that is strictly speaking neither soul nor God nor world. And that the light painted as *trompe l'oeil* can make its relief visible only by dissimulating this obscure other side, this unnamable support (this *sub-stance*) on whose chaotic weave it is painted. Thus it will never be possible to remove or to raise the veil of the painting without running the risk of never seeing anything more, seeing nothing there but blackness—a blackness that no light has yet separated from itself, and which does not assume even the figure of a shadow. And yet it is also through the "vision" of this invisible support—*formless substance of the eye itself*—that illumination first takes place. Behind the painting, what in fact does the face of Descartes resemble? Behind the lifeless eye, which deceives the eye, what does the eye (of the) subject resemble? Which *chaogito*?

IGNOTUS MORITUR SIBI

If the chaogito paints itself, this means both that it *cannot* paint itself, and that it can present itself only in painting. The reason is the same in both cases: the chaogito resembles nothing. Resemblance is required because it is impossible.

It is impossible first of all for the *cogito* itself. It is the subject who cannot recognize *himself*, not without entering into a complex process whereby the *trompe l'oeil* converts into vision the blindness of substance, of the support that can neither see nor be seen without exposing the surface of light and of the gaze. It is thus necessary to have recourse to the gaze of another, which is not without danger, that of having the vision of oneself absorbed within an alienated image. Descartes stated later that he took as his motto the following lines from Seneca, which extend the *"bene latuit"* of his first motto:

> *Illi mors gravis incubat,*
> *Qui, notus nimis omnibus,*
> *Ignotus moritur sibi.*[25]

Descartes delivers this motto in one of those passages (whose frequency is well known) in which he declares himself to be henceforth resolved to "abstain from writing books." This resolution was already made at the end of the *Discours*, and I shall return to this point. For in the book, that is, upon the painting in which the subject exhibits himself, there is brought into play in its entirety the difficulty of acceding to self-vision through the self-portrait's deceptive appearance, the difficulty of acceding to the face by way of the mask, to substance by way of the surface.

This difficulty is verified by the *Discours* in two respects, framing it so to speak: the *Discours* is anonymous, and it purports to be the first and last book published by its author.

The anonymity of the *Discours* does not have the function of ordinary anonymity—unless it "unveils" the hidden activity of all forms of anonymity. It does not simply hide its author. It hides the author who presents the painting of his life, thus it hides him who discovers himself in his truth. This anonymity thus states expressly that it is a deceptive appearance, and at the same time, lacking the author's name—and *through* this lack—it proclaims that there *is* an author, a single, irreducible author, or rather an author of whom a single, irreducible example will be depicted for us. It thus proclaims that the dissimulated name is the *most proper* of proper names: the name of the one who alone gave himself the method of certitude, and hence of the one who gives *himself* out as the method of certitude and the certitude of method.[26] But the identity of this subject is valid only on the condition that it be identity *itself*, stripped entirely of the accidental, the empirical (the name René Descartes, for example), and presented in its substance as subject. Perhaps this is actually the complex reference to the author implied by the *trompe l'oeil* in general, in other words by all painting that operates under the sway of resemblance. There should be *no* author if the perfect illusion joins with the identity itself that is (re)presented, and if the author of such a perfect resemblance can be none other than the author par excellence.[27] Anonymously once again *larvatus pro Deo*.

Moreover, yet confirming what we just said, Descartes intends for this anonymity to be only temporary. In this sense it is no longer a simple dissimulation. It is a mask to be removed, but it must be removed only once the public in reading the *Discours* has taken cognizance of its author. For the moment the mask allows "that what I shall do be not less than what would have been expected."[28] If Descartes fears deceiving with respect to what may be expected from René Descartes, it is because the *Discours* (the method) must not be measured against its author, but rather the author against the method, that is, against the very certitude of science. The feint must be deciphered here as well: beneath "I am perhaps not equal to what is expected of me" must be read "I am only the unheard(—of) equal of what I exhibit." My identity is valid only as the exorbitant identity of the subject of truth—*I think*. "René Descartes" will be unveiled only once he is identified with this I (which, as we know, is identical only to itself and resembles nothing).[29]

The anonymous subject of the method exhibits a feigned subject in portrait so as to find therein his truth of subject impossible to feign.

Without this operation the subject would never appropriate his own image (his idea), but with it perhaps he never appropriates anything but his own painting.

This is probably why Descartes intends never to publish anything else. Whether it be *Le Monde*, hidden behind the *Discours*, or what he continued writing later, Descartes believed that he should "in no wise agree that they be published during my life so that neither the opposition and controversy to which they would perhaps be subject, nor even whatever reputation I might obtain from them might give me occasion to lose the time that I intend to employ in my own instruction."[30] Thus it is no longer a question of gaining instruction from the judgment of another: the viewer's gaze was apparently necessary only for the presentation of the subject, not for the verification of science. In being published, however, Descartes would expose himself to losing himself, to "dying unknown unto himself," or to not knowing himself, which for the subject amounts to dying. The *exhibited* subject stands to win his own substance and to lose his own identity. Or vice versa. Henceforth he will only be published posthumously—once he has returned in himself unto himself, to "this indefinable something that has no name in any tongue."

And yet Descartes continues to write. "I thought," he writes, "that as I discovered their truth, I should actually continue to write down all things that I judged to be of some importance, and that I should bring to this the same care as if I wished to have these things printed: as much in order to have a greater opportunity to examine them carefully, since one certainly looks more closely at what one believes must be seen by many (. . . as in order that they might be read after my death)."

It is thus as if writing, deficient and flat prior to the *Discours*, had been discovered or transformed by means of painting into a necessary instrument of thought. Or rather, writing itself has become painting. To write is to paint for oneself a *trompe l'oeil* reader. In order to "examine more closely," Descartes pictures to himself the deceptive appearance of another's gaze. The exhibitionist contrives for himself the fiction of a voyeur. This is a feint, and yet is not one: the voyeur will exist after my death; it is there that I see him. Through his own lifeless eye Descartes sees the one who beholds him. He needs this added *trompe l'oeil* in order not to die unknown to himself.

LARVATUS ERGO

A fictive viewer is thus always required for the exhibition of the portrait, that is, for the *conception* of the *subject* of the painting, for *truth*. The truth that Cartesian mathesis institutes as the certitude of the subject is at the same time determined as being the auto-conception of this subject, or the auto-conception that *is* this subject. The ontology of subjectivity is not that of a subjective "interiority" or of a consciousness; it is the ontology of the auto-conception of being.

But this is the same determination that through the exposing of the subject radically destroys the possibility of self-apprehending. Descartes' entire discourse pertains to nothing other than the appropriation of self. But its organization or position—emphasis having been laid here upon the manner in which it is presented as a discourse of the painting of self—conforms to the constraints of the impossibility of this appropriation: the ontology of the *thinking substance* stands by principle in contradiction with the exhibition of the surface covered with signs. Moreover, this is what metaphysics had always said. The ontology of the *subject*, however, posits exhibition itself, together with the production of signs, as the locus and the being of substance itself. Such an ontology seeks to show the support, or rather that the support show *itself*. And without fail what it exposes and exposes to itself is the lure of its surface. In the very instance of appropriation the subject appropriates only the *sans-fond* of the still surfaceless substance*, or the formlessness of the support that has not taken pictorial form.[31]

So "true" it is that the surface forms the *fond*—and that in order for the latter to see itself it must see its surface—and that to see the surface it has only the gaze of others. Consequently, so true is the fiction of the viewer.

"Fictive" here does not mean "imaginary," but rather designates a position or a *role* that is structurally indispensable in the production of the *theoretical* truth of the subject. Cartesian fiction designates the feint (the same word) whereby the truth of an unexhibitable identity is given—where it at once presents and represents itself. This is the very feint of painting and perspective, as set forth by the *Dioptrique*.

For instance, copperplate engravings, which consist of a bit of ink spread here and there on paper, represent for us forests, towns, men and even battles and storms. And yet, in the infinity of diverse qualities that they cause us to conceive of in these objects, there is not one in respect of which they actually resemble them except shape. Even this is a highly imperfect resemblance, given that on a totally flat surface they represent raised and sunken objects in various manners, and according to the rules of perspective, they often represent circles better by ovals rather than by other circles, and squares by diamonds than by other squares. Such is the case with all other figures, so that often in order to perfect the quality of the image, and to represent an object better,

---

* In French, the word *fond*, signifying bottom, depth or foundation, as well as content or meaning, stands opposed to both *forme* and *surface*.—Trans.

these figures should not resemble it. We must hold a quite similar thought of the images that are formed in our mind. . . .[32]

It is clear that the "fictive" is not the "imaginary," or rather that it is, in the sense that the imaginary itself, the order of the image, is henceforth the order of thought. Cartesian imagination inextricably compounds the value of irrational and dangerous "fantasy" with that of the image as *sketch* [*tracé*] that reproduces the thing. But once the thing exists in and through its figure, this sketch is also *the sketch that produces the thing*. One thing alone has no figure—the thinking substance. But for all things, and thus for thought as well, there is only one law of presentation: its figure must be sketched. Thus the ticklish connection of the "figureless" and of the law of the sketch constitutes what is called the "subject." Moreover, via a long story, it is this connection that initiates the future privilege of (re)presentation for Kant of space over time, with all its consequences. Cartesian theory is fundamentally that which provides true thought of the thing itself with the condition of spatial representation—and for this reason it is the theory of the *subject*, that is, of the "homogeneity of the substratum of representation" of which Panofsky speaks with regard to perspective.[33] This homogeneous substratum is the substance of the "single and immobile" eye, as it is *supposed* by perspective. Descartes' philosophy is grounded in the ontology of this *position* required by *per-spective*, that is, by "clear and piercing vision." Since this position is as unassignable (being always on the reverse side of the support) as it is rigorously determined, this same ontology supports itself only through the representation by which one deceives the eye by painting the eye itself. The subject does not imagine himself, but because he can be only the subject of his representation, at each moment he bestows upon himself his *image*, he *pictures himself*.

The vision (the theory) of the subject is not "fictive." This may be better expressed by a judicial cognate of the word, "*fictice*." A fictitious action in Roman law is one in which the judge extends the validity of the law to a case where it does not apply. Yet this is a real action, and not a scholastic exercise. The law of Cartesian truth is the law of the vision of the subject, the law of evidence ("natural light") that produces certitude, per-spective. The method extends its validity to the case where it cannot apply: the subject's viewing himself, the vision of vision. *Speculation* is fictitious, therefore it exhibits itself not by means of mirrors, but portraits—which are masks.

The mask's eye is double. It is the painted eye of the picture, which does not see but appears to see (*videre videor*), and which masks the blind eye of the painter who hides himself. At the same time it is the eye of a mask, in other words the only thing in a mask that is neither feigned nor figured. A mask does not have eyes, it has holes. Behind the holes is the actual eye of one knows not whom. The structure of the mask is thus equivalent to the structure of the face (this is why it deceives and figures, deceiving by figuring a figure that resembles), if the face indeed corresponds to what is expressed by Lichtenberg's aphorism referred to by Freud: "He found it strange that in place of eyes cats have two holes slit flush with the skin." But this structure is still that *of the eye itself*, which has at its center, as Descartes could not fail to note, "a little round hole called the pupil, which appears so black in the center of the eye when one looks at it from the outside."[34] To see the eye is to see the mask, and this always means seeing the glaringly truthful figuration of the hole. To see the mask is to see the eye: by masking himself Descartes has shown everything.

Let us now re-read the "larvatus prodeo."

In order that the blush of their faces does not show, actors on the stage put on a mask. Like them, when I go out into this theater of a world, where hither I have been but a spectator, masked I go forward.

It is not clear where Descartes got the idea connecting the function of the theatrical mask with modesty,[35] or whether this explanation is traditional or of Descartes' invention. Finding this passage somewhat troublesome, Adam and Tannery state that it must involve a recollection of grammar school theater: only young amateur actors need to hide their bashfulness about appearing on stage. This is clearly less than convincing. In return, however, we might pause for a moment to consider those plays in which Descartes might have had occasion to act at La Flèche: *Les Fausses vérités ou Croire ce qu'on ne voit pas et ne pas croire ce qu'on voit* by Ouville, *L'Innocente infidélité* by Rotrou, *La Fidèle tromperie* by Gougenot, *Les Apparences trompeuses* by Boisrobert, or *Le Semblable à soi-même* by Alarcon? Was it he who as Lidias, one of the secondary characters in *La Ressemblance* by Rotrou, declaimed, "I believe myself to have a mask," or as one of the two Dromios in *The Comedy of Errors*, "I am to myself disguised"?[36] Is not the *Discours de la méthode* the theory of baroque esthetics, of tragi-comedy as *trompe l'oeil* (plot and decor) that takes over the stage during the very period when Descartes was writing the *Discours*? Descartes' thought is then the most exemplary form of *baroque thought*, finally in other words, and as I think may now be "seen," less the theory *of* the *trompe l'oeil* than *theory as* TROMPE L'OEIL, with all that this expression means.

. . . or rather, with all that this expression cannot state without collapsing in upon itself.

In any case it is known that Descartes wrote at least three acts of a comedy, which according to Baillet "was just like a woodland Pastoral or Fable" (the first form of tragi-comedy, an edifying fable employing masks, false pretenses, and metamorphoses). Also according to Baillet, in this play Descartes "wanted to cloak the love of wisdom, the quest for truth and the study of philosophy in the figured speeches of his characters." We shall never know what these masks were like. In any case, I know with total certainty that in this scenography (the ancient word for the science of perspective) *I* set upon the stage from beginning to end a spectator, myself, whom I never saw and whom I always took for another, myself.

But let us return to the mask. It does not hide the subject as much as it does his shame. This is to say as well that it shows the subject, that it allows him to show himself relieved of all shame. The mask at once hides and shows the shamelessness of the subject who exposes himself, this "blush of the face" which according to Ferenczi is the equivalent of an erection. The portrait of Descartes that no one has ever seen, and which however is his only portrait, is that of an erect Descartes.

However, through the wiles of Medusa, as unavoidable here as elsewhere, this is also the portrait of Descartes' *confusion*. If there can be no subject except erect, this erection itself plunges him in confusion. The mask dissimulates the subject in disarray, in disorder, ashamed of himself and bereft of assurance the moment he presents himself. But since the subject *was not* before coming out upon the stage where he will say "I am," the mask also dissimulates the confusion in which he comes unto himself (thus unto being), obscure to himself beneath the black reverse side of the mask, losing himself in this other whose role he plays in the attempt to appear to himself.

Behind the mask is no one; there is no figure for thought, if "by body I understand all that may end in some figure."[37] There is someone beneath the mask, since masked "he" goes forward. There is someone confused with no one, since "he" resembles nothing, someone who is confused with no one [*personne*], that is, in Latin, with the role or mask with which "he" hides his shame.

But this modesty is the condition of knowledge of the subject. The text of *Les Préambules* adds: "Science is like a woman; if she is chaste and remains by her husband she is honored; if she gives herself to all, she debases herself."

Bene latuit: behind the mask science remains by her husband, Descartes. Or rather Descartes, a masked woman, remains by God. In this intimacy behind the mask, shame could be gotten rid of; truth could bare itself. "At present the sciences are masked; the masks removed, they would appear in all their beauty." This is still in the same text, and a singular way of throwing off the mask. Descartes and science, or God and Descartes, in short the subject and himself, naked could *conceive the subject in complete purity.* But perhaps this is precisely what is impossible, and in any case never visible. Descartes' children, little Francine and the *ego* of the *cogito,* always remain hidden.

Larvatus pro Deo: in all initiations, in all sacred rituals, the sole function of the mask has always been to hide a person *who was not a person,* who ceased to be a person once he masked himself. In his place the mask shows the figure of the god, never visible without a mask. The subject of Descartes is initiated into the theory of the subject by uttering *larvatus ergo sum.* "In its own terms the *cogito* signifies nothing. It signifies as mimic," writes Valéry.[38]

(Translated by Daniel A. Brewer)

NOTES

1. One has only to look through the literature on Descartes to find these various fluctuations. Special reference may be made to the work of Maxime Leroy, *Descartes, le philosophe au masque,* 2 vols. (Paris, 1929), and concerning the text *Les Préambules,* to the commentary of Adam and Tannery, H. Gouhier, *Les premières pensées de Descartes* (Paris: Vrin, 1958), J. Sirven, *Les années d'apprentissage de Descartes* (Paris: Albi, 1928), as well as S. de Sacy's *Descartes par lui-même* (Paris: Seuil, 1956).

2. *Préambules,* in Descartes, *Oeuvres philosophiques,* 3 vols., edited by F. Alquié (Paris: Garnier, 1963–73). I shall refer to this easily accessible edition, designating the volumes by roman numerals (I, II, III). In this case, I, 45.

3. "He who was well hidden lived well" (*Tristes,* III, 4, 25). Cf. Descartes' letter to Mersenne of April 1634.

4. Hence in general the *narrative* mode of Cartesian exposition, whose specificity Hegel strongly emphasizes in his *History of philosophy.* I shall return to this later. However, it should be pointed out here that this mode, closely related to the pictorial model, concerns the three texts that founded Cartesian philosophy: the *Regulae,* the *Discours,* and the *Méditations* (and in part *Le Monde* and *L'Homme*). (As for the *Principes,* they are an exposition designed for schools, at least according to the wish of their author). In this sense the present study is the continuation of a sketch of the history of philosophical exposition begun elsewhere concerning Hegel and Kant.

5. I, 570–71.

6. October 17, 1630. I, 278.

7. October 8, 1629. I, 224.

8. At issue is not—not only—the "psychology" of Descartes. How could he have confidence in frankness who singly has just invented frankness as method, in other words who has just invented the very conditions of veracity?

9. I, 640.

10. I, 651.

11. I, 654. A more general area of examination would be all the procedures of comparison, metaphor and model whereby Cartesian light is always presented as the object of *indirect* sight.

12. I, 687.

13. II, 422, 428.

14. The material concerning Apelles has been taken from the remarkable documentation brought together by Dominique Bergougnan throughout the *Enciclopedia dell'arte classica e orientale* (Rome: 1958—); by Pauly in the *Real Encyclopâdie der Classischenaltertumswissenschaft* . . . (Stuttgard: J. B. Metzler, 1894–19—); by E. Bénézet, *Dictionnaire critique et documentaire des sculpteurs, dessinateurs et graveurs* (Paris: Grund, 1948); by L. Hourticq, *Encyclopédie des Beaux-Arts* (Paris: 1925).

15. One should open up the gap formed here by the correspondence between the theoretical apparatus and the situation, both of which oblige the author to hide himself. The situation is that of the Galileo affair—Galileo who later will have *lost his sight* when Descartes will wish to have him read his works.

16. I, 614.

17. II, 453.

18. II, 817. The two pages that follow in Descartes' text repeatedly name the painter and refer in particular to his portraits of Alexander.

19. II, 818.

20. I, 615.

21. The admission in turn dissimulates, however, another proposition, which is to be analyzed at a later stage in this work, namely, that only the fictive creation of another possible world provides, according to certitude, the true science of our world. The theoretical status of fiction, such as it governs all of modern science, is thereby instituted.

22. I, 347.

23. It must at least briefly be recalled that the *cogito* makes it known *that there is* a substance, in other words a *subject* of the operation, but not— in the moment of the cogito itself—*what* this substance is. The knowledge of the *cogito* itself, strictly limited to what constitutes it as such, is but the knowledge of something as a subject, in other words the knowledge of a subject as something that *nothing*, in this *instant*, yet determines either as "consciousness," nor even as "thought" in a definite meaning of the term. In the instant of the cogito, thinking is but the self-positioning of the fiction-making operation of doubt, which substantiates itself exactly there where its feint occurs. This is what substantiates itself, or "materializes" according to the following passage from the *Réponses* to Hobbes: "The subjects of all acts are in truth understood as substances (or if you will as things of matter, that is, as metaphysical matters)" (II, 604). Insofar as the word "matter"—with and despite Descartes' precautions—designates something here (and is not simply the equivalent of "something," in other words of "anything"), it can designate only that which escapes all assignation or designation: the formlessness and unnamableness of the subject that indeed *here* has no form, and that cannot be named *since its pure nomination is equivalent to its self-statement* (SON AUTO-ÉNONCIATION), *which states only the act of stating itself* . . . Pure anonymity (to which we shall turn) and full identity here are rigorously the *same* "thing."

24. Letter to Mersenne, December 23, 1630. I, 287.

25. Letter to Chanut, November 1, 1646. III, 684. "A grievous death awaits him, too well known by all, who dies unknown to himself."

26. Which will later have to be extended by analyzing the special exemplariness set in play by the *fable* of the *Discours*.

27. This is why only anonymity is acceptable, and not a pseudonymity such as that of Polybius the Cosmopolitan.

28. Letter to Mersenne, February 27, 1637. I, 523.

29. Cf. the text of Voetius, quoted by Descartes in his *Epitre* to Voetius: "His name, for a while kept secret, and which he himself revealed, is René Descartes" (III, 29). If it were not somewhat superfluous, one might add here the analysis of the feint with which Descartes presents his *Discours*. It was a response to the false rumor that was spread, according to which he had a philosophy. He claims that he fashioned himself one so that the false rumor would stop being one: the argument thus reproduces the process for separating the true from the false, this time probably with a scarcely concealed irony, yet perhaps revealing the constant irony that governs this process throughout the *Discours*: as if certitude were certain only of feigning to be certain . . . (cf. I, 600–601).

30. I, 638.

31. This is clearly what must be established by examining the fable of the *cogito*. In this regard let us point out that the present study consists of plunging into the breach in the *cogito* as it was situated by J. Derrida in "Cogito et histoire de la folie" in *L'écriture et la différence* (Paris: Seuil, 1967).

32. I, 685.

33. *La perspective comme forme symbolique*, trans. G. Ballangé (Paris: 1975), pp. 174, 42, for the following quotation. The entire work by Panofsky would require commentary along the lines of the Cartesian motif.

34. *L'Homme*, I, 416.

35. Masks have been known to be used because of modesty, such as those found in the doorless *cabinets d'aisance* of certain Venetian homes of the Renaissance. Masks are also known to have been worn to the theater during the Elizabethan period by women of title. We shall see later that a masked woman, a spectator, is appropriate for the show that Descartes will present.

36. Still more directly related would be an examination of plays of Jesuit theater from this period, such as the *Cenodoxus* by Bidermann, a story of hypocrisy and feint, in which Death repeats as in Calderón that "life is a dream." One would then have to examine this moral theater designed to uphold the ethics of life conceived of as theater, an ethics that we find in Descartes (cf. for example the letter to Elizabeth, May 18, 1645).

37. Second *Méditation*, II, 417.

38. Paul Valéry, *Cahiers*, ed. Judith Robinson, 2 vols. (Paris: Gallimard [Pléiade], 1973–74), 1: 609.

THREE

CATARACT: DIDEROT'S DISCURSIVE POLITICS, 1749–1751

Jeffrey Mehlman

Il y a des nuages, il pleut et voilà tout.

Michel Serres

In 1749, Réaumur, in couching the cataracts of a girl born blind, presided at what literary history has come to regard as the "experiment of the century."[1] The event was decisive for Diderot and was integrally linked to the emergence of his philosophical and political "maturity." For the text that he was prompted to write by Réaumur's experiment, *La lettre sur les aveugles*, marks the first coherent articulation of his atheism.[2] And his ensuing imprisonment and act of submission at Vincennes was to necessitate a subsequent strategy of characteristic circumvention and ruse. It is to that strategy that these pages are devoted. For our reading of the 1749 text shall be oriented toward a consideration of the bracing implications of the deviousness of the first major essay which Diderot, with "tacit permission" from Malesherbes, was to publish after emerging from Vincennes, *La lettre sur les sourds et les muets*.[3]

We should do well to observe initially that whereas Diderot's contemporaries were transfixed by the spectacle of a blind sensibility emerging into light, he, on the contrary, was above all concerned with the new understanding that might accrue by sharing philosophically the experience of the blind. Whence the essay's center, the fictive deathbed discourse of Saunderson, the blind professor of optics. For Saunderson speaks from the discursive position in which the cosmological proof of God's existence turns short. Eyeless, he is the missing link in the infinite chain of an allegedly ordered universe, the gentle Cambridge monster who can but smile in irony at every appeal to the self-evident splendor of the cosmos.

Diderot, of course, was careful to delineate his own difference from Saunderson in a letter of reply to Voltaire: "Le sentiment de Saunderson n'est pas plus mon sentiment que le vôtre. . . ."[4]* But he continues: "C'est ordinairement pendant la nuit que s'élèvent les vapeurs qui obscurcissent en moi l'existence de Dieu; le lever du soleil les dissipe toujours. . . ." The image recalls the discomfort of the deist in *La Promenade du sceptique* (1747), interrupted in his discourse by a storm: "le ciel s'obscurcit; un nuage épais nous déroba le spectacle de la nature."[5] The discourse of atheism, the core of Diderot's text, is the language of a cloud (*nuage, vapeurs*). Emblematically, returning to the point of inception of the *Lettre*, we may designate that cloud a *cataract*. Littré: "*Cataracte*: opacité du cristallin ou de sa membrane . . . qui empêche les rayons lumineux de parvenir jusqu'à la rétine et qui cause ainsi la perte de la vue."

In its most virulent core, Saunderson's discourse—and Diderot's text —comes close to transcribing a series of passages from Book V of *De Rerum Natura*. Paul Vernière, in particular, has been insistent and persuasive in maintaining that it is Lucretius—"Lucrèce et Lucrèce seul"—(and not Diderot's contemporary physiologists) who dictates Saunderson's quasi-delirium of a universe of chance worlds monstrously emerging and fading away.[6] Diderot takes us to a hypothetical origin of things: "si nous remontions à la naissance des choses et des temps, et que nous sentissions la matière se mouvoir et le chaos *se débrouiller*, nous rencontrerions une multitude d'êtres informes" (p. 121). Thus our cataract—or cloud—takes on a certain positivity. Far from being a simple obstacle to the vision of God's splendor, it becomes a stochastic chaos, a suspended fog, out of which things and times in their plurality are precipitated. Diderot's cataract ceases to be privative, and emerges —potentially—saturated with the entire universe of Lucretius.[7]

One index of the positivity of Diderot's blind universe is the extent to which it is dominated by what he regarded as the most fundamental of senses: touch. (See, most succinctly, the third *Entretien sur le 'Fils naturel'*: "Les sens ne sont qu'un toucher . . .").[8] It is in this realm perhaps that a more essential and idiosyncratic relation to Lucretius

---

* French quotations in the text are translated in the appendix.

than that traced by Vernière in his search for "sources" may be approached. For *De Rerum Natura* as well offers a universe bizarrely subordinated to touch. Consider, on the one hand, Diderot's blind man defining a mirror: "une machine . . . qui met les choses en relief loin d'elles-mêmes . . ." (p. 84). And symmetrically: "un miroir est une machine qui nous met en relief hors de nous-mêmes" (p. 85). And now, Lucretius, in Book IV, on the cause of vision: "there exist what we call images of things; which, like films drawn from the outermost surface of things [*quasi membranae summo de corpore rerum dereptae*], flit about hither and thither through the air. . . ."[9] "In the first place, from everything we see there must of necessity continually flow and discharge and scatter bodies which strike our eyes and excite vision."[10] The blind man's mirror in Diderot, estranging an object—or subject—from itself, and Lucretius' *simulacrum* both appeal primarily to touch. So much so, in fact, that we are tempted to confront the Lucretian "proof" of the existence of *simulacra*, on the one hand:

In the first place, since amongst visible things many throw off bodies . . . as often when cicadas drop their neat coats [*tunicas*] in summer, and when calves at birth throw off the caul from their outermost surface, and also when the slippery serpent casts off his vesture amongst the thorns . . . since these things happen, a thin image must also be thrown off from things, from the outermost surface of things [*ab rebus mitti summo de corpore rerum*].[11]

and Diderot's terse assertion, on the other:

Saunderson voyait donc par la peau. (P. 117)

For whether the skin (*tunica, peau*) be that of subject or object, a phenomenology of vision is displaced by an energetics of touch.

But what are we to make of this unorthodox connection between Diderot's text and what Diderot scholarship has long recognized to be its principal source? More simply, what is the relation between sight and touch in Lucretius? It is here that we shall draw on the analyses of France's most imaginative adept of Lucretius, Michel Serres.[12] For we shall attempt to demonstrate that his own "untimely" reading of Diderot's Latin source provides as well the unexpected elements for a reading of the *philosophe*. First off, a confirmation of our earlier comments: "La physique épicurienne . . . est du tact plus que de la vue. . . ."[13] Now along with the theory of *simulacra*, the other main oddity of Lucretian—or Epicurean—physics is the celebrated *clinamen*: "that while the first bodies are being carried downwards by their own weight in a straight line through the void, at times quite uncertain and uncertain places [*incerto tempore ferme incertisque locis spatio*], they swerve a little from their course, just so much as you might call a change of motion. For if they were not apt to incline, all would fall downwards like raindrops through the profound void, no collision would take place and no blow would be caused among the first-beginnings: thus nature would never have produced anything."[14] And further on: "bodies must incline a little; and not more than the least possible [*nec plus quam minimum*]." From the stochastic cloud—or cataract—of Diderot's letter on blindness, we have come to the Lucretian downpour—or cataract—of atoms. But more immediately we are concerned with two infinitesimal deviations in the Epicurean scheme: the *simulacrum* or emission of an extremely tenuous surface, and the *clinamen* or minimal swerve in the vertical fall of atoms.

And now, in what is only apparently a digression from our subject, several remarks on statistical thermodynamics from the "history of heredity" that François Jacob entitled *La Logique du vivant*:

1. "The properties of a gas can be described by the purely mechanical model of balls that collide, and entropy can be interpreted in terms of molecular agitation. If a man is unable to prevent the degradation of energy, it is because he is unable to distinguish each molecule and observe its characteristics. But it is perfectly possible to imagine a being with a better brain and finer senses, whose faculties, according to Maxwell, 'are so sharpened that he can follow every molecule in its course; such a being, whose attributes are still as essentially finite as our own, would be able to do what is at present impossible to us.' This tiny being or demon has to be imagined as capable of 'seeing individual molecules,' and able to move a sliding door which causes no friction, in a partition separating two compartments of a gas-filled vessel. When a rapidly moving molecule arrives from left to right, the demon opens the door; when a slow moving molecule arrives, he closes it; and conversely. The rapid molecules will then accumulate in the right-hand compartment, which will get warmer, and the slow molecules in the left-hand compartment, which will cool down. 'Without expenditure of energy,' the demon will have converted non-utilizable energy into usable energy. He will have circumvented the second law of thermodynamics."[15]

2. The decrease of entropy, or increase of "negentropy," is plainly an increase in order and information within the contingent universe of cloud or gas.

3. Maxwell's demon was exorcised by Szilard and Brillouin: "For Szilard and Brillouin, on the contrary, information has to be paid for. The demon can 'see' the molecules only if he has with them some physical connection, such as radiation. Not only the gas, but the whole system composed of the gas and the demon tends toward equilibrium. Sooner or later, the demon becomes 'blind' to the gas."[16]

4. The resultant image of the organism: "Living or not, every system that functions tends to wear out, to fall into disrepair, to increase in entropy. By means of a certain regulation, each local loss of energy is compensated by work provided by another part of the organism; hence another increase in entropy, in turn compensated by further work carried out at another point in the body. And so on, *in a sort of waterfall*, by which loss in one place is compensated by increased order elsewhere. The coordination of the system depends on a network of regulatory circuits by which the organism is integrated. But as in a waterfall, the total change of energy always takes place in the same direction, that imposed by the second law of thermodynamics. The statistical tendency to disorder gradually dilapidates any system that is closed to all exchanges with the outside world. Ultimately, the maintenance of a living system in good repair has to be paid for: the return to the ever unstable equilibrium leads to a deficit of surrounding organization, that is, to an increase in disorder of the total system composed of the organism and its environment. The living organism, therefore, cannot be a closed system. It cannot stop absorbing food, ejecting waste-matter, or being constantly traversed by a current of matter and energy from outside. Without a constant flow of order, the organism disintegrates. Isolated, it dies. Every living being remains in a sense plugged into the general current which carries the universe towards disorder. It is *a sort of local and transitory eddy* which maintains organization and allows it to reproduce."[17]

Thus the historian of science spontaneously rediscovers the imagery of Lucretius. In a stochastic universe, the transitory eddy in the waterfall corresponds to the turbulence resultant from the *clinamen* in the atomic downpour. Systems relate in that cataract not through any process of contemplation, but rather by a transmission of energy, order, or information: whence the aptness of the Lucretian *simulacrum*. Finally, the irreversible direction of the flow, the fact that the cloud (cataract) in suspension has become rain (cataract) is testimony to the second principle of thermodynamics. At the center of Serres' recent work has been a remarkable articulation of the concerns of statistical thermodynamics with the aleatory grandeur of the Lucretian universe. To which achievement we shall return.

But what of Diderot? If it has yet to *rain* in our reading of the *philosophe*, we have nevertheless discovered a world that is aleatory and tactile, essentially Lucretian. For the world of virginal perception, in which Réaumur's experiment renewed interest, posed philosophical questions that Diderot was content to relinquish to others. Thus notice the delight with which he pairs off idealist (Berkeley) and sensualist

(Condillac) in what he takes to be a thoroughly futile struggle: "Selon l'un et l'autre, et selon la raison, les termes essence, matière, substance, support, etc., ne portent guère par eux-mêmes de lumières dans notre esprit; d'ailleurs remarque judicieusement l'auteur de *l'Essai sur les connaissances humaines*, soit que nous nous élevions jusqu'aux cieux, soit que nous descendions jusque dans les abîmes, nous ne sortons jamais de nous-mêmes; et ce n'est que notre propre pensée que nous apercevons; or c'est là le résultat du premier dialogue de Berkeley, et le fondement de tout son système. Ne seriez-vous pas curieuse de voir aux prises deux ennemis dont les armes se ressemblent si fort? . . ." (p. 115). The extremes of sensualism and idealism tend, mirror-like, to oscillate into each other, based as they are on the primacy of perception, the division between subject and object. To which we would oppose, speculatively, Diderot's blind and tactile world of energy and information.[18] With Serres, the neo-encyclopedist, on the horizon: "Et peut-être n'y a-t-il pas une grande différence entre ce que nous appelons sujets, nous, et ce que nous nommons les objets. . . ."[19]

Consider the problem of Molyneux, inherited from Locke and Condillac, in this perspective. To the question of whether a man born blind, upon gaining sight, could distinguish and identify at a distance the cube and sphere which were familiar to him from touch, Diderot is alone in answering in the affirmative, i.e., in dissolving the problem. Moreover, Diderot's treatment of the problem is marked by repeated recourse to the one figure—chiasmus—that structures what will be seen to be the pseudo-problem par excellence of the *Lettre sur les sourds et les muets*, that of inversion.[20] Thus: "Ces objets pourraient fort bien se transformer dans mes mains et me renvoyer, par le tact, des sensations toutes contraires à celles que j'en éprouve par la vue" (p. 142). Then: "Mais aurait-il continué avec Locke, peut-être que, quand j'appliquerai mes mains sur ces figures, elles se transformeront l'une en l'autre . . ." (p. 142).

Now in Lucretius, in the section concerning trouble in vision, we find an odd analogue to the problem of Molyneux: "And when afar off we see foursquare towers of a city, they often appear to be round, for this reason, because every angle at a distance is seen blunted or rather it is not seen at all, its blow is lost and the stroke does not glide across to our eyes; because while the images are rushing through a great space of air, the air with frequent buffeting forces it to become blunt."[21] It may be suggested, emblematically, that the minute difference between circle and square might serve as an approximation of the tenuous surface film constituting the simulacrum itself. But in that case the "trouble in vision" referred to would be not contingent but essential; it would refer to that breach in perception marked by an essentially tactile *simulacrum*. Such might have been a version of the problem of Molyneux which Diderot would not have hastened to dissolve.

One of the most striking observations on the blind realm of touch concerns an experimental tracing on a hand of the shape of a familiar mouth. When asked whose mouth it is, the blind man proves the best subject of the experiment, for: "la somme des sensations excitées par une bouche sur la main d'un aveugle est la même que la somme des sensations successivement réveillées par le crayon du dessinateur qui la lui représente" (p. 118). We would suggest that the mouth indistinguishable from its own simulacrum be regarded as that of Lucretian Venus, the muse of his sensual physics. Or perhaps it should be read as the organ of a logos which, in the world of the blind, proves to be contaminated originarily by a form of writing (*trace*). . . . We touch here on what might be elaborated as the opposition "Serres"-"Derrida," a question to which we shall return. . . .

La Lettre sur les aveugles was published June 9, 1749. On July 24, Diderot was taken to Vincennes. On August 13, he confessed to Lieutenant General Berryer as follows: "I therefore avow to you, as my worthy protector, what the tediousness of a prison and all imaginable penalties would never have made me say to my judge: that the *Pensées*, the *Bijoux*, and the *Lettre sur les aveugles* are excesses that slipped out of me; but that I can on the other hand pledge my honor (and I have some) that they will be the last, and that they are the only ones."[22] Diderot was released from Vincennes on November 3. He immediately set to work on his tasks for the *Encyclopédie*, but in the course of the following year wrote a sequel to the text that had resulted in his imprisonment, the *Lettre sur les sourds et les muets*. It is to that work's odd relation to the discourse on blindness, in the context of the "neo-Lucretian" remarks already made, that we now shall turn.

Early in the second Letter, addressed with mock deference to the newly named occupant of the chair in Greek and Latin philosophy at the Collège de France, Diderot imagines an experiment in which a series of "conventional mutes" would be obliged to answer questions in the language of gestures: "Ne serait-ce pas une chose, sinon utile, du moins amusante, que de multiplier les essais sur les mêmes idées; et que de proposer les mêmes questions à plusieurs personnes en même temps. Pour moi, il me semble qu'un philosophe qui s'exercerait de cette manière avec quelques-uns de ses amis, bons esprits et bons logiciens, ne perdrait pas entièrement son temps. Quelque Aristophane en ferait, sans doute, une scene excellente; mais qu'importe: on se dirait à soi-même ce que Zénon disait à son proselyte: [*Greek omitted*], si tu veux être philosophe, attends-toi à être tourné en ridicule" (p. 98). The final barb seems ironically intended for the *abbé* Batteux, the addressee of the *Lettre*. In brief, the comedy sketched would be emblematized by Diderot's text itself. But the name of that comedy, of course, is *The Clouds*. Whereas the image of the cloud (*vapeurs*) in the letter to Voltaire seemed essentially privative, here "clouds" constitute the positive content of the 1751 text. Or as Diderot says of his own procedure later in the *Lettre*: "moi qui m'occupe plutôt à former des nuages qu'à les dissiper, et à suspendre les jugements qu'à juger . . ." (p. 125). Now the comedy of a mass interrogation demanding response in an other than oral medium is precisely the scenario of *Les Bijoux indiscrets*: gesture has replaced the discourse of the *bijou*. We need but transcribe Diderot's own subsequent translation of a segment of Lucretius' invocation to Venus—"Parle, o déesse"—at the beginning of *De Rerum Natura* to see how potentially saturated with Lucretian values the "clouds" of the second *Lettre* may be.[23] The text, then, is, at some level, the assemblage of "clouds" through which Venus speaks.

We have clouds, but not yet any rain: neither downpour nor *clinamen*, the infinitesimal deviation (Lucretius: *nec plus quam minimum*). And yet as early as the *Lettre* on the blind, the premonitions of a Lucretian storm have been entertained: "Saunderson avait de commun avec l'aveugle du Puiseaux d'être affecté de la moindre vicissitude qui survenait dans l'atmosphère . . ." (p. 116). Let that sensitivity to the slightest aerial vicissitude serve as a transition to the torrent we shall soon see drenching the text of 1751. . . .

Perhaps the section of the *Lettre sur les sourds* that most crucially links it to its predecessor concerns Diderot's mocking request of the *abbé* Batteux, his addressee, that he clear up the question of what is meant by "la belle nature." In his concluding summary, the *philosophe* states: "j'ai tâché, Monsieur, de vous faire entendre que ceux qui ont lu vos *Beaux-Arts réduits* à l'imitation de la belle nature, se croyaient en droit d'exiger que vous leur expliquassiez clairement ce que c'est que *la belle nature*" (p. 155). Now that exchange between Diderot and the *abbé* Batteux may be read, I would suggest, as a simulacrum, transposed into the realm of esthetics, of Saunderson's deathbed colloquy with Mr. Holmes in the earlier text. It was precisely the untenability of any appeal to the "beauty" of nature that vitiated Holmes' cosmological argument for God's existence; but it is the failure to include a chapter on what "la belle nature" *is* that renders Batteux's entire treatise "sans fondement" (p. 146). And the multiple ironies of Diderot toward his well-placed interlocutor are so many affirmations that the "foundation" requested is not about to be supplied. Thus, whereas the *philosophe* in 1749 had pretended to be merely translating Saunderson, and had distinguished his position from the Englishman's in a letter to Voltaire, in 1750–51 Diderot was implicitly assuming as his own the discursive position whose simple presence in the earlier text had led to his imprisonment. All this under the guise of a submissive surrender to authority. . . .

Now the final section of the second *Lettre*, in which Diderot taunts Batteux on the subject of beautiful nature, is as well studded with short verse quotations from both "ancients" and "moderns," examples—or elements—of the Diderotian "sublime." Although our author demonstrates no interest in the thematic content of the fragments selected, a remarkable mutuality of *orientation* among them may nevertheless be demonstrated. Thus toward the center of the section we find two exemplary passages of verse discussed. First, from the conclusion of the second *chant* of *Le Lutrin*:

> Soupire, étend les bras, ferme l'oeil et s'endort. (P. 133)

Then, from the ninth book of the *Aeneid*:

> Pulchrosque per artus
> It cruor; inque humeros cervix collapsa recumbit,
> Purpureus veluti eum flos succisus aratro
> Languescit moriens; lassove papavera collo
> Demisere caput, pluvia cum forte gravantur.

> the blood spread over his lovely limbs, and his neck, relaxing, sank on his shoulder. He was like a bright flower shorn by the plough, languishing and dying, or poppies, weighted by a sudden shower of rain, drooping their heads on their necks. (P. 135)[24]

In these two remarkably dissimilar verse achievements, the first from a seventeenth-century satire, the second from a Latin epic, we are nevertheless confronted with a sudden—potentially fatal—drooping of . . . the head. (In the context of the imprecation to Batteux to define "la belle nature," it is a bit as though Diderot's nature were presided over by a Divine Thug silently, sublimely "rubbing out" his victims.) It is for that reason that a subsequent passage quoted from the *récit de Théramène* in Act V of *Phèdre* takes on an odd resonance:

> Il suivait pensif le chemin de Mycènes,
> Sa main sur les chevaux laissait flotter les rênes.
> Ses superbes coursiers qu'on voyait autrefois
> Pleins d'une ardeur si noble obéir à sa voix,
> L'oeil morne maintenant, *et la tête baissée*,
> Semblaient se conformer à sa triste pensée. (P. 142, my emphasis)

Jeffrey Mehlman

Once again, in an entirely different context, we find a characteristic lowering of the head, or rather, in Diderot's terms, a "nutation," an inclination (p. 143). Now toward the very beginning of the *philosophe's* sequence of examples we are offered another fragment from the *récit de Théramène*:

> . . . Les ronces dégouttantes
> Portent de ses cheveux les dépouilles sanglantes. (P. 125)

With this initial precipitation of drops, we approach a second associative chain, along with the inclination of the head. For it may be noted that the decline of the head in the passage from Virgil was accompanied by a jet of blood metaphorized as the weight of rain. Whereupon the verb *flotter* in our earlier Racine fragment may be assumed to take on an added resonance. For we are touching here on the associated theme of *liquid descent*. That dimension passes through a playful allusion to Petronius' parody of the Virgilian passage, in which the liquid may be assumed to be sperm, but reaches catastrophic magnitude in a key passage cited from Voltaire's *Henriade*:

> Et des fleuves français les eaux ensanglantées
> Ne portaient que des morts aux mers épouvantées. (P. 133)

We may conclude the series in the midst of Diderot's skeptical observations about the possibility of transposing poetry into paint. For he there quotes again *The Aeneid*:

> Interea magno misceri murmure Pontum,
> Emissamque hiemen sensit Neptunus, e imis
> Stagna refusa vadis; graviter commotus, e alto
> Propisciens summa placidum caput extulit unda.

> But meanwhile Neptune had been made aware by the ocean's roaring commotion, and the currents eddying even in the sea's still depths, that a storm had been unleashed. Gravely provoked, he raised his head from the waves . . . (P. 147)

Diderot's comment is: "Par quelle singularité . . . ce peintre ne pourrait prendre le moment frappant, celui où Neptune élève sa tête hors des eaux? pourquoi, le dieu ne paraissant alors qu'un homme décollé, sa tête si majestueuse dans le poème, tenait-elle un mauvais effet sur les ondes?" (p. 147). With this concluding image our two series converge. The descending torrent has reached the sea and the declining head has been washed along with it.

Now in the course of discussing the earlier fragment from Virgil—Euryalus, his head declining midst a spurt of blood—Diderot, just prior to commenting on the accuracy of Virgil's rendering of the "jet de sang," observes: "Je ne serais guère plus étonné de voir ces vers s'engendrer par quelque jet fortuit de caractères que d'en voir passer toutes les beautés hiéroglyphiques dans une traduction" (p. 135). The liquid (*jet de sang*) whose precipitation we have been charting comes into contact with the chance casting of letters (*jet fortuit de caractères*). But in the most audacious of the *Pensées philosophiques* of 1745 (XXI), "jets fortuits de caractères" had been assimilated to the thoroughly convincing genesis of our world through a "jet fortuit des atomes." That equivalence, of course, is fundamentally Lucretian. The torrent of descending liquid is less the *theme* of Diderot's "sublime" than the chance cataract of characters or atoms out of which every theme *per se* is precipitated.[25]

Perhaps our reading thus far may be described in terms of two models. First, from the "Letter on the Deaf," the example of Diderot stuffing his fingers into his ears in order to block his hearing as soon as the curtain rose in the theater. His purpose in so doing was, of course, to better gauge the import of that crucial dimension of the actor's art: gesture. Whence the bizarre decision to refuse to listen in order to understand better ("pour mieux entendre") (p. 109). I would suggest that in deliberately deafening ourselves to Diderot's argument, in charting the odd narrative tendentially inscribed into the heterogeneous, multilingual fragments of verse that stud Diderot's text, we have attempted something akin to the *philosophe*'s experiment in the theatre.

But a second case, in which Diderot this time imagines himself in the situation of the blind, offers a still more telling model. Consider Diderot on the language of Saunderson: "Ceux qui ont écrit sa vie disent qu'il était fécond en expressions heureuses . . . Mais qu'entendez-vous par des expressions heureuses, me demanderez-vous peut-être? Je vous répondrai, madame, que ce sont celles qui sont propres à un sens, au toucher, par exemple, et qui sont métaphoriques en même temps à un autre sens, comme aux yeux; d'où il résulte une double lumière pour celui à qui l'on parle, la lumière vraie et directe de l'expression, et la lumière réfléchie de la métaphore" (p. 110). The speech of the blind is thus doubly inscribed, and bears with it an unintended, metaphorical dimension. That second stratum, split off from the intentionality of the speaker, offers the image of a rudimentary "unconscious": "Il est évident que dans ces occasions Saunderson, avec tout l'esprit qu'il avait, ne s'entendait qu'à moitié, puisqu'il n'apercevait que la moitié des idées attachées aux termes qu'il employait" (p. 111). But Saunderson's case is soon generalized to the two cases of *Witz* and parapraxis: "Mais qui est-ce qui n'est pas de temps en temps dans le même cas? Cet accident est commun aux idiots, qui font quelquefois d'excellentes plaisanteries, et aux personnes qui ont le plus d'esprit, à qui il échappe une sottise, sans que ni les uns ni les autres s'en apercoivent" (p. 111). Soon, however, the felicitous estranging of linguistic terms turns out to be the special achievement of foreigners speaking an alien tongue, and writers to the extent that they are in the situation of foreigners *vis-à-vis* their own language: "J'ai remarqué que la disette de mots produisait aussi le même êffet sur les étrangers à qui la langue n'est pas encore familière: ils sont forcés de tout dire avec une très petite quantité de termes, ce qui les contraint d'en placer quelques-uns très heureusement. Mais toute langue en général étant pauvre de mots propres pour les écrivains qui ont l'imagination vive, ils sont dans le même cas que des étrangers qui ont beaucoup d'esprit; les situations qu'ils inventent . . . les écartent à tout moment des façons de parler ordinaires" (p. 111). Now it is in the light of the preceding passage that we may interpret our entire analysis as an exploitation of the single word *cataracte*, from blinding cloud (*La Lettre sur les Aveugles*) to torrential downpour (*La Lettre sur les sourds et les muets*). Yet lest that splitting of meaning be regarded as the artifice of an ingenious foreigner, we would do well to consult that writer gifted with an "imagination vive," Littré. For he apprises us that the original meaning of *cataracte* is a barrier: "sorte de herse placée aux portes des villes," whence, in the plural, *cataractes* came to mean floodgates: "portes ou écluses qui sont supposées retenir les eaux célestes." It is from this sense that the optical use of the term—a visual opacity preventing the passage of light—is derived. A second and stranger derivation, however, resulted in the sense of torrential downpour. Littré accounts for it as follows: "Etymologiquement, la *cataracte* est l'engin qui, rompant avec force, bouche un pertuis; on a passé sans peine du sens de cet engin à celui de chute d'eau." Thus the term *cataracte* is imperceptibly split between the meanings of "barrier" and "transgression." We can constitute the term—and our reading—as a tripartite apparatus or "cataract": cloud/dike/downpour. In which case the "cloud" would be the focus of the first *Lettre*, the ensuing "downpour" that of the second, and the—ineffective—"dike" would figure the sheer fact of censorship most dramatically encountered in the prison at Vincennes. As a discursive machine, the "cataract" is thus fundamentally political, allowing one to effect a transgression while affirming the terms of the barrier, to press forward one's articulation of the Lucretian scheme of things even as one pretends to recant one's initial moves in that direction. Such are the ruses of our "cataract" and the *simulacra* it calls into play.

We are now in a position to broach the central question of the *Lettre sur les sourds*: the inevitable gap between the necessary simultaneity inherent in every act of thought (or sensation), on the one hand, and the successiveness of the discourse that would convey it, on the other. Thus, for example: "mais la sensation n'a point dans l'âme ce développement successif du discours; et si elle pouvait commander à vingt bouches, chaque bouche disant son mot, toutes les idées précédentes seraient rendues à la fois . . ." (p. 120). Diderot's discussion, pursued at length, ultimately invalidating the premises of the debate on temporal inversions—for "il ne peut y avoir d'inversion dans l'esprit"—reaches its exemplary formulation in a celebrated passage: "Notre âme est un tableau mouvant d'après lequel nous peignons sans cesse: nous employons bien du temps à le rendre avec fidélité; mais il existe en entier et tout à la fois: l'esprit ne va pas à pas comptés comme l'expression . . ." (p. 124). Time erupts with the materiality of discourse ("la langue se traîne sans cesse après l'esprit"), and manifests an essential incompatibility with and betrayal of the spatiality of mind or thought (p. 120).

Now it is a paradox worth noting that Diderot's elaborate image for conveying the essential simultaneity—or atemporality—of the activity of understanding ("l'entendement") should be the clock of classical mechanics: "Monsieur, considérez l'homme automate comme une horloge ambulante." In a development whose principal "sources" are Descartes and La Mettrie, Diderot proceeds: "que le coeur en représente le grand ressort, et que les parties contenues dans la poitrine soient les autres pièces principales du mouvement. Imaginez dans la tête un timbre garni de petits marteaux, d'où partent une multitude infinie de fils qui se terminent á tous les points de la boîte: élevez sur ce timbre une de ces petites figures dont nous ornons le haut de nos pendules, qu'elle ait l'oreille penchée comme un musicien qui écouterait si son instrument est bien accordé; cette petite figure sera l'âme. *Si plusieurs des petits cordons sont tirés dans le même instant, le timbre sera frappé de plusieurs coups, et la petite figure entendra plusieurs sons à la fois*" (pp. 121–122, my emphasis). As the model is developed, it eventually is assumed to accommodate discourse itself, but in its inception Diderot's clock is designed essentially to illustrate the simultaneity of perceptions in an act of thought. And consequently, to the extent that time—as discourse—has been deemed fundamentally incompatible with the atemporality of individual thoughts, we are faced with a paradoxical discrepancy between time and the clock.

Diderot's esthetics in the *Lettre*, however, are intended to obliterate that discrepancy. For such is the import of the crucial notion of "hieroglyphics," introduced in the course of an effort to define the "spirit" (*esprit*) of poetry: c'est lui [*l'esprit*] qui fait que les choses sont dites et représentées tout à la fois; que dans le même temps que l'entendement les saisit, l'âme en est émue, l'imagination les voit et l'oreille les entend; et que le discours n'est plus seulement un enchaînement de termes énergiques qui exposent la pensée avec force et noblesse, mais que c'est encore un tissu d'hiéroglyphes entassés les uns sur les autres qui la peignent. Je pourrais dire en ce sens que toute poésie est emblématique" (p. 133). The virtual wads of hieroglyphics are thus intended to redeem —or deny—time, to stem the temporal flow of discourse in its incompatibility with the timelessness of mind.

There follows a discussion of an initial example of a hieroglyph that we have already encountered: "Mais l'intelligence de l'emblème poétique n'est pas donnée à tout le monde; il faut être presque en état de le créer pour le sentir fortement. Le poète dit:

> Et des fleuves français les eaux ensanglantées
> Ne portaient que des morts aux mers épouvantées.

Mais qui est-ce qui voit, dans la première syllabe de *portaient*, les eaux gonflées de cadavres et le cours des fleuves comme suspendu par cette digue? Qui est-ce qui voit la masse des eaux et des cadavres s'affaisser et descendre vers les mers à la seconde syllabe du même mot?" (p. 138). The lines from Voltaire were a key element in the torrential *cataract* we constructed above. Here the initial hieroglyph that would suspend the flow of time is the first syllable of *portaient*—thus: *porte*—stemming the flow of the current; it is a dike (*digue*) or cataract (floodgate). And yet what this primal example of a hieroglyph comes to narrate is the catastrophic rush of water beyond the dike. The hieroglyph—indistinguishable in this case from our cataract—would appear to have its own failure (or transgression) inscribed within it.

Consider now the irreversible flow of time, discourse, cataract in its opposition to that emblem of simultaneity, the clock ("horloge ambulante") of classical mechanics. More specifically, we would inscribe what must be the inclined *head*—in view of its "oreille penchée"—atop the clock into that increasingly declining series of inclined heads—from Virgil, Boileau, Racine—that marked the verse fragments in the *Lettre* and culminated in the image of a solitary head apparently afloat on the Virgilian waters. In brief, the irreversibility of the cataract would succeed in decapitating the "man" imagined by Diderot in terms of classical mechanics.

The "time of poetry," however, may also be interpreted as the history of poetry or, in a still broader perspective, of language itself. That history narrates an irreversible loss. For what is the situation of French in relation to earlier idioms? Diderot is univocal: "Ou pour continuer le parallèle sans partialité, je dirais que nous avons gagné, à n'avoir point d'inversions, de la netteté, de la clarté, de la précision, qualités essentielles au discours; et que nous y avons perdu de la chaleur, de l'éloquence et de l'énergie" (p. 128). Similarly, referring to Amyot and Montaigne, Diderot later invokes "cette noblesse prétendue qui nous a fait exclure de notre langue un grand nombre d'expressions énergiques" (p. 152). Thus the temporality of poetry, the history of the language is an irreversible flow—or cataract—figuring a progressive loss of heat and energy. To enter into that current is quite simply to participate in beheading the man of classical mechanics, to encounter the reality of entropy. Littré: "*cataracte*: appareil qui, dans les machines à vapeur à simple effet, sert à régler le mouvement." With stunning untimeliness, Diderot's epistemologico-esthetic meditation on the sublime—"sublimation: passage de l'état solide à l'état gazeux"—has culminated in the realm of thermodynamics.

François Jacob: "The second law of thermodynamics imposes a direction on phenomena; no event can go in a direction different from that observed, for that would mean a decrease in entropy. No part of the universe's substance can return to a former condition, as might be imagined in a purely mechanical system such as an imaginary clock."[26] Michel Serres: "Le temps du moulin décline vers le temps du feu . . . L'éternel retour du même ne peut avoir lieu, ni en statique, ni en dynamique, ni en théorie de l'information. Ni pour le balancier, ni pour le moteur, ni pour la page d'écriture."[27]

The meteorology of Lucretius, the thermodynamics of Serres, and somewhere in between, on the descent, the "cataract" of Diderot. . . .[28] In the structure we have elaborated, our intention has been to indicate the surprisingly rigorous coherence of a genealogy. Surely, a critical generation schooled in the imperialist techniques of psychoanalysis will not smart at the apparently anachronistic reference to thermodynamics. For a crucial relation to that discipline is present in Freud at the inception of his undertaking in 1895 and continues through the critical work of his later years. Indeed, it may be demonstrated that whereas Freud's enterprise reached its culmination in a marrying of the Empedoclean duality Love and Strife with the concerns of thermodynamics, Serres' work has led him to a similar mating of Lucretian Mars and Venus with terms of the same discipline. But it is precisely at that juncture that the difference between Serres and those whose efforts derive essentially from Freud and Nietzsche becomes manifest. For whereas Freud read into the entropaic death instinct repetition *per se* as the ground of psychical—or cosmic—functioning, entropy for Serres is precisely the physicist's access to an irreversibility of time corrosive of the repetitiveness of a reversible, minimally entropaic classical mechanics. Whence the periodic disparagements of both Nietzsche and Freud which traverse his writings.

And Diderot in all this? If Serres has seemed to us, in important ways, the Diderot of our times, it is in part because the locus of just such a disparagement of the current cult of repetitive textuality seems devastatingly present in the *Lettres* we have analyzed: in the vain stuffing of hieroglyphics into the floodgate—or cataract—through which time, irreversibly, would flow. In the current critical context, the implications of that disquieting vision loom among the most forceful that a reading of Diderot may impel us to pursue.

POSTSCRIPT

A postscript, *à la Diderot*, on an additional segment of his work all but saturated by our *cataract*: the "moral tales." Offered as an extension, but, as well, as a provisional summary of our earlier findings.

If one were to pinpoint the formal specificity of Diderot's "fiction," it would lie in the extent to which the activity of narration (*récit*) comes to interfere—or coincide—with the events narrated (*histoire*). Thus, most impressively, in *Jacques le Fataliste* the dialogue between narrator and reader is perpetually interrupting the dialogue between Jacques and his master, the putative subject of the novel. Moreover, the tonality of those two dialogues is diametrically opposed: on the one hand, the "fatalism" of Jacques ("ce qui est écrit là haut"); on the other, the anarchical freedom of the narrator, perpetually taunting the reader with new fictive possibilities he feels at liberty to complicate the plot with. Let these comments on *Jacques* (Serres: "Comment, du hasard, émerge une nécessité? . . . Tous les textes, sans doute, le mien, celui d'Aurevilly, ou *Jacques le Fataliste*, sont des modèles de cette question") serve as an introduction to our reading of the tales.[29]

Upon superimposition, the "quatre contes" yield a surprisingly unvarying *histoire*. Three ("Mystification," "Ceci n'est pas un conte," "Madame de la Carlière") of the four are plainly concerned with the disastrous physical and moral effects undergone by a woman betrayed in love. "Mystification," for example, turns on the advice given by a bogus doctor to Mlle Dornet, abandoned by Galitzine, in order to "rétablir une machine usée par le peine et par le plaisir" (p. 16).[30] But the name of the exhaustion from which she and later Madame de la Carlière explicitly—and Mlle de la Chaux in "Ceci" at least by implication—suffer is "des vapeurs." That term is, in fact, sufficiently marked in the text to merit a scholarly appendix on that ailment in the critical edition of the tales. The apparently *fated* situation with which Diderot presents us repeatedly is the decline of physical and moral energy in what we may call, combining his words, a *machine . . . à vapeurs*.

If we turn now from the *histoire* to the dialogue through which it is narrated, we find a surprising recurrence. For the beginning of "Madame de la Carlière" offers, as well, a meditation on "vapeurs":

Voyez-vous ces nuées?—Ne craignez rien; elles disparaitront d'elles-mêmes et sans le secours de la moindre haleine de vent.—Vous croyez?—J'en ai fait souvent l'observation an été dans les temps chauds. La partie basse de l'atmosphère que la pluie a dégagée de son humidité va reprendre une portion de la vapeur épaisse qui forme le voile obscur qui vous dérobe le ciel. La masse de cette vapeur se distribuera à peu pres également dans toute la masse de l'air, et par cette exacte distribution ou combinaison, comme il vous plaira de dire, l'atmosphère deviendra transparente et lucide. (P. 105)

These meteorological observations between narrator and reader thus serve as a raising of the curtain before the action begins. And yet that impression is deceptive. For the vapor is not removed or liquidated, but expanded, generalized to the point of invisibility. Moreover, the beginning of the *Supplément au voyage de Bougainville*, which, to all appearances, occurs on the day following that of "Madame de la Carlière," gives the lie to the narrator's confidence in the dissipation of the cloud:

A. Cette superbe voûte étoilée, sous laquelle nous revînmes hier, et qui semblait nous garantir un beau jour, ne nous a pas tenu parole.
B. Qu'en savez-vous?
A. Le brouillard est si épais qu'il nous dérobe la vue des arbres voisins. . . .[31]

There is thus an irreducibility of the vapor out of which the action of the *conte* emerges. But that action can as well subside back into it. For within "Madame de la Carlière," the drama of the heroine gives way to a discussion of the chaotic manner in which the public—including reader and narrator—perceives it. We are treated to a description of random agglomerations of opinion within "la foule imbécile" (p. 126). This is the stochastic realm of *inconséquence* that gives the tale one of its titles ("Sur l'inconséquence du jugement public de nos actions particulières"), and it resembles nothing so much as the process of cloud formation with which narrator and reader had earlier been preoccupied: "Dans les circonstances les plus équivoques le parti de l'honnêteté se grossit sans cesse de transfuges" (p. 127). More telling still: "car ils se poussent tous les uns les autres, et comme ils n'ont point de règles dans leurs jugements, ils n'ont pas plus de mesure dans leur expression . . ." (p. 133).

If we turn to "Ceci n'est pas un conte," we find that the opening discussion of "vapeur" between narrator and reader in "Madame de la

Carlière" may be superimposed on a discussion of a discursive analogue to the meteorological phenomenon. For the tale to be told will no doubt initiate a frenetic and random circuit of communication: "un sujet aussi intéressant devrait mettre toutes les têtes en l'air, défrayer pendant un mois tous les cercles de la ville, y être tourné et retourné jusqu'à l'insipidité, fournir à mille disputes, à vingt brochures au moins et à quelques centaines de pièces en vers pour et contre" (p. 73). A further aftereffect of the tale: "une litanie d'historiettes usées qu'on se décochait de part et d'autre" (p. 74). *Pour et contre; de part et d'autre*: plainly, we are in an aleatory medium, the discursive equivalent of the clouds discussed at the beginning of "Madame de la Carlière."

Consider now the relation between *récit* and *histoire* as we have constituted them in the tales. We find a fated and irreversible degradation of moral and physical energy (*vapeurs*) emerging from a stochastic, cloudlike space of communication (*vapeur*). Diderot has assigned the same name to "chance" and "necessity."

To the question of the etiology of "vapeurs," Diderot supplies at least three answers:

1. In "Mystification," the bogus doctor Desbrosses offers an interesting theory explaining Mlle Dornet's illness. But before discussing it, we should note that his theory occurs at the point of intersection of a remarkable number of motifs with which we have been concerned in this essay:

    a. Desbrosses, examining Mlle Dornet: "Je n'écoute pas, je regarde" (p. 7). Explaining the constraints of "Turkish" medicine: "C'est qu'il n'est pas permis d'interroger sa malade . . . On juge la maladie aux gestes. . . . "(p. 13). The reader recognizes here an odd repetition of the scenario in the Letter on deaf-mutes.

    b. Desbrosses is an expert at "la Chiromantie ou la connaissance de sa fin par les traits de la main" (p. 14). He proceeds to read Mlle Dornet's hand, thus enacting a strangely displaced version of the crucial form of writing—of shapes inscribed on a hand—proposed by Diderot in the Letter on the blind.

    c. Desbrosses defines the retina as "une toile d'araignée tissue des fils nerveux les plus déliés, les plus fins, les plus sensibles du corps, qui tapisse le fond de l'oeil" (p. 22). That "textual" image, crucial to *Le Rêve de d'Alembert*, is continuous with the generally centrifugal meditation (hands vs. eye) of the Letter on the blind. To find it situated here in the core of vision ("au fond de l'oeil") is a striking, implicit affirmation of the thesis of that Letter.

Now at the center of this minor text, so studded with fragmentary simulacra of essential motifs of Diderot's thought, the author, through Desbrosses, offers a pseudo-theory of the etiology of *vapeurs*: "On dirait qu'il s'échappe des choses qui ont appartenu, qui ont touché à un objet aimé, des écoulements imperceptibles qui se portent là. Cette idée n'est pas nouvelle; c'est la vieille doctrine d'Epicure. Ces Anciens-là en savaient plus que nous. Cela tient à la vision, et la vision comment se fait-elle? Par des simulacres minces et légers qui se détachent des corps et s'élancent vers nos yeux" (p. 20). Thus at the point of intersection of these various simulacra of Diderotian theory, we are presented with . . . Lucretius' theory of simulacra. Behind the "vapeurs," "des écoulements. . . ." As the Lucretian storm—or cataract—gathers, one understands the precipitation with which J. Proust, in the critical edition, footnotes, "bien entendu," Diderot's lack of sympathy with Desbrosses' theory (p. 164).

2. A second cause—or precipitating factor of "vapeurs" is tendered in "Madame de la Carlière." For the heroine discovers the betrayal of her beloved when his love letters—to another—come fluttering out of a sealed chest that accidentally falls and breaks in her presence: "Là l'anneau casse, le coffret tombe, le dessus se sépare du reste, et voilà une multitude de lettres éparses aux pieds de Madame Desroches . . ." (p. 118). Whereupon: a recognition of betrayal and . . . les vapeurs. But the narrator prepares this sequence with a warning to his reader: "J'ai dit cent fois aux amants: N'ecrivez point, les lettres vous perdront; tôt ou tard le hasard en détournera une de son adresse. Le hasard combine tous les cas possibles, et il ne lui faut que du temps pour amener la chance fatale" (p. 118). The language is remarkably close to *Pensée philosophique* XXI, in which the world is assumed to be explicable through an infinite series of castings of atoms even as a masterpiece could be fortuitously composed through an infinite series of castings of "caractères." *Atomes, caractères*, and now, in "Madame de la Carlière," *lettres*. Out of the stochastic chaos or "vapeur" at the beginning of the tale comes a disastrous and fortuitous cataract of Lucretian "letters" (*détournement* for *clinamen*), and the moral stability of the tale's world is ruined in the process. (Note that in Pynchon's *The Crying of Lot 49*, the figure for entropy is a surreptitious and renegade postal system, disrupting for centuries the West's channels of communications.) The definitive reading of "Madame de la Carlière" may well be the epigraph we have chosen from Serres: "Il y a des nauges, il pleut, et voilà tout."

3. A third observation on *vapeurs* occurs in *Le Réve de d'Alembert*, where Mlle de l'Espinasse refers to it as a "sorte d'anarchie qui nous est si particulière."[32] Anarchy, moreover, is defined as that situation in which "tous les filets du réseau sont soulevés contre leur chef, et où il n'y a plus d'autorité suprême." Order or authority here is largely the illusion of autonomy emergent at the point of maximal intersection of the strands constitutive of the network. When that fortuitous center breaks down, the stochastic chaos from which it emerges—and which insists on its fringes—asserts itself (Diderot's "anarchie"). The political image

here will allow us to account for the case of the one male ruined by a treacherous mate in the *contes*: Tanié in "Ceci n'est pas un conte." For he is destroyed by two voyages to the colonies dictated by his rapacious mistress (Reymer). His fate, that is, is to be ruined by his estrangement from the *métropole* ("le chef"), first in Santo-Domingo, then in the far North where he dies: "J'ai été lui chercher la fortune dans les contrées brûlantes de l'Amérique, elle veut que j'aille la lui chercher encore au milieu des glaces du Nord" (p. 81). If *vapeurs* is the name of a principle of moral and physical—or thermic—degradation which irreversibly governs the constitutive fringes of an order whose center is thereby threatened, Tanié, as much as any of Diderot's women, has been devastated by *vapeurs*.

Thus *vapeur*—stochastic chaos and irreversible degradation of energy—comes to repeat in the *contes* the division within the *cataract* we elaborated earlier: cloud and torrent. Meteorology as the measure of morals? What seems perhaps archaic in Lucretius and magnificently perverse in Serres is, of course, explicit in Diderot: "Le premier serment que se firent deux êtres de chair, ce fut au pied d'un rocher qui tombait en poussière; ils attestèrent de leur constance un ciel qui n'est pas un instant le même; tout passait en eux et autour d'eux, et ils croyaient leurs coeurs affranchis de vicissitudes."[33] Lucretius, Diderot, Serres: beyond the science(s) they have drawn upon—might Serres not have found all the thermodynamics he needed in Diderot's *machine . . . à vapeurs?*—it is the prodigious spiral of discursive energy circulating through that genealogy that promises to yield—feedback or *après-coup*—interpretative possibilities we are only beginning to gauge.

APPENDIX: TRANSLATIONS OF FRENCH QUOTATIONS IN THE TEXT

"Saunderson's sentiment is not my own any more than it is yours."   38

"It is ordinarily at night that the vapors arise which obscure within me the existence of God; the rising sun invariably disperses them . . ."   38

"the sky darkened; a thick cloud hid from us the spectacle of nature."   38

"Cataract: an opaqueness of the crystalline lens or its membrane . . . which prevents rays of light from reaching the retina, thus causing a loss of sight."   38

"if we were to go back to the birth of things and of times, and feel matter move and the chaos disentangle itself (literally: de-fog itself), we would encounter a multitude of amorphous beings."   38

"The senses are but varieties of touch . . ."   38

"a machine . . . that casts things into relief outside of themselves . . ." 39

"a mirror is a machine that casts us into relief outside of ourselves." 39

"Sanderson thus saw by his [the] skin." 39

"Epicurean physics . . . is one of touch rather than sight." 39

"According to one and the other, and according to reason, the
terms essence, matter, substance, support, etc., hardly provide by
themselves any illumination for our mind; moreover, the author of
the *Essay on Human Knowledge* observes judiciously that whether
we climb to the heavens or ascend into the abyss, we never step out
of ourselves; and it is only our own thought that we perceive; now
that is the conclusion of Berkeley's first dialogue, and the basis of his
entire system. Would you not be curious to see in combat two adversaries whose weapons resemble each other so greatly?" 42

"And perhaps there is not a great difference between what we
call subjects, ourselves, and what we call objects . . ." 42

"The objects could very well undergo transformation in my
hands, and return to me, by touch, sensations quite contrary to those
I experience by sight." 42

"But, he would continue with Locke, perhaps when I apply my
hands to the figures they will be transformed into each other . . ." 42

"The sum of sensations excited by a mouth on the hand of a
blind man is the same as the sum of sensations successively awakened by the quill of the artist who represents it to him." 43

"Would it not be amusing, if not useful, to multiply the attempts
with the same ideas, and to pose the same questions to several persons simultaneously. For my part, I believe that a philosopher who
would exercise himself in this matter with several of his friends—
good minds and good logicians—would not entirely waste his time.
An Aristophanes would, no doubt, make an excellent scene out of it;
but never mind; one would tell himself what Zeno told his proselyte:
if you want to be a philosopher, be prepared for ridicule." 43–44

"I who am more concerned with forming clouds than with dis-
persing them; with suspending judgment than with judging . . ." 44

"Saunderson had in common with the blind man of Puiseaux to
be affected by the slightest vicissitude in the atmosphere . . ." 44

"I have attempted, sir, to make you understand that the readers
of your *Fine Arts Reduced* to the imitation of beautiful nature believed themselves entitled to require of you a clear explanation of
just what *beautiful nature* is." 44

Boileau: "Sighs, extends her arms, shuts her eye, and falls
asleep." 45

Racine: "He followed pensively the Mycene road/His hand let
the reins afloat above the horses/His superb steeds that had been
seen in an earlier time,/Filled with so noble an ardor, obeying his
voice,/With a mournful eye now, *their head lowered*,/Seemed to
conform to his sad thoughts." 45

Racine: "The dripping thorns/Bear the bloody remains of his
hair." 46

Voltaire: "And the bloodied waters of the rivers of France/Carried only corpses to the frightened seas." 46

"By what singularity could a painter not seize the striking moment, when Neptune raises his head out of the water? Why, the god appearing at this point to be merely a decapitated man, would his head, so majestic in the poem, produce a poor effect on the waves?" 46

"I would barely be more astonished to see those lines of verse engendered by a chance casting of letters than to see all of their hieroglyphic beauties transmitted in translation." 47

"Those who have written his life claim that he was fertile in felicitous expressions . . . But what do you mean by felicitous expressions, you will perhaps ask me? I shall respond, madame, as follows: those which are literal for one sense, touch, for example, and at the same time metaphoric for another sense, such as the eyes; whence there comes a double illumination for the person addressed, the true and direct light of the expression, and the reflected light of metaphor." 47

"It is evident that on such occasions, Saunderson, for all his wit, understood only half of his utterance, since he perceived only half of the ideas attached to the terms he used." 47

"But who is not from time to time in an identical situation? Such accidents are common among idiots, who are at times capable of excellent jokes, and among the wittiest individuals, who utter occasional blunders, without either the idiots or the wits ever realizing it." 47–48

"I have observed that the dearth of words had the same effect on foregners to whom the language is not yet familiar: they are forced to say everything with a very small quantity of terms, which forces them to place some of them quite felicitously. But every language in general being poor in proper words for writers gifted with a lively imagination, they are in the same situation as foreigners endowed with great wit; the situations they invent . . . constantly divert them from ordinary ways of speech." 48

"a kind of portcullis placed at the gates of the city." 48

"a floodgate intended to retain the celestial waters." 48

"Etymologically, *cataract* is the machine which, breaking forcefully, stops an opening; the transition was made without difficulty from that machine to a waterfall." 48

"but sensation does not have within the soul the sequential development of discourse; and if it could dispose of twenty mouths, each mouth having its say, all the preceding ideas would be rendered simultaneously." 49

"there can be no inversion in the mind." 49

"Our soul is a moving *tableau* according to which we paint endlessly; we employ much time to render it faithfully; but it exists entirely and all at once: mind does not progress step by step as does discourse . . ." 49

"The tongue—language—drags endlessly after mind." 49

"Sir, consider man the automaton as an itinerant clock." 49

"the heart represents the mainspring, and the parts contained in the chest are the principal pieces in its movement. Imagine in the

head a bell equipped with small hammers, to which are attached an
infinite multitude of wires ending in all the points of the case: mount
onto the bell one of those small figures used to adórn clocks, its ear
cocked like that of a musician determining whether his instrument is
on pitch; that figure will be the soul. If several of the small strings
are pulled in the same instant, the bell will be struck with several
blows, and the tiny figure will hear several sounds at once."   49

"it allows for things to be said and thought at the same time, for
understanding to grasp them at the same time that the soul is moved
by them, the imagination sees them and the ear hears them; for discourse no longer to be simply a concatenation of energetic terms that
expose thought forcefully and nobly, but as well a tissue of hieroglyphs piled atop each other and that paint it. I could say in this
sense that all poetry is emblematic."   49–50

"But the intelligence of the poetic emblem is not given to all:
one must be almost in a position to create it in order to feel it
strongly. The poet says: 'And the bloodied water of the rivers of
France/Carried only corpses to the frightened seas.' But who sees, in
the first syllable of *portaient*, the waters swollen with cadavers and
the course of the rivers suspended, as it were, by a dike? Who sees
the mass of waters and cadavers collapse and descend toward the
seas in the second syllable of the same word?"   50

"Or to continue our parallel impartially, I would say that we
have gained (through not having inversions) neatness, clarity, precision, qualities essential to discourse; and that we have lost heat,
eloquence, and energy."   50–51

"that feigned nobility that has made us exclude from our language a great number of energetic expressions."   51

"cataract: an apparatus that is used to regulate the movement
in a simple steam engine."   51

"sublimation: a passage from the solid to the gaseous state."   51

"The time of the mill declines toward the time of fire . . . The
eternal return of the same cannot take place, neither in statics, nor
in dynamics, nor in information theory. Neither for the pendulum,
nor the engine, nor the written page."   51

"What is written above"

"How, from chance, does a necessity emerge? . . . All texts, no
doubt, mine, d'Aurévilly's, or *Jacques le fataliste*, are models of that
question."   52

"restore a machine worn out by pain and pleasure."   52

"Do you see those clouds?—Don't fear; they will disappear of
themselves and without the aid of the slightest breath of wind.—
You think so?—I have often observed as much on hot days in summer. The lower part of the atmosphere that rain has freed of its hu-
midity will absorb a portion of the thick vapor forming the dark veil
that hides the sky. The mass of that vapor will be distributed fairly
equally throughout the entire mass of the air, and by that exact distribution or combination, as you please, the atmosphere will become
transparent and clear."   53

"A: The superb, starry vault beneath which we returned yester-

day, and which seemed to guarantee us a beautiful day, has not kept
its word. B: How do you know? A: The fog is so thick that we can't
see the nearby trees." 53

"In the most equivocal circumstances, the party of decency
swelled incessantly with deserters." 53

"For they all jostle each other, and since they have no rules in
their judgments, they have no measure in their expressions . . ." 53

"so interesting a subject should thrill everyone, be the life of
conversation in town for a month, be turned over and again to the
point of insipidness, furnish matter for a thousand disputes, twenty
brochures, and hundreds of plays in verse for and against." 54

"a litany of worn out stories that came flashing out of one quar-
ter or another." 54

"I don't listen, I look." "It is not permitted to interrogate sick
women . . . Sickness is judged by gesture." 54

"Palmistry or the knowledge of one's end by the lines of one's
hand." 54

"a spider's web woven with the finest, most sensitive nerve
strands of the body, which covers the base of the eye." 54

"It is as though there escape from things that have belonged to
or touched a love object imperceptible flows which stream there. This
idea is not new; it is the old doctrine of Epicurus. The Ancients knew
more than us about it. It is a matter of sight, and how does sight
occur? By thin and light simulacra, which separate from bodies and
dart toward our eyes." 54–55

"whereupon the ring breaks, the chest falls, the top separates
from the rest, and behold a multitude of letters spread before Madame Desroches' feet." 55

"I have told lovers a hundred times: Don't write, letters will de-
stroy you; sooner or later chance diverts one from its address.
Chance combines all possible cases, and needs only time in order to
bring about the fatal case." 55

"There are clouds, it rains, and that's it." 55

"a kind of anarchy so particular to us." 55

"all the segments of the network rise against their chief, and in
which there is no longer a supreme authority." 55

"I have sought fortune for her in the burning countries of America; she wants me to find her still more midst the ice of the North." 56

"The first oath two creatures of flesh ever took occurred at the
foot of a rock crumbling to dust; they called to witness their con-
stancy a sky which is not a single instant the same; everything
passed within and around them, and they believed their hearts free
of vicissitudes." 56

"there are, in bodies which have been struck, infinitely small
oscillating parts, and nodes or immobile parts which are infinitely
close together." 62

"We must return from Hell to earth." 63

"Ah, Mr. Philosopher, poverty is a terrible thing. I see her
crouched, mouth wide open, in order to receive a few drops of ice
water escaping from the Danaid's urn . . . You cannot sing well be-

neath that urn. Happy still is he who can place himself beneath it. I
was there. I couldn't keep myself there."   63

"How is it that with so fine a tact, so great a sensitivity to musical beauty, you are blind to the beauties of morals?"   63

"waters, which either murmur in a solitary, cool place, or descend in a torrent from mountainous heights."   63

NOTES

1. J. Chouillet, *La Formation des idées esthétiques de Diderot* (Paris:
Armand Colin, 1973), p. 132.

2. Page references in the text to *Lettre sur les Aveugles* are to *Oeuvres
philosophiques*, ed. P. Vernière (Paris: Garnier, 1964).

3. Page references in the text to *Lettre sur les sourds et les muets* are to
Premières oeuvres, ed. N. Rudich (Paris: Editions sociales, 1972), 2.

4. Cited in the critical edition of the *Lettre*, ed. R. Niklaus (Paris: Mi-
nard, 1963), p. 89.

5. *Oeuvres complètes*, eds. J. Assézat and M. Tourneux (Paris, 1875–
1877), 1: 235.

6. *Oeuvres philosophiques*, p. 122.

7. For the passages virtually translated from Book V of *De Rerum Natura*
in Saunderson's discourse, see *Oeuvres philosophiques*, pp. 121–23.

8. *Oeuvres esthétiques*, ed. Vernière (Paris: Garnier, 1965), pp. 167–68.

9. Translation by W. H. D. Rouse, Loeb Classical Library (Cambridge:
Harvard, 1975), p. 279.

10. Ibid., p. 295.

11. Ibid., p. 281.

12. Serres lectured extensively on Lucretius at Johns Hopkins in the
spring of 1976, and those lectures are the matter of a forthcoming volume.
Serres' reading of Lucretius informs a recent article on Barbey d'Aurevilly,
"Analyse spectrale: Barbey d'Aurevilly," *Critique* (June–July 1976), pp. 349–
350, to which reference is made below. It is hoped that the reading of Diderot
attempted in this paper will simultaneously offer access to recent developments
in the writings of one France's most iconoclastic thinkers.

13. Serres, "Analyse spectrale," p. 566.

14. Lucretius, p. 113.

15. F. Jacob, *The Logic of Life: A History of Heredity*, trans. B. Spillmann
(New York: Vintage, 1976), p. 196.

16. Ibid., p. 250.

17. Ibid., p. 253, my emphasis. The Maxwell-Brillouin juncture has as
well furnished one of the orienting schemes of the novels of Thomas Pynchon.
This is nicely captured by R. Poirier in an article on that author in which he
is obliged to explicate Brillouin's paper, "Maxwell's Demon Cannot Operate":
"The rage to order, Pynchon seems to say, is merely a symptom of accelerating
disorder," in "The Importance of Thomas Pynchon," *Mindful Pleasures: Essays
on Thomas Pynchon*, eds. G. Levine and D. Leverenz (Boston: Little, Brown &
Co., 1976), p. 20. A worthwhile point of departure for any "grafting" of French
thought on and in American cultural reality might well be a consideration of
why Maxwell-Brillouin should figure centrally in America in the work of a

novelist (Pynchon) and in France in that of someone (Serres) whose efforts lead him to claims normally—or not so normally—those of a critic.

18. That world may be elaborated as a reading of Diderot's *De l'Interprétation de la nature* (1753). The continuity with the *Lettre sur les Aveugles* is marked by the epigraph from the section on "trouble in vision" in Book IV of *De Rerum Natura:* "Quae sunt in luce tuemur/E tenebris" ("we see out of the dark what is in the light"). Scientific activity, in Diderot's text, is interpreted as favorable to a general reversal of the traditional hierarchy in which "experimental philosophy" has been subordinated to "rational philosophy." Thus, in the exemplary Pensée XXIII, experimental philosophy—metaphorized in terms of its tentative, tactile ("tâtonnant"), blind ("les yeux bandés") activity—ends up by disproving the arrogant claims of rationalism—metaphorized as the bearer of a torch ("flambeau")—by demonstrating that light can be decomposed. But the "tactile" is generalized to the principle of the constitution of the world in the "extravagant" series of conjectures on the "general laws of the communication of movement" in Pensée XXXVI. Arguing against the thesis of the *homogeneous* transmission-distribution of movement in cases of impact ("le choc"), Diderot maintains that in the transmission of force, what is communicated is subject to elaborately coded constraints ("il y a, dans les corps choqués, des parties oscillantes infiniment petites, et des noeuds ou points immobiles infiniment proches . . ."). In brief, what is communicated may be thematized as order, information, energy. . . . Finally, the world as the generalized system of such communication is imagined by Diderot, pressing Maupertuis' intuition to the limit, as "une copulation universelle" (Pensee L). Thus the Venusian motif comes to join, under the epigraph from Lucretius, the dimensions of "touch," "blindness," and aleatory "communication" in their opposition to a metaphysics—"rational philosophy" or "geometry"—of light.

19. Serres, p. 598.

20. "Inversion" would be a reversal of order in the passage from a natural medium to a conventional language. But since thought, the *most* natural medium of mentation, is, according to the *Lettre sur les sourds*, atemporal in its essence, there can be no natural *order* of grammatical parts in thought.

21. Lucretius, p. 305.

22. Quoted in A. Wilson, *Diderot* (New York: Oxford, 1972), p. 108.

23. "Salon de 1767," *Oeuvres complètes*, 11: 77.

24. Translation by W. F. Jackson Knight in *The Aeneid* (Baltimore: Penguin, 1956), 9. 433–37.

25. A passage of Lucretius (1. 810–811), twice quoted in the *Lettre* occurs in *De Rerum Natura* just prior to the poet's assimilation of atoms to letters.

26. Jacob, p. 198.

27. Serres, pp. 563, 568.

28. The median position of Diderot may be elaborated as the rudiments of a reading of *Le Neveu de Rameau*. . . . In Book III, Lucretius, in his onslaught on religion, informs us that the myths of infernal punishment are simply metaphors for more earthly torments. Thus the case of the Danaids: "Then to be always feeding an ungrateful mind, yet never able to fill and satisfy it with good things . . . this, I think, is meant by the tale of the damsels in the flower of their age pouring water into a riddled urn, which, for all their

trying, can never be filled" (p. 269). Serres, playing the latter-day Lucretius, *grounds* the same myth ("Il faut remonter des Enfers sur la terre") by taking account of the inevitable degradation of energy—or entropy— introduced into the perfect circularity of the waterclock constituted by Danaids, water, and urn. The cycle would never be quite complete, and only an infernal regime could expect the damsels to perform with ideal efficiency. Thus with every cycle there is a departure from equilibrium, and the ideal circle of the (water)clock gives way to the descending spiral of eddy-within-the-waterfall referred to by Jacob. Consider now the situation of Rameau: "Ah, monsieur le philosophe, la misère est une terrible chose. Je la vois accroupie, la bouche béante, pour recevoir quelques guottes de l'eau glacée qui s'échappe du tonneau des Danaïdes . . . On ne chante pas bien sous ce tonneau. Trop heureux encore, celui qui peut s'y placer. J'y étais; je n'ai pas su m'y tenir." Thus the parasite lives off of the cycle of the Danaids and is superimposable on the function of entropy in Serres's version of the myth. Rameau, after all, is diabolically attuned to Diderot's·materialism ("le grand branle de l'univers"). *Le Neveu de Rameau*, a meditation on degradation . . . of energy?

Diderot's dialogue may in fact be constituted at the intersection of the two *Lettres* we have read:

a. The characteristic response to Rameau is either flight or sticking one's fingers in one's ears, and at the conclusion of the dialogue even the chess players have recourse to the latter. The *neveu* at his most intense, however, is driven to pantomime ("On ne *chante* pas bien sous ce tonneau . . ."). With an audience whose hearing is blocked responding to a remarkable practitioner of gesture, we rediscover the scenario of the *Lettre sur les sourds et les muets*.

b. "MOI: Comment se fait-il qu'avec un tact aussi fin, une si grande sensibilité pour les beautés de l'art musical, vous soyez aussi aveugle sur les belles choses en morale . . . ?" Here the opposition between ethics and esthetics is superimposed on that between sight and touch, the focus of the *Lettre sur les aveugles*. To that extent, we may imagine the esthetic (tact) coming to englobe the ethical (light), thus confirming the Nietzschean reading of *Le Neveu* that Foucault (*Histoire de la folie*), most recently, has undertaken.

c. Just prior to the Danaid reference, Rameau imagines himself as one of the many who *fail* to be the mythical statue of Memnon, his archetype of genius. *They remain mute upon being struck by light.* Thus is the nephew's failure located at the intersection of the two texts we have read.

Perhaps we should think of Rameau, a genius only in abjection, perspiring ("tout en eau") in his vile pantomime, imitating with greatest effectiveness "des eaux ou qui murmurent dans un lieu solitaire et frais, ou qui descendent en torrent du haut des montagnes. . . ."

29. Serres, p. 580.

30. References in the text are to *Quatre contes*, ed. J. Proust (Geneva: Droz, 1964).

31. *Oeuvres philosophiques*, p. 456.

32. Ibid., p. 346.

33. *Oeuvres romanesques*, ed. H. Benac (Paris: Garnier, 1962), p. 604.

FOUR

THE ACT
Michael Ryan

Beware even of every great word, every great pose!
Nietzsche, *Ecce Homo*

Ecce Homo[1] is a theatrical performance that strains to be performative, an act whose language attempts to act. An act, in both senses, is Nietzsche's only recourse if he is to teach what he insists he *has* to teach—the revaluation of all values: "Seeing that before long I must confront humanity with the most difficult demand [that of revaluating all values] ever made of it, it seems *indispensable* to me to say *who I am* . . . Under these circumstances I have a *duty*. . . ."[2] The rhetorical strategy of obligation dramatizes an essential element of the revaluation, the necessity of affirming, by submitting oneself to, the power of fate, instinct, physiology. (According to the book's subtitle, one should become what one necessarily *has* to be, that is, what one is—"How One Becomes What One Is.") the repeated gestures of obligation reflect Nietzsche's belief that his language is inspired, unconscious, obligatory. One could apply his own words to his text: "It is *not* morality that speaks thus; thus speaks physiology" (p. 271; p. 231). The aim of his teaching in *Ecce Homo* is to make language become as fateful, as obligatory, in relation to his student/readers as it is in relation to himself. Language would no longer be the servant of knowledge, but would be rather an obligatory performance, an obliging performative. At least, this is what Nietzsche promises.

Like *Ecce Homo*, the revaluation is a sort of autobiographical act: "*Revaluation of all values [Umwerthung aller Werthe]*: that is my formula for an act of supreme self-examination on the part of humanity, become flesh and genius in me" (p. 363; p. 326). But the book might not only be an exemplary self-examination. Autobiography is also obligatory because the revaluation is inseparable from Nietzsche. It is what makes him unique:

It is my fate that I have to be the first decent human being; that I know myself to stand in opposition to the mendaciousness of millennia.—I was the first to *discover* the truth by being the first to experience lies as lies. (p. 363; p. 326) . . . My task of preparing a moment of the highest self-examination for humanity . . . this task follows of necessity from the insight that humanity is *not* at all by itself on the right way, that it is by no means governed divinely, that, on the contrary, it has been precisely among its highest value concepts [*Wertbegriffen*] that the instinct of denial, corruption, and decadence has ruled seductively. (P. 328; p. 291)

In teaching the revaluation, then, Nietzsche is in effect teaching himself:

The good fortune of my existence, its uniqueness perhaps, lies in its fate [*Verhängniss*]:[3] I am, to express it in the form of a riddle, already dead as my father, while as my mother I am still living and becoming old.[4] This dual descent, as it were, both from the highest and the lowest rung on the ladder of life, at the same time a *decadent* and a *beginning*—this, if anything, explains that neutrality [*Neutralität*], that freedom from all partiality in relation to the whole problem of life, that perhaps distinguishes me. I have a subtler sense of smell for the signs of ascent and decline than any other human being before me; I am the teacher [*Lehrer*] *par excellence* for this—I know both, I am both [*Ich bin Beides*] (p. 262; p. 222) . . . Looking from the perspective of the sick toward *healthier* concepts and values [*Werthen*] and, conversely, looking again from the fullness and self-assurance of a *rich* life down into the secret work of the instinct of decadence—in this I have had the longest training, my true experience; if in anything, I became master in this. Now I know how, have the know-how, to *reverse perspectives*. . . . (P. 264; p. 223)

To teach himself *is* to teach the revaluation, since what the revaluation espouses is "selfishness," becoming oneself: "At this point the real answer to the question, *How one becomes what one is*, can no longer be avoided. And thus I touch on the masterpiece of the art of self-preservation—of selfishness [*Selbstsucht*]" (p. 291; p. 253). Nietzsche's repeated claims of uniqueness and his exaggerated self-vaunting throughout *Ecce Homo* can be considered, therefore, as strategies for dramatizing selfishness.

Selfishness works against knowledge in favor of obligation. Nietzsche also calls it the Dionysian and *amor fati*. It differs from the "mendaciousness" of idealism by calling for the acceptance or affirmation of what is fated—instinct, the physiological concerns of life—rather than inventing a false, ideal world which forbids "physiology." In order to be selfish, to save one's energy by affirming life instead of reacting against it, one must not know oneself; one must actively forget oneself:

Another counsel of prudence and self-defense is to *react as rarely as possible* . . . (p. 290; p. 253) . . . in all these matters—in the choice of nutrition, of place and climate, of recreation—an instinct of self-preservation issues its commandments, and it gains its most unambiguous expression as an instinct of self-defense. Not to see many things, not to hear many things, not to permit many things to come close—first prudence, first proof that one is no mere accident [*Zufall*] but a necessity [*Necessität*] (p. 290; p. 252) . . . To become what one is, one must not have the faintest notion *what* one is. From this point of view even the *blunders* of life have their own meaning and value . . . where *nosce te ipsum* [know thyself] would be the recipe for ruin, forgetting oneself, *misunderstanding* oneself . . . become reason itself. (P. 290; p. 254)[5]

Everything in existence, including the self, will be remembered—eternally returned—because it has been forgotten, become involuntary, hence, necessary and fated.

The movement away from knowledge towards fate or obligation can be described as an attempt to foreclude woman. In *Ecce Homo*, which is one of Nietzsche's more polemically anti-feminist texts, woman is associated with idealism. She is the figure of figures, representation, metaphor, that is, of the grounds of knowledge. Because truth, for Nietzsche, is always false, an appearance, woman is also the figure of error, arbitrariness, and contingency. Like idealism in general, she is an accident, not a necessity. In the paragraph that Peter Gast suppressed from the first edition of *Ecce Homo*, a simulacrum of castration emerges in the text. Nietzsche first speaks of his mother and sister in terms that are far from adulatory:

The treatment [*Behandlung:* also dressing of wounds] which I have undergone on the part of my mother and sister up to this moment inspires me with an unspeakable horror: here works a consummate hell machine, with inevitable certainty at the moment when one can wound me bloodily—in my highest moments . . . because there one lacks power to defend oneself against poisonous worms . . . Physiological contiguity renders such a disharmony praestabilita [pre-eminent]. (P. 266; my translation)

Then, he turns to a father, or, at least, a possible father:

I do not understand it, but Julius Caesar could have been my father—or Alexander, that love-bound Dionysus . . . At this moment, as I write this, the postal service is bringing me a head of Dionysus [*Dionysos-Kopf*]. (P. 267; my translation)

The most important feature of this apparent fantasm of castration is a lack or failure of knowledge—of how Caesar could be the father and of who the father is. The vehicle of castration is the postman, a letter as cutting edge, one perhaps from Nietzsche's mother and sister, since letters were their only means of communication. Moreover, Nietzsche's own act of writing is associated with castration. What the postman brings must be read, known, passively, like a woman as Nietzsche describes her. Writing, one's own performance, might keep castration at bay. Furthermore, Dionysus, *the* Dionysian considered as *amor fati*, that which castration threatens, might also, by converting accidents into necessities, work to neutralize castration. The contrast between passive reading and active writing, between language as a vehicle of communication and language as a means of action, describes a movement, a desire, similar to the one inscribed in the passage from knowledge to obligation in the revaluation.

A trajectory from representation to performance can be deciphered in both the history of Nietzsche's books and that of his life in *Ecce Homo*. The history of his books begins with *The Birth of Tragedy*: "I had discovered the only parable and parallel in history for my own inmost experience" (p. 309; p. 271). By the time he reaches *The Case of Wagner*, the last book discussed, he has turned his claim around: "My whole life is the demonstration *de rigeur* of these propositions" (p. 361; p. 324). Rather than his books representing his life, his life now performs his books. The history of his books intertwines with the history of his progress towards selfishness: "The name of Voltaire on one of my essays—that really meant progress—*toward me*" (p. 320; p. 283). The essay he means is *Human All-Too-Human*, which he calls "the monument of a crisis" (p. 320; p. 283). The book occurs at that moment in the history of his life when his instinct made its "inexorable decision," and he gave up the "unseemly 'selflessness' " that had characterized him up to that point and "got hold of [his] task" (p. 325; p. 288). This liberates him from the "book," his "parable" of decadence and selflessness, since books bury and silence the "nethermost self . . . under the continual pressure of having to listen to other selves (and that is after all what reading means)" (p. 324; p. 288). Freed from reading and philology, that self "spoke again" (p. 324; p. 288). While Nietzsche's life history seems inseparable from the history of his books, it paradoxically describes his liberation from books, from *the* book, considered as the passive, selfless acceptance of what others represent to you in the act of reading.

In teaching the revaluation, Nietzsche attempts to circumvent idealism—that is, "bookishness," knowledge, representation, reading, feminism—in four ways.

First, by means of autobiography itself—his gesture of uniqueness or exemplariness. I have said that the teaching of the revaluation is inseparable from the teaching of "who" or "what Nietzsche is. But who or what is "Nietzsche"? The gesture of exemplariness which is the title— "Ecce Homo," "Behold the man"—makes of "Nietzsche" both Pilate and Christ, both the speaker and the addressed, both the mocker and the mocked. The subtitle is more explicitly impersonal—"How One Becomes What One Is" [*Wie man wird was man ist*]. The impersonal construction makes of the revaluation an empty category capable of being filled by anyone. What the "Nietzsche" of *Ecce Homo* exemplifies is a "contrast" [*Gegensatz*]: "I am a disciple of Dionysus; I should prefer to be even a satyr to being a saint. This essay had no other meaning than to give expression to this contrast in a cheerful and philanthropic manner" (p. 256; p. 217). Both Pilate and Christ, so also both Dionysus and the Crucified—the self is the stage of this contrast. To understand "Nietzsche" is to know not a subject, but the place where a certain ethical battle, a certain difference of force takes place, taking the place of the subject: "Have I been understood? Dionysus against [*gegen*] the Crucified . . ." In this the last line of the book, "Nietzsche" presents himself as Dionysus, a name signaling joy and affirmation, placed against the Crucified, a name that carries the weight of guilt and sacrifice. Dionysus is the "against"-ness of Christ, not so much his antithesis as his eternal return, the same but different: "The devil is merely the leisure of God on that seventh day" (p. 349; p. 311). The subject "Nietzsche," therefore is exemplary only as it is also a non-subject. To learn the revaluation by following "Nietzsche's" example, by oneself becoming "what one is," one must learn that "what one is" might have little to do with "one"-self considered as a subject. Were this not so, the sub-title might have read "wer man ist" instead of "was man ist." As it stands, what-ness is all.

"What" Nietzsche is is a certain "contrast," a "tension" [*Spannung*] which is not an opposition, since each term is itself only as it is also the other. In this sense, Nietzsche *is* the revaluation, the possibility of "being both," hence, of reversing perspectives—"Neutrality:"

Considered in this way, my life is simply wonderful. For the task of a *revaluation of all values* more capacities may have been needed than have ever dwelt together in a single individual—above all, even contrary [*Gegensätze*] capacities that had to be kept from disturbing, destroying one another. An order of rank among these capacities; distance, the art of separating without setting against one another; to mix nothing, to "reconcile" nothing. . . . (P. 292; p. 254)

This contrast does not lend itself to a dialectic which would reduce it to a synthesis, "reconcile" it, and make it available to knowledge. Nietzsche, therefore, is an improper subject. By grounding the revaluation in his own life and within the self,[6] he seems to evade the trap of idealist conceptualization, of knowledge and representation, the "book:" "Finally, I speak only of what I have lived through [*Erlebten*], not merely 'what I have thought through' [*Gedachten*]; the contrast [*Gegensatz*] of thinking and life is lacking in my case. My 'theory' grows from my 'practice,' oh out of a in no way harmless and unthinking [*unbedenklichen*] practice."[7] What the litotic phrase "in no way . . . unthinking" seems to suggest is that just as the distinction theory/practice collapses in Nietzsche's case, so also will the distinction upon which he bases his undertaking in *Ecce Homo*, that between knowledge and involuntary, obligatory, "unthinking" performance.

Nietzsche also tries to short-circuit idealism by means of a rhetoric of contradiction. If the book and the act of reading are equated with selflessness for Nietzsche, then what links up with selfishness might be called non-reading, in the sense of not understanding. In his irony the neutrality of selfishness, of being both, appears as an undecidability of meaning, saying one thing while simultaneously saying its opposite, thus neutralizing the first. For example, he condemns reaction while himself being in reaction against woman. He subsumes difference into identity by asserting his identity as his difference from all others. On the one hand he claims to follow his instincts while on the other calling the autobiography he must undertake something against which his instincts revolt. This irony puts in question the very notion of decidable opposition and what it has always implied—knowledge. Irony, because it can never be reduced to a single representation of truth, precludes knowledge, hence also, the imposition of one's thoughts on another in the invitation to read. As such, irony is a rhetorical performance which serves no other end than its own self-destructive functioning.[8] The most striking example of irreducible irony is Nietzsche's account of his mother and father. Being "already dead as [his] father" is the "highest . . . run on the ladder of life," but it also makes of Nietzsche a "decadent," and it doesn't give him "life": "[such a father] explains whatever else I have of privilege—*not* including life, the great Yes to life."[9] Similarly, being "still living" as his mother is the "lowest rung," but it also is what allows a "beginning."[10]

Nietzsche's third maneuver for avoiding idealism in his teaching is not to teach at all: ". . . a 'revaluation of all values' is perhaps possible for me alone" (p. 264; p. 223). First, at the end of the preface, he narrows the field of his students: "Such things reach only the most select. It is a privilege without equal to be a listener here" (p. 288; p. 220). Then, on the page that separates the preface from the first chapter, he follows Schopenhauer's example and excludes his audience altogether: "—and so I tell my life to myself [*erzähle ich mir mein Leben*]" (p. 261; p. 221). This gesture of self-enclosure works to prevent his students from turning him into an idol, since, in effect, he is not teaching them. In so doing, he gives them an example of what he teaches—return to oneself—while simultaneously creating a lure to follow the example. It is fitting that this gesture should follow Zarathustra's farewell to his students in the quotation that closes the preface:

Now I go alone, my disciples. You, too, go now, alone. Thus I want it . . . One repays a teacher badly if one always remains nothing but a pupil. And why do you not want to pluck at my wreath? You revere me; but what if your reverence *tumbles* one day? Beware lest a statue slay you . . . You had not yet sought yourselves; and you found me. Thus do all believers; therefore all faith amounts to so little. Now I bid you lose me and find yourselves; and only *when you have all denied me* will I return to you. (Pp. 258–59; p. 220)

What Nietzsche seems to teach ultimately is how not to be taught—through perpetual self-teaching.

Nietzsche may avoid idealism in his teaching stance, but it is impossible for him to avoid his own text. It cannot avoid being what he condemns as the "parable" of selflessness—a book. In order to teach his lesson of selflessness, he must resort to an instrument of selflessness. He must write a book. He cannot help but ask his pupils to do what he teaches them not to do at the very moment of teaching—read. *Ecce Homo*, then, is at once an advertisement for the revaluation and an unavoidable betrayal of it.

This problem gives rise to Nietzsche's final strategy for circumventing idealism. It centers on an explicit attempt to convert the language of teaching from an instrument of knowledge to a means of action, from something plagued by error and accident to an obligation which, like a performative, necessarily obliges something to happen.

As one might expect, it is in the chapter entitled "Why I Write Such Good Books" that Nietzsche manages to find an apparent way out of his book bind. It has to do with a theory of reading and writing that he sets forth in that chapter. He begins by discussing the question of his writings' "being understood or *not* understood" (p. 296; p. 259), and he decides that "the time for this question certainly hasn't come yet. The time for me hasn't come yet" (p. 296; p. 259). It is his "triumph" that he neither is nor will be read: "*non legor, non legar*" (p. 297; p. 259). Even those who do read him will not understand him because "ultimately, nobody can get more out of things, including books, than he already knows. For what one lacks access to from experience one will have no ear" (p. 298; p. 261). Reading, then, is essentially autobiographical, since one in effect reads only what is in oneself. It follows that if

Nietzsche is the only one ever to have experienced the revaluation, then he is the only one capable of reading his own text. He seems to have his own text in mind when he writes:

Now let me imagine an extreme case: that a book speaks of nothing but events that lie altogether beyond the possibility of any frequent or even rare experience—that is the first language [*erste Sprache*] for a new series of experiences. In that case, simply nothing will be heard, but there will be the acoustic illusion that where nothing is heard, nothing is there. (P. 298; p. 261)

Ecce Homo, in other words, is unreadable (except proleptically) because the language of the text has no knowable referent for the reader. The reader cannot understand the text unless he has already experienced what the language describes, but since the experiences are so new that they pertain only to Nietzsche, the reader's understanding of it is impossible. Nietzsche, for this reason, is inevitably misread:[11] "This is, in the end, my average experience and, if you will, the originality of my experience. Whoever thought he had understood something of me, had made up something out of me after his own image—not uncommonly an antithesis to me; for example, an 'idealist' " (p. 298; p. 261).

Nietzsche's remarks on writing in the same chapter suggest a conclusion similar to the one he reaches concerning reading. He describes "style" in terms of autobiography: "Good is any style that really communicates an inward state" (p. 302; p. 265). Once again, he asserts his own uniqueness: "considering that the multiplicity of inward states is exceptionally large in my case, I have many stylistic possibilities—the most multifarious art of style that has ever been at the disposal of one man" (p. 304; p. 265).[12] And, as before, his self-description issues in a claim of incomprehensibility: "Always presupposing that there are ears —that there are those capable and worthy of the same pathos, that there is no lack of those to whom one may communicate oneself.—My *Zarathustra*, for example, is still looking for those—alas, it will have to keep looking for a long time yet!—One must be worthy of hearing him" (p. 302; p. 265). Because no one else has experienced the "same pathos" as he, no one can understand what he writes—at least not yet. His writing, therefore, can be nothing more than a promise of its one day being read and understood. That is, a promise that the revaluation will one day affect all men, thus providing him with readers: "Some day institutions will be needed in which men live and teach as I conceive of living and teaching; it might even happen that a few chairs will then be set aside for the interpretation of *Zarathustra*. (p. 296; p. 259) . . . The calm in promising, this happy gaze into a future that is not to remain a mere promise!" (p. 318; p. 281).

If *Ecce Homo* can only be a proleptically readable text, one which can only promise that it will one day be understood, then how does it work to effect this promise? That is, if the absolute uniqueness and newness of the experiences described prevent the book from teaching by means of knowledge, then by what alternate way can it teach? The direction one should take to find an answer might be suggested by the quotation that closes the chapter on "Good Books." It is taken from *Beyond Good and Evil* and is placed there "to give an idea of [Nietzsche] as a psychologist" (p. 305; p. 268). What is described is a teacher,

the tempter god and born pied piper of consciences whose voice knows how to descend into the netherworld of every soul; who does not say a word or cast a glance in which there is no consideration and ulterior enticement. (P. 305; p. 268)

He works by means of luring and coercion—"temper," "pied-piper," "enticement." His

mastery includes the knowledge of how to seem . . . what is to those who follow him one *more* constraint to press ever closer to him in order to follow him ever more inwardly and thoroughly. (P. 305; p. 268)

He does not so much teach a doctrine or an idea as act upon his students to change them:

the genius of the heart who silences all that is loud and self-satisfied, teaching it to listen; who smooths rough sound . . . who teaches the doltish and rash hand to hesitate. (P. 305; p. 268)

Who teaches, in other words, those who would, but should not, write, not to write, "rash hand to hesitate."

Finally, Nietzsche's description of himself clearly plays off an antithetical concept of teaching, that of Christian morality or idealism:

the genius of the heart . . . is a divining rod . . . from whose touch everyone walks away richer, not having received grace and surprised, not as blessed and oppressed by alien goods [*fremden Gute*], but richer in himself, newer to himself than before, broken open . . . (P. 306; p. 269)

This genius' "constraint" to follow him has the effect not of producing understanding but of acting upon the student in such a way that he is changed within himself, and not encumbered with the ideas of others— books, "alien goods."

By placing this quotation at the end of the chapter that introduces the review of each one of his books, Nietzsche gives the impression that he is describing what has been, and probably still is his own method of teaching. It is one that would accommodate the bracketing of knowledge by taking as its means the lure and constraint to follow. Words would act to produce change in those who are caught. They would no longer merely represent something that is understood, but that must be tolerated as being "alien." Instead, they would coerce the student into changing himself—"more inwardly and thoroughly."

This particular kind of teaching would seem to be Nietzsche's alternative in *Ecce Homo*. In order for his book to be "understood," its language must pose, as well as represent, what it teaches.[13] It must, in effect, provoke the experience it represents in its readers. Its purpose, then, would be to instigate, not only to communicate, to produce, not only to reproduce, a performance of the revaluation.

This teaching[14] requires a language that is capable of action. Nietzsche conveys this sense of action through dynamic, physical images:

I am no man, I am dynamite.[15] (p. 363; p. 326) What I am today, where I am today—at a height where I speak no longer with words but with lightning bolts. (p. 318; p. 281) . . . This proposition, grown hard and sharp under the hammer blow of historical insight [read: *revaluation of all values*], may perhaps one day, in some future—1890!—serve as the ax swung against the 'metaphysical need' of mankind. (p. 326; p. 289) . . . But my fervent will to create impels me ever again toward man; thus is the hammer impelled toward the stone. (p. 347; p. 309) . . . From this moment forward all my writings are fish hooks. (P. 348; p. 310)

To change man, one must change his values, since values, like language, derive from physiology. Because the revaluation is, before all else, a re-education, this change can only be carried out in language. Nietzsche's ideal teacher, Zarathustra the "seducer," "says No and *does* No [*Nein sagt, Nein thut*] to an unheard-of degree" (p. 343; p. 306). The revaluation consists of a simultaneity of saying and doing, of speech and performance, a simultaneity of language and action that resembles the traditional notion of truth as the adequation of sign and referent, in which reference is *aufgehoben*. Nietzsche adds to the adequation of sign and meaning, the traditional telos of representational language, the adequation of speech and act, that action must follow immediately from speech, that what is said is also done: "I obey my Dionysian nature which does not know how to separate doing No [*Neinthun*] from saying Yes [*Jasagen*]" (p. 364; p. 327).

The one most often repeated definition of the revaluation in the autobiography is saying/doing No: "the turn had come for the No-saying, *No-doing* [*neinsagende, neinthuende*] part: the revaluation of all values so far" (p. 348; p. 310). To say/be Yes to all things while also saying/doing No "to everything to which one has so far said Yes" (p.

Michael Ryan

343; p. 306) constitutes an action, a designation of value which changes existing valuations. Interpreted "physiologically," this revaluation of all values consists of breaking the names used to designate the old values, since values, in a revalued world, can no longer be thought of as ideal entities separate from their physical embodiment, the words used to designate (or, as Nietzsche would have it, to pose) them.

The revaluation, I shall now argue, is an attempt to change belief, to teach, whose vehicle is a change of names.

At one point, Nietzsche defines the revaluation as the "conjuring up" [*Heraufbeschwörung*] of "a day of decision" (p. 348; p. 310). The verb "to conjure" re-appears at the beginning of the final chapter—"Why I Am A Destiny": "I know my fate. One day my name will be associated with the memory of something tremendous—in crisis without equal on earth, the most profound collision of conscience, a decision that was conjured up [*heraufbeschwören*] *against* everything that had been believed, demanded, hallowed so far" (p. 363; p. 326). Conjuring is, of course, the use of words to make something happen, in this case, "an act of supreme self-examination on the part of humanity" (p. 363; p. 326). This act should consist of experiencing "lies as lies" (p. 363; p. 326), and this includes realizing that "so far one has called *lies* truth [*man hiess bisher die Lüge Wahrheit*] (p. 363; p. 326). . . . Everything that has hitherto been called 'truth' [*was bisher 'Wahrheit' hiess*] has been recognized as the most harmful, insidious, and subterranean form of lie" (p. 371; p. 334). In other words, morality has been founded on an antiphrasis, calling something by the name which belongs to its opposite. To recognize this is already to break values: "Whoever uncovers morality also uncovers the disvalue of all values [*Unwerthe aller Werthe*] that are and have been believed" (p. 371; p. 334). To recognize that the former truth is, in fact, a lie is at the same time to call it a lie, to reverse and correct the antiphrasis. Just as this recognition is inseparable from a certain language act, a naming, so also the personal belief of those who followed the Christian "holy men" was linked to a particular kind of naming. "Slander" [*Verleumdung*] is the word Nietzsche uses most often to characterize this naming or mis-naming:

And whatever harm those do who slander the world [*Weltverleumder*], the harm done by the good is the most harmful harm (p. 367; p. 330) . . . Who before me climbed into the cavern from which the poisonous fumes of this type of ideal—slander of the world [*Weltverleumdung*]—are rising? (p. 369; p. 331) . . . one looks for the evil principle in what is most profoundly necessary for growth, in *severe* self-love (this very word constitutes slander [*verleumderisch*]). (P. 370; pp. 332–33)

All that has been suppressed and excluded by the idealist value system has been given names that express disvalue:

an ideal fabricated from the contradiction [*Widerspruch*] against the proud and well-turned-out human being who says Yes, who is sure of the future, who guarantees the future—and he is now called *evil [heisst nunmehr der Böse]*. (P. 372; p. 335)

According to this passage, at least, the ideal is fabricated [*gemacht*] from this slander, this speaking against—"contradiction," "*Widerspruch*" —and not the other way around, as one might expect. Misnaming, antiphrasis, lies at the origin of idealism: "The condition of the existence of the good is the *lie*: put differently, not *wanting* to see at any price how reality is constituted fundamentally" (p. 366; p. 329). Each idealist value concept exists at the expense of something Nietzsche would value, and when he discusses these concepts, he usually places each one within quotation marks, thus underlining its metaphoric or catachrestic nature:

The concept [*Begriff*] of "God" invented as a counter-concept of life . . . The concept of the "beyond," the 'true world,' invented in order to devaluate [*entwerthen*] the only world there is . . . The concept of the "soul" . . . invented in order to despise the body. (Pp. 371–72; p. 334)

In each case, the quotation marks direct the reader's attention to the fact that each one of these concepts is a lie, a metaphor, an invention, and an antiphrasis. At the same time, Nietzsche makes it clear that the lies of idealism have acted to make believe, that is, to pose values contrary to physiology and to educate man in such a way that the decadent instincts have dominated over the life instincts:

the *lie* of the ideal has so far been the curse [*Fluch*] on reality; on account of it, mankind itself has become mendacious and false down to its most fundamental instincts—to the point of worshipping the opposite values of those which alone would guarantee its health, its future, the lofty *right* to its future. (P. 256; p. 218)

A language act—"curse," *Fluch*—can change man's physiology. Idealism, therefore, both is and is not merely a matter of words.[16]

The action Nietzsche takes against morality is itself contradiction: "I contradict [*widerspreche*] as has never been contradicted before" (p. 364; p. 327). His contra-diction consists of making new value-posing metaphors, or of remaking old ones, that correct the idealist antiphrasis and privilege the values "forbidden" by idealism. To counter-act idealism, however, these new names or value concepts must work to re-educate man, to change his physiology, since the idealist antiphrasis has succeeded in over-turning the right order of rank in his instincts. This is necessary not only because values are determined by man, but also because man is determined by values, and Nietzsche's ultimate goal is to change man. Such a revaluation is possible only because, for Nietzsche, to change the name a thing is called by is to change the thing. The "thing" is itself already only an identity-posing metaphor (*Gleichsetzung*). As he writes in his chapter on *Zarathustra*, "It actually seems to allude to something Zarathustra says, as if the things [*Dinge*] themselves approached and offered themselves as metaphors [*Gleichnisse*] (. . . On every metaphor [*Gleichniss*] you ride to every truth [*Wahrheit*] . . .)" (p. 338; p. 301). In this sense, to say No is to do No. For Nietzsche, there is an adequation of word and act (although he does question the notion of the actor, the privileging of the doer in terms of the deed, especially in the passage preceding the one just cited: "Everything happens involuntarily . . . The involuntariness of image and metaphor [*des Bildes, des Gleichnisses*] is strangest of all" (p. 338; p. 300)). He displays an insight into the nature of being as "art," in the sense of a posing of identity—metaphor—where none exists. He then immediately calls for a forgetting of the metaphoric nature of "truth" and espouses the necessity of art. Similarly, at this juncture, he seems to suggest that there might be such a thing as a good metaphor, that is, a good speech act, and that metaphoricity as posing (especially in the form of the involuntarily inspired, hence instinctual and fated philosopher/poet's language) might lead to a practical triumph, a modification of being.

What is seductive about the last line of the book—"Dionysus against the Crucified"—the way in which it teaches or acts, is the way in which it changes names or metaphors. "Good over Evil," or "Virtue over Egotism," or "The Saint over the Satyr," are three alternate versions that might be offered by an idealist as Nietzsche describes him. Instead, Nietzsche radically reverses and displaces the hierarchy implicit in the "slander" perpetrated by morality. What the idealist would call "satyr," he calls "Dionysus." What was branded slanderously is now given a name indicating value. The renaming revalues by turning a negative valuation into a positive one. Similarly, he replaces the positive valuation of the word "saint" with the negative value carried by the name "the Crucified." What was evil becomes good, is shown to have always been good but for its name. What was called good is re-named for what it is, according to Nietzsche, castration. The absoluteness of idealist values is thus taken away, and the weapon of morality is shown to be antiphrastic misnaming.

The reader, in reading the line, has already performed the renaming. His reading is itself a first step towards an act of revaluation. One is caught in Nietzsche's fish hook simply by reading, because in reading one already begins to call things differently. One already begins to revalue. Again, according to Nietzsche's own definition, one cannot answer the question— "Have I been understood?"—one cannot understand him, unless one performs the revaluation oneself, unless one begins calling things by different names. For this reason, "Dionysus against the Crucified" is the only kind of answer which could be given to the question. Understanding, like Nietzsche's own "theory," will only arise from performance, from "practice."

"Dionysus against the Crucified . . ." is exemplary of the revaluation. The two terms are defined as a difference of force rather than as an opposition. The necessity of the Crucified, its eternal return, is recognized. Dionysus, the new value, is not only taken from the tradition it attacks, but is also defined in terms of that tradition, in terms of the Crucified. In this sense, the revaluation is more parodic than pathetic. Rather than step outside idealism to attack it from without—what amounts to confirming it—Nietzsche opts to undermine it from within: "[Human All-Too-Human] is war, but war without power and smoke, without warlike poses, without pathos and strained limbs: all that would still be 'idealism'" (p. 321; p. 284). He takes over idealism and uses it against idealism. The paradox implied in this ironic appropriation and displacement is that by preserving one destroys.

The revaluation itself is borrowed wholesale from idealism:

Indeed, this is *my* insight: the teachers, the leaders of humanity, theologians all of them, were also, all of them, decadents: *hence* the revaluation of all values [*Umwerthung aller Werthe*] into hostility to life, *hence* morality. (P. 371; p. 333)

As "teachers" [*Lehrer*] have been responsible for propagating idealism, so it is that by teaching alone Nietzsche can set right the error. In his teaching, he is obliged to retain the names used by idealism, since idealism seems to have permeated all language: "When mendaciousness at any price monopolizes the word 'truth' for its perspective, the really truthful man is bound to be branded with the worst names" (p. 368; p. 330). Along with Dionysus, two of Nietzsche's contra-dictory names are Zarathustra and the Immoralist. Zarathustra represents "the self-overcoming [*Selbstüberwindung*] of morality, out of truthfulness . . . into its opposite—into me" (p. 365; p. 328). Since "Zarathustra created this most calamitous error, morality, consequently, he must also be the first to recognize it" (p. 365; p. 328). As Zarathustra is a turning of morality against itself, the word "immoralist," because it like "Dionysus" is a negative word within the context of morality, also becomes a weapon against it: "What defines me, what sets me apart from the whole rest of humanity is that I *uncovered* Christian morality. That is why I needed a word that had the meaning of a provocation for everybody" (p. 369; p. 332). Doing what seems to go against one's interests, for example, accepting the eternal return of idealism (as the other which

Michael Ryan

is the same as the Dionysian, it's seventh day's sleep), can in the end—strategically, ironically—serve one's interests: "This is the exception where, against my wont and conviction, I side with the 'selfless' drives: here they work in the service of *self-love, of self-discipline*" (p. 292; p. 254).

In that he desires a performative rhetoric in his teaching, one which would necessarily oblige something to happen—a revaluation which would simultaneously transform man—Nietzsche borrows another tactic from idealism, that of the imperative:

> The morality that would unself man is the morality of decline *par excellence*—the fact, "I am declining" [*ich gehe zu Grunde*], transposed into the imperative, "all of you ought to decline" [*ihr sollt alle zu Grunde gehn*]. . . . This only morality that has been taught so far, that of un-selfing [*Entselbstungs-Moral*], reveals a will to the end; fundamentally, it negates life. (P. 370; p. 333)

Rather than negate life, which means also to decline to the ground [*zu Grunde*] of a single, absolute value that excludes what it opposes, Nietzsche's imperative demands a simultaneous ascent and decline—a strategic decline to the ground of an absolute value (Dionysus) but only insomuch as it is constituted as an ascent to a new value that comprises both the Crucified as well as Dionysus, that affirms both. This double affirmation is the neutrality of selfishness. As such, it cannot take the form of a law of the idealist type: "You should all leave the ground of absolute and exclusive values; you should accept and affirm everything; you should become yourself." Nietzsche's entire pedagogical undertaking can be read as an attempt to avoid such a law, since what he teaches—becoming oneself—implies ceasing to listen to such laws, such "alien goods." The paradox of his theory of education, from *Wir Philologen* on, is that it requires a teacher who obliges the student to discover his own law, a law that demands that he break whatever law the teacher proposes. Nietzsche's pedagogical imperative, then, must be more subtle, more seductive, more enticing than the idealist imperative. It must almost not be there—like a promise.

Perhaps this is why the idea of the future is so important to the revaluation and why the entire text seems to be written in the future tense: "Seeing that before long I must confront humanity with the most difficult demand ever made of it . . ." (p. 255; p. 217). There will always be a temporal delay in the relationship between Nietzsche's textbook and the action it hopes to produce. Words are not themselves—here and now—acts that touch physiology. They must pass by way of education and the changing of convention before reaching the instincts. In this sense, although Nietzsche's text escapes its book bind by trying to be a performance that instils performance, thus defusing knowledge and representation, that is, the book considered as "alien goods," it can only do so at the expense of falling into a rhetorical trap, one which, because it is the condition of possibility of the revaluation, cannot be escaped without also destroying the revaluation—that of the promise.

The revaluation will always carry a future inscribed in it, the future in which the words by which it acts will take effect on their readers. The only means it has, therefore, of carrying out its promise is the promise. And the future promised by the promise can never be reduced to a present in which the promise, the word, becomes the act it promises. Any seeming fulfillment of the promise merely generates another promise. The "fulfillment" would itself be a promise. If the word or promise acted immediately on the student, it would be "alien goods." The delay allows the word to act as a pointer, an example, an enticement, a promise that draws the student into the enterprise of revaluing as an autonomous agent. The delay is thus a delay of understanding, of reflexivity. In relation to the word that inspires it, the student's action cannot be "fated" or involuntary. There must be a difference between the word that inspires action and the action inspired if the action is to be truly autonomous—becoming what one is rather what someone else tells you to be. This gap constitutes the revaluation, allows it to work, while simultaneously undoing it, making it fall short of the "rhetoric" Nietzsche uses to describe it. Nietzsche's words can never be the fish hooks or the lightning bolts he pretends they are. The revaluation must pass by this gap—of education, of understanding—in order to do what it promises to do, and because of this, it must forever fall short of an immediate adequation of word and act, of promise and fulfillment as the transformation of even the involuntary movements of instinct and the body.

For this reason, Nietzsche can only pretend to act. His performative rhetoric can only be a performance, a ruse, a pose—precisely what he condemns in idealism. He must make believe in order to make believe, act in order to act. As I pointed out earlier, he laces his text with gestures of obligation: "Seeing that before long I *must* confront humanity . . . it seems *indispensable* to me . . . Under these circumstances I have a *duty* against which my habits . . . revolt. It is my fate that I *have* to be the first decent human being . . . the truth speaks out of me [*redet aus mir die Wahrheit*]" (pp. 225, 363; pp. 217, 326). He pretends to act under the power of an unavoidable imperative, the fatedness of inspiration or instinct. Like a character in a Greek tragedy, he acts, acting out the will of the gods. At the same time, he is like the actor who plays the role of the character, someone who knows his lines well but who, because the lines are not his "own," must look on them with a certain irony, a certain "neutrality." To act, for Nietzsche, to act out fate and to act with words to teach others to do the same, to become actors, is also to act—to dramatize as well as to pose. And when one poses, even when one poses not to know, he knows one is posing.

Nietzsche, therefore, in order to go beyond knowledge in his teaching, must resort to a mode of knowledge—pretense, acting. If all knowledge is a posing (a pro-posing of identity where only a difference of force exists), so all posing is just that—a pose, pretense, hence cognitive. His promises can never be anything but false. If we are to believe Nietzsche's rhetoric (words that would be fish hooks, lightning bolts, hammers), he desires to cross the line between language and physical action to the extent that his words would become immediate acts, immediate modifications of man's physiology. The teacher would become the student, the self the other—*"Ich bin deine Wahrheit."*[17] This impossible desire for a performative rhetoric forces him to resort not only to promises (". . . before long . . .") but also to excuses: "From this moment forward all my writings are fish hooks: perhaps I know how to fish as well as anyone?—If nothing was caught, I am not to blame. *There were no fish*" (p. 348; p. 310). An actor, an ironic apologist, intervenes during the scene of teaching, at the moment where language doesn't live up to its promise—to act immediately. His irony is in fact symptomatic of that incapacity. It points out, while attempting to efface, the aporia between knowledge and performance. Hence, even though he *knows* his lines, knows that they are lines (even in the sense of feeding someone a line—an excuse), he is himself part of the performance. His excuse for the performance (or, for the lack of performance) is itself a fish hook, a lure.

The last line of the book poses a kind of rhetorical question, one to which Nietzsche (as well as the reader, if he's been reading the book) already knows the answer—"Have I been understood?" (In German, the question is more active, thus placing more responsibility on the reader—*"Hat man mich verstanden?"*) By asking if one has understood him, Nietzsche would seem to ask—ironically: "Are you acting without understanding either me or yourself? Are you renaming, like this—'Dionysus against the Crucified? . . .'" The answer to the question is undecidably both yes and no. To understand Nietzsche, to be able to say "Yes," is to say "No, I have not understood you; I don't even know you." To say "No" would thus be a more affirmative response, what is demanded by the question, indeed by the entire revaluation. It would be a less sincere response, since in order to say "No," one would have to have understood Nietzsche; one would have to be able to say "Yes." I would be (did such a thing exist) a rhetorical answer. If the entire last line stakes out the limit of Nietzsche's undertaking as a moment of undecidability or reversibility between knowledge—the question of being understood—and performance—the exemplary re-naming—it also puts the reader in the same ironic bind. He is caught in the same act. In order to answer the question, he, too, must act, in both senses.

The final question also opens up the possibility of another take on the word "rhetorical," since what the question invites is a disclosure of the rhetorical nature of values and a simultaneous transformation of that rhetoric—"*Dionysos gegen den Gekreuzigten* . . ." Pedagogical rhetoric here forms a hinge with political rhetoric. Teaching, as a rhetorical exercise, is already a mode of political action. One way out of the undecidable aporia of knowledge and performance is, to resort to Nietzsche's tactic, to affirm it. If it reduces all performance to knowledge, it also allows a conception of knowledge as performance.

To interpret the world, to perform the rhetorical exercise of naming things, is, in a certain sense, already to transform it. What Nietzsche's rhetorical question provokes is such a gesture of interpretation/transformation. Nietzsche teaches, if anything, in *Ecce Homo*, the rhetorical nature of man's world and the capacity of rhetoric to change it. (With a future attached, to be sure, the delay of education or self-education. To use Nietzsche's word, it has to *dawn* upon you.) It's no wonder, then, that when he gives examples of the "basic concerns of life" that idealism has suppressed (read: misnamed), he chooses three things that are always in one way or other associated with rhetoric—"politics . . . social organization, and education" (p. 294; p. 256). To debunk rhetoric in the sense of a rhetorical question, therefore, because it is inauthentic, insincere, a pose, an act, is to overlook the fact that the concept of authenticity is itself a rhetorical act. Every pose, even the pose of authenticity when it is placed against artifice, poses something. Every act acts, even if it is only to pose itself as an act. The actor always performs, although you may not *know* it until later, until after the sun has gone down.

APPENDIX

Nietzsche seems to have been inspired to undertake an autobiography by George Brandes to whom he sent a summary of each of his books and a *curriculum vitae* in a letter of April 10, 1888. In an earlier letter dated February 19, 1888, he describes a moment which would become the most important moment of his life in *Ecce Homo*:

> Between the *Unzeitgemässige Betrachtungen* and *Menschliches, Allzumenschliches* came a crisis and a sloughing. Physically, too, I lived for years next door to death. This was my great good fortune: I for-

got myself, I survived myself. (*Werke in Drei Bänden*, 3; 1279; *Selected Letters*, P. 286)

Similarly, in the letter of April 10, he writes:

> From 1882 on, very slowly to be sure, my health was in the ascendant again: the crisis was passed (my father died very young, at exactly the age at which I myself was nearest to death) . . . my sickness . . . has restored to me the courage to be myself. (*Werke in Drei Bändan*, 3: 1287; *Selected Letters*, P. 294)

One could also see the book as having a more intrinsic origin, as being more than a mere accident inspired from without. For instance, I argue that the revaluation of all values and autobiography—considered as *Selbstüberwindung* or *Selbstaufhebung*, self-overcoming—are inseparable, and that it is this necessity which creates problems for Nietzsche. How does one teach the revaluation if that implies something one can only do oneself to oneself? It would be feasible to argue that Nietzsche took the opportunity Brandes offered him to teach the revaluation by means of autobiography, that is, by means of the only way it could be taught. Since autobiography is, as Nietzsche claims, against his own instincts, to undertake it is an example of self-overcoming, of revaluation. When he first mentions *Ecce Homo* to Peter Gast in a letter of October 20, 1888, Nietzsche presents it as a harbinger of the revaluation:

> Not only did I want to present myself *before* the uncommonly solitary act of revaluation; I would also just like to *test* what risks I can take with the German ideas of freedom of speech. (*Werke in Drei Bänden*, 3: 1328; *Selected Letters*, P. 319)

In a later letter to Brandes, November 20, 1888, Nietzsche writes again of *Ecce Homo*: "The whole work is the prelude [*Vorspiel*; foreplay?] to the 're-valuation of all values,' of the work that lies finished before me [*das fertig vor mir liegt*]." (*Werke in Drei Bänden*, 3: 1334; *Selected Letters*, p. 326). What Nietzsche means by the work that lies finished [*fertig*] before him is hard to guess. One could argue, as does Montinari, that *Der Antichrist* was intended to be the whole revaluation and that for this reason Nietzsche changed the list on the page separating the foreword from the first chapter of *Ecce Homo* to read "the revaluation of all values" instead of "the first book of the revaluation of all values" (See Montinari, p. 397). Nietzsche's manuscript letter to Paul Deussen of November 26, 1888, seems to indicate that at one point he did conceive of *Der Antichrist* as the entire *Revaluation:* "My *Revaluation of All Values* with the title *der Antichrist* is complete" (*Werke*, 8, pt. 3: vi). It is also true, however, that Nietzsche, in the first days of his insanity, deleted the sub-title "Umwerthung aller Werthe" and substituted for it "Fluch auf das Christenthum." One should also consider an entry in the *Nachgelassene Fragmente* for September 1888, which presents *Der Antichrist* as the first book of the *Revaluation*, that which Nietzsche also called it on the original title page of the book:

> Revaluation of All Values. First Book: The Antichrist. Attempt at a critique of Christianity. Second Book. The Free Spirit. Critique of philosophy as a nihilistic movement. Third Book. The Immoralist. Cri-

tique of the most fateful [*verhängnissvollsten*] kind of ignorance, morality. Fourth Book. Dionysus. Philosophy of the eternal return. (*Werke*, 8, pt. 3: 347)

The "Revaluation of All Values" was at one timé to be the sub-title of the *Nachlass* fragments entitled *Der Wille zur Macht*. If Nietzsche considered the *Revaluation* completed on November 20, 1888, then, it is conceivable that he also considered using parts of the *Nachlass* which were originally intended for *Der Wille zur Macht* in the *Revaluation*. If this is so, then the *Revaluation* was to consist of not just *Der Antichrist*, but of the *Nachlass, Ecce Homo*, and *Der Antichrist*. The second, third, and fourth books of the projected *Revaluation* seem to be accounted for in this way by the *Nachlass* as it was organized in *Der Wille zur Macht*: by the first book, "Der europäische Nihilismus," by the second part of the second book, "Kritik der Moral," and by the last two parts of the fourth book, "Dionysos" and "Die ewige Wiederkunft." One could argue against this by saying that the divisions of the book now known as *Der Wille zur Macht* were made by the editors. This is true, but it is also true that they took these divisions from an outline Nietzsche himself left behind, one similar to the outline of the *Revaluation*. Since Nietzsche himself did not do the arranging, it would probably be wiser to speak of thematics instead of sections, although a good number of the entries for each section fall adjacent to each other both in *Der Wille zur Macht* and in the *Nachlass*.

The third book of the *Revaluation, Der Immoralist*, seems to describe *Ecce Homo*. Nietzsche in the autobiography plays the role of immoralist against morality, frequently calling himself the "first immoralist." Also, the word "fateful," from the notebook description of *Der Immoralist*, certainly is not foreign to *Ecce Homo*. I should like to suggest that Nietzsche decided to use what he had originally intended to be the third book of the *Revaluation* as a prelude to it, to test the "ground," so to speak. As *Der Antichrist* presents the psychology of the priest, *Ecce Homo* might be said to portray the physiology of the immoralist. Many of the ideas of *Ecce Homo* appear in the second part of Book Two of *Der Wille zur Macht*, that is, within the thematic of the critique of morality, the one which would correspond to *Der Immoralist*—the attack on selflessness and the praise of selfishness, the questioning of Christian value concepts as false names invented to degrade life, the polemic against idealist psychology as opposed to physiology, the preaching of the great "economy" and the denial of moral "castration." To all this one should add that both the sub-title and the last line of *Ecce Homo* also appear within this thematic of the *Nachlass*, that is, in the spring notebook of 1888, the one which contains most of the entries for the second part of what was to be the second book of *Der Wille zur Macht:* "in spite of all, one will become only what one is" and "Dionysus against the Crucified" (*Werke*, 8, pt. 3: 82, 113; *The Will to Power*, tr. Walter Kaufmann [New York: Vintage, 1968], pp. 182, 217). The word "immoral," "immorality," and "immoralist" appear a number of times within the thematic in connection with ideas that re-emerge in *Ecce Homo*. Perhaps the most important of these ideas, in terms of my own argument in this essay, is the "slander" [*Verleumdung*] perpetrated by morality against everything Nietzsche would value. The word Nietzsche uses in the *Nachlass* to designate the work of re-naming is the same one he uses in *Ecce Homo*—task [*Aufgabe*]: "my task is to translate the apparently emancipated and denatured moral values [*naturlos gewordenen Moralwerthe*] back into their nature—i.e., into their natural 'immorality'" (*Werke* 8, pt. 2: 44; *The Will to Power*, p. 168). One would have to disagree with Colli and Montinari, then, by saying that *Der Immoralist* was not broken off, but continued in *Ecce Homo*: "after this the plans and drafts for the second [actually the third] book of the *Revaluation of All Values* under the title *Der Immoralist* soon broken off because of the composition of *Ecce Homo*: until the middle of October . . ." (*Werke*, 8, pt. 3: vi). Those plans and drafts seem precursors of *Ecce Homo*. They treat several themes that are significant in the autobiography—the fictivenes of the ego, selflessness as decadence, the strength of the instinct of self-defense, humanity's desire not to see the truth, the good conceived as parasites against life, and, finally, the worthlessness of the "improver" [*Verbesserer*] of mankind, a word that Nietzsche uses several times in *Ecce Homo* to describe the teachers in opposition to whom he defines himself (Leipzig edition, 8: 315–22).

NOTES

1. Whether or not it is "Nietzsche's" *Ecce Homo* that I am dealing with is questionable. Mazzino Montinari, in a highly important essay on the manuscript of the book, "Ein neuer Abschnitt in Nietzsches *Ecce Homo*," *Nietzsche Studien*, 1 (1972): 380–418, argues convincingly that some "shocking" parts of the book, notably parts that condemned Nietzsche's mother and sister, were suppressed by Nietzsche's censors, Peter Gast and Elizabeth Forster-Nietzsche: "Nietzsche left behind a finished *Ecce Homo*, but we do not have it" (p. 401). Perhaps the most telling piece of evidence cited by Montinari is Peter Gast's letter to Franz Overbeck dated February 27, 1889: "I would like that you, Honored Professor, should first get to know the manuscript [of *Ecce Homo*] from my copy, thus without the places which give me the impression of a greater self-intoxication or of a far too broad scorn and unfairness—so that you receive the impression firsthand, which I cannot myself sufficiently communicate, that the omissions [*Ausgefallene*] are slight."

2. Friedrich Nietzsche, *Ecce Homo* in Nietzsche, *Werke*, ed. Giorgi Colli and Mazzino Montinari (Berlin: deGruyter, 1960), 6, pt. 3: 255; *Ecce Homo*, trans. Walter Kaufmann (New York: Vintage, 1969), p. 217. All further references given in the text will be to these two editions, first the German, then the English. Some passages of Kaufmann's translation do not appear in the Colli-Montinari edition because he relied on the former standard editions. At those points, I provide references to one of those editions—*Nietzsche's Werke* (Leipzig: C. G. Naumann, 1905–13)—hereafter referred to as the Leipzig edition. Similarly, certain passages suppressed by Gast that appear in the *Kritische Gesamtausgabe* but that don't turn up in the translation I have translated myself.

3. The draft of a letter to his sister Elizabeth dated December 1888 reads: "The task which is imposed *upon* me is, all the same, my nature . . . there attaches to my name a quantity of doom [*Verhängnis*, fate] that is beyond telling" (*Nietzsche in seinen Briefen und Berichten der Zeitgenossen*, ed. Alfred Baeumler (Leipzig: A. Kröner, 1932), p. 508; *Selected Letters of Friedrich Nietzsche*, ed. and tr. Christopher Middleton (Chicago: Univ. of Chicago Press, 1969), p. 355. In terms of this sense of "fate," see also his account of his dream of his dead father in his first autobiography, "Aus meinen Leben,"

Werke in drei Bänden, ed. Karl Schlecta (Munchen: Hanser, 1960), 3: 38. In *Ecce Homo*, he describes a time in his life when he wanted to go to Aquila, for him the "counter-concept" of Rome, "but some fate [*Verhängniss*] was at work; I had to go back."

4. The father/mother dichotomy is also, within the context of Nietzsche's parody of the Christ story throughout *Ecce Homo*, a version of the Immaculate Conception. Nietzsche's conception comes about immaculately through the agency of a heavenly father, "already dead," and an earthly mother who still lives. Each one corresponds to one of the ends of the ladder of life, which, much like Jacob's, stretches between heaven and earth. Any irony against Christianity—"idealism"—in nineteenth-century Europe will probably also be irony against Hegel, and that seems to be the case with *Ecce Homo*. The book's sub-title seems an obvious mockery of Hegel's notion of the spirit becoming what it already is through history. One means of becoming for Nietzsche is active forgetfulness, a parody of Hegel's *Erinnerung*, the way in which the spirit remembers itself and is re-membered after its fall or crucifixion in the process of self-division.

5. From the notebook fragments for *Ecce Homo*: "one must only do one's commands, not wishing to know, what one is, as one commands . . . one must have no thoughts, formulas, or attitudes about oneself,—one must suffer, without knowing, one must do the best, without therein understanding oneself" (*Werke*, 8, pt. 3: 446).

6. The revaluation itself is grounded historically. *Ecce Homo*'s title and its last line combine synchrony and diachrony, eternity and history, and make the book itself seem synchronic in its temporality. At the same time, the teleology of the sub-title lends it a perennial or universal dimension. However, the use of phrases like "the turn had come" and "all values so far" place Nietzsche's undertaking in history. This move toward diachrony undermines the book's pedagogical intent by steering it away from universality, from universal applicability, but it simultaneously works to save it from idealism.

7. Friedrich Nietzsche, *Werke des Zusammenbruchs*, ed. Erich F. Podach (Heidelberg: W. Rothe, 1961), p. 252; p. 340.

8. Paul de Man, "The Theory of Irony" (Seminar Notes), Spring, 1976.

9. Leipzig edition, 15: 14; p. 226.

10. To demonstrate the irrepressibility of the desire to reduce the undecidability of irony, I cite an earlier version of this essay: "His attitude towards each one [of his parents] is undecidable, and I over-simplify for the sake of argument by taking what appears in each case to be the dominant attitude as the only one." What is a "dominant attitude" if not a *sens unique*? And isn't this contrary to what Nietzsche shows, namely, that life, like love, is a two-way street?

11. One other consequence of Nietzsche's theory of reading, one he fails to notice, is that if his writing is unreadable, then it is superfluous, in no way "alien" to its readers. Since all reading is autobiographical, there can be no such thing as an "alien" book. All books are acceptable, therefore, because all reading is not-reading.

12. Nietzsche's variations on the title of the book in the notebook are often relevant. One of them goes as follows: "*Ecce Home: Notebooks of a Multiple One*," and is followed by a list of possible styles: "1. The psychologist speaks 2. The philosopher speaks 3. The poet speaks 4. The musician speaks

Michael Ryan

5. The writer speaks 6. The educator speaks." The multiplicity of stances is further reflected in the alternate titles which follow: *"Fridiricus Nietzsche: de vita sua Translated into German,"* and *"The Mirror: Attempt at a Self-Appraisal"* (*Werke*, 8, pt. 3: 445).

13. Nietzsche's theory of metaphor, especially as he gives it in "Ueber Wahrheit und Lüge im aussermoralischen Sinne (Pfulligen, 1961), 1: 636," always carries the undecidable, double charge of representation and posing [*setzen*]. Metaphors represent man's desire for power while positing a world of self-identical things where only chaos exists. Martin Heidegger put it this way: "This assimilation [of chaos] is not adequation to something given which it imitates and reproduces, but: an imperatively-poeticizing, perspective-horizon fixing transfiguration [*befehlend-dichtendes, perspektivisch-horizonthaftes, festmachendes Verklären*]." It may not be "adequation to something given," but it is nonetheless representational, if only of itself, of the act of posing. Just as all representation is also posing, so also all posing is representational.

14. It is a kind of teaching that accords with Nietzsche's earlier theories of education set forth in *Wir Philologen* (1874), *Ueber die Zukunft unserer Bildungs-Anstalten* (1872), and *Schopenhauer als Erzieher* (1874). In *Wir Philologen*, he first attacks those who should not teach: "I believe 99 philologists out of a 100 *should* not be philologists . . . If they had education in their hands they *would educate* consciously or unconsciously, after their *own* image." In other words, the rash hand should hesitate, and pathos should be avoided. He writes further: "The substance of study lies in this: only what provokes imitation . . . should be studied," which foreshadows the teaching by example of *Ecce Homo*. Finally, he writes near the end: "We do not want to build prematurely: we do not know, whether we will ever be able to build, and whether it would not be better not to build," in other words, not to teach at all (Leipzig edition, X: 344, 345, 413–14; *The Complete Works of Friedrich Nietzsche*, ed. Oscar Levy (London: T. N. Foulis, 1909), 8: 110, 111, 183, 190). The idea is carried further in *Ueber die Zukunft* where Nietzsche addresses his audience with the following words: "[those who understand] actually need only to be reminded and not to be instructed." In the fifth lecture, he describes education in terms resembling those of the ideal educator in *Ecce Homo* who simultaneously constrains the student and inspires independent action: "At that time the student sensed at what depth a true educational institution must take root, namely in an inward renovation and inspiration of the purest moral faculties . . . great leaders are needed, and . . . all culture begins with obedience" (*Werke*, 3, pt. 2: 136, 241; *Complete Works*, 3: 8, 139). The peculiar mixture of self-reliance and constraint that one finds described in the autobiography as a whole appears also in Nietzsche's early theory of education. The combination is even more pronounced in his essay on Schopenhauer: "Set up in a row before you these honored things, and maybe, they will reveal to you, in their being and their order, a law [*Gesetz*], the fundamental law of your real self . . . The true educators and moulders reveal to you what is the real groundwork and meaning of your being, something thoroughly uneducatable and unmouldable." If one recalls that he says in *Ecce Homo* that the real subject of the essay is "Nietzsche as Educator," one understands why he attributes to Schopenhauer a teaching method he himself uses in the autobiography: "But Schopenhauer spoke to himself [*redet mit sich*]; or if one likes to imagine an auditor, then one imagines the son

whom the father instructs" (*Werke in Drei Bänden*, 1: 290, 295; *Complete Works*, 6: 107, 114).

15. A letter to Peter Gast dated December 9, 1888 reads: "[*Ecce Homo*] so transcends the concept of 'literature' that there is no parallel to it even in nature itself; it blasts, literally, the *history* of mankind in two—the highest superlative of *dynamite*" (*Werke in Drei Bänden*, 3: 1338; *Selected Letters*, p. 331).

16. In *Ecce Homo*, Nietzsche quotes twice from the chapter of *Thus Spake Zarathustra* entitled "On Old and New Tablets." There, he links the breaking of the old tablets, the old laws, with the breaking of words: "Such words were once called holy . . . where have there been such better robbers and killers in this world than in such holy words? . . . Break the maxims of those who slander the world [*Welt-Verleumder*] . . . Human society is a trial . . . and not a 'contract.' Break, break this word of the softhearted and half-and-half." The inscribing of new tablets follows the destruction of the old: "Therefore, my brothers, a *new nobility* is needed to be the adversary of all rabble and of all that is despotic and to write anew upon new tablets the word 'noble' " (*Werke*, 6, pt. 1: 249, 250, 253, 261; *The Portable Nietzsche*, ed. Walter Kaufmann (New York: Viking Press, 1968), pp. 314, 315, 317, 324).

17. The last line of the last poem, "Von der Armut des Reichsten," in the *Dionysus Dithyramben*, *Werke*, 6, pt. 3: 408.

FIVE

REPETITION, MUSEUMS, LIBRARIES:
JORGE LUIS BORGES
Alicia Borinsky

This animal, common in the north, is four or five inches long; its eyes are scarlet and its fur is jet black, silky and soft as a pillow. It is marked by a curious instinct, the taste for India ink. When a person sits down to write, the monkey squats cross-legged nearby with one forepaw folded over the other, waiting until the task is over. Then it drinks what is left of the ink, and afterward sits back on its haunches quiet and satisfied.

Wang Thai Hai (1791)

Borges, *The Book of Imaginary Beings*

THE MONKEY sits back quiet and satisfied after having drunk what is left of the ink, what has been left unwritten by the writer. The monkey drinks the residue of ink and its silence is made of that which has been left *outside* but which is, nevertheless, also *there* as an excess that can only be brought forth by de-monkeying the monkey. What would that de-monkeying consist of? What would be the twist of the relationship—mimicry—that could escape from the specularity entailed by that sitting back, by the monkey's sameness to the writer, by the dependence of the inkpot? But in posing this question we veil yet another: who or what is the monkey? Who performs the role of silent imitator? Who works with the excess, with the residue of ink?

The texts by Jorge Luis Borges weave in the image of the monkey of the inkpot as an image for the kind of "originality" attained by the work of art. Borges' well known notion of writing as an exercise of repetition of certain key metaphors approved by time, eternal because they come back said in a simpler tone suggests that the basic scene of writing is precisely a double relationship, at least, between a hypothetical writer and something or somebody assimilating what has been left *unsaid*, a something that is both unnecessary and pertinent. It belongs to the *same* inkpot but it has been left out. Nevertheless, the monkey is silent. The very notion of a simpler tone, of a certain economy of speech, a bareness, acquires simultaneously the qualities of silence, reticence, and excess. Why repeat what has been said before, why work out of the same inkpot? The inkpot, that *same* ink, performs the role of the language of *truth*. It is not a truth to be found out *outside* writing. It is the production of writing as a rereading, an interplay between sameness and difference that produces its own effects of clarity, economy, and bareness in a differential system of readings. That particular truth which Borges is talking about seems to elude the naiveties of realism; there seems to be no pointing outside the text, no belief in extraliterary referentiality. It is the inkpot. The position of the monkey regarding the writer is the double nature of authorship; no text is ever complete and finished; the authors are always two, one who writes the text and another one—at least—who profits from its excess.

Borges also speaks about authority, difference between monkey and writer. But the fragment about the monkey of the inkpot appears *already* as the result of the monkey's work. It is part of an anthology prepared by Borges, the author of the text is someone else. The anthologist sits behind Wang Thai Hai (fictional or not, it does not matter), his silence consists in showing that signature; the excess is worked into the very notion of an anthology, it is that which makes the arrangement possible, that *other* arrangement that takes it away from its context and integrates it as part of a miscellany. The anonymity implied by an anthologist is illusory; the disorganization of an order and the organization of a disorder effected by the selection, position and choice of quotes is hidden behind it. The monkey *is* the writer if every writing is a rewriting as Borges would have us believe.

> The yellow carrousel of horse and lion
> Whirls in the hollow while I hear the echo
> Of those tangos of Arolas and Greco
> I watched danced on the pavement

> On an instant that today stands out alone,
> Without before or after, against oblivion,
> And has the taste of everything lost,
> Everything lost and recovered[1]

Alicia Borinsky

The monkey is a recoverer; his passivity in drinking the ink left in the inkpot is a way of preserving the materiality of the text written by the writer. Borges' texts tend to weave this preservation in a way that is apparently antithetical because the terms that come to mind to explain the relationship of rewriting are parody, lie, hoax, the building of versions. But it is precisely at that point, when the texts are telling us that they are not original, that they have already been written somewhere else, by somebody else, seemingly putting forth the notion of derivation versus originality, of a collective writing versus the individual authorship, that we may start to wonder about how collective this writing is, how radical the displacement is, what kind of substitution has taken place. This bracketing of the notions about writing to be "found" in Borges' texts takes, in the first movement of our reading, the form of posing the terms in which the monkey works as a witness of the others' writing. Our position entails a certain kind of specular exercise. For we—as many of Borges' narrators—are going to look for the Aleph, for that minimum that functions as a reduced model for the Universe, understanding by Universe, language.

It is not by chance that the image of the monkey of the inkpot does not tell us anything about what the writer is writing. The only things we know concern the economy of the ink. And that is precisely what Borges' texts will tend to effect: an effacement of that which is said by displacing any fixed information for the movement of informing itself. The proliferation of "witnesses" of all sorts (readers, reviewers, participants in events, friends, and family figures) helps to produce the illusion of secondariness and derivation at the same time that it is faithful to the kind of exchange between subject and object ridiculed in "Tlon, Uqbar, Orbis Tertius," according to which once you stop perceiving something, it disappears. But if this last development of the idealistic psychology of Tlon is devalued in the form of the example of the horse that faded after a man stopped looking at him, it is also strongly repeated in a displaced way in the very movement of the text that makes of the question of translation and reconstruction of Uqbar a task that can only be carried out by a group that is constantly defining its own "presence" by taking part in the kind of investigation that assures a bond between the belief in the "existence" of the subject matter and the researcher. The *emergence* of Uqbar is the result of the *convergence* of a mirror and a library. Whatever *outside* referent is attempted for the discourse appears already intertwined in a certain machinery of production, so that the task of naming it becomes a description of the obstacles that exist for pushing it back to a non-problematical identity to itself. That possibility of "going back to" functions as a certain otherness implied in the text, as the kind of opposition that would put into play what is involved in this fragment from Chesterton's *The Scandal of Father Brown,*

From the very first minute I entered that big empty bar or saloon, I knew that what was the matter with all this business was emptiness; solitude; too many chances for anybody to be alone. In a word, the absence of witnesses,

with this fragment from Lactantius quoted by De Quincey in *Murder as One of the Fine Arts,*

Now if merely to be present at a murder fastens on to a man the character of an accomplice; if barely to be a spectator involves us in one common guilt with the perpetrator, it follows, of necessity, that, in these murders of the amphitheatre, the hand which inflicts the fatal blow is not more deeply imbrued in blood than his who passively looks on; neither can *he* be clear of blood who has countenanced its shedding; nor that man seem other than a participator in murder, who gives his applause to the murderer, and calls for prizes on his behalf.

In Chesterton's fragment there are no witnesses; the "event" acquires the bareness of the lack of any versions about it. The orator's speech in de Quincey's text makes of the question of murder essentially a matter of complicity. Participation in a murder is rendered possible by being a witness, someone who can build versions about the "event." In very much the same way, Borges' texts show the departure from a non-problematic original language, intensifying that departure through the narrator's participation in what makes the displacement more acute: the construction of further versions of an *event* torn from its source.[2]

LAUGHING IN THE LIBRARY

The most obvious embodiment of the monkey's work is probably "Pierre Menard, Author of *Don Quixote.*" For Menard's attempt is to produce *Don Quixote* while preserving, at the same time, the difference between himself and Cervantes. At first, Menard thinks of the possibility of becoming Cervantes but he soon abandons his attempt because he finds it too easy, "To be, in some way, Cervantes and to arrive at *Don Quixote* seemed to him less arduous—and consequently less interesting —than to continue being Pierre Menard and to arrive at *Don Quixote* through the experiences of Pierre Menard. (This conviction, let it be said in passing, forced him to exclude the autobiographical prologue of the second part of *Don Quixote.* . . ."[3]

Whatever verisimilitude we find as the final effect of a reading comes from the strength with which a narrative builds for itself the fictionality of a voice organizing it from "behind." A persuasive machinery of effects creates the illusion of the existence of something or somebody at the very origin of its production who is the giver of the information that we receive from the reading. But that persuasiveness, the kind of hallucination—to use Macedonio Fernández' term—that makes us believe in a source of truth is there only because of a certain arrangement, a certain web by which the texts point outside themselves to create an authority that will give them a status different from fiction. When Pierre Menard decides to say the monkey's truth—since that is what is involved in his wish to be himself and Cervantes simultaneously—he puts into play the question of authorship as the production of voice and, in doing so, he questions the kind of continuity that exists between that hypothetical voice and its discourse. Menard learns the Spanish of Cervantes as a doubly foreign tongue (another language and another time), sets himself at the *other* end of the process and tries to posit his own voice as responsible for the text. Understanding the text becomes an understanding of the one who produced it because the only difference in the sense of the fragment reproduced lies in the separation between Menard and Cervantes. That is why we are asked to read the fragment twice. The interpretation provided by the reviewer constantly points to the question of authorship, "Equally vivid is the contrast in styles. The archaic style of Menard—in the last analysis of a foreigner—suffers from a certain affectation. Not so that of his precursor, who handles easily the ordinary Spanish of his time."[4] The difference between Menard and Cervantes is pointed out in terms of style, tone, ideology, mastery of the language. Menard's work turns out to be superior because it is a higher level of artifice; he is a master of displacement and anachronism. A symbolist from Nimes, Menard has been able to produce his own voice by rewriting with the exact words several fragments from Cervantes. It is through the reading of the text as voice that the reviewer is able to stress the artistry of Menard; the reviewer believes in the existence of such an entity behind the fragments and is, thus, able to exercise admiration for the producer. Menard has *reenacted Don Quixote*.

But let us read closely the fragment that serves to build the difference between two producers and stress, at the same time, their existence as the voices responsible for what is said. It is precisely that part in *Don Quixote* where one is told that the novel may be a translation of a work by a Moor—all liars in the coded literary morality of the time—Cid Hamete Benengeli. Cervantes would have been a Menard already; his relationship to that text is no different from Menard's. Cervantes had a monkey relationship to his own text; the question of original authorship is pushed back to an undecidable "before."

He remembered that the dreams of men belong to God, and that Maimonides wrote that the words of a dream are divine, when they are all separate and clear and are spoken by someone invisible.[5]

The reviewer warns us from the beginning that there are two main divisions in the works of Menard, his *visible* works and his invisible ones. The fact that he first discusses the visible ones in order to have material for the invisible is important. Menard's visible work is mostly some kind of displacement of other writings. He plays with irony, translation, attributions. What we read, therefore, is the intellectual biography of a symbolist whose task consists in creating illusions of duplication or a critique of univocal meanings. The invisible work is nothing but the culmination of the same nihilistic esthetic; in the last analysis an esthetic that is supported by a notion of derivation. Rewriting *Don Quixote* is part of the same attempt; it is the production of a double of the novel through the preservation of the words and a redefinition of meaning by the voice that produces it. The particular situation of the fragment in the original work functions as a bracketing of the very notion that the rewriting wants to convey. For if Cervantes was not himself the author of *Don Quixote*, what sense is there in his having become split, in being at the same time Cervantes and Menard? Menard does not understand the status of the piece he has written. He believes that the "original" has been the result of Cervantes' spontaneous work. In a letter quoted in the review he says "My affable precursor did not refuse the collaboration of fate; he went along composing a little a la diable, swept along by inertias of language and invention. I have contracted the mysterious duty of reconstructing literally his spontaneous work."[6] What Menard believes to be a new task is already inscribed in *Don Quixote* so that his rewriting is, in fact, a misreading. But the form of his error is such that it turns out to be the most faithful kind of reconstruction; it is a simulacrum of the "original" situation which is, already, devoid of the kind of anteriority conveyed by a fixed producer.

What is the status of the reviewer? To what extent is his own account outside of Menard's system of false derivations? The reviewer signs his text in Nimes, 1939. In doing so he repeats De Quincey's speech about murder; his exercise will take him back to Pierre Menard and his followers. His snobbish discourse, the way in which he quotes the supporters and friends of Menard, the enemies he builds in order to sort out arguments for his credibility are there in order to introduce him as a character and bracket his objectivity. What does this bracketing involve? How important is it for the understanding of the Menard enterprise? The reviewer himself has participated in the Nimes cenacle; the many digressions in his text suggest a complex network of personal intrigues that link him to Menard's friends and enemies. His

Alicia Borinsky

review is but one of the elements through which he attempts to make an intervention in the same literary circle. In this way, the reviewer emerges from the "beginning" as *the character* hidden in the surface of his own discourse. In talking about Menard, he talks about himself, he gains a literary voice which coincides with Menard's; his text is one of the figurations (*figuraciones*) of a conspiracy for granting sense to the Nimes project; his specular relationship with Menard is revealed by the complicity involved in the belief in his invisible works. As soon as we pose the way in which the reviewer becomes a displaced version of Menard who is a displacement of Cervantes who, in turn, is a displacement of an undecidable Cid Hamete Benengeli, we realize that this kind of interplay effects a figure (*figura*) for another exchange, which is the virtual exchange that makes humour possible. It is now time to work our way out from the specular movement of our reading, to abandon the monkey's position and to pose the question that will help us come to terms with the interplay that overdetermines our laughter in reading this text. What is it in the rewriting of this project of rewriting that builds the possibility for the detached laughter?

In the last analysis, says Lane, it's always best to stand in front of a mirror with the pipe in your mouth and study the effect. Some pipe smokers consider it vanity to scrutinize themselves in the mirror. But it is well worth their while. After all, a pipe is an investment in a man's future.[7]

Menard and the reviewer have chosen for themselves a pipe that does not belong to them. The reviewer and Menard are each other's mirror; they are trying to smoke—to use up—Cervantes who, in turn was using up Cid Hamete. But if Cervantes was able to write a masterpiece, Menard can only come up with a faulty artifact praised by a reviewer who shares his *bad* taste for useless intellectual games.

The reason why the pipe smoker has to study the effect of the pipe in the mirror is *class*; he has to discover which one really corresponds to him. It is hopeless to get a pipe that will not fit you because your looks and your manners will clearly indicate to *us* that in spite of your being able to get through all the motions of smoking, there exists a basic discontinuity between you and the pipe. Some characteristics of that discontinuity—according to Schnitzer—are lack of elegance, subtlety, etc. In short, a certain "I don't know what" that indicates very precisely, nevertheless, good and bad in the world of taste. Who are *we*, the ones who know about the pipe? Who are we, readers, laughing against Menard and the reviewer and why is that inevitable? The answer lies in the kind of interplay liberated by the signature of the article in Nimes. That signature—a reduced model for the games showing the pettiness and ignorance of the reviewer, his bad Spanish, the admiration for Menard's most useless enterprises, his friendship with lady readers, the general participation in a shallow cultural circle—serves the purpose of producing the space of separation that will be taken over by another complicity; the one between a narrator writing the text behind the reviewer and a reader who shares his grammar, his library, his sense of good Spanish; a complicity between good pipe smokers, owners of the strict set of rules of that "I don't know what" which is the same "I don't know what" that separates good repetition from pointless rewriting. The monkey of the inkpot is the qualification of the distance that separates it from the writer; it works out of the *same* inkpot but it still remains a monkey; it has not been able to produce an inkpot that would be a repetition in difference of the "author's" work; it has a derivative relationship to the text it wants to rewrite; in very naive terms: there is a good and a bad repetition. Menard is the bad difference. He has read the question of repetition literally. Although he has been able to produce a simulacrum of *Don Quixote* by reproducing the movement already present in Cervantes, what he does puts him in the position of the silly monkey. The reader and the narrator behind those explicitly at play in the text conspire to reveal that the Nimes enterprise is to be scorned because it involves a basic misunderstanding of what good literature is all about.

Our laughter is the effect of that conspiracy overdetermining the reading. It is a laughter *with* the owners of the library of good literature and correct language; it pushes aside certain literary movements seen as the result of ignorance. (At this point let us remember that we find in Borges numerous texts of this nature. *El Libro de arena* is perhaps one of the clearest examples. The loss of the infinite book in the story that gives a title to the collection is a substitute for the destruction of that book and, perhaps, the volume in which the reader finds the story. The intricate network leading to this "end" alludes to the dialogue between an implied reader and a narrator who conspire to deny credibility to the one explicitly in charge of telling the story.) In laughing at Menard, then, we participate as accomplices in the enterprise of building the figure of the able practitioner of repetition.

We know that the pipe is not being well smoked; Menard and the Nimes cenacle are not the ones to master the art of literature because they have a naive, literal understanding of repetition. The literal understanding of repetition *is* Menard and, to a certain extent, the monkey. It involves preserving the earliest appearance of the thing and taking it up as the source for further work—a map of natural size, as we read in *Las Crónicas de Bustos Domecq*—or the loss of voice by preserving the

Alicia Borinsky

ownership of the inkpot as we learn from the fact that there is an inescapable difference between author and monkey.

What is involved in the scorn for Menard is not a simple opposition between originality and rewriting; it is rather a complication of the notion of *going back to*. Due to our mistrust we have gone back to *Don Quixote* and found out that the passage is not *even* the earliest appearance of the thing. The method is suspect from the very start; going back in search for a univocal source is hopeless because the "event" is torn from the beginning. Rewriting is, nevertheless, what Borges attempts to do in his literature. His works suggesting the constant recurrence of the same metaphors with the effect of producing one single anonymous text, the enlargement of the notion of text by posing, as in "The Garden of Forking Paths," a system of exchanges where a detective plot that leads to a real crime may be better inscribed in a newspaper or in marble or, perhaps, in an in-between that is neither one nor the other; the games with false attributions where the Aleph and the Zahir may operate as reduced models for a simultaneity that includes succession. These are but ways in which he takes part in attempts not altogether different from Menard's.

But Borges' repetition has little to do with a historical anteriority. It is the building of a system of translations and reinscriptions where the original source is blurred to effect a neutral space for what is "said," a radical anonymity that makes Menard's reviewer a fool because he believes in the importance of voice and individual producers. In posing the ways in which Menard and the reviewer become characters punished by laughter, we have started to doubt the anonymity, we have discovered that it hides an exchange between good readers. It is now time for thinking about the library of these good readers, their authority, the ways in which they earn their right to laugh, their card catalogue.

TOWARDS A MUSEUM

. . . but it wasn't a voice it was voicing
John Bricuth, *The Heisenberg Variations*

The explicit project in Borges is the substitution of the notion of *voice* by *voicing*; there is no locus for the one's overdetermining the texts. Their neutrality is their truth, the truth of undecidability. But the undecidability that wants to dissolve itself as having any single effect attempts, nevertheless, to teach us how to read well. It wants to remain hidden not as voice, but as the eternal recurrence of a neutral *voicing*.

Our bracketing of laughter returns it, nevertheless, to a locus where neutrality becomes impossible. In searching for clues against neutrality a rather brutal move is required, the dating of the aristocracy of intelligence in Argentine political history.

After the wars of Independence a conflict between Buenos Aires, the port city, and the rest of the country developed. The economic problems involved in these struggles are obscured in the years that follow the Independence by the cultural dichotomy posed by Sarmiento in terms of "Civilización y Barbarie." By a twist not altogether foreign to the rest of the Romantic movement in Latin America, the native groups of the country are seen as the evil forces of Barbarism and ignorance. The project of gaining the hegemony of Buenos Aires over the rest of the land is closely linked to an educational campaign where European culture is equated with the only possible literacy; the fight for democracy becomes, in Argentina, an effort of importing the model of the American Constitution and the ideas of French Liberalism. Sarmiento, praised as the great pedagogue, founder of the first schools, becomes simultaneously one of the most influential ideologues against the local provincial caudillos and their task force, the Montoneros. Bartolomé Mitre founds the most important organ of opinion for the epigones of the port city, the newspaper *La Nación* and becomes the translator of Dante. Literacy is seen as a violent battle for Europe; whatever exists already in the country is perceived as an obstacle, to the extent that the campaign to eradicate the Indians from the South is called euphemistically "Campaign of the Desert" thereby presenting itself as a populating effort. The killing necessary to turn the region into a real desert is hidden by the name of the campaign.

This group does not see itself as particularly violent; on the contrary, it fights against violence and irrationalism. Its project is to speak the language of a neutral truth, to integrate Argentina in the world scene as a European country, the only kind of country to be considered educated; the model of progress in America being the United States. Two distinct lines are formed in the country, one that poses the continuity of the anti-liberal forces in the triad San Martin-Rosas-Perón and another one that takes up the Mitre tradition. It is still puzzling to see the recurrence of the terms of the old struggle in contemporary Argentine politics. The left wing of Peronism takes up the name of Montoneros in direct reference to the provincial soldiers; the anti-Peronists speak against the barbarism of Perón in very much the same terms they spoke against Rosas. The cultural battle is re-enacted time and again, both sides claiming to represent one of the old lines.

Borges' notion of an aristocracy of intelligence, which emerges from

Alicia Borinsky

the kind of complicity between good readers that we have discovered in the reading of Pierre Menard, is one of the figurations of this old struggle. The infinitude of the Library of Babel hides in its surface the refusal of another card catalogue (the one we discover as being punished by humour); the neutrality of its truth is the one of the good pipe smokers. He is teaching us how to read well by exercising the right of laughter against ignorance. It is already a commonplace to say that Borges' literature blurs all distinctions between dreaming and reality, sanity and madness. But this undecidability only gives way to another opposition, intelligence versus ignorance. A pair of opposites putting into play the great fight for literacy that currently assumes the form of a sense of "good" Spanish fighting against any attempts at destroying syntactic laws.

In one of the many fictional genealogies that Borges attributes to himself he posits his own name as the result of the recurrence of certain political figures in his own blood:

> This, here, is Buenos Aires. Time which brings
> to men either love or money, now leaves to me
> no more than this withered rose, this empty tracery
> of names from the past recurring
>
> out of my blood: Laprida, Cabrera, Soler, Suárez . . .
> names in which secret bugle calls are sounding,
> the republics, the horses and the mornings,
> glorious victories and dead soldiers.[8]

The names that recur are the ones of distinguished soldiers of the educational effort; the cycle will be constantly repeated—differently—as for Perón. Perón heard the names of Rosas and the Montoneros. He saw himself as nothing but one instance of their repetition. The duel beween those two recurrent forces does not take place any longer in a space where their efforts are contradictory. They come to be united—as in "La Milonga de los dos hermanos"—under a common flag by dint of a third term in the political struggle, that new class that has redefined the fighters and displaced the neutrality of their libraries to an ideological museum.

ON CURATORS

> Not that I believe that people raised this statue to me,
> I know as well as you that I commissioned it.

> Nor that I thereby hope for inmortality:
> I know the people will one day destroy it.
> Nor that I wished to give myself in life
> the monument you will not raise when I am dead:
> but that I had it raised knowing you haté it.
>
> Ernesto Cardenal, "Somoza unveils the statue of Somoza
> in Somoza Stadium," *Marilyn Monroe and Other Poems*

Who would be the curators of such a museum? Who the cataloguers, the ones to tell us what is what? How would that present tense able to build a history for the fighters be elaborated?

The narrative that has presented two opposing traditions—the *sarmientista* founding of the schools vs. the *montoneros's* barbarism—as forces that jointly disregard their previous disagreements to fulfill the task of oppressing a new class implies the existence of a third term delineating a new battlefield. The anecdotal history of this phenomenon would present us a Borges that celebrates the military dictatorship in Argentina, one who is decorated in the Chile of Pinochet. The Perón that emerges in this context is the theoretician of what he called "El Pacto Social," an attempt to efface the nature of the class struggle in Argentina by posing the problems of the country in terms of a fight between the *pueblo* and the *antipueblo* while forcing the left wing of his own Peronist movement into the underground. The fight against the left initiated by Perón's last government is being continued by those who were seemingly his adversaries, the Army praised by Borges. At this level, the story has the devastating clarity of a news item in the daily paper. The Montoneros praised by Perón in their common opposition to *Sarmientismo* become enemies of the people in much the same way as for Borges. The tradition of intelligence-and-truth-versus-the-ignorance-of-*barbarie* makes it possible for Borges to praise the barbaric practices of a fascist military elite that continues the task started by Perón.

But our reading has attempted to produce something that is located in a different node of the same network; it has tried to show how the neutrality of Borges' discourse may be re-inscribed as the interested discourse of an ideological elite. By thinking of some of the humorous effects of his texts as the result of a complicity among good readers we have found a *place* for an exchange that would otherwise remain unmarked, neutral, universal. Our reading opens up puzzling analogies between the Borges we encountered and a Perón eager to dilute any direct reference to class antagonism through his Social Pact.

An ideological museum. Freezing some effects of texts in a way that would seem to be faithful to their most intense reading. All of this cataloguing and exhibiting is rendered possible not by a romantic belief in any wisdom of a militant working class but by the suspicion that "neutral" discourses work against themselves.

NOTES

1. Jorge Luis Borges, "The Tango," *A Personal Anthology* (New York: Grove Press, 1967), p. 159.

2. A witness bestows "reality" on whatever he describes as a result of his observation. As he becomes a character in his own narrative the level of objectivity of his statements can be determined only by a reading of the role he plays in producing the results of his "observation." Borges' works play in that *in-between* indicated by the quoted fragments: on the one hand (Chesterton), the impossibility of saying anything about the "event" (lack of witnesses) although we know that it took place; on the other (De Quincey), the impossibility of taking anything that is said into account because of the politics of complicity involved in being a witness.

One of the most explicit examples of what is involved in the first case is Borges' short story "The Intruder." A number of "witnesses" introduced by a narrator are disqualified for different reasons, the common denominator being that they have not seen the event or that their prejudices are too great to report it accurately. The exercise of selection and subsequent rejection occupies a large part of the text and serves as an introduction to the discourse of a narrator who takes up the task of telling the event after warning us that he is a literary man who knows things second hand and is not able to report anything in its bareness, without literary distortions. That is why we read a classic story of male friendship winning over sexual passion; the recurrence of a commonplace has been substituted for the specificity of an elusive event without witnesses. The "Aleph" takes us to the other possibility. The Aleph is simultaneously an object and an event (this distinction is effaced in Borges' writings: objects are always constituted as events). The narrator reports with scorn the works of a poet who has given himself the task of embodying the universe in a poem. His text—quoted in the story—is mannered and altogether worthless, mostly because of its clumsy relationship to literary tradition. But the task itself—being the witness of an object that embodies the whole universe—is not to be discounted. The narrator *sees* the Aleph and attempts to describe the obstacles that make it impossible for him to write an accurate report of the way it looks. He is not part of the literary world of the poet, he is not an accomplice in the perpetuation of its language, and that is why he may attempt a certain bareness of discourse in his effort to "tell" the Aleph. He comes out the winner in a contest to choose the most reliable observer. His success takes the form of a failure because of the irreducible nature of the Aleph. The perfect, noncomplicitous witness is only an ideal possibility; his statement will never be uttered.

The political character of narration, the right to report, to tell, the many distinctions between good and bad observers pervades Borges' texts in a way that makes it necessary to read them as careful selections of privileged witnesses.

3. Jorge Luis Borges, "Pierre Menard, Author of Don Quixote," *Ficciones* (New York: Grove Press, 1962), p. 49.

4. Ibid., p. 53.

5. Borges, "The Secret Miracle," *A Personal Anthology* (New York: Grove Press, 1967), p. 189.

6. Borges, "Pierre Menard, Author of Don Quixote," p. 51.

7. Raymond L. Schnitzer, *Leaves from a Tobaccoman's Log* (New York: Vantage Press, 1970), p. 56.

8. Borges, "The Cyclical Night," *A Personal Anthology*, pp. 155–56.

SIX
WRITING AND TRUTH IN POE'S
THE NARRATIVE OF ARTHUR GORDON PYM
John Carlos Rowe

Language, as sense that is sounded and written, is in itself suprasensuous, something that constantly transcends the merely sensible. So understood, language is in itself metaphysical.

Heidegger, On the Way to Language

That the signified is originally and essentially (and not only for a finite and created spirit) trace, that it is *always already in the position of the signifier*, is the apparently innocent proposition within which the metaphysics of the logos, of presence and consciousness, must reflect upon writing as its death and its resource.

Derrida, Of Grammatology

IN THE PAST two decades critical interest in Poe's *Narrative of Arthur Gordon Pym of Nantucket* (1838) has resulted in various interpretations of the work's coherence and organization. Most commentators agree basically with Edward Davidson's summary of Pym's spiritual education: "It is a study of emerging consciousness, a very special intelligence and awareness which is Arthur Gordon Pym's (and, to an extent, Poe's). . . . The self-as-imagination begins with the real, substantial world, and then goes even farther in order to set up on 'the other side' certain symbols and keys to the mind's perception of reality."[1] Davidson's general characterization of the work as *Bildungsroman*, however, has been challenged by various ingenious critics, each offering some historical or contextual key to unlock the secret of *Pym*'s form and meaning. Recent American criticism in particular either tries relentlessly to fit the *Narrative* into some predetermined generic category or marshalls impressive evidence to demonstrate basic flaws and inconsistencies in the text. In both cases, the same standard continues to operate: a good work of literature ought to demonstrate internal coherence and narrative consistency. Such an attitude implies that criticism is a process of making intelligible difficult or extraordinary texts. The degree to which a work meets the criteria of unity and coherence may frequently be a measure of its conventionality or its susceptibility at least to analytic "translation." Since literature depends upon its ability to disrupt and violate accepted meanings and ordinary expectations, the most original work characteristically frustrates established methods and categories of interpretation. It does not, of course, follow that the text's resistance to interpretation is a guarantee of its literary value, but more attention ought to be paid to the ways in which our critical traditions tend to privilege certain "major works" and exile other "eccentric" texts. One need only review the diverse generic characterizations of *Pym* to realize that this work is either a monumental bungle or the achievement of transcendent genius. The title of Joseph Ridgely's recent review of the criticism suggests some of the prevailing confusion: "Tragical-Mythical-Satirical-Hoaxical: Problems of Genre in *Pym*."[2]

Contemporary French critics find *Pym* and Poe's works in general appropriate pretexts for the consideration of basic literary and theoretical questions. The *Tel Quel* theorist Jean Ricardou closely examines the episode on the Island of Tsalal as an exemplary demonstration of how all writing is inevitably concerned with its own inscription. *Pym* is a "Journey to the Bottom of the Page" that explores the possibility of its own textual existence at the same time that it prefigures its own erasure: "No text is more complete than *The Narrative of Arthur Gordon Pym*, for the fiction it presents points to the end of every text, the ultimate establishment of 'blank paper defended by whiteness.'"[3] Ricardou's interpretation, however, concentrates on only one restricted part of the narrative and disregards the formal strategies of the narration. Focusing on the hieroglyphs carved in the chasms and the "singular character" of the water on the island, Ricardou only hints at a comprehensive reading of the metaliterary possibilities in *Pym*. In "Le tombeau d'Edgar Poe," Maurice Mourier adds some important remarks on the "Preface" and "Note" in relation to the inscriptions in (and *of*) the chasms. Mourier parodies the critical desire for "hidden" meaning by forcing the shapes of the chasms to spell out "E. A. Poe" and deciphering the alphabetical characters carved in the marl as "A. G. Pym" and "E. A. P." He con-

John Carlos Rowe

cludes that the narrative displaces and hides any "narrating subject," an idea that relies on Jacques Derrida's concept of *"écriture"* as the graphic mark of the "trace" or "difference" that characterizes the productive play of all signification: "the text of *The Adventures of Arthur Gordon Pym* mimes/refuses/exorcises the death of the narrator (of any narrator), the death of the *I* and its text wherein the narrator-character conceals the languishing scriptor who slips away, childishly placing onto the character all responsibility for the fictional *mise-en-scène* (it does not belong to *I*)."[4]

The metaliterary character of *Pym* clarifies a number of problems concerning the work's form and thematic intention. In its fundamental investigation of the problematics of writing, *Pym* also questions the nature and possibility of literary form. What critics have considered difficulties and inconsistencies in the text may also be considered self-conscious disruptions of the impulse toward coherent design and completed meaning. Forever holding out the promise of a buried signified, *Pym* offers a sequence of forged or imitation truths: delivered messages, deciphered hieroglyphs, a penultimate vision. And yet the inability of each successive sign to present its truth is ironically disclosed, increasingly entangling any reading in the signifying web it attempts to unravel.

Poe's writings have also provided the occasions for Lacan's reading of Freud in "Seminar on 'The Purloined Letter'" and Derrida's deconstruction of Lacan in "The Purveyor of Truth."[5] Derrida's objections to Lacan's psychoanalytic treatment of "The Purloined Letter" might be applied generally to certain implicit assumptions made by literary critics. Derrida demonstrates how Lacan's disregard for the formal strategies of the narration of the tale tends to reduce the text to an "exemplary content" in the analyst's own argument. Thus Derrida suggests how all criticism (psychoanalytic, literary, historical) tends to neutralize the constraints of the pretext that continue to operate in the critical discourse. What Derrida terms Lacan's "ideality of the signifier" —the "indivisible" presence of the signifier—subtly shares the "ideality of a meaning" that governs the critical tendency to employ texts to illustrate "general laws."[6] The violence of interpretation—the displacement of the signifier with a supplementary signifier—is repressed in the history, formalist scholarship, psychoanalysis, or psychobiography that presumes to make the historical event of the pretext semantically present. The "work" in question must always be the differential relation of pretext and criticism, a "work" produced in the interpretative supplementation of its ostensible subject. If any "literary history" is to be salvaged, then it ought to be a narrative of this disguised critical appropriation (neither by "authors" nor "critics," but *in* language), an unveiling of the ways in which a signifying potential is generated and used.

A "history" of how literature is invented ought to begin with those texts that have rendered our conventional conceptions of poetic form most problematic. We might explore the gaps and deletions disguised by the continuities and genealogies of our traditional literary histories. On the other hand, the nature of critical appropriation is most marked in those works by "established" literary figures that remain the most eccentric to their critically defined *oeuvres*. In the nineteenth-century American literary tradition, one thinks of such troublesome works as Poe's *Pym*, Thoreau's *A Week on the Concord and Merrimack Rivers*, Hawthorne's *The Blithedale Romance*, and Melville's *The Confidence-Man*. A reinterpretation of these works might tell us a good deal about how our criticism has standardized the thought of these writers and the complexity of their works. Each of these works escapes conventional generic categories; each is concerned explicitly with the problem of how one writes. Viewed as reflections on how literature is made possible, they can be made to question the literary tradition and their authors' own assumptions concerning literary meaning and value.

I do not propose to privilege these texts by claiming some metaliterary genre for them; their semantic indeterminacy is shared by every effort to signify. Their "eccentricity," however, has been determined largely by the critical tradition that has attempted to "account for" or "make consistent" their meanings within the cultural period, the authors' respective *oeuvres*, and the prevailing conception of historical order. I propose to interpret these works as "marginal" texts that share the modern awareness of the displaced center, the divided present, the irrecoverable origin. Such a project follows the strategy of Derridean deconstruction summarized by Gayatri Spivak: "To locate the promising marginal text, to disclose the undecidable moment, to pry it loose with the positive lever of the signifier; to reverse the resident hierarchy, only to displace it; to dismantle in order to reconstitute what is always already inscribed."[7] This "moment" in which the tradition is questioned is profoundly "historical," not in the sense of a diachronic development but as the synchronic play of interpretations. Thus it is the modernity of Poe that is at stake in this essay, a Poe whose writings may be said to disclose our own critical dilemma. In Joseph Riddel's analysis, the "Poe" who:

. . . carried his discourse into an aestheticism which brought itself into such severe question and subjected itself to such acute guilt that only an utterly idealistic aestheticism could reconstitute the world with a center. It was this Poe whom the *Symbolistes* discovered, an implicit Poe who most crucially

John Carlos Rowe

realized the Modernist rupture in an art which accentuated the center as the presence of an absence, the music of nothingness.[8]

The "idealistic aestheticism" that appears to control most of Poe's writings is precisely what is threatened by *The Narrative of A. Gordon Pym*, superficially a "romance" relying on conventions that would support such an idealist intention. This work deconstructs the idea of representation as the illusion of the truth and dramatizes the contemporary conception of writing as the endless production of differences.

In its main outlines, *Pym* appears to follow the basic argument of Poe's poetry and prefigure the gnostic cosmology of *Eureka* (1848). In the course of his sea-voyage, Pym proves himself to be one of Poe's least perceptive characters. Pym's lack of insight in his early adventures is comparable to the myopia of the narrator of "The Fall of the House of Usher"; both characters epitomize the dangers of relying on the illusory world of sense impressions and misleading empirical data. Repeatedly baffled and frustrated by his experiences, Pym is forced to rely on various helpers and companions during his voyage. In the poetry, psychic guides generally assist the persona to interpret the cosmic message obscurely inscribed in nature. Nesace is charged by the deity with conveying his Word to the world in "Al Aaraaf," Psyche reads " 'What is written' " on the " 'legended tomb' " for the "I" in "Ulalume," and the "pilgrim shadow" points the way toward "Eldorado" for the "gallant knight." Pym's companions, however, are far less effective in helping him to understand either the progress or purpose of his voyage. Augustus dies of gangrene as the survivors drift aimlessly on the wreck of the *Grampus*, Tiger the Newfoundland dog simply disappears shortly after he has served his narrative function, Parker is eaten by the others, and Captain Guy and his crew are buried alive by the natives on the island of Tsalal. Dirk Peters alone accompanies Pym to the furthest limit of the voyage and returns alive, but not to tell the tale. Daniel Hoffman sees Peters as the "resilient dwarfish savage" who replaces the "rational, Prefect of Police side of Pym's mind" represented by his earlier friend and guide, Augustus.[9] Peters calls Pym's attention to the "singular looking indentures in the surface of the marl," and Peters rather than Pym judges them to have "some little resemblance to alphabetical characters."[10] Although Peters has a basic intuitive sense of natural order, he can neither articulate nor communicate this understanding. To the end of the voyage, Pym remains blind to the metaphysical and spiritual implications of his adventures.

The failure of Pym's companions to help him understand his journey gives special importance to his editorial relationship with "Mr. Poe," who must be considered another character in the drama and distinct from the historical Poe. The elaborate framing devices of Pym's "Preface" and the appended editorial "Note" have been generally viewed as part of Poe's parody of the scientific-voyage narratives that were in such vogue in the nineteenth century. The deliberate confusion of Pym and Mr. Poe as narrative voices also seems to reinforce the parabolic character of the tale and its relation to Poe's own inner voyagings. Mr. Poe, however, is neither a simple *Doppelgänger* of Pym nor identical with Edgar Allan Poe. As the writer of the adventure, Mr. Poe transforms the "facts" afforded by Pym into the poetic expression that constitutes Pym's education and knowledge. Pym explains why he has not undertaken the writing of his own story: "A distrust in my own abilities as a writer was, nevertheless, one of the principal causes which prevented me from complying with the suggestion of my advisers" (p. 724). And in spite of the encouragement of Mr. Poe "to prepare at once a full account of what I had seen and undergone," Pym fears he "should not be able to write, from mere memory, a statement so minute and connected as to have the *appearance* of that truth it would really possess. . . ." Thus Pym's lack of talent as an imaginative writer is bound intimately to his failure to understand the significance of his voyage.

The authorship of the text is further complicated by the alternation between journal entries and sequential narration. Only about twenty-five percent of the tale is told in journal form, and even this minimal contribution cannot be attributed exclusively to Pym. The entries in chapter six, for example, are employed for the sake of literary economy, in an effort to include events "of little importance" which "had no direct bearing upon the main incidents" of the narrative (p. 763). In fact there is no explicit reference to Pym's journal until the beginning of chapter eighteen, in which the *Jane Guy* is boarded by the natives. In a note Pym remarks: "I cannot, in the first portion of what is here written, pretend to strict accuracy in respect to dates, or latitudes and longitudes, having kept no regular journal until after the period of which this first portion treats. In many instances I have relied altogether upon memory" (p. 819). A similar qualification of the extent and accuracy of Pym's actual journal is given in chapter twenty-five. We may thus speculate with some certainty that Mr. Poe is intended to be the main writer of the text, relying on Pym's oral account and such necessary memoranda as the drawings of the chasms and their figures in chapter twenty-three. Pym's claim at the end of the "Preface" smells strongly of red herring: "This *exposé* being made, it will be seen at once how much of what follows I claim to be my own writing; and it will also be understood that no fact is misrepresented in the first few pages which were written by Mr. Poe. Even to those readers who have not seen the Messenger

John Carlos Rowe

[*Southern Literary Messenger*], it will be unnecessary to point out where his portion ends and my own commences; *the difference in point of style will be readily perceived*" (p. 725; my emphasis). Pym's contribution to the text remains simply the germ of Mr. Poe's poetic idea, which is the true story behind this improbable romance.[11] Pym still plays a crucial role in this drama of poetic composition; Mr. Poe's story is an interpretation of what is already part of Pym's psychic experience. Narrative authority is in question from the beginning, because the writing must rely on both the formlessness of Pym's unconscious and the poetic interpretation of Mr. Poe.

As we shall see, there are several other writers involved in Pym's story, all of whom are controlled by the poetic composition. The multiple authorities for the narration appear to contradict Poe's general concern in his works with poetic unity. For Poe, poetic expression moves toward the origin and end of all language: the energetic cosmic unity described in the pseudo-science of *Eureka*: "In sinking into Unity, it [Matter] will sink at once into that Nothingness which, to all Finite Perception, Unity must be—into that Material Nihility from which alone we can conceive it to have been evoked—to have been *created* by the volition of God."[12] In its referential function, language sustains the spatial and temporal dimensions of our material condition. Poetry does violence to this mode of representation and attempts to constitute itself as a self-referential system of signs. The poem imitates cosmic design and symmetry, rather than offering a reflection of empirical phenomena. Thus poetic expression strives for a physical presence in the word itself as the embodiment of psychic and cosmic truth. The aim is literally to construct a poem *in* its being rather than *through* its meaning. The poetic process involves the ontological effacement of the self-conscious Ego, and thus the "annihilation of self" becomes ironically the ground for one's identity in Being. The poem approximates this spiritual completion by transforming the self into a full poetic image rather than a mere "name."

Straining against ordinary temporality and its own materiality, poetic writing imitates the cosmic dialectic of "Attraction and Repulsion," the consolidation and dispersion which together define the "throb of the Heart Divine."[13] Writing inaugurates a desire for completion that its own inscription is destined to frustrate. Unity is nowhere present for Poe, because the original act of creation "was that of a determinate irradiation—one finally *dis*continued."[14] Bearing as it does both nostalgia and desire for divine silence, writing substitutes the *idea* of order and unity as a simulacrum for the lost presence. The poetic act may prefigure a future reconciliation of all things, but in so doing it only asserts more fully its own lack. Thus the poetic image presents itself as a complex play between the extremes of self-conscious alienation and the dissolution of self in metaphysical unity. Such writing embodies the essential doubleness of Poe's cosmic metaphor: both irradiation and concentralization. We may recall at this point Poe's definition of the "Poetic Principle" as "strictly and simply, the Human Aspiration for Supernal Beauty. . . ." The dialectic of desire and repression informs Poe's idea of "the Poetry of words as *The Rhythmical Creation of Beauty.*"[15]

In *The Narrative of A. Gordon Pym*, the differential process of writing is enacted as the subject and object of the work. The tale "progresses" from an ordinary referential discourse to a poetic expression in which the metaphoric structure of language materializes in a landscape of signs. For both Pym and Mr. Poe, the true journey is into the text itself, in which a paradoxical kind of "self-definition" might be found. Their mutual silence at the end opens the play of writing to its necessary interpretation, marked by the appended "Note" penned by yet another hand. Neither in form nor content does this "Note" satisfy our expectation of a conclusion. We learn of "the late sudden and distressing death of Mr. Pym" only to discover "that the few remaining chapters which were to have completed his narrative . . . have been irrecoverably lost through the accident by which he perished himself." The limit of the voyage is itself the incompletion of writing, which must be supplemented by the author of the Note or by Peters, who is "still alive, and a resident of Illinois . . . and will, no doubt, afford material for a conclusion of Mr. Pym's account" (p. 852). Yet, Mr. Poe declines "to fill the vacuum," as if the disclosure of the difference of writing has been the end and beginning of his poetic task. Thus the "Preface" and "Note" formally define Pym's metaphysical adventure by questioning beginnings and endings. Within this frame, the text explores the nature of writing in such a way as to render ambiguous what we thought we had understood to be Poe's gnostic philosophy of composition.

Pym's motivation for going to sea originates with the stories told by his friend and occasional bedfellow, Augustus Barnard. Their brief voyage on the *Ariel* and their rescue by the *Penguin* prefigures their subsequent adventures at sea. It is Augustus' "manner of relating his stories of the ocean" that reinforces Pym's "somewhat gloomy although glowing imagination." Pym subsequently suspects these stories "to have been sheer fabrications," but it is just this air of unreality that sparks the boys' desire for adventure. Both of them seem to long for some alternative to the superficially ordered world of Edgarton. Thus it seems especially appropriate that their "scheme of deception" enables them to escape as well as to expose the illusions of control and order maintained by this conventional society. Augustus forges a note to Pym's father, which purports to be a formal invitation for Pym to spend a fortnight with the sons of a family friend, Mr. Ross. Augustus thus displaces the acceptable signified of such a message and calls into question the habitual methods of reference supporting social intercourse. Like all forgeries, this note plays upon the notion that we read a text according to a specific author, in this case the authorizing signature of "Mr. Ross." The writing of the note marks the boys' departure from society, antedating their physical embarkation on board the *Grampus*. The deception threatens the fundamental rules of social behavior and communication; the boys' departure is made absolute in the act of writing the forgery.

When he boards the *Grampus*, Pym enters a space that is implicitly textual. Before he "stows away" in the darkness of the ship's hold, Pym has a brief glimpse of Augustus' spacious stateroom and notices "a set of hanging shelves full of books, chiefly books of voyages and travels" (p. 734). In the hold, Pym finds that his coffin-like "iron-bound box" is also equipped with "some books, pen, ink, and paper." Presumably these things will serve him as substitutes for the more tangible adventures on deck. Thus Pym discovers the realm of romance through a succession of intertwined metaphors of textuality: preface, fabricated stories, forged notes, books, writing implements, paper. Derrida remarks that in the opening of "The Purloined Letter": "Everything begins 'in' a library: among books, writing, references. Hence nothing begins. Simply a drifting or a disorientation from which one never moves away."[16] The voyage in Pym is only nominally conducted by sailors, ships, and oceans. These are mere figures for the writing itself, which is characterized by a "drifting" and "disorientation" from its own origin or end. Every effort at representation merely discloses another representation, and we are quickly entangled in an inescapable metaphoric play. *Pym* is a narrative about a journey toward a metaphysical and geographical center, but in the very effort of writing such a story that center is displaced, disrupted, deferred.

The hidden textuality of Pym's voyage gradually emerges from the darkness to enter the body of the world. Shortly after he accustoms himself to his cramped quarters, Pym falls into a deep sleep that marks the gap between Edgarton and the poetic space of the voyage. Pym dozes off while reading "the expedition of Lewis and Clark to the mouth of the Columbia," another narrative of a voyage in quest of undiscovered origins. This episode also serves to distinguish the psychological time of the voyage from ordinarily measured temporality. Augustus has left his watch with Pym, but it runs down while Pym is asleep. When he awakens, he can only guess that he has slept "for an inordinately long period of time" (p. 737). Despite frequent references to dates in the remainder of the narrative, Pym's temporal disorientation in the hold continues throughout the rest of the voyage. Measured time is gradually replaced by a temporal sense closely related to the length of particular episodes and other kinds of narrative emphasis.

Pym's fears multiply when Augustus fails to return for him. Imprisoned by mutineers, Augustus manages to scrawl a note to Pym. Pym's Newfoundland dog, Tiger, conveniently materializes in order to deliver the message. Pym is awakened from his delirious dreams of monsters, demons, and ferocious beasts by "some huge and real monster . . . pressing heavily upon my bosom . . ." (p. 738). Only after an elaborate attempt to escape from the hold does Pym discover the note that is buried beneath the fur of Tiger's left shoulder. The contiguity of the dog with both Pym's dream-images and Augustus' note suggests a more general movement in the *Narrative* from a conception of language as a system of abstract referential signs to the material facts of a poetic landscape. Tiger may bear the message, but he destroys the means by which it might be read. Pym finds that the dog has "mumbled" the candles and scattered most of Pym's phosphorus. Left in the dark by Tiger's ravenous appetite, Pym contrives a "multitude of absurd expedients for procuring light" before finally deciding to rub the paper with his few remaining fragments of phosphorus: "Not a syllable was there, however—nothing but a dreary and unsatisfactory blank; the illumination died away in a few seconds, and my heart died away within me as it went" (p. 743). Pym's frustration and his growing delirium cause him to tear the note into three pieces and cast them aside. Only after this impetuous act does he realize that he has looked at only one side of the paper.

Pym must appeal to Tiger and his sensitive nose to fetch the pieces from the dark recesses of the hold. Pym then carefully feels each piece in hopes that the letters might show "some unevenness." What he discovers instead is an "exceedingly slight, but discernible glow, which followed as it proceeded" (p. 744). Assuming that the glow must emanate from the phosphorus he had rubbed on the blank sides of the note, Pym finds the proper combination by turning each piece dark side up. In his excitement, Pym is unable to read the entire message, even though "there would have been ample time enough for me to peruse the whole three sentences before me." Nevertheless, the seven-word fragment he does read is sufficient to convey the urgency of Augustus' warning: *"blood— your life depends upon lying close"* (p. 745).

Pym's personal concern for his own survival blinds him to the

John Carlos Rowe

philosophic implications of this written message. The entire episode, from Tiger's arrival to the reading of the fragment, is an education in language and its expressive function. The blank side of the note at first exasperates Pym, but it is in fact the means whereby the message itself is made legible. Like the "white curtain" at the end of the narrative, blankness and silence motivate human discourse. Unlike reflected light, the phosphorus glow is an internal radiation analogous to the illumination of the poetic imagination. Augustus' note deals with man's fundamental situation, stressing as it does both "blood" and "life." Pym ought to have learned already the arbitrariness of human interpretation, which has been suggested both by the forged note from "Mr. Ross" and Pym's own willful scattering of Augustus' warning. Subject to myriad combinations and the intentions of endless "authors," language generally disseminates its truth.

The crucial word "blood," of course, is the very medium in which the message is written. Augustus subsequently explains that he was forced to use his own blood; the "red ink" perceived by Pym is in fact a synecdoche for the body of Augustus. Evelyn Hinz considers this detail an extension of the satiric intentions of the work: "Whereas Augustus used his blood to write the word, Pym turns the word back into flesh."[17] The significance of this episode is governed by the general narrative movement from referential discourse to a system in which signs refer only to other signs. Augustus' first note employs the false reference of familiarity and social custom—Mr. Ross's invitation—to cover the boys' escape. In this second message, the key word "blood" refers to the writing of the note itself: "*I have scrawled this with blood. . . .*" Augustus' ostensible communication is carried by the second clause, but Pym, Mr. Poe, and the reader concentrate on the disjointed word "blood."

The narrative itself makes the association between these two notes explicit. Pym learns from Augustus that: "Paper enough was obtained from the back of a letter—a duplicate of the forged letter from Mr. Ross. This had been the original draught; but the handwriting not being sufficiently well imitated, Augustus had written another, thrusting the first, by good fortune, into his coat-pocket, where it was now opportunely discovered" (p. 755). This coincidence of the two notes contradicts Pym's earlier perception of the blank obverse of Augustus' message. Yet, what critics have generally considered an error made in the haste of composition offers an important illustration of the doubleness of writing. Poe's poetic theory seems to argue that human discourse is grounded in a principle of unity that is silence: a paradoxical emptiness and fullness. In *Pym* the act of writing carries the trace of a prior representation, which defers the desired approach to an undifferentiated meaning or central signified. This minor textual "error" helps to illustrate the general metaphysical crisis being enacted in the narrative. As a simple warning to Pym, the note is little more than a convention of the popular romance. As another reflection on the question of "poetic" writing, the note demonstrates the difficulty of transcending the differential system of language to deliver a unified truth. Writing appears to defer the presence it desires by constituting a divided "present" that prefigures its own erasure.[18] Meaning may be situated only within the functions produced by this play of differences. Augustus' message serves as a signifier whose signified is yet to be read by Pym. In this context, the blank side provides the "space" of such an interpretation. No such innocent reading is possible, however, since that supposedly "blank" sheet is already inscribed with a prior signification—a clumsy duplicate of a forgery. Such retention and protention characterize the temporalizing function of writing, which replaces the less adequate "measures" of time in the text, such as Augustus' mechanical watch or the duration of Pym's "consciousness."

Pym's experiences in the darkness of the hold with dreaming, reading, writing, and interpreting prefigure the world he enters on deck. In the referential world of Edgarton, referential signs are employed as secondary mediations of reality. In the dynamics of deciphering Augustus' message, Pym gives the sign "blood" the status of an object in its own right. He is subsequently "reborn" into a poetic landscape where external phenomena have the characteristics of written signs. In this world cut off from such familiar bases for meaning as family, home, school, law, and society, the ordinary distinctions between appearance and reality no longer signify. Every "natural" phenomenon may be understood only according to what it may be said to "produce" within a semiotic system. Daniel Hoffman refers to the "regressive imagination" that seems to govern the images in this latter portion of the narrative.[19] Davidson claims that a spiritual progress takes place "by the steady recession of any 'fact' world . . . and the gradual domination of a chimera or the world as it really is behind the mask of ostensible reality."[20] Every experience and phenomenon contribute to an emerging psychic landscape. Rescued from the drifting wreck of the *Grampus* by the *Jane Guy*, Pym returns to a world of apparent order. The narrative devotes increased space to factual explanations, extracts from accounts of historical voyages, and scientific discourses on subjects as various as navigation and the drying of *biche de mer*. But the marked discrepancy between these realistic details and the alien symbolism of nature merely emphasizes the ineffectiveness of any empirical account of Pym's voyage.

John Carlos Rowe

On the island of Tsalal, the psychic drama is enacted in the confrontation of "civilized" whites with "primitive" natives. Regardless of how we view the natives in relation to Pym's inner voyage, their associations with darkness, burial, and deceitful behavior make them emblematic of a subterranean level of psychological reality. Their close ties with their surreal environment are suggested by their expressive language, which is "a loud jabbering . . . intermingled with occasional shouts" in apparent imitation of natural sounds. In fact, the word for the taboo of white is "Tekeli-li," which is the cry of the "gigantic and pallidly white birds" that fly from beyond the veil in the final episode.[21] The natives treat nature as though it were sentient, a conventional indication in Poe's writings that we have entered a "landscape of the soul." Unlike the whites, the natives apparently do not recognize their own reflections. Glimpsing his image in the cabin mirrors, Too-wit throws himself on the floor and buries his face in his hands. In order to identify a photograph or reflected image with his own person, the viewer relies on a concept of iconic representation whereby the signifier and signified share an actual resemblance. The inability of the natives to view reflections as icons reinforces the notion that we have left the realm of signs and things to enter a textual space in which reference is possible only among differing signs.[22]

This outlook may help us synthesize a number of the more extraordinary interpretations of the curious water on the island, which is both veined and limpid, varied purple in hue and unreflecting. Both Marie Bonaparte and Walter Bezanson emphasize the veined character of the water in order to equate it with blood.[23] Ricardou, of course, considers the water a metaphor for the text itself, ingeniously arguing: "If an imaginary perpendicular line is made to sever a given line of writing, the two severed fragments remain united in the idea by an intense syntactic cohesion. If, on the other hand, a horizontal separation is made between the two lines, the broken link, essentially spatial in nature, provides a very inferior sort of adhesion. This double complicity of the liquid with written language—by contiguity and similitude—encourages us to believe that what we are faced with is a text."[24] Mourier also concentrates on the peculiar divisiblity of the water—the separation of the veins along their boundary lines, the cohesion of the fluid across the veins—in order to draw an analogy between the stream and human musculature.[25] Rather than selecting any one of these interpretations, we ought to acknowledge that they all suggest that the stream is a metonymy for another physical thing: body or text. And this confusion of "body" and "writing" / "thing" and "word" has been taking place from the beginning of the narrative. We have entered a realm composed of "objects," but of a sort that frustrate ordinary representation. Patrick Quinn's conclusion regarding Ricardou's reading helps relate these various views: "The water-text analogy holds up primarily in this respect: neither offers a mirroring surface. Anti-realism is the key."[26] As the episode in the chasms will illustrate, we have entered a world in which word and thing are no longer distinguishable, frustrating the illusion of "self-presence" that operates explicitly in iconic representations but is implicit in other forms of mediating representation.

Burying the crew of the *Jane Guy* and driving Peters and Pym deep into the interior of the island, the natives help to uncover what the writing of the text has been performing: the interplay of the unconscious and the conscious. In the final episodes of *Pym*, this psychic relation is established as the very scene of writing and the generative source of human interpretation. Just as Tiger emerges from Pym's dream to deliver the message of blood, so the natives open a path for Peters and Pym to discover the writing on the chasm walls. The "alphabetical characters" carved in the marl, however, are already inscribed within the enveloping textuality. The relation between the irreducibly figurative landscape and the graphic nature of the narrative is made explicit in Pym's drawings of the shapes of the chasms themselves. These sketches (figures 1, 2, 3, and 5) indicate the scriptural characteristics of the "world" in which the message of figure 4 is inscribed. As the anonymous editor of the final "Note" explains: "Figure 1, then figure 2, figure 3, and figure 5, when conjoined with one another in the precise order which the chasms presented, and when deprived of the small lateral branches or arches (which, it will be remembered, served only as a means of communication between the main chambers, and were of totally distinct character), constitute an Ethiopian verbal root—the root ଥ∧Ꮧ᛬ 'To be shady'—whence all the inflections of shadow or darkness" (p. 853). Mr. Poe's narrative has thus reached a point at which his language and that of the world coincide. Concerned as it is with the inner voyage of Pym, the narrative reveals at this point the extent to which its re-presentation of the adventure must begin with that which is already a system of representation. The relation between the chasm shapes and the carvings on the walls ought to indicate how any account of Pym's voyage must inevitably expose the originating metaphorics of such a journey.

What is in fact inscribed at the heart of the island is the doubleness of writing which we have seen enacted as the major theme of the work. The chasms present themselves as signs of the darkness and ambiguity in which man finds himself imprisoned. Carved as they are in the black marl, the "alphabetical characters" identified by Peters seem to repeat this message. Yet, if we grant the validity of the translation of these

figures offered in the Note, then we recognize that what is signified—
"To be white" in "The region of the south"—denies both the black
signifiers and the field of their inscription. Throughout the narrative, the
apparent opposition of white and black is gradually transformed into a
reciprocal relationship. Neither doubles of each other nor polar opposites, white and black constitute one of several binary images employed
by the narrative to express metaphysical difference.

In the foregoing interpretation we have argued that writing itself is
the central subject of *Pym*, and we have attempted to rethink the "educational" aim of the work in terms of its reflection on the function of
language. Assuming a paradoxical materiality in the shapes of the
chasms and the traces in the marl, this writing serves to constitute an
illusion of psychic depth by means of a complex interplay of metaphors.
Thus Mr. Poe makes visible through inscription what could never be
discovered by any empirical journey of exploration. The implicit poetics
of such a theory of writing seems to pose no problem for Georges
Poulet: "To create a beauty that cannot exist in time, the poet is obliged
to recompose the elements of that time and to invent with the help of
their multiple combinations a new, imaginary duration, analogous to the
divine eternity. This imaginary duration is that of dream."[27] Yet, the
"duration" of the "dream" in *Pym* has been expressed in terms of fundamental differences contributing to the temporalizing function of psychic
inscription. The "wholeness" of consciousness presented in the poetic
"dream" is an illusion disguising the interplay of past and future traces.
Poe may have longed for a writing that would imitate the lost presence
of cosmic unity, but this work relies on writing itself to stage the differential "throb" of the cosmic or psychic process. The "energy" of thought
is constituted by the endless struggle of language both to transcend its
spatio-temporal bounds and yet defer its ends. *The Narrative of A.
Gordon Pym* prefigures Harry Levin's interpretation of the cosmic order
in *Eureka*: "the perfection of indeterminacy."[28]

Thus the final image in Pym's journey toward a metaphysical and
psychological center betrays the duplicity of the sign we have witnessed
throughout the voyage: "And now we rushed into the embraces of the
cataract, where a chasm threw itself open to receive us. But there arose
in our pathway a shrouded human figure, very larger in its proportions
than any dweller among men. And the hue of the skin of the figure was
of the perfect whiteness of snow" (p. 852). The offered "embrace" of the
opening "chasm" is checked by the exaggerated "human figure" that
appears to block the path. This is the complex that has already been
inscribed in the text, particularly in the relation of the chasm shapes to
the carvings in the marl. Pym's vision of the end bears the traces of those

prior representations, which had already offered in the pictograph of figure 4, "a human figure standing erect, with outstretched arm" (p. 843). Death and deferral, revelation and repression all serve to compose the shifting "center" of this psychic voyage. We can find no fault with Marie Bonaparte's reading in this instance; her Freudianism seems especially appropriate to describe the originary difference of this creative principle:

For now we behold the form to which all Pym's wanderings and adventures led; the great maternal divinity whose sex, though unmentioned, must be that of the "shrouded" figure, the "woman in white," who appeared to the raving Poe in Moyamensing Prison; it is the mother reclaiming her son. . . . On the one hand, she is white as the South Pole and warm with milk and with life, so recalling that blessed time when he was suckled at his mother's breast but, on the other, now related not to milk but to snow, representing *coldness* and death and so recalling unconscious memories of his pale, dead mother. Given the indifference to time characteristic of the unconscious, we see condensed in this figure the two main attributes Poe successively attached to his mother: *milk* and *death*.[29]

An interpretation already written in *Eureka*: "Their [atoms of fragmentation] source lies in the principle, *Unity. This* is their lost parent. *This* they seek always—immediately—in all directions—wherever it is even partially to be found; thus appeasing, in some measure, the ineradicable tendency, while on the way to its absolute satisfaction in the end."[30] Found only "partially," such "unity" is in fact displaced by a contrived facsimile or clumsy duplicate. To borrow from Bonaparte's lexicon, we might suggest that the center remains the mother without the father, a lack which is disclosed in the son's attempts to supplement it.

The end has already been deferred by those inscriptions which have prepared for this ultimate representation, this final forgery. All of which is displaced again by a postscript, an appended note subverting its customary function as a final word. The "Note" is offered as yet another "reading," a supplementation of those inscriptions in the text that have constituted the play of the psychic structure. This editorial interpretation relies on the "roots" of various languages—Ethiopian, Arabic, Egyptian, and hints of Biblical Aramaic and Greek—to translate the universal writing of the psychic journey. The text itself has become a machine for the production of surplus signifiers. The figures in the marl and the chasms themselves may serve as signifiers for the final vision, but that image itself remains unread in the "Note." Concentrating on the problem of translating the inscriptions, the anonymous editor emphasizes the impossibility of escaping the hermeneutical circle in which any "truth" must be figured. Thus the signifiers graven in the hills are dis-

John Carlos Rowe

placed by those of the "Note," both sets of which emphasize the generative qualities of a text whose signified remains "shady." In this process of inscription and re-inscription a kind of psychic palimpsest has been constructed, the illusory "depth" of which involves an inevitable encounter with the "surface" of writing itself.

In his reading of Freud's "Note Upon the Mystic Writing-Pad" and Freud's general use of a graphic figure to describe the functioning of the psychic apparatus, Jacques Derrida argues that the relation between psychic strata cannot be viewed as a simple "translation" or "transcription" duplicating in consciousness "an unconscious writing." Freud himself had demonstrated that the text of the dream is a system of signifiers lacking "a permanent code" that would allow "a substitution or transformation of signifiers while retaining the same signified."[31] The dream content according to Freud is "expressed in a pictographic script (*Bilderschrift*)," which for Derrida is "not an inscribed image but a figurative script, an image inviting not a simple, conscious, present perception of the thing itself—assuming it exists—but a reading." The content of the dream assumes "meaning" in the traces it carries and the series of events (always textual) it activates. Derrida's analysis has the effect of deconstructing the Freudian hierarchy extending from the conscious to the unconscious, and substituting instead a fundamental *differance* of which every written sign bears the mark:

Let us note that the *depth* of the Mystic Pad is at once a depth without bottom, an endless reverberation, and a perfectly superficial exteriority: a stratification of surfaces each of whose relation to self, whose inside, is but the implication of another similarly exposed surface. It joins the two empirical certainties by which we are constituted: infinite depth in the implication of meaning, in the unified envelopment of the present, and, simultaneously, the pellicular essence of being, the absolute absence of a grounding.[32]

In *The Narrative of A. Gordon Pym*, such distinctions as inner and outer, lower and higher, unconscious and conscious merely metaphorize two functions in the ordinary movement of signification. In this narrative and in *Eureka*, the desire for "Unity" operates as part of a generative system for dissemination and the production of differences. Doubtless Poe would hesitate at such an unexpected swerve in his metaphysical project and blindly reassert the transcendent ground of a "divine volition." But the writing in *Pym* and *Eureka* continues to betray any such monism. As Hoffman argues with some emotion: "A double motion, where what Poe sought, what he ached to discover and return to, was a *single* motion. . . . But the nature of existence betrayed that desire. At the deepest level of his being Poe felt, Poe *knew*, that there can be no such unitary stasis."[33]

In *The Narrative of A. Gordon Pym*, Poe lingers on the verge of establishing writing itself as the constitution and facilitation of psychic experience: "a writing advanced as conscious and acting in the world (the visible exterior of the graphic, of the literal, of the literal becoming literary, etc.) in terms of that exertion of writing which circulates like psychical energy between the unconscious and the conscious."[34] Derrida demonstrates how Freud moves through neurological and optical metaphors for the functioning of the psychic apparatus only to establish tentatively the graphic metaphor of the "Mystic Writing-Pad" as an *inadequate* representation. Poe transforms the scriptural metaphor into a poetic "actuality" that facilitates the divided perception at the end of Pym's Antarctic voyage. Language may still appear to be a limitation for Poe that "veils" a signified behind and within the ambiguous drift of signifiers leading to the end of the journey. But it is not a "veiled" but a "shrouded" figure baring the winding sheet of finitude that is at once disclosed and repressed in the supplementary movement of psychic signification. Thus deferral and supplementarity describe the *difference* of a writing activity carried out by a diverse cast of interpreters in *Pym*: Poe, Pym, Mr. Poe, the "editor" of the Note as well as such lesser factorers of script as Augustus, Dirk Peters, even Tiger.

The writing itself has performed an unsettling of thought and intention we might never have expected from the ostensible author of *Eureka: An Essay on the Material and Spiritual Universe*. Poe's gnostic and idealist attitudes appear to have been questioned by the very theory of writing that ought to have confirmed their values for the artist. It should no longer be necessary to account for the "accidental" death of Pym or the reluctance of Mr. Poe to offer a final explanation. They have been written *into* the text and have thus "discovered" themselves in their facilitation of the movement of signification. They have situated themselves in both the time and space of writing by effacing the metaphysical presence that would obliterate their text. Further readings and writings are always already inscribed in this narrative, which provides its own appendix as the sign of the necessary *Nachträglichkeit* of voyaging: a literal, a literary footnote:

NOTES

1. Edward Davidson, *Poe: A Critical Study* (Cambridge, Mass.: Harvard Univ. Press, 1957), pp. 160–61.
2. Joseph Ridgely, "Tragical-Mythical-Satirical-Hoaxical: Problems of Genre in *Pym*," *American Transcendental Quarterly*, 24 (Fall 1974): 4–9.
3. Jean Ricardou, "The Singular Character of Water," trans. Frank Towne, *Poe Studies*, 9 (June 1974): 4.

4. Maurice Mourier, "Le tombeau d'Edgar Poe," *Esprit*, 12 (December 1974): 924.

5. Jacques Lacan, "Seminar on 'The Purloined Letter,'" trans. Jeffrey Mehlman, *Yale French Studies*, 48 (1972): 39–72; Jacques Derrida, "The Purveyor of Truth," trans. Willis Domingo, James Hulbert, Moshe Ron, and Marie-Rose Logan, *Yale French Studies*, 52 (1975): 31–113.

6. Derrida, "The Purveyor of Truth," pp. 45, 84.

7. Gayatri Spivak, "Translator's Preface," in Derrida, *Of Grammatology* (Baltimore: The Johns Hopkins Univ. Press, 1976), p. lxxvii.

8. Joseph Riddel, *The Inverted Bell: Modernism and the Counterpoetics of William Carlos Williams* (Baton Rouge: Louisiana State Univ. Press, 1975), pp. 264–65.

9. Daniel Hoffman, *Poe Poe Poe Poe Poe Poe Poe* (Garden City, N.Y.: Doubleday and Co., Inc., 1972), p. 275.

10. Poe, *The Narrative of Arthur Gordon Pym of Nantucket*, in *The Complete Poems and Stories of Edgar Allan Poe*, ed. Arthur Hobson Quinn and Edward H. O'Neill, 2 vols. (New York: Alfred A. Knopf, 1964), 2: 843. Further references included in the text.

11. Evelyn Hinz also considers *Pym* to be centrally concerned with the problem of narration rather than with Pym's questionable "adventures." See "'Tekeli-li': *The Narrative of Arthur Gordon Pym* as Satire," *Genre*, 3 (1970): 382.

12. Poe, *Eureka: A Prose Poem*, ed. Richard P. Benton (1848; rpt. Hartford, Conn.: Transcendental Books, 1973), p. 139.

13. Ibid.

14. Ibid., p. 54.

15. Poe, "The Poetic Principle," in *Complete Poems and Stories*, 2: 1039, 1027.

16. Derrida, "The Purveyor of Truth," p. 101.

17. Hinz, "'Tekeli-li': *The Narrative of Arthur Gordon Pym* as Satire," p. 393.

18. See Derrida, "Difference," in *Speech and Phenomena and Other Essays on Husserl's Theory of Signs*, trans. David B. Allison (Evanston, Ill.: Northwestern Univ. Press, 1973), pp. 142–43: "Differance is what makes the movement of signification possible only if each element that is said to be 'present,' appearing on the stage of presence, is related to something other than itself but retains the mark of a past element and already lets itself be hollowed out by the mark of its relation to a future element. . . . And it is this constitution of the present as 'primordial' and irreducibly nonsimple, and, therefore, in the strict sense nonprimordial, synthesis of traces, retentions, and protentions . . . that I propose to call protowriting, prototrace, or differance."

19. Hoffman, *Poe Poe Poe Poe Poe Poe Poe*, p. 271.

20. Davidson, *Poe: A Critical Study*, p. 170.

21. The word, of course, echoes Daniel's interpretation of the writing on the wall warning Belshazzar and his kingdom of God's judgment: "Mene, Mene, Tekel Upharsin" (*Daniel* 5:25). See Hinz, "'Tekeli-li': *The Narrative of Arthur Gordon Pym* as Satire," p. 381.

22. See Jonathan Culler's discussion of the icon in *Structuralist Poetics: Structuralism, Linguistics, and the Study of Literature* (Ithaca: Cornell Univ. Press, 1975), p. 16.

23. Marie Bonaparte, *The Life and Works of Edgar Allan Poe: A Psycho-Analytic Interpretation*, trans. John Rodker (London: Hogarth Press, 1949), p. 332. Walter Bezanson, "The Troubled Sleep of Arthur Gordon Pym," in *Essays in Literary History Presented to J. Milton French*, ed. Rudolf Kirk and C. F. Main (New York: Russell and Russell, 1965), p. 169: "Even fresh water runs purple, and the use of the word 'veins' to describe its peculiar structure suggests a fantasy on negro blood. . . ."

24. Ricardou, "The Singular Character of Water," p. 4.

25. Mourier, "Le tombeau d'Edgar Poe," p. 905.

26. Patrick Quinn, *"Arthur Gordon Pym:* 'A Journey to the End of the Page?'" *Poe Newsletter*, 1 (April, 1968): 13–14.

27. Georges Poulet, *Studies in Human Time*, trans. Elliott Coleman (Baltimore: The Johns Hopkins Univ. Press, 1956), p. 330.

28. Harry Levin, *The Power of Blackness: Hawthorne, Poe, Melville* (New York: Vintage Books, 1958), p. 129.

29. Bonaparte, *The Life and Works of Edgar Allan Poe: A Psycho-Analytic Interpretation*, pp. 350–51.

30. *Eureka*, p. 44.

31. Derrida, "Freud and the Scene of Writing," trans. Jeffrey Mehlman, *Yale French Studies*, 48 (1972): 93, 90.

32. Ibid., p. 109.

33. Hoffman, *Poe Poe Poe Poe Poe Poe Poe*, p. 294.

34. Derrida, "Freud and the Scene of Writing," p. 93.

SEVEN

THEATRUM ANALYTICUM
Philippe Lacoue-Labarthe

> The pleasure produced by tragic myth has the same heritage
> as the impression of pleasure that dissonance provokes
> in music.
> Nietzsche, *The Birth of Tragedy*

> *Eros:* You ask too much, Thanatos.
> Pavese, *Dialogues with Leuco*

THE FOLLOWING remarks concern a text of Freud published by Max Graf in 1942, "Psychopathic Characters on the Stage." There are at least two principal reasons that make this an interesting text. First of all, among all the posthumous texts this one stands alone as an enigma, not only because Freud did not publish it (nor want it published, or write it for publication), but because he seems to have "forgotten" its very existence, or in any event to have *lost touch* with it.[1] If this occurrence is not unique, it is still sufficiently uncommon to make the text intriguing, to provoke our attention and to demand an investigation that would consider both the history of Freud's thought and the position that this semi-clandestine text was able to assume (and maintain) within it. The second reason, less limited in scope, pertains to the subject-matter of this text, the theater. If this essay is now generally admitted to be one of the most important written by Freud on this subject, it is because it poses directly and in terms probably not found elsewhere a decisive question that has since come to be the focus of an entire critique of Freud: the question of the relation of psychoanalysis to theatricality or, more generally, to *representation*.

At a certain point, it seems likely that these two apparently unrelated reasons are in fact one and the same, and this is what we shall endeavor to indicate here, albeit in summary fashion.

To do so we must begin by referring to the situation (or the "scene") in France, and in particular to the philosophical and political debate concerning Freud that has been going on for several years, above all since the publication of *Anti-Oedipus* and, less superficially, of Girard's work.[2] Here several developments must be considered. First, there was the growing recognition that theatricality functions as a *model* or even a *matrix* in the constitution of psychoanalysis; established theoretically by Lacan, of course, it was then confirmed by diverse commentators, such as Starobinski and Green.[3] This resulted not merely in justice being meted out to would-be "applied psychoanalysis," but also in the rigorous delineation of one of the most pervasive metaphorical networks in Freud, as well as in the construction of the "analytical scene" itself. At the same time, but elsewhere, the consequences of the Heideggerian questioning of representation had begun to make themselves felt and, accentuated and displaced, to *work* effectively.

The reaction—with or without quotation marks—was not long in coming. Yet, however problematic the newly discovered psychoanalytical "sceno-morphics" may have appeared, and despite the strict precautions invoked and practiced by those who reintroduced the "closure of representation" (beginning with the very concept of "closure" itself), a critical tendency emerged which, in its haste, was only too happy to free itself of one of the more cumbersome of those "cultural cadavers," whose time—it was rumored—had come. Such criticism should not necessarily be deemed to be beneficial simply because it shakes up academic habits a bit, or because it opposes to Capital precisely what the latter tends to encourage. At any rate, the great discovery of this critical movement was that Freud had remained a pure and simple prisoner of the Western system and of the mechanics of representation— of Graeco-Italian sceno-graphy, of classical dramaturgy, etc.—and that he had even added to its coercive power by presenting it as a structural necessity of the human subject in general.[4] This was then held to explain both the timorous, relatively sterile and conservative aspect of his esthetics, and more importantly, the repressive character (institutionally, but also theoretically) of psychoanalysis itself. This description is obviously schematic and in need of further "discrimination" (that would include explanations of our grievances with regard to the obscure prem-

Philippe Lacoue-Labarthe

ises of anti-Freudism as well as our reticences concerning all movements that are simply "anti-"). It does give, however, a general idea of what has been happening in France, and probably elsewhere, during the past few years.

A recent page of Jean-François Lyotard bears witness to the situation just described (and will also permit us to continue a discussion initiated under other circumstances). Commenting on the text of Freud with which we propose to deal, Lyotard summarizes the essence of this critical motif:

The privileged status of the theater in Freudian thought and practices, with respect to the other arts, has already been noted. Freud not only acknowledges this, but on at least one occasion makes an apparent effort to justify it. In a short text of 1905–6 entitled "Psychopathic Characters on the Stage," he suggests a genesis of psychoanalysis that would be oriented by the questions of guilt, indebtedness and repayment. Sacrifice, destined to appease a divinity angered by man's revolt, would constitute the matrix. Greek tragedy, itself arising from the sacrifice of the goat—as Freud believes—would engender the socio-political drama, then its individual (psychological) form, of which psychopathology and—we would add—psychoanalysis would in turn be the offshoots. This genealogy not only permits us to discern that the analytical relationship is organized along the lines of a ritual sacrifice; it also suggests the identity of the spaces in which the operation of acquittal takes place. The temple, theater, political chamber and office are all *de-realized* spaces, as Laplanche and Pontalis put it, spaces circumscribed by and exempt from the laws of so-called reality, in which desire can play itself out in all of its ambivalence, a region where the "things themselves" of desire are replaced by tolerated *simulacra* that are assumed not to be fictions, but authentic libidinal productions, simply exempted from realist censorship. . . .[5]

None of this, of course, is false. On the contrary, it should be stressed that this reading is entirely necessary, for it in fact uncovers something in Freud that should not be ignored, even though Ehrenzweig was one of the few commentators to have called attention to it. Nor do we intend, as is often done in such cases, to object on "philological" grounds, by reproaching Lyotard, for instance, for forcing the text to produce a genealogy of psychoanalysis that is not really there (Freud himself does not go beyond comparison),[6] or for "mixing up" the text, without further ado, with the celebrated seventh section of the fourth chapter of *Totem and Taboo* (where Freud places considerable emphasis on questions involving the origin of the theater, issues which in this text are present only in embryonic form. In the later text Freud does in fact speak of the "tragic fault," guilt, payment of debt, etc.). Such reproaches, however, would only be of secondary importance.

Let us say, then, that by and large, Lyotard is right.

But he is right only on one condition—or rather on two, which are merely two sides of the same coin. The first condition involves posing, or imagining, that there is a *reality* "outside representation"; that this reality, far from being what Bataille called and Lacan calls the impossible, is that which can present itself actually and as such; and that consequently there is, in general, the possibility of presentation, of presence, and of plenitude as something whole, virginal, unadulterated, and uncorruptible. A primeval state where we could and would be *ourselves*, subjects (in whatever form that might be), unalienated and integral, prior to all fault and to every prohibition, to wars and rivalry—prior also, it is clear, to all institutions. The condition thus amounts to nothing less than relegating, once and for all, the reality principle to the obsolescent arsenal of the metaphysical police-force. But there is still the other condition: that the *necessity* of the representational scheme [*dispositif*] for psychoanalysis (affirmed by Freud and determining the practice of analysis) be derived solely from *desire* (and from a pleasure without hiatus, full, whole, etc.), or more precisely, from "drive productions" [*"productions pulsionnelles"*] that in turn derive solely from the *libido*. If what analysis deals with are merely drives insofar as they are libidinal; if, in general, there is nothing but libido—and a libido that is invulnerable, never frayed, marred, or riddled (that is, shot through and blackened, or furrowed and doomed to die), then it is certain that the function of de-realization in what Luce Iragaray has described as the "possible practices of analysis" [*le practicable analytique*] can, and indeed must be called into question. The whole problem consists in knowing whether analysis is concerned only with the libidinal, or whether there is an aspect of the drives (not, however, one that simply *manifests itself*) that is irreducible to the libido, above all in the sense of a univocally "positive" striving.

If we raise this question, it is obviously not out of respect for "Freudian orthodoxy." Orthodoxy as such is of little interest to us and we are only too well aware of the role played by orthopedics—that is, of a rectification that is ontological, virile, committed to domination, and properly political—in all forms of orthodoxy, as in all submission to a discourse that is tutorial and paternalistic. It is also clear that we have not broached this question in order to "save" Freud from a *univocal* reading (he needs no help in this regard), since no one can be interested in reintroducing ambiguity for its own sake. Our concern is to extricate Freud, or rather "his" text, from a critique committed precisely to the opposing values "univocal" versus "equivocal." The question thus becomes one of the usage of texts and of criticism, which is also a "political" question. With Freud, however, things are always much more

Philippe Lacoue-Labarthe

complicated. Regardless of his own desire and of the unquestionable (but *reversible* . . .) critical power of analysis, there is ultimately nothing in Freud that permits a *decision*, i.e. the determination of a decisive meaning (be it primary, final, hidden, etc.), that in turn would be sufficiently certain to enable us either to appropriate or to exclude it. Or, for that matter, to allow for appropriation or exclusion in general. Our intention, therefore, is not to preserve a benevolent "neutrality," but rather to call a certain kind of doctrinal *identification* into question, in the name of a notion that is less simple, less self-assured, less triumphant—and hence, less apt to be "confiscated" by any type of critique. And, given the importance of what is at stake here, a little subtlety is perhaps not too much to ask.

The charge that Lyotard addresses to Freud is, in fact, two-fold. On the one hand, it is directed at the representational scheme as being one of derealization, i.e. as the closure (the *temple*) of the tragic site—the stage, insofar as it is a substitute for the place of the actual ritual sacrifice, commemorating the murder of the *Urvater* (that this is the version of *Totem and Taboo* is of little matter here). If one can read between the lines, this accusation already includes that pre-theatrical phenomenon, ritual, or the religious as such, whether or not the latter is understood to imply real violence, sacrifice, exclusion, etc. In this respect, Lyotard's position converges with the critique developed by Girard, for whom Christianity stands alone as the sole explicit acceptance of violence ever manifested, by contrast to the totality of vicarious formations (whether religious, political, aesthetic) intended to channel such violence but which, by masking it and causing it to be forgotten, actually exacerbate it. On the other hand, however, Lyotard's accusation bears on the "psychic" *instrumentality* or *support* of this derealization, which transforms the evocation of sacrifice, murder, and of suffering into something not merely tolerable but even desirable (to the point of producing therapeutic effects). This is to say that Lyotard calls into question the libidinal formalism of Freudian aesthetics—the hypnotic, anesthetizing power of form, as he puts it,[7] including the intricate network of *Lustgewinn, Nebengewinn, Vorlust, Verlockungsprämie*, etc. This formalism is held responsible for Freud's inability to consider or even to perceive what Ehrenzweig has termed the *disruptive* function of art, and in particular of modern art, as opposed to its merely vicarious aspect. The notion of art as disruption, of course, implies that its function must be other than merely "secondary," that it have the power to put us in the presence of the Real itself (of *présence*), that in one way or another it can become an *event*: in short, that it *affects*, one might say, *effectively*.

It is hardly difficult to see that the genuine target of this two-fold accusation is not so much Freud himself as a (if not *the*) entire philosophical tradition, and in particular Aristotle, whose authority Freud invokes explicitly at the beginning of "Psychopathic Characters on the Stage," although implicitly he probably never ceased to appeal to it, be it out of prudence, "academism," or for other less anecdotal reasons that will appear in due course. In thus taking refuge in an appeal to the philosophical, Aristotelian tradition, Freud profers, so to speak, the tool of his own undoing. All that is left unsettled, it would seem, is the question of how this apparently unreserved submission actually functions. But this is precisely where the difficulties begin.

How in fact does "Psychopathic Characters on the Stage" "function"? How does this text present itself? Modestly, as is almost always the case with Freud; namely, as a simple development of Aristotle's poetics of drama, intended merely to render the latter more "precise": "If, as has been assumed since the time of Aristotle, the purpose of the play (*Schauspiel*) is to arouse 'terror and pity,' to bring about a 'purification of affects,' it is possible to describe that goal in rather more detail by saying that it concerns opening up sources of pleasure or enjoyment in our emotional life."[8] But this gesture obviously serves to cover up— and this is *also* always the case—Freud's scarcely concealed desire of producing the *truth* of those poetics, of taking its measure and of revealing its ultima ratio. In other words, "Psychopathic Characters on the Stage" presents itself as nothing more nor less than a psychoanalytic reading—as an interpretation and hence as a *translation* of the *Poetics* (albeit an active and, as we shall see, a transformational one). This reading, it is true, reduplicates the analogous or homologous translation given by "German Romanticism" to a question first posed in Germany during the time of Lessing, concerning the difference between the Ancients and the Moderns (between the Greek and the Occidental, the Oriental and the Hesperian, etc.). This question, that dominated the entire field of historical aesthetics from Hölderlin, Hegel, and the Schlegels to Nietzsche, finally produced a general theory of culture or of civilization.

Hence, in order to evaluate the meaning and import of Freud's gesture with some precision, it may be sufficient to compare it with an operation that is similar, even though its initial purpose may have been entirely different: that of Nietzsche in *The Birth of Tragedy*. That this comparison is not entirely arbitrary should be clear, for whatever Freud's "denials" concerning this relationship may have been, it is now generally recognized that psychoanalysis is closely bound up with certain major intuitions of Nietzsche. Indeed, the question raised by Nietzsche, one concerning not only tragedy but art in general (since tragedy, in entirely classical, even Hegelian fashion, is its paragon), is exactly the same question that Freud, through Aristotle, poses in the very first two paragraphs of "Psychopathic Characters on the Stage." Even the terminology employed (particularly in chapter 22 of *The Birth of Tragedy*) is identical. It can be formulated as follows: How can the spectacle of suffering, annihilation, and death be enjoyable, and indeed more so than any other spectacle? It is true that Nietzsche (who, of course, was not unaware of the Aristotelian origins of the question) rejects any response that does not ultimately refer to "aesthetical principles," including therefore and above all Aristotle himself. In other words, Nietzsche dismisses the *cathartic* interpretation of tragedy, and moreover not without vehemence. But in the name of what? Here is the bill of indictment:

> Never since Aristotle has an explanation of the tragic effect been offered from which aesthetic states of an aesthetic activity of the listener could be inferred. Now the serious events are supposed to prompt pity and fear to discharge [*Entladung*] themselves in a way that relieves us; now we are supposed to feel elevated and inspired by the triumph of good and noble principles, at the sacrifice of the hero in the interest of a moral vision of the universe. I am sure that for countless men precisely this, and only this, is the effect of tragedy, but it plainly follows that all these men, together with their interpreting aestheticians, have had no experience of tragedy as a supreme *art*.
>
> The pathological discharge, the *catharsis* of Aristotle, of which philologists are not sure whether it should be included among medical or moral phenomena, recalls a remarkable notion of Goethe's. "Without a lively pathological interest," he says, "I, too, have never yet succeeded in elaborating a tragic situation of any kind, and hence I have rather avoided than sought it. Can it perhaps have been yet another merit of the ancients that the high-point of pathos was with them merely aesthetic play, while with us the truth of nature must cooperate in order to produce such a work?"
>
> We can now answer this profound final question in the affirmative after our glorious experiences, having found to our astonishment that the deepest pathos can indeed be merely aesthetic play in the case of musical tragedy. Therefore we are justified in believing that now for the first time the primal phenomenon of the tragic can be described with some degree of success. Anyone who still persists in talking only of those vicarious effects proceeding from extra-aesthetic spheres, and who does not feel that he is above the pathological-moral process, should despair of his aesthetic nature.[9]

We have chosen to quote this text at length in order to show just how far removed we seem to be from the discourse of Freud. Ultimately no one would appear more open to such an indictment than Freud himself, even at the risk of attributing a strange gift of prophecy to Nietzsche. In reality, however, things are quite different. Once one takes into account the specifically Nietzschean oppositions (the Dionysian and the Apollinian, music and the plastic arts, the "immediate reproduction" of the original Unity versus its mediate, reduplicated reproduction) the answer becomes perfectly clear: tragedy, however it is approached, including its "properly" musical or Dionysiac aspect, never *presents* as such the suffering that it (re)presents (*darstellt*); on the contrary, it presupposes an already circumscribed space, of derealization if one insists, and by virtue of which the "high-point of pathos" is always an *aesthetic play*. Even music, it should be stressed, including its worst varieties (that of *Tristan*, for example)—even *dissonance* still (or already) produces enjoyment. And it is clear why: at some point, ontologically, but also aesthetically, if the world is to be understood as an "aesthetic phenomenon," or if art, in the narrow sense is to be understood as the "imitation" of the production of things that are—at some point, then, *suffering itself is enjoyment*, even if it is only as the *discharge (Entladung)*, i.e., as the *catharsis* of the contradiction that constitutes it.

If one makes allowances for the ontological "speculation," all this is not very different from the type of response that Freud puts forth, prudently, in "Psychopathic Characters on the Stage." His apparent submission to the Aristotelian model should not be misconstrued. Certainly, at no time does Freud go beyond the limits attributed by Nietzsche to the "pathological-moral" interpretation of tragedy. On the face of things, at least. And it seems no less certain that he is satisfied simply to translate Aristotle. The first lines are in fact an almost literal translation of the *Poetics*: for if Freud, at the outset, seems to commit or to repeat the well-known misinterpretation of the catharsis of emotions in general,[10] it becomes clear in the course of the text, when the discussion focuses on the drama, i.e. on tragedy, that he understands catharsis in the limited sense of a "purgation" of suffering alone (that is, of terror and compassion). And there is no doubt that it could be demonstrated, based on the texts concerned, that "libidinal derealization," in the sense of an economical law (of economizing), both governs aesthetic enjoyment and also transcribes faithfully the χαρὰν ἀβλαβῆ, "the joy without harm or loss" that Aristotle, in the Politics (VIII, 1342 a), attributes to catharsis, precisely in its medical, homeophatic, "pharmaceutical" function (catharsis utilized φαρμακείας χάριν).[11] The fact nevertheless remains that on one fundamental point, this "faithful" translation in reality upsets Aristotelian theory. This takes place when, intentionally or not, Freud moves from medicine back to what was probably the origin of catharsis, to religion, and raises the question of mimesis (i.e. "mimicry," or, in his language, *identification*) as that which renders the "cathartic machine" itself possible. It is true that Freud, in conformity with Aristotle, will continue to maintain the analogy of art with the play of the child until, but not including *Beyond the Pleasure Principle*,[12] and that like Nietzsche in the final chapters of *The Birth of Tragedy*, he transfers the Aristotelian *recognition* (ἀναγνώρισις) onto the relation between scene and audience, thus involving the spectator.[13] Yet despite all this, Freud still introduces an element that is foreign to the Aristotelian "program," but that explains the link between catharsis and mimesis, something that had remained unthought throughout the entire tradition (with the exception of Nietzsche).[14] This is simply the notion that tragic pleasure is *masochistic* in essence and hence—although this is not made explicit in 1906, for reasons that will appear shortly—that it is closely bound up with *narcissism* itself:

Being present as an interested spectator at a spectacle or play [written here *"Schau-spiel"*: *"Schau,"* "spectacle," and *"Spiel,"* "play" or "game"] does for adults what play does for children, whose hesitant hopes of being able to do what grown-up people do are in that way gratified. The spectator is a person who experiences too little, who feels that he is a "poor wretch to whom nothing of importance can happen," who has long been obliged to damp down, or rather displace, his ambition to stand in his own person at the hub of world affairs; he longs to feel and to act and to arrange things according to his desires—in short, to be a hero. And the playwright and actor enable him *to identify himself* with a hero. They spare him something, too. For the spectator knows quite well that actual heroic conduct such as this would be impossible for him without pains and sufferings and acute fears, which would almost cancel out the enjoyment. He knows, moreover, that he has only *one* life, and that he might perhaps perish even in a *single* such struggle against adversity. Accordingly, his enjoyment is based on an illusion; that is to say, his suffering is mitigated by the certainty that, firstly, it is someone other than himself who is acting and suffering on the stage, and, secondly, that after all it is only a game, which can threaten no damage to his personal security. . . .

   Several other forms of creative writing [*Dichtung*], however, are equally subject to these same preconditions for enjoyment . . . But drama [*Drama*] seeks to explore emotional possibilities more deeply and to give an enjoyable shape even to forebodings of misfortune; for this reason it depicts the hero in his struggles, or rather (with masochistic satisfaction) in defeat. This relation to suffering and misfortune might be taken as characteristic of drama, whether, as happens in serious plays, it is only *concern* that is aroused, and afterwards allayed, or whether, as happens in tragedies, the suffering is actually realized.[15]

The reference to masochism in no way undermines the *economic* character of tragic pleasure (as is proven later in the essay by the exclusion of physical illness from the space of the scene; this is a result of the law according to which suffering must be compensated, a law that governs theatrical identification and hence provides the norm for the dramatic form itself).[16] But the economic system here put in place is not a simple one. Already a paradox begins to emerge that will be of great consequence once the question of masochism (and of narcissism) has begun to transform, metapsychologically, the theory of drives. This is the question of the role played by the "supplementary gain," the *Nebengewinn*, in the "economy" of "enjoyment." Freud explains that the "purification of affects [of emotions]" signifies the total release, in our emotional life, of the "sources of pleasure [*Lust*] and of enjoyment [*Genuss*];" and he adds immediately (it is the era of the book on Jokes) "just as in the comical, the *Witz*, etc., the same effects are produced by the workings of our intelligence, which (otherwise) has rendered many of these sources inaccessible."[17] The dissymetrical character of the comparison (in which the "workings of the intelligence" appear as an agent of repression) should not surprise us: the appeal to the *Witz* ushers in what the final paragraph of "Psychopathic Characters on the Stage" will identify as the "preliminary pleasure" (*Vorlust*) discussed in the *Three Essays* and the *Witz*,[18] This "supplementary gain" in the position of an "incitement bonus" (*Verlockungsprämie*[19]), far from implying, as Lyotard suggests, some kind of "anesthetizing power of form," supposes on the contrary a specific pleasure involving an "elevated tension" (*Höherspannung*) or, if one prefers, an "intensification" (involving the augmentation of pain) for its own sake:

In this connection the prime factor is unquestionably the process of getting rid of one's own emotions by "blowing off steam" [*das Austoben*]; and the subsequent enjoyment corresponds on the one hand to the relief produced by a thorough discharge [*Abfeuern*] and on the other, no doubt to an accompanying sexual excitation; for the latter, as we may suppose, appears as a supplementary gain [*Nebengewinn*] whenever an affect is aroused, and gives people the sense, which they so much desire, of an intensification [*Höherspannung*] of their psychical state.[20]

Theatrical enjoyment, in other words, is totally masochistic. Suffering causes pleasure only when *formally* prepared by this supplement of pleasure which itself, however, implies pain. As in Nietzsche, or in Goethe, the "high-point of pathos" is consequently nothing more than "aesthetic play" (would this be a possible definition of masochism?). And as in Nietzsche, this is moreover just what explains the superiority of Greek tragedy to the drama of the Moderns:

Suffering of every kind is thus the subject-matter of drama, and from this suffering it promises to give the audience pleasure. Thus we arrive at a first precondition of this form of art: that it should not cause suffering to the audience, that it should know how to compensate, by means of the possible satisfactions involved, for the sympathetic suffering which is aroused. (Modern writers have particularly often failed to obey this rule.)[21]

This is why the second psychoanalytical "translation" proposed by Freud here should be that of the relation between Greek and modern (Shakespearean) dramaturgy, in conformity to the constant association opposing *Hamlet to Oedipus* which this text, all appearances notwithstanding, does not deny.[22] Genealogically, the modern "break" occurs when the unconscious—that is, the difference between the repressed and the non-repressed—is introduced into the tragic conflict. Up to and including the psychological drama—which, according to Freud's typology, comprises not simply the theater of "characters" or social theater, but also the "tragedy of love" and the opera—the theater is still situated within the horizon of the Greek system of representation. But once what is described in *The Interpretation of Dreams* as the "secular advance of repression"[23] has taken place; once, that is, the general space of neurosis has been established, the modern epoch of drama has begun:

> But the series of possibilities grows wider; and psychological drama turns into psychopathological drama when the source of the suffering in which we take part and from which we are meant to derive pleasure is no longer a conflict between two almost equally conscious impulses [which was the case for Oedipus], but between a conscious impulse and a repressed one. Here the precondition of enjoyment is that the spectator should himself be a neurotic, for it is only such people who can derive pleasure instead of simple aversion from the revelation and the more or less conscious recognition of a repressed impulse. In anyone who is *not* neurotic this recognition will meet only with aversion and will call up a readiness to repeat the act of repression which has earlier been successfully brought to bear on the impulse: for in such people a single expenditure of repression has been enough to hold the repressed impulse completely in check. But in neurotics the repression is on the brink of failing; it is unstable and needs a constant renewal of expenditure, and this expenditure is spared if recognition of the impulse is brought about.[24]

This explains why, in order to maintain the thesis of catharsis apparently intact, it was necessary to modify the Aristotelian scheme of "recognition" by introducing identification. For only the principle of identification authorizes the recognition of the repressed. In no way, however, does this prevent modern catharsis from being as "economical" as that of the Greeks (if one makes allowances for certain rules, more subtle and sophisticated than in the past, such as that of *averted attention*, formulated by Freud in regard to *Hamlet*, and that aims at the weakening of resistances inherent to neurosis).[25] Otherwise, as was the case before, the establishment of the system implies an exclusion—in this case not only that of suffering and physical illness but of mental illness, of a successfully constituted neurosis, which is "alien" (and hence that resists recognition); an exclusion, one could doubtless say, of *alienation* or of *madness.*

The entire operation is thus devoid of mystery, if not of difficulties. The "economically oriented" aesthetics is already present, in a condensed form, even though as late as *Beyond the Pleasure Principle* Freud will (still) feel compelled to formulate it as a project.[26] But when he mentions it again, it will only be to deny its importance with regard to the far more serious and difficult question concerning what is prior to the "pleasure principle," or beyond it, or in any event "independent" of it "and, perhaps, more primitive than it." All this is well known, as is the fact that this question is introduced in the space opened by the break with the Aristotelian analogy, maintained until then, between the play (of the child) and the play on the stage [the *Schau-spiel*]. The allusion to Aristotle is even made perfectly explicit: "Whatever the case may be," writes Freud [*that is, whatever the insurmountable difficulties presented by the* indecidable *character of play may be*], "it emerges from this discussion that to explain play by means of an imitative instinct is to formulate a useless hypothesis."[27] But this is not all. For it is clear that if play is thus to be separated from "artistic play and artistic imitation," it is essentially for two reasons: First, because play does not imply the mechanism of representation or, to be more exact (since there is always the crib of the *Fort/Da* player as counter-example), the mechanism of the spectacle. If there is mimicry involved, it is one that is effective, direct, and *active*, comparable to that of the actor (and not of the spectator). The process of identification thus implied is more immediate, but also more compromising than the actor's, since the difference that constitutes the scene has vanished (or exists only in an embryonic state). Hence, the derealizing closure of the theatrical site has not yet been really established (or at least only in part, if we accept the necessity of a *primitive* interiorization of the representational cleavage). The second reason for the separation is that play—which is ultimately and necessarily part of a *libidinal economy* (but is an economy conceivable that would not be libidinal or "erotic"?)—by virtue both of its very nature, reproducing and repeating the "disagreeable," and of its function (i.e., abreacting and striving for mastery), presupposes an indirect way to pleasure, by contrast with the participation of the spectacle. Thus, in implying a renunciation (albeit a provisional one) of pleasure, or a reiteration (be it ephemeral and simulated) of suffering, play involves a break (however brief, furtive, or tentative) with the economic system. At one moment or another (and at a point impossible to localize), there is thus an element of *loss* in play. And hence a risk. One must get lost in play (and take risks) to win (back oneself). There, in an inverted form, is the entire difficulty of the *generalized economy* in the sense of Bataille. The economy of play is not just another simple economy, like the theatrical-spectacular economy, at least in its Aristotelian version. It is an economy of difference and deferral [*une économie différée*]. What it lacks, in short, is precisely the anesthetizing form (if something of the sort indeed exists), even if play is the birth of form. And we can hardly ignore what is revealed and also concealed by this differance—in the Derridean sense—deferring gain, pleasure, security, and even sur-vival; namely, (the) death (drive) "itself."

And yet, by virtue of a kind of chiasmus, marking both the disorientation of psychoanalysis and the manifestation of an inextricable question, all this is not very far from emerging, apropos not of play but of dramatic mimesis, when Freud, in "Psychopathic Characters on the Stage" introduces the notion of masochism in order to account for tragic pleasure. If this use of the notion is especially problematic at the time, it is because it is situated at the very frontier between stage and auditorium, actor and spectator, and because "masochistic satisfaction" is opposed from the very beginning to "direct enjoyment" (a contradiction that explains the necessary scenic, and hence epic "elevation" of the victim). In this connection Freud writes, "Heroes are first and foremost rebels against God or against something divine: and pleasure must be derived from the feeling of anguish experienced by the weaker being confronted by divine might. This pleasure is due to masochistic satisfaction, but also to direct enjoyment of an individual whose greatness is nevertheless accentuated."[28] But this is also what Freud betrays by submitting to the constraint of a system, and by the double exclusion of illness and madness. In each case it is the ambivalence of *identification* that is at stake; and once the dualism of the drives has been established, it is identification that will provide the center around which both the description of the Oedipus complex and the construction of that "scientific myth"—here still in a stage of germination—of the "primal horde" will be reorganized (albeit not without difficulty).[29]

It is obvious that it is impossible, in a sketch of this kind, to follow, in all of its complexity, the textual network in which the Freudian notion of death is precariously elaborated, and in which, as Freud always indicated in his numerous historical recapitulations of the *Trieblehre*, the questions of masochism, narcissism, identification etc. intersect. However, in terms of our immediate interest here, that is, the question of theatricality itself, we can at least point out something that never becomes explicit in the text of 1906 (which, however, it therefore renders aporetic),[30] but which will be directly stated in a text of 1916: namely, that the split of representation does not take place *within* the libido but rather *between* the libido (desire) and death, and that it is therefore, to use another terminology, the limit of the economic scheme in general: "Our own death is indeed unrepresentable [*unvorstellbar*], and whenever we make the attempt to represent it we can perceive that we really do so only as spectators. Hence, the psychoanalytic school could venture on the assertion that at bottom no one believes in his own death, or to put the same thing in another way, in the unconscious every one of us is convinced of his own immortality."[31]

Like the female, or maternal genitals, death cannot present itself as such, or as Lyotard would say, "in person." Just as the female abyss has an apotropaic structure (as obscenity),[32] death is submitted to the ineluctable necessity of re-presentation (in the sense of a *mise-en-scène*, of a *Darstellung*), and hence of identification and of mimicry as well:

in the world of fiction, in literature or in theater we seek a substitute [*Ersatz*] for loss of life. There we still find people who know how to die . . . there alone we can enjoy the condition which makes it possible for us to reconcile ourselves with death, namely, that behind all the vicissitudes of life there remains for us another life intact. . . . In the realm of fiction we discover that plurality of lives for which wc crave. We die by identifying with a given hero, yet we survive him, and are ready to die again with the next hero just as safely.[33]

If it is permissible to play on a "popular" etymology, we might say that death is *ob-scene*. At the very least, Freud is convinced that death "cannot be looked in the face" and that art (like religion) has the privilege of being the beginning of economic representation—that is, of libidinal representation. Death never appears as such, it is in the strict sense unrepresentable, or the unrepresentable itself, if this expression has any meaning: *the death drive works in silence; all the noise of life emanates from Eros.* "It" (the Id) works, "it" unsettles all manifestation, but it never manifests "itself" and if it ever does become "manifest," it has long since been "eroticized"—as in art, including modern art, and no matter what havoc has been wrought with the form or the work it has dared to assume. All we ever apprehend of death is its *ebb*.[34] This is the origin of the "economic problem of masochism." This is why representation and its machinery [*dispositif*] does not comprise an enclave within the libidinal but rather the libidinal itself. Or the *economy of death* (in the double sense of the genitive, of course). And to introduce the opposition of primary and secondary process here, as do Ehrenzweig and Lyotard, does not change matters. On the contrary. It is precisely the unconscious that does not know death (negation), or, if one prefers, that does not want to hear about it (denial, *Verneinung*).

All this defines Freud's thought as being essentially "tragic." Certainly, this is nothing new; unless, perhaps, one begins to investigate the precise relation of the tragic, in the modern sense (including that of Nietzsche), to philosophy, from which—by contrast with ancient tragedy—it proceeds or, if you like, succeeds. What in fact tragic thought reveals is that the *necessity of representation* exceeds the limits of mere art or religion, and that "thought" itself is condemned to representation. And this in turn explains why, for Freud as for Nietzsche (albeit for diverse reasons) both philosophy and science are themselves to be comprehended as "works of art," or even as myths or rational fictions. "Thought" is condemned to representation because death, in the final analysis, is precisely what "the life of the Spirit" is terrified of, for it compels the Spirit, whether it wants to or not, to avow its incapacity to "maintain itself." The unconscious, as Hyppolite and Lacan have shown with the famous example of the *Verneinung*,[35] obeys a logic comparable to that of Hegel: it "supercedes" [*aufhebt*] death, it denies it and is only willing to speak or to "know" anything about it on the condition of imagining itself to be exempt from it, i.e. of refusing to "believe in it." Inversely (and even if this reversibility is not absolute), the logic at work in philosophy ignores death in its own fashion, and all the more so when it claims to have internalized it. But death is precisely what cannot be internalized and it is this, perhaps, that constitutes the Tragic (including what Bataille called *dramatization*): the "consciousness" or rather—which is the same—the *avowal* that all one can do with death is to theatricalize it. In any event, what is certain is that to protest in the name of the alleged mission of art to look death in the face[36] has never amounted to anything more than making Freud into a pre-Hegelian rather than a Hegelian, which is hardly a step forwards. And what is worse is that this attitude tends to miss entirely the place in Freud where the function of theatricality as matrix comes to impose itself in a decisive manner: namely, beyond the constitution of the *"analytical scene* (and hence a fortiori beyond the beginnings of the "cathartic method"), in the metapsychology itself: in the irreducible dualism of the drives.

The fact remains that the fundamental theatricality of analysis is confusingly similar to that of philosophy itself. Which, in turn, is an almost certain indication of the fact that analysis *also* is a part of philosophy, depending upon it and subordinate to it. Its "tragic thought" in no way transgresses the closure of philosophy. And up to a point, it is true, it cannot be denied that analysis as a whole is constructed along the lines of philosophical representation, which is to say, within the space delimited by the (political) scenography of Plato. This holds even if it is equally true that analysis *subsequently* makes possible the recognition and deconstruction of this system by distinctly revealing the hopes of royalty and of mastery, the "basilic" desire at work in the philosophical *deflection* of tragedy. But all this is perhaps not what is essential. For even without taking into account the minute and "systematic" disruption to which Freud practically, empirically submitted the machinery of representation,[37] his texts reveal consistently the troubled concern that, in spite of everything (and with Freud, this "everything" is impressive), haunts the philosophical (and medical) desire for mastery. Here, we will cite only one example, because it closely involves one of the major motifs of "Psychopáthic Characters on the Stage." We have seen that modern dramaturgy supposes the cultural or social establishment of neurosis. A quarter-century later (i.e. really very late), while he is once again reworking the same hypothesis, Freud will ask himself to what extent, exactly, and above all how one can speak of a society's or a civilization's being neurotic. It is an apparently harmless question, but one that in fact brutally undermines the power of medicine itself (in the Nietzschean, philosophical sense of a "medicine of civilization"), both in the diagnosis and in the therapy. This occurs in *Civilization and its Discontents,* and it does not require an excess of imagination to recall what such a text might have represented in 1930:

. . . there is one question which I can hardly evade. If the development of civilization has such a far-reaching similarity to the development of the individual and if it employs the same methods, may we not be justified in reaching the diagnosis that, under the influence of cultural urges, some civilizations, or some epochs of civilization—possibly the whole of mankind—have become "neurotic"? And analytic dissection of such neuroses might lead to therapeutic recommendations which could lay claim to great practical interest. . . . But we should have to be very cautious and not forget that, after all, we are only dealing with analogies and that it is dangerous, not only with men but also with concepts, to tear them from the sphere in which they have originated and been evolved. Moreover, the diagnosis of communal neuroses is faced with a special difficulty. In an individual neurosis we take as our starting point the contrast that distinguishes the patient from his environment, which is assumed to be "normal". For a group all of whose members are affected by one and the same disorder no such background could exist; it would have to be found elsewhere. And as regards the therapeutic application of our knowledge, what would be the use of the most correct analysis of social neuroses, since no one possesses authority to impose such a therapy upon the group?[38]

It goes without saying that these few remarks are too brief to want to be "decisive." Such could hardly be their purpose, since the intention that has dictated them was rather to mark the "constitutive" *undecidability* of Freud's treatment of representation. The critical disruption of the medical-philosophical discourse does not exclude the possibility of itself being translated into "conservative" terms, as often happens. But one should not simply abandon its interrogative, subversive power to be picked up and superceded—*aufgehoben*—by whoever happens along. In this (Hegelian) sense, Freud himself never "picked up" anything. His "academism," his economic and libidinal formalism, however questionable they may be, are not without reason, and it is one that is far more audacious than the prudence and circumspection that seem to be the cause. Which is not, however, to say—and here, at least, we are in agreement with Lyotard—that they are not without problems.

This is why, far from *reinforcing* Freudianism, we will finish here with a *question*. In the text from which we began, Lyotard speaks of the "credence accorded by Freud to the Sophoclean and Shakespearean libretti."[39] This is the same criticism that Nietzsche, at the time of *The Birth of Tragedy*, directed at the entire Western tradition of commentary on Greek tragedy and "operatic culture." Lyotard goes no further. There is, however, a symptom involved that should not be neglected. It is no accident that Freud repeatedly avows himself to be devoid of all sensibility for music and to be incapable of being interested in it. In such declarations he is perhaps only being consistent with the Aristotelian (and also Platonic) elimination of *musical* catharsis—that is, as Rohde demonstrated, of Dionysian (and feminine) Carybantianism. On this point, Nietzsche himself "hesitated," as one says. He was highly suspicious, for instance—and not just because of prudery or of "protestant" severity—of all experience that claimed to be free and wild, "barbarian" or Dionysian. Rather, it was because he *also* knew that the Dionysian *itself* was inaccessible, or, which amounts to the same, that music *itself* has always been plastic, figural—Apollinian. And, had he not refused to read him, Freud might have *recognized* something in a text of this genre:

We need not conjecture regarding the immense gap which separated the *Dionysian Greek* from the Dionysian Barbarian. From all quarters of the ancient world—to say nothing of the modern—from Rome to Babylon, we can point to the existence of Dionysian festivals, types which bear, at best, the same relation to the Greek festivals which the bearded satyr, who borrowed his name and attributes from the goat, bears to Dionysus himself. In nearly every case these festivals centered in extravagant sexual licentiousness, whose waves overwhelmed all family life and its venerable traditions; the most savage natural instincts were unleashed, including even that horrible mixture of sensuality and cruelty which has always seemed to me to be the real "witches' brew." For some time, however, the Greeks were apparently perfectly insulated and guarded against the feverish excitements of these festivals, though knowledge of them must have come to Greece on all the routes of land and sea; for the figure of Apollo, rising full of pride, held out the Medusa's head to this grotesquely uncouth Dionysian power.[40]

This "resurrection" or "consolidation" (which is that of Doric art) confronted with the Dionysiac—this apotropaic gesture is precisely the moment that, in the history of Greek culture, precedes the "reconciliation" of the Apollinian and the Dionysian, which only the "noble art" of Greece (the tragedy) revealed itself capable of assuring. One can think whatever one cares to about such a reconciliation. For us there is no doubt that it must be deconstructed, if only in its (surviving) dialectical aspect, which is to say in all that still masks the recognition of the ineluctable representation that it implies. There is no need, it is true, to mobilize Apollo for that, and Nietzsche himself, moreover, will end up doing without him. For it is within the Dionysian itself that the *interdiction* of presence takes place, or, to put it in another language (one that Freud uses in an enigmatic text to justify the desire of art),[41] death incessantly undermines and deports all "presence" irrevocably, dooming us to repetition. A thought that should not be cast aside as an embarrassment, or indicted as a symptom of nihilism, as a "pious and depressed thought." Rather, it is what Nietzsche called "heroism"; and heroism—that is, the impossible ethical (and not pathetical) trial of the abyss—has never been known to signify nihilism.

(Translated by Robert Vollrath and Samuel Weber)

NOTES

1. This manuscript was given by Freud, at an undetermined time, to the historian and music theorist, Max Graf, a long-time member of Freud's circle of friends and disciples. Graf published it for the first time in 1942, in an English translation by H. A. Bunker. The text, which was entitled "Psychopathic Characters on the Stage," appeared in the *Psychoanalytical Quarterly* 11, no. 4. This is the version included in volume 7 of the *Standard Edition*. The original was first published in 1962 (*Neue Rundschau*, 73) before appearing in volume 10 (*Bildende Künste und Literatur*, 1970) of the *Studienausgabe* published by Fischer in Frankfurt. It is not included in Freud's *Gesammelte Werke*. Despite Graf's belief that the text was written in 1904, it is now generally considered to have been composed in 1905, or at the latest, early in 1906. Thus it is roughly contemporary with the *Three Essays on the Theory of Sexuality, Jokes and their Relation to the Unconscious*, and perhaps even *Delusions and Dreams in Jensen's "Gradiva"*. It is not clear, however, why Freud decided to give the text to Graf, without indicating the slightest intention of having it published (or even of correcting it).

The present text appeared orginally in an earlier version entitled "A Note on Freud and Representation" [*Note sur Freud et la représentation*] and was designed to accompany the first French translation of Freud's text, done in collaboration with Jean-Luc Nancy, which appeared in the review *Digraphe* 3 (Autumn 1974).

[English citations of "Psychopathic Characters on the Stage" are from the *Standard Edition of the Complete Psychological Works of Sigmund Freud*, ed. James Strachey et al., 23 vols. (London: Hogarth Press, 1953–66), 7: 305–310 (henceforth: S.E.). In order to maintain continuity with Lacoue-Labarthe's and Nancy's French translation of this text, we have retranslated where necessary. Trans.]

Philippe Lacoue-Labarthe

2. See in particular, René Girard, *La Violence et le sacre* (Paris: Grasset, 1973).

3. Jean Starobinski, "Hamlet et Freud," preface to the French translation of E. Jones, *Hamlet et Oedipe*, (Paris: Gallimard, 1976); André Green, *Un Oeil en trop—Le complexe d'Oedipe dans la tragédie* (Paris: Editions de Minuit, 1969); and *Shakespeare, Freud et le parricide* (in *La Nef* 32 [July–October 1967]). Concerning the reading of "Psychopathic Characters on the Stage," see also O. Mannoni, *Clefs pour l'imaginaire ou l'Autre scène* (Paris: Seuil, 1969), and Sarah Kofman, *L'enfance de l'art* (Paris: Payot, 1972).

4. See, in particular, Jacques Derrida, "Le théâtre de la cruauté et la clôture de la représentation," and "Freud et la scène de l'écriture," in *L'écriture et la différence* (Paris: Seuil, 1967).

5. Jean-François Lyotard, "Beyond Representation" [*Par delà la représentation*], preface to the French translation of Anton Ehrenzweig, *The Hidden Order of Art* (Paris: Gallimard, 1974). Although we only cite what closely concerns "Psychopathic Characters on the Stage," the entirety of Lyotard's critical treatment of Freudian esthetics should be taken into account, including texts such as "Jewish Oedipus" and "Current Major Trends in the Psychoanalytic Study of Artistic and Literary Expressions," in *Dérive à partir de Marx et de Freud* (Paris: U.G.E., 1973) or "Freud according to Cézanne" in *Des dispositifs pulsionnels* (Paris: U.G.E., 1973).

6. Freud probably *never* goes beyond comparison. The model here is the famous phrase, "the tragedy of Oedipus unfolds like an analysis." But if Lyotard is thus able to "literalize" this figure, it is because he has previously interpreted the text as deducing the psychopathics (the neurosis) of Greek tragedy, and then psychopathology itself from psychoanalysis. Freud, however, simply says that, at a given moment and for determinate reasons, the tragic scene becomes the site of a neurotic type of conflict. Which is not quite the same thing, since it implies that the theater enters the space of neurosis, but it does not produce it. Just as tragedy does not produce the Oedipus complex, even if the form of that complex is *necessarily* dramatic, and even if the structure of the scene, in general, is *necessarily* Oedipal.

7. Lyotard, "Beyond Representation," p. 12: "The seductive enticement [*prime de séduction*]," says Lyotard in particular, "operates no differently in Freud's thesis than does sleep in his theory of dreams, which functions to lower the defenses and with which all of secondary revision conspires."

8. Freud, "Psychopathic Characters on the Stage," p. 305.

9. Friedrich Nietzsche, *The Birth of Tragedy*, trans. Walter Kaufmann (New York: Vintage, 1967), pp. 132–33.

10. This is the classical misinterpretation par excellence, to which the entire French seventeenth century, almost without exception, succumbed.

11. In still other words, Freud follows the Aristotelian thesis in all respects: namely, that catharsis is doubled (and constituted) by an "accompaniment of pleasure"; i.e. the thesis of the κάθαρσις μεθ' ἡδονῆς, of relief or alleviation through pleasure (see *Politics*, VIII, 1342a).

12. The analogy can be found, for instance, in "Creative Writers and Day-Dreaming" (1908), S.E. 9: 141–153, or in §6 of "Formulations on the Two Principles of Mental Functioning" (1911), S.E. 12: 218–26.

13. See Starobinski, "Hamlet et Freud," p. ix. This is obviously what renders possible the analytical "verification" of the paradigmatic character as-

sumed by *Oedipus Rex* in Aristotle's *Poetics*, and thus of the matricial function of theatricality with regard to analysis, including the elevation of "Oedipus" in general to the rank of an absolute paradigm. In *Beyond the Pleasure Principle*, identification will retain its Oedipal character, even as primary identification (and notwithstanding the practically insurmountable difficulties that it provokes, discussed in Postscript B of *Group Psychology and the Analysis of the Ego*, S.E. 18: 135–37).

14. See in particular his analysis of the tragic effect developed from the viewpoint of the "artist as spectator" in chapters 21–24 of *The Birth of Tragedy*. This analysis concerns essentially the exemplary function of tragic myth. Here can be found in embryonic form the Nietzschean theory of identification, whose place in his general "typology" is well known.

15. Freud, "Psychopathic Characters on the Stage," pp. 305–6.

16. "But the suffering represented is soon restricted to *mental* suffering; for no one wants physical suffering who knows how quickly all mental enjoyment is brought to an end by the changes in somatic feeling that physical suffering brings about. If we are sick we have one wish only: to be well again and to be quit of our present state. We call for the doctor and medicine, and for the removal of the inhibition on the play of phantasy which has pampered us into deriving enjoyment even from our own sufferings. If a spectator puts himself in the place of someone who is physically ill he finds himself without any capacity for enjoyment or psychical activity. Consequently a person who is physically ill can only figure on the stage as a piece of stage-property and not as a hero, unless, indeed, some peculiar physical aspects of his illness make psychical activity possible—such, for instance, as the sick man's forlorn state in the *Philoctetes* or the hopelessness of the sufferers in the class of plays that center around consumptives." Ibid.

17. Ibid., p. 305.

18. "In general, it may perhaps be said that the neurotic instability of the public and dramatist's skill in avoiding resistances and offering fore-pleasures [*Vorlust*] can alone determine the limits set upon enjoyment of abnormal characters on the stage." Ibid., p. 310. Cf. *Three Essays on the Theory of Sexuality*, 3: 1, S.E. 7: 208–11, and *Jokes*, B: IV and V, S.E. 8: 117–58. The difficulty in this text lies in the fact that fore-pleasure, which normally should permit the *avoidance* of intolerable tensions, here appears to overlap with another species of pleasure, to which Freud, moreover, attributes an independent mechanism: this is the sexual pleasure bound up with the deferral of discharge, which thus becomes a "super-tension" that is desired for its own sake. Here, in condensed form, lies the whole (future) problem of masochism. The reading we are attempting here tends not to resolve the problem, but to intensify it.

19. See "Creative Writers and Day-Dreaming" (1907).

20. Freud, "Psychopathic Characters on the Stage," p. 305.

21. Ibid., p. 307.

22. The heroical-mythical figure invoked here as the emblem of tragedy in a way reminiscent of *Totem and Taboo* (IV: 7), is that of Prometheus: "The fact that drama originated out of sacrificial rites (the goat and the scapegoat) in the cult of the gods cannot be unrelated to this meaning of drama. It appeases, as it were, a rising rebellion against the divine regulation of the universe, which is responsible for the existence of suffering. Heroes are

first and foremost rebels against God or against something divine . . . Here we have a mood like that of Prometheus. . . ." But just as the sacrificial origins of drama, in *Totem and Taboo*, are inscribed in the Oedipal matrix (revised, so to speak, by Nietzsche: Dionysus' laceration as a reminder of the original murder), here it is Oedipus who governs the entire genealogy of the drama and who accounts for the psychopathological drama (in conformity with the Oedipal version of Hamlet proposed in *The Interpretation of Dreams*).

23. Freud, *The Interpretation of Dreams* V: IV, §2, S.E. 4. If we were retracing the overall movement of Freud's interpretation of *Hamlet*, "Psychopathic Characters on the Stage" would be situated—following the argument advanced by Starobinski (who was apparently unaware of this text) midway between *The Interpretation of Dreams* and the *Introductory Lectures on Psycho-Analysis* (the *Vorlesungen* of 1916). Concerning the interpretation of a *hidden conflict* in *Hamlet* (". . . the conflict in *Hamlet* is so hidden that at first I had to guess that it was there"), cf. also Lyotard, "Jewish Oedipus," and in particular everything concerning the "non-fulfillment of the paternal utterance as the difference between the Modern and the Greeks."

24. Freud, "Psychopathic Characters on the Stage," pp. 308–9.

25. "The first of these modern dramas is *Hamlet*. It has as its subject the way in which a man who has so far been normal becomes neurotic owing to the peculiar nature of the task by which he is faced, a man, that is, in whom an impulse that has hitherto been successfully suppressed endeavours to make its way into action. *Hamlet* is distinguished by three characteristics which seem important in connection with our present discussion. (1) The hero is not psychopathic, but only *becomes* psychopathic in the course of the action of the play. (2) The repressed impulse is one of those which are similarly repressed in all of us, and the repression of which is part and parcel of the foundation of our personal evolution. . . . As a result of these two characteristics it is easy for us to recognize ourselves in the hero . . . (3) It appears as a necessary precondition of this form of art that the impulse that is struggling into consciousness, however clearly it is recognizable, is never given a definite name; so that in the spectator too the process is carried through with his attention averted, and he is in the grip of his emotions instead of taking stock of what is happening. A certain amount of resistance is no doubt saved in this way, just as, in an analytical treatment, we find derivatives of the repressed material reaching consciousness, owing to a lower resistance, while the repressed material itself is unable to do so." Ibid., pp. 309–10.

26. Freud, *Beyond the Pleasure Principle*, chapter II, in fine.

27. Cf. *Poetics*, 1448b: "Imitation is natural to man from childhood, etc." Concerning the "undecidable" nature of play, Freud makes a note of it twice during the course of this development. At the very least this renders problematic Lyotard's claim that the *fort/da* analysis attests to "the recurrent power of the theatrical process in Freud's epistemological unconscious," "Beyond Representation," p. 13.

28. Freud, "Psychopathic Characters on the Stage," p. 306.

29. Cf. Freud, *Group Psychology and the Analysis of the Ego*, Postscript B.

30. Would this account for his "forgetting" the text?

31. Freud, "Thoughts for the Times on War and Death," (chapter 2, "Our Attitude towards Death"), S.E. 14: 289–300.

32. Cf. "The Head of Medusa." Suffice it to say that in pursuing a certain number of Rohde's indications in Psychè, in particular concerning the catharsis of impurity or the union of the apotropaion with catharsis, the relation between catharsis and femininity invites examination in the light of the relation of death (and suffering) to catharsis.

33. Freud, "Thoughts for the Times on War and Death," S.E. 14: 291.

34. This renders the Jungian deviation denounced by Freud, for instance in chapter VI of Civilization and its Discontents, a constant possibility. That is, the reduction of the drives to a single libido is always possible, as the most recent discourse of Lyotard confirms—see in particular Economie libidinale (Paris: Editions de Minuit, 1975).

35. Lacan, Ecrits, (Paris: Seuil, 1966).

36. See Lyotard, "Current Major Trends," where, in "fulfillment" of the interpretation proposed by Blanchot of the Orpheus allegory, Lyotard writes the following: "But the story of the legendary adventure continues. Orpheus turns around. His desire to see the figure exceeds his desire to lead it back to the light. Orpheus wants to see in the night, to see the night. In attempting to see Eurydice, he loses all possibility of letting her be seen: the figure is that which has no face, killing whomever dis-figures [dévisage] her because she fills him with her own night . . . But Orpheus has gone to search for Eurydice precisely because of this disfigurement, and not in order to produce a work; the artist has not descended into the night in order to render himself capable of producing a harmonious song, or the reconciliation of night and day, or to earn laurels for his art. He has gone to search for the figural instance, that other of his own work, to see the invisible, to see death. The artist is someone in whom the desire to see death even at the price of dying triumphs over the desire to produce." But all this is only conceivable on the condition that one considers death to be a "figure," and correlatively, the artist's descent into the inferno—frequent enough in modern art—to be itself, "biographically," a "work of art." The equivocation of Lyotard with which we take issue stems ultimately from Discours, Figure (Paris: Klincksieck, 1971), the terminology of which reemerges here. Theoretically, Lyotard's point of departure is his determination of the figure, or the figural, against our every expectation, as something pertaining not to the realm of manifestation (and correlatively, his determination of writing as designating the order of constituted discourse). This is without a doubt the origin of our disagreement.

37. Refer to Luce Irigaray, "La philosophie par derriére," a paper given to the "Groupe de recherche sur les théories du signe et du texte" at the University of Strasbourg II.

38. Freud, Civilization and its Discontents, chapter VIII.

39. Lyotard, "Beyond Representation," p. 10.

40. Nietzsche, The Birth of Tragedy, chapter 2.

41. Freud, "On Transience," S.E. 14: 305–7.

EIGHT
KENNETH BURKE'S LOGOLOGY:
A MOCK LOGOMACHY
Timothy C. Murray

The system is a *coherent* and *total vision*, a *self-contained* and *internally consistent way of viewing man*, the various scenes in which he lives, and the drama of human relations enacted upon those scenes.
　　W. H. Rueckert, *Kenneth Burke and the Drama of Human Relations*
　　　　　　　　　　　　(my emphasis)

And whereas a statement about the grammatical principles of motivation might lay claim to a universal validity, or complete certainty, the choice of any one philosophic idiom embodying these principles is much more open to question. Even before we know what act is to be discussed, we can say with confidence that a rounded discussion of its motives must contain a reference to *some kind* of background.
　　　　　　　　　Kenneth Burke, *A Grammar of Motives*

Speculative technique made available by speech would seem to single out the human species as the only one possessing an equipment for going beyond the criticism of experience to a criticism of criticism. We not only interpret the character of events. . . . We may also interpret our interpretations.
　　　　　　　Kenneth Burke, *Permanence and Change*

METACRITICISM is more than the affirmation of a "consistent way of viewing man." Kenneth Burke would have us take a step beyond the mechanical motions of neutral critical commentaries. Metacritical work is the active and forceful questioning of the motivating background—"the sub-stance"—of any criticism of experience. The critic's purpose is not only to evaluate the total vision of a work, but to put to a thorough test the philosophical idioms informing the symbolic grammar of an interpretation. Such a responsibility goes beyond the merely holistic analysis of W. H. Rueckert, Burke's most devoted interpreter. For Burke constantly reminds us of our critical obligations: "the reader may encounter the same formulations put forward with a different attitude, or used for different purposes, at different points in our text. . . . For the most part, however, I should prefer not to be 'forgiven' these inconsistencies" (PLF,* p. 22).[1] In this statement of 1941, Burke underlines the inherent role of dissonance in any critical presentation. His metacritical stance prefigures by thirty years the contemporary concern of such a critic as Paul de Man who denies "the notion that a literary or poetic consciousness is in any way a privileged consciousness, whose use of language can pretend to escape, to some degree, from the duplicity, the confusion, the untruth that we take for granted in the everyday use of language."[2]

The avowed solicitation of dissonant statements should be of utmost concern to the critic who wants to perform a metacritical *act*. Required of the interpreter is a thorough knowledge of the similarities and differences within the script to be represented. Having gone through the repetitive motions of rehearsal—the memorizing of the author's script—the metacritic can then begin the drama. Freed from the director's pleas to stick to the coherent and total vision of the script, the critic-as-actor is able to make his own interpretative presentation. He might speak dissonant lines that seem to reveal the motivational strategies of the text, and he acts out these motivations in terms of his own critical concerns. On a metacritical stage, the actor also goes beyond the normative limits of his script to enter into a playful dialogue with an extended audience. He hopes to engage them in the active evaluation of his own critical performance. If the metacritic is a polished actor, he will mimic Kenneth Burke's style "of getting along by dodges, the main one being a concern with tricks whereby I could translate my self-involvements into speculations about 'people' in general" (DTE, p. 26). Any *critical* discussion of Kenneth Burke must consider his message in terms of his critical *plays*. In rehearsing this particular act, I realized that a profitable analysis of

---

* See n. 1 for key to abbreviations.

Kenneth Burke's numerous performances need account for the tricks and dodges with which he translates his self-involvements into a drama of human relations. The first and only scene of this one act play opens with a few lines on Burke's own interpretative strategy.

In "Freud—and the Analysis of Poetry," Burke writes glosses on Freud's interpretative strategy that are analogous to strategies of literary criticism. Burke's intent is to "characterize [Freud's] strategy of presentation with reference to interpretative method in general" (PLF, p. 258). These glosses also highlight the interpretative stakes of Kenneth Burke's criticism. In Burke's words, "they would concern a distinction between what I should call an essentializing mode of interpretation and a mode that stresses proportion of ingredients." Elaborating on Freud, Burke claims that

the tendency in Freud is toward the first of these. That is, if one found a complex of, let us say, seven ingredients in a man's motivation, the Freudian tendency would be to take one of these as the *essence of motivation* and to consider the other six as sublimated variants. We could imagine for instance, manifestations of sexual impotence accompanying a conflict in one's relations with his familiars and one's relations at the office. The proportional strategy would involve the study of these three as a cluster. The motivation would be synonomous with the interrelationships among them. But the essentializing strategy would, in Freud's case, place the *emphasis* upon the sexual manifestation, as *causal ancestor* of the two. (PLF, Pp. 261–62, my emphasis)

Implicit in these two stances are radically different ways of approaching a text. A proportional reading looks upon the text as a zone of free play. Any part of a text can be used in any fashion to provide a different focus for its viewing. Freud's exercise in free association and Burke's method of "joycing"—the reshaping of pliant phonetic resemblances—are fair and common games. By "joycing," for instance, Burke states that the last line of Keats's "Ode on a Grecian Urn," "Beauty is truth, truth beauty," can be read "Body is turd, turd body" (AS, pp. 20–22). All levels of language and culture are understood as interchangeable and as potential signifiers of each other. The concerns of such an open reformulation of duplicious communication and textuality "have such important bearing upon matters of culture and conduct in general that no sheer conventions or ideals of criticism should be allowed to interfere with their development" (GM, p. 451). The essentializing strategy, however, places these limits on the activity of reading. The critic feels obligated to identify in the text but one essential motivation from which all other elements causally derive. This purely symbolic method "as used in the restricted sense (in contrast with free association), would refer to the imputation of an absolute meaning to a crossing, a meaning that I might impute even before reading the book in question" (PLF, p. 267). Restriction here applies to not only *what* is read in(to) the text, but also *how* the text should be read. For the primacy of causal relations implies the efficiency of a causal, linear reading. Formal attention to the linear succession of the text overrides an emphasis on striking or peculiar moments in any piece of writing. A particularly informative sign may be quietly dismissed as not essential to the text's causal progression.

As with Freud, both interpretative strategies are prevalent in the work of Kenneth Burke.[3] And as Burke does with Freud, we can lament Burke's tendency toward the essentializing gloss. A closer look at this tendency will illuminate the critical shortcomings of such a method. But in accounting for the self-involvements of his criticism—his motives, purposes, and philosophical idioms—we will learn from Burke how the slightest maintenance of proportion undermines essential boundaries of criticism. In short, an active look at Burke will revive and replay his metacritical tricks.

Burke's inclination to essentialize is clearly illustrated by his attitude concerning the presence of duplicity and dissonance in his work. There are recurring discussions and applications of dissonant strategies throughout Burke's texts. Yet, the particular grammar utilized by Burke restricts duplicity to the latent level of recessive strategies. While dissonance comprises parts of Burke's criticism, it does not endure as a force of its own:

A sound system of communication, such as lies at the roots of civilization, cannot be built upon a structure of economic warfare. The discordant "sub-personalities" of the world's conflicting cultures and heterogeneous kinds of effort can be reintegrated only by means of a unifying "master-purpose," with the logic of classification that would follow it. The segregational or dissociative cannot endure—and must make way for an associative or congregational state. (PC, P. 163)

The shift from dissociative to associative is the philosophical motive for Burke's "sound system of communication." Communication, he contends, is the hortatory call to a *social* language of action. The "master-purpose" of communication is signified by Burke as dramatistic logology. Burke's compulsion to translate his own self-involvement with communication into a master-purpose of human relations results in his transgression of metacritical responsibilities. He is motivated more by the mechanical motions of essentializing than by creative acts of proportion.

Although my metacritical motive is not to outline Burke's complex theory of dramatism—such a task is ably carried out by Rueckert—a brief summary of this system will delineate its displacement of dissonance and proportion.

In formulating an "empirical definition of man," Burke puts aside the classical conception of man as "the rational animal." In its place he promotes man as a symbol-using animal. Man not only communicates, but he creates modes of communication. Utilizing his power of *logos*, he assigns symbolic names in four realms. In the natural realm, names comprise words for things, material operations, physiological conditions, etc. Names in the socio-political realm are for social relations, law, rule, etc. Third is the verbal realm where names are assigned to words. "Here is the realm of dictionaries, grammar, etymology, philology, literary criticism, rhetoric, poetics, dialectic—all that I think of as coming to a head in the discipline I would want to call "Logology" (RR, p. 14). It is from the verbal realm of *logology* that Burke analyzes the associative condition of language.

The logological study of language depicts two basic movements of signification: 1) *substitution*: words are the signs of things in terms of what they are *not*, signifying the natural and socio-political realms; 2) *negativism*: a function peculiar to symbol-systems, is the making present of what is not—be it signs for things, expectations, or proscriptions. Affected by his invention of the negative, man gravitates toward naive verbal realism. Man's central concern is with words as a substitute reality. He is then separated from what Burke romantically calls his "natural" condition by instruments of his own making. Peculiar to this verbal displacement is man's development of a "logic of titles." Titles, or titular signs, of generalization are universals ("man," "dog") substituted for entire groups of signs. The individual "men" become particularized instances of the "perfect" form embodied in the title "man" (LSA, p. 361). In an emptying movement, a *via negativa*, the linguist rises in dialectical progression "to ever and ever higher orders of generalization." A Title of Titles results (RR, pp. 21–23). Representing the ultimate point of this negativistic "dialectic of transcendence . . . *in terms of a Beyond*," the Title personifies the realm of the supernatural. Because the "god-term" is farthest removed from "nature" and symbolizes the dialectical movement of symbolicity and all within it, a second level of signification reverses the direction of symbolic reference: things become the signs of words (RR, p. 21; LSA, pp. 9–13, 419–79). Burke explains that "the realm of the symbolic corresponds to the realm of the 'supernatural': the natural is pervaded or 'inspirited' by the realm of the verbal or symbolic" (RR, p. 17). By this reversal, the flexibility of verbal signification is arrested. The supernatural is treated as "prior" to the other three realms of language, "and as their 'ground.' " Meaning is consequently a non-temporal—though embodied in a temporal series—and a timeless *fixed* definition.

The logic of entitlement, not to mention its results, comprises the logological activity. It follows then that Burke is justified in maintaining that his own critical dealings in "logology could properly be called central, and all other studies could be said to 'radiate' from it, in the sense that all '-ologies' and '-ographies' are guided by the verbal . . . all specialization can be treated as radiating from a logological center" (RR, p. 26). Burke's critical activity is here essentialized as the causal ancestor of any other criticism or discipline. Logology is not, however, all that motivates Kenneth Burke.

Dramatism is "a technique of analysis of language and thought as basically modes of action rather than as means of conveying information" (LSA, p. 54). The primary unit of action is "the human body in conscious or purposive motion" (GM, p. 14). Consideration of pure verbal internality delineates the dramatic function of human language as attitudinal or hortatory, not derivative or descriptive. Thus dramatistic criticism must act on a text and call forth the audience to perform its own act on both texts. Dramatism provides the impetus for a sort of metacriticism.

More specifically, Burke maintains that language elicits action in the form of "terministic screens." Being linguistic titles of complex nonverbal situations of action, these screens bid their users to act (LSA, p. 361). To illustrate the relation of screen and action, Burke presents a contiguous series of terministic screens that become symbolic of his entire project. *Drama* is taken to be the culminative form of action. The central instrument of dramatic action is *mimesis*, the *purposeful* response to the logological paradigm. Anyone who grasps this ordering principle will mimetically "embody it or represent it in any mode of action he may choose" (RM, p. 137). But subsequent action will inevitably catalyze a situation of crisis. For if *drama*, then *conflict*. Conflict is inherent in the socializing of action, a not always harmonious "joining-with" the Other. But if *conflict*, then *victimage* (LSA, pp. 54–55). The victim facilitates neutralization of conflict. Burke here develops a scapegoat theory. Movement beyond conflict is best guaranteed if, through the agency of the scapegoat, conflictive danger—in whatever form—is expressed, but not harmful. *Catharsis* results from the scapegoat's "draining-off of dangerous [as in Aristotle's lightening] charges" (CS, p. xii; LSA, p. 94). Purified action is the scapegoat's product. Dissonance is escaped.

Missing in this discussion of dramatism is, returning to our second epigraph, any clear grammatical principle of motivation that might lay claim to the universal validity of dramatism. We have yet to clarify the *purpose* implied in action (LSA, p. 389). In the "Introduction" to *A Grammar of Motives*, Burke appends a comment to his definition of dramatism: "We hope to make clear the ways in which dialectical and metaphysical issues necessarily figure in the subject of motivation" (GM, p. xxii). Logology, the dialectical and metaphysical realm of language, provides such a purpose.

The logological movement to and from transcendence sustains the "entelechial" principle of perfection. Likewise the "entelechial" perspective provides the dialectical and metaphysical pulse of dramatism. For it locates "the 'principles' of a form not in temporally past moments that a form develops *from*, but in possibilities of perfection in the form as such toward which all sorts of stories might gravitate" (LSA, pp. 390–91). Dramatic action is symbolic movement *beyond* conflict toward perfection. The scene of the "entelechial" movement is within the form of *hierarchy*. The hierarchical principle includes the "entelechial tendency, the treatment of the 'top' or the 'culminating' stage as the 'image' that best represents the idea" (RM, p. 141). Symbolic of the logological activity as a whole, hierarchical form, according to Burke, permeates all levels of human activity.

Logological dramatism and its hierarchical form culminate in the Title of Titles. The structure of logological dramatism can be summarized by two concepts. *Synecdoche* stresses the dramatistic part for the transcendent whole. This principle symbolizes the logological counterpart of time: "*the one-directioned rectilinearity of narrative*" (RR, p. 144, my emphasis). *Tautology* is the logological counterpart of eternity. It refers to the combined movements of dramatism and logology,

insofar as the entire structure is infused by a single generating principle, this principle will be tautologically or repetitively implict in all the parts. . . . in so far as man is a symbol-using animal, his world is necessarily inspirited with the quality of the Symbol, the Word, the Logos, through which he conceives it. (LSA, P. 55)

The quality of this system is guaranteed to be perfect. It is an *associational* system synonomous with universal order. Analogous to it is an essentializing mode of interpretation—emphasizing its logological source and one-directioned rectilinear reading.

That Burke's logological dramatism presents "a coherent and total vision" is apparent. We have yet, however, to test the philosophical idiom upon which this tautology rests. No substantive assertion of the system's internal consistency, thus positing its maintenance of the logological and essentializing standards, can be made without reference to its foundational language.

The textual entrance into the disclosure of this idiom is suggested by Burke himself:

> . . . *in terms* of derivation from a transcendent super-personality . . . there is this area wherein analogies may *fold back on themselves*, reilluminating the place they started from. (RR, P. 37)

It is no coincidence that Burke suggests his texts' tendency to "fold back on themselves." The internal consistency of his vision can be tested by its own deconstruction: reilluminating the idiom that it started from. Burke also provides us with the particular investigative area of a transcendent super-personality. The super-personality is defined by Burke in terms of authority:

> the concept of *auctor* includes both senses of originator, either as progenitor, father, ancestor, and the like, while out of both senses grows the third sense, the sense of the *auctor* or head or leader, from which we derive our usual meaning for "authority." It is the principle of group cohesion, and of cohesion among groups pitted against the group. (GM, P. 123)

The authoritarian fitting together of the *auctor's* groups of creation is observable in Burke's own attempts to bring his already written texts under control. Burke's many prefaces, forewords, prologues, and introductions are attempts to gather up groups of texts, be they groups of chapters or volumes.[4] By what he calls "looseleafing," Burke uses the preface "opportunistically" to reformulate his texts "in accordance with the shifts of public attention" (PLF, p. xx), not to mention the shifts of his own intentionality as the synthesizer of an ever increasing number of texts. Burke's prefatory efforts are attempts at the re-shaping of *past* writings—already interpretable by substitute authorities (readers)—to conform with his interpretations that are intended to last *beyond* (transcend) the moment of gathering. Burke here posits himself as the transcendent super-personality: the father of logological texts who creates and renews fixed timeless meanings.[5]

The analyzable area of the transcendent super-personality is now understood to be the preface. The "Preface to the First Edition" of *Counter-Statement* suggests a code for the analysis of the background of Burke's critical motives. In referring to the "Lexicon Rhetoricae," "intended as a . . . machine for criticism," Burke states that

> it is, in general, an attempt to schematize many critical concepts which have been more or less vaguely in the air since psychology took the place of metaphysics as a foundation for aesthetic theory. (CS, P. ix)

Timothy C. Murray

This passage provides the first term of our code, *psychology*. The machine for criticism outlines the interdependency of form and psychology: "literature [form] is an arousing and fulfillment of desires." And, in part, the psychological function confirms the linear stages of dramatism: "one part of it leads a reader to anticipate another part, to be gratified by sequence." But in acknowledging psychology over metaphysics as the foundation for aesthetic theory, Burke questions the efficacy of the entelechial perspective. " 'Perfection' as applied to literature is a meaningless term. The naturalness of progressive and repetitive form is impaired by divergence in the ideologies of writer and reader" (CS, p. 178). The dismissal of "entelechy" as an intrinsic literary principle challenges the validity of "dialectic" as *the* motivating force of literature. It also provides the basis for the second term in our code, a "negative" one: *metaphysics* is not an intrinsic trait of literature. The third term describes the condition of any text: "our 'Lexicon' would look upon literature as the thing added." If literature is an adding to what already exists, then the interpretation of a literary text is the multiplication of the addition. The result is a possible infinity of "imperfect" texts.

Furthermore, a profusion of texts might do much to arouse desire, but their duplicity and disassociation are likely to confuse and delay gratification. Dependency on sequential development and clarity is not the most efficient manner of dealing with the inherent ambiguity of literary texts. It is too likely to result in frustration rather than satisfaction. A different system of reading is required to make the chaos of textual multiplication both intelligible and gratifying. Yet, Burke's prefaces illustrate his motives for devising a system of reading, which would thereby catalyze an essentializing and programmatic activity of reading grammar, rhetoric, religion, and symbols.

In the "Prologue" to the 1953 edition of *Permanence and Change*, Burke analogically links his professional motives to the code outlined above. He writes of a preoccupation with his own "compulsion neuroses" and his " 'occupational psychosis' as a writer" (PC, p. liii). The source of his dilemma is "the piously fearful study of ourselves through the methodic or haphazard study of ingenious texts" (LSA, p. viii). If we interpret literary texts as the calling forth to action, we must be able to rise up to the subsequent mimetic act. The infinity of imperfect texts, however, frustrates action by representing only "the muddle." Some of the reader's

decisions merely apply to ways of thinking with which the deliberator was already quite at *home*. Other decisions, made at times of "Crisis" (which is but the Greek word for "judgment"), characteristically also involve an *unsettling*, an attempt (or temptation?) to think in ways to which the deliberator was not accustomed. (PC, P. xlvii)

For Burke, the temptation to think in unsettling ways derives from repetitive divergence in literary texts. A certain helplessness to deal with (judge) recurrent textual incongruity forces Burke to exercise his occupational psychosis: the promotion of "certain specific patterns of thought" assisting in the productive and distributive functions of criticism (PC, p. 38).

The disposition of his compulsion neuroses enhances Burke's entrapment in an essentializing criticism. His customary response to an unsettling strategy is first "fear" and then displacement. Burke histrionically illustrates this very same process in the "Preface to the Second Edition" of *Counter-Statement*:

As for my remarks on Spengler, I should add: Spengler made a tremendous impression on me. He scared me, much as the Theater Guild's production of Capek's *R.U.R.* scared me, or much as a child (or the child in our adult selves) is scared by the story of some monstrous invader from an alien planet. No, he scared me even more than that; for he pictured an invader already here, from within (an invader derived from mankind's best logic, mankind's best genius). When "disposing" of Spengler with such dispatch, I could have been more judicious. (PC, P. xiv)

What scares Burke is Spengler's destruction of the *one-directioned* rectilinearity of historical perspective. Spengler emphasizes a unique concept of the contemporaneous—things existing at corresponding stages in different cultures and ages. Spengler clearly operates according to a *multi-directional* method of proportion "by taking a word usually applied to one setting and transferring its use to another setting" (PC, pp. 90–91). Burke's reaction to Spengler is essential. Burke's tendency toward "symbolic displacement" motivates his critical activity.

His personal "neuroses" and "occupational psychosis" compel him to devise a way by which variant texts could be "joined" in one symmetrical and linear communication transcending the threat of duplicity. The satisfaction of establishing a *statement* or form of normative social communication would *counter* the individual's frustration with his own interpretative functions. Reflecting on *Counter-Statement* thirty years after much of its writing, Burke summarizes his motives and its result:

I refer to the fact that this book begins on the word "perhaps" and ends on the word "norm." . . . the quest of the norm must bring one to feel great sympathy, and even kinship, with many kinds of "abnorm." But the over-all trend is *through* Perhaps *towards* the norm (even though I unconsciously reveal my tentativeness with regard to it by ending on it—not outright, but in quotation marks).

Add the theory of form that is developed in these pages . . . and I believe you have, in these three moments, the gist of this book, and *maybe also of the books by me that grew out of it.* (my emphasis here—CS, P. xi)

The shortcomings of this critical project are also made clear by Burke: "the attempt was later to turn from "inconsistency" to a systematic search from a dialectic of many voices. The quest of the "norm" led to a study of the varied ways in which men seek *by symbolic means to make themselves at home in social tensions.* And the theory of form led to *problems* that, while they may seem to some readers far from this theory, are logical developments from it" (CS, p. xi, my emphasis). The problems arising from Burke's metacriticism derive from its model. As Burke himself tells us, the "perfection" of any literary system is an unreal possibility.

Still, his occupational psychosis transforms any problem with the actuality of his "symmetry" into a moot point. He is adamant in his defense:

Call it fallacious if you want. That need not concern us here. We are discussing the rhetorical advantages of an ultimate vocabulary as contrasted with a vocabulary left on the level of parliamentary conflict. We are but pointing to a notable formal advantage, got by the union of drama and reason, a wholesome rhetorical procedure in itself. (RM, P. 197)

Psychosis is, according to Webster, a "lasting mental development characterized by defective or lost contact with reality."[6] Reality is thus forgotten and a personal poetics is embraced—"namely: the thought of an ideally weighted vocabulary, grounded in an ideally ordered mode of material cooperation. And with such a *non-existent ideal condition*, one joins 'in principle'" (PC, p. liv). Moreover, the logological dramatism embraced "in principle" in this preface of 1953 had already been established as a new critical reality in the "motivorum" texts of 1945 and 1950.

The same "Lexicon Rhetoricae" that distinguished between metaphysics and literature discusses the literary effect of Burke's transcendent symbolism:

A Symbol appeals: *As the interpretation of a situation.* It can, by its function as name and definition, give simplicity and order to an otherwise unclarified complexity. The schematization is done . . . by idealization, by presenting in a "pure" and consistent manner some situation which, as it appears among the contingencies of real life, is less effectively coordinated; the idealization is *the elimination of irrelevancies.* (CS, P. 154, my emphasis)

For the logological critic—self-defined as a neurotic—simplicity means elimination of duplicity. Burke's use of the "scapegoat" is keenly illustrated when he revises the second edition of *Permanence and Change* by removing five or six pages: "Since, under present conditions, the pages could not possibly be read in the tentative spirit in which they were originally written, the omissions help avoid troublesome issues not necessary to the book as such. There is even a sense in which the omissions could be called a kind of "restoration," since they bring the text closer to its original nature" (PC, p. xlix).[7] The eternal return here means the infusion of symbol systems with "entelechial" metaphysical purposes. Logology is the displacement of duplicity. By folding the transcendent super-personality back on itself, the motivating philosophical idiom of Burke's entire "consistent way of viewing man" is reilluminated as dis-placement. Keeping dis-sonance from the place of critical activity, logology has a literal foundation of negativism, loss, and absence. Or in Burke's authorial prefatory words of 1952, "By adding one thing to my purpose nothing" (CS, p. xv).

We should beware, however, of a deconstruction that leads only to nothing. For the super-personality of old warns us that "Nothing can be made out of nothing." As a metacritical activity, deconstruction shares the risk that Burke enumerates—and that we validate as more than a risk—for the "entelechial" approach: "that it may maneuver us into too great a love for the 'finishedness' of such a method" (LSA, p. 405). Just because Burke's system is motivated by a move *beyond* dissonance does not mean that it fails to generate a vocabulary by which dramatism might constructively serve the neurotic. "Rhetorically, the neurotic's every attempt to legislate his own conduct is disorganized by rival factions within his own dissociated self" (RM, p. 23). Factional incongruities are often expressed by the inherent *recalcitrance* of metacritical language (PC, pp. 255–61).

Traces of recalcitrance are scattered as seductive and welcome ambiguities throughout Burke's texts. Since the ordering process of the preface is itself derived from recalcitrance—the author's showing strong objection or resistance to the "iterability" or independence of his texts[8] —we can benefit from a heavy residue of refractory statements settled into the form of the preface. Indeed these statements signify the rich form of the metacritical text. Central to the metacritical task is its antinomian point of view. Its "very accumulation (its discordant voices arising out of many systems) serves to undermine any one rigid scheme of living" (CS, p. viii). The metacritical text gives way to its own deconstruction. In addition, it relies on "terms that clearly reveal the strategic spots at which ambiguities arise" (GM, p. xvii).

An entire catalogue of "spots" comprises "Instead of a Foreword to Third Edition" of *The Philosophy of Literary Form.* For instance, one "spot" pits metaphysician against diacritic: long-pull investment vs. in-out-trader. But "perspective by incongruity" is perhaps the most illuminating "spot" in any Burke preface. It suggests a motive for reading

Timothy C. Murray

other than dramatistic logology. "Perspective by incongruity" is the methodic merger of terms that had been considered mutually exclusive" (PC, p. lv). There is no transcendence away from the ambiguous "substance" of such a merger. "It appeals by exemplifying relationships between objects which our customary rational vocabulary has ignored" (PC, p. 90). Armed with this perspective, the psychotic steps forward to face crisis. He can now feel at home with duplicity; he is not threatened by, say, the unsettling effacement between imagination and reality.

Yet, Burke's logology exemplifies how much easier it is to displace dissonance than to own up to it. Consequently "perspective by incongruity" must be cultivated with serious intent. For instance, Burke cites "the grotesque" as a peculiarly effective model of incongruity "wherein the perception of discordancies is cultivated without smile or laughter . . . even the most destructive nonsense is seen to be an upholder of things" (PC, p. 112). In the revised "Prologue" to *Permanence and Change*, he provides the plan for just such a grotesque merging of imagination and reality:

the author had had a plan for a kind of melodrama (or perhaps modernized morality play) constructed around two orders of motivation. In the foreground of the stage, there was to be a series of realistic incidents, dealing with typical human situations, such as family quarrels, scenes at a business office, lovers during courtship, a public address by a spellbinder, etc. In the background, like a set of comments of this action, there was to be a primeval forest filled with mythically prehistoric monsters, marauding and fighting in silent pantomime.

These two realms were to have no overt connection with each other. The monsters in the "prehistoric" background would pay no attention to the everyday persons of the foreground; and these everyday persons would have no awareness of the background. But the pantomime of the background would be in effect a "mythic" or "symbolic" way of commenting upon the realistic action of the foreground . . . Such correspondences, it was intended, would indicate the "jungle motives" that underlie such practices as the use of an ethical vocabulary for goading men to the slaughter of one another.

Gradually, however, with increasing frequency, there were to be fleeting moments when the two realms seemed in more direct communication. And the play was to end with a sudden breaking of the frame, whereat the monsters of the background would swarm forward, to take over the entire stage, in a kind of Total Revolution that completely overwhelmed the powers of Reason, insofar as Reason was represented by the "normal" ways of moralized polemics. (PC, Pp. li–lii)

This ideal dramatistic plan for a perspective by incongruity would overwhelm the "norms" of essentializing interpretation. But whether or not ideal, Burke dismisses it as unreasonable. Of the play he writes, "Symbol-wise, the author has never regretted that he was unable to carry out this project. He doesn't think it's the sort of plot one should be able to imagine convincingly" (PC, p. lii). This is certainly Burke's *problem*. Comparable plots were imagined—if not also performed—convincingly by Sartre (*Les Mouches*) and Ionesco (*Rhinocéros*). More recently, a segment of the movie public has been mesmerized by a resurgence of King Kong films. A Total Revolution of thought is being pushed by even Hollywood (however much it is motivated by "normal" economic incentives).

But no matter how ambivalently Burke might openly embrace certain recalcitrant acts, his critical activity confirms his attraction to "perspective by incongruity." His essays suggest his repressed desire to let King Kong loose in his texts—thus wreaking havoc among the powers of logology. As a testament to this desire, many of his essays treating (or reflecting) incongruity are gathered in the volume *Perspectives by Incongruity* (PI), edited by Stanley Edgar Hyman. And in a recent position paper, Burke acknowledges the dissonant side of his strategy:

I doubt whether it's remotely possible for Wellek to understand my ways, or give an adequate summarized characterization of my work insofar as he fails to lay considerable emphasis upon the kind of thinking first formulated in the outlawed subject of my concern with the *stylistics* of "perspective by incongruity," a critical tool for which I am almost traumatically indebted to a combination of Nietzsche and Remy de Gourmont . . . Such thinking is as characteristic of my linguistic theories now as it was when *Permanence and Change* . . . was first published in 1935. (AS, P. 19)

It is typical of Burke that he undermines the one-directioned rectilinearity of his tautological criticism by outlining a plan for incongruous, multidirectional action.

In terms of the act of interpretation, success at "perspective by incongruity" is contingent on the critic's sensitivity to the elasticity of language. "Any deliberate attempt at analogical extension," Burke warns, "can be accomplished only by going beyond the conventional categories of speech" (PC, p. 118). Required is the recognition of new patterns of signification based, for instance, on the linguistic concept of the "free-floating signifier." Language's own repeatability generates new significations that frustrate authorial efforts to limit the meaning. To go "beyond incongruously" is to avoid the associational pitfalls of conventional speech. A different meta-use of *logos* is required: *logomachy*.

Lacking an "-ology" or "-ography," logomachy's first referent is not to its own center from which all else radiates. Instead, logo-machy stresses the inherent ambiguous nature of human communication giving rise to metasystems: "manifestations of the logomachy . . . for presenting real divisions in terms that deny division" (RM, p. 45). In fact, Burke's subordination of logomachy to logology is nothing but a mockery of his emphasis on division. His critical ruse is uncovered by the definition of logomachy in *Webster's Third New International Dictionary*:

1. a dispute over or about words.
2. contention in words that are used wholly or most wholly without real awareness of their meaning or that have little or no actual relation to reality.
3. a game of cards with which words are formed.

Logomachy, then, disputes the associational dependence on logology, a system valorized by the user's defective or lost contact with reality. The substitution of dramatistic logomachy for dramatistic logology is also to perform Burke's critical trick of "misnaming." He discusses "perspective by incongruity" as an effective means of dispelling a child's fear of ghosts in a closet. Instead of pretending to bring the ghosts out of the closet, in order to cast them away, the adult will be more successful at picking up a coat and calling it a coat. The feared object is misnamed "as regards its nature in the child's precious orientation. . . . One casts out demons by a vocabulary of *conversion*, by an incongruous naming, by calling them the very thing in all the world they are not: old coats" (PC, p. 133). In the same way that King Kong is misnamed as unconvincing and thereby dismissed by Burke, dramatistic logomachy is the literal act of misnaming ("contention in words . . . without real awareness of their meaning") and exorcising the precious orientation of logology.

Webster's definition of logomachy also points to another example of recalcitrant residue in the "Prologue" to *Permanence and Change*. Spurred on by his logological suspicion of the adequacy of dreams (LSA, p. 357), Burke attributes little significance to the fact that "during his work on 'perspective by incongruity,' the author once dreamed of playing a new kind of card game" in which cards were renamed so "that its new name made it into a higher denomination" than the face value of the opponent's cards. "But the new assigned identity of the card had to persist from then on, and be remembered, until all the cards in the deck had been transformed" (PC, p. lv). Might we interpret this as the card game of logomachy transforming the "face value" of logological discourse into the *language of a higher denomination* until such a discourse no longer exists? In turn, we should not be surprised that "the dreamer awoke while the game was still in its earlier stages—but already it had become like a fever dream." The -machy is indeed a game of high stakes for any -ologies or -ographies.

In adopting logomachy's rules, dramatism would consist of a new sort of activity. It would no longer depend on scapegoats for the rise to hierarchical perfection:

the matter may not be one of active forgetting [dis-placement], but may involve *the nature of attention* in the "first place." We are proposing that the metaphor be tentatively shifted from a legalistic one suggesting repression to an optical one suggesting focus. (PC, P. 141, my quotation marks)

A relaxed field of action would result where the strategy of interpretation would be grounded in the duplicities of focus. Burke describes it in one of his prefaces: "When they [the proportional pentad of dramatism: act, scene, agent, agency, purpose] become difficult, when we can hardly see them, through having stared at them too intensely, we can all of a sudden relax, to look at them as we always have, lightly, glancingly. And having reassured ourselves, we can start out again, once more daring to let them look strange and difficult for a time" (GM, p. xvi). Relaxation at the time of unsettling crises provokes the vision of a critical tying together of dissociative and free-floating "manifestations of the ethical or creative impulse . . . the lines connecting these concepts could be drawn at *random*. We can go from any point in the series to any other point in the series without ellipsis" (PC, pp. 262–63). Such a vision might be called "anamorphic." Anamorphosis, commonly known as a method of painting, is the distortion of an image that requires a special lens, device, or perspective for its normalization.[9] As a strategy of interpretation, anamorphosis would be the reader's ability to decipher distorted textual images by means of his flexible and playful perspective. Thus, the isolation of certain objects from a one-directioned linear narrative or from any clearly delineated enclosure of objects—as with my deconstructive presentation of bits and pieces of Burkean verse—renders these elements unintelligible without the aid of some reconstructive device. Our lens for regaining perspective is dramatistic logomachy. The visual perspective of such a method is suggested by Burke: "the concern with 'perspective by incongruity' could be likened to the procedure of certain modern painters who picture how an object might seem if inspected simultaneously from two [or more] quite different positions" (PC, p. lv). If we consider a variant *Webster's* definition of rectilinearity: critical vision "corrected for distortion so that the straight lines are imaged accurately ($\approx$lens)," we can see that anamorphic logomachy even meets Burke's demands for rectilinearity.

Through the metacritic's efforts to develop a detailed method of logomachical reading, we can benefit from the philosophical, psychological, and critical implications of an *assured* foundation in "the segregational or dissociative state" that *always* endures. However much the interpreter tries to maintain "an associative or congregational" view of human relations, duplicity remains. Furthermore, language's inherent "pliancy" sets the conditions by which "philosophic systems can pull one

Timothy C. Murray

way and another" (GM, p. xxii). Satisfying man's deepest desires, logomachy permits him to act, however unsettlingly, at home. The resilience of ambiguity is, I suggest, the very "sub-stance" of Burke's many tricks and dodges. His holistic analysis is but a deflection of an anamorphic logomachy. It is to Burke's credit that his texts, in their free-floating signification, lead the metacritic to the articulation of logomachy. The act of interpretation is rightly titled logomachy. For by "joycing" logomachy is the sign for: *logo(s)-n'-acting* or *log-on-acting*.[10]

NOTES

1. I have referred to Burke's works using the following titular abbreviations:

AS   "As I Was Saying," *Michigan Quarterly Review*, 11, no. 1 (1972), 9–27.

CS   *Counter-Statement* (Los Altos, Ca.: Hermes Publications, 1953).

DTE   "Dancing with Tears in My Eyes," *Critical Inquiry*, 1, no. 1 (September, 1974), 23–31.

GM   *A Grammar of Motives* (New York: Prentice-Hall, 1945).

LSA   *Language as Symbolic Action: Essays on Life, Literature, and Method* (Berkeley: Univ. of California Press, 1966).

PC   *Permanence and Change* (Indianapolis: Bobbs-Merrill Co., 1965).

PI   *Perspectives by Incongruity*, ed. Stanley Edgar Hyman (Bloomington, Ind.: Indiana Univ. Press, 1964).

PLF   *The Philosophy of Literary Form: Studies in Symbolic Action* (Berkeley: Univ. of California Press, 1973).

RM   *A Rhetoric of Motives* (Berkeley: Univ. of California Press, 1969).

RR   *The Rhetoric of Religion: Studies in Logology* (Boston: Beacon Press, 1961).

2. Paul de Man, *Blindness and Insight* (New York: Oxford Univ. Press, 1971), pp. 8–9.

3. Burke elaborates on interpretative methodologies in "The Philosophy of Literary Form," (PLF, pp. 66–102). This detailed discussion is fully illustrated with applications to specific literary texts. A comprehensive discussion of "The Philosophy of Literary Form," however, would take us beyond the scope of this essay. The frustrations of choosing specific texts and passages from Burke's corpus are well described by his statement regarding his condensation of Freud: "the desire to write an article on [Burke] in the margins of his books, must for practical reasons here remain a frustrated desire" (PLF, p. 258).

4. While Cary Nelson never expounds on Burke's motives, results, or even content for that matter, he does suggest the topic of this study: "Kenneth Burke, whose books are often a patchwork of prefaces, appendices, and footnotes, has transformed these formulaic structures into quite conscious vehicles for intellectual play." "Reading Criticism," *PMLA*, 89, no. 5 (October, 1976), 802.

5. Burke's statements on the title of a book suggests that his prefaces are attempts to resurrect the book from a "fall": "Insofar as the title of a book

could be said to sum up the nature of that book, then the breakdown of the book into parts, chapters, paragraphs, sentences, words would be technically a "fall" from the Edenic unity of the title, or epitomizing 'god-term.' The *parts* of the book reduce its 'idea' to 'matter' " (RR, p. 175).

In "Hors Livre," Jacques Derrida elaborates on the significance of the preface in relation to its author. *La dissémination* (Paris: Seuil, 1972), pp. 9–67.

6. More technical definitions of neurosis and psychosis will clarify how a combination of personal neurosis—with an end of "sociability"—and an occupational psychosis—a personal giving-in to the occupational desires for unlimited clarity in communication—might drive anyone from the reality of language as the unsettling vehicle for both personal and social desires: "Whereas in neurosis the ego bows to the demands of reality (and of the super-ego) and represses instinctual claims, in the case of psychosis a rupture between ego and reality occurs straight away, leaving the ego under the sway of the id; then at a second stage—that of the onset of delusions—the ego is supposed to reconstruct a new reality in accordance with the desires of the id . . . the distinction fades between libidinal cathexis and the ego-interest." Jean LaPlanche and J.-B. Pontalis, *The Language of Psychoanalysis* (New York: W. W. Norton, 1973), p. 372.

7. The passages omitted from the 1953 edition presented Communism as the form that "material cooperation should take" (PC, p. xlix). Political pressure was undoubtedly the reason for these omissions. This fact, however, does not lessen the implications of textual alterations for Burke's editorial motives. The attention called to these omissions not only highlights the act of alteration, but also its underlying critical stance. Of Communism, Burke writes that "its underlying concept of vocation is radical—for it does not permit our sense of duty to arise simply from the contingencies which our ways of production and distribution force upon us, but offers a point of view from which these contingencies themselves may be criticized" (PC [New York: New Republic, Inc., 1935], p. 344). As an interpretative strategy, Communism would arrest the occupational psychosis fed by the contingencies of essentializing production and distribution. Its tendency is more proportional than essentializing.

8. Derrida discusses the importance of iterability in regard to speech acts (the philosophical counterpart to dramatism) in "Signature Event Context," *Glyph I* (Baltimore: The Johns Hopkins Univ. Press, 1977), pp. 172–97.

9. A very lucid discussion of anamorphosis is provided by Jurgis Baltrusaitis in *ANAMORPHOSE ou magie artificielle des effets merveilleux* (Paris: Olivier Perrin, 1969). The intracacies of *anamorphic reading* are discussed in my article, "A Marvelous Guide to Anamorphosis," *MLN*, 91, no. 6 (1976), 1276–95. A superb exhibition of anamorphic games and pictures, "Anamorphosis: Games of Perception and Illusion in Art," is currently touring the United States (1976–77). A catalogue of this exhibition has been published (New York: Harry N. Abrams, Inc., 1976). See Markus Raetz's "Portrait of Mickey Mouse" (plates 54–55) for a modern illustration of anamorphic logomachy.

10. "By 'joycing' we mean the deliberate and systematic coaching of such transformations for heuristic purposes. They can't often prove anything, but they may lead to critical hunches" (RM, p. 310).

NINE

LIMITED INC
a b c ...
Jacques Derrida

d

I COULD HAVE pretended to begin with a "false" beginning, my penchant
for falsity [*pour le faux*] no longer requiring special demonstration. I
could have simulated what in French is called a *"faux départ"* (I ask
that the translator retain the quotation marks, the parentheses, the italics, and the French). And I shall place in the margin (I ask the publish-
ers to follow this recommendation) the following question. I address it
to Searle. But where is he? Do I know him? He may never even read
this question. If he does, it will be after many others, myself included,
and perhaps without understanding it. Perhaps he will understand it
only in part and without judging it to be *quite* serious. Others will
probably read it after him. How is all that possible? What does it imply?
That is precisely what interests me.

When I say that I do not know John R. Searle, that is not "literally"
"true." For that would seem to mean that I have never met him "in
person," "physically," and yet I am not sure of that, with all these col-
loquia; moreover, although I have read some of his work (more, in any
case, than he seems to have read of mine—my first compliment), what I
read in *"Reiterating the Differences: A Reply to Derrida,"* strikes me as
being very familiar. It is as if I had known him forever. I will have
occasion to return to this strange, uncanny familiarity.

Thus, I place in the margin (but why must I already repeat it? I "mets à gauche"—placing it on the left, but also putting it aside, in reserve) the question that begins with "What is the nature of the debate . . ."

What is the nature of the debate that seems to begin here? Where, here? Here? Is it a debate? Does it take place? Has it begun already? When? Ever since Plato, whispers the prompter promptly from the wings, and the actor repeats, ever since Plato. Is it still going on? Is it finished? Does it pertain to philosophy; to serious philosophy? Does it pertain to literature? The theater? Morals? Politics? Psychoanalysis? Fiction? If it takes place, what is its place? And these utterances —are they "serious" or not? "Literal" or not? "Fictional" or not? "Citational" or not? "Used" or "mentioned"? "Standard" or not? "Void" or not? All these words are, I assure you and you can verify it yourselves, "citations" of Searle.

And I repeat (but why must I repeat again?) that I could have pretended to begin with a false start [*faux-départ*] with whatever seemed to me the "first" or "primary" utterance used or mentioned—I don't know which—in the *Reply*, as I read it, "originally," in manuscript.

On top, at the left, above the title, I then read the following:

"Copyright © by John R. Searle"

And handwritten above the ©, the date: 1977. I received the manuscript shortly before Christmas, 1976. The use of this mention (which I rediscovered in the text published by *Glyph*, this time in its proper place *at the bottom* of the first page) would have lost all value in 1976 (no one abused it then) or in another place, or between quotation marks, as is *here* the case, in the middle of a page that no normal person (except, perhaps, myself) would dream of attributing to the hand of John R. Searle.

I had, first of all, to resist the temptation of contenting myself with a commentary (in the American sense) on the thing. I say thing because I don't know how to name it. What kind of a performance is it, if it is one? The whole debate might boil down to the question: does John R. Searle "sign" his reply? Does he make use of his right to reply? Of his rights as author? But what makes him think that these rights might be questioned, that someone might try to steal them from him, or that there could be any mistake concerning the attribution of his original production? How would this be possible? Can the thing be expropriated, alienated? Would anyone dream of countersigning or counterfeiting his signature? Why would anyone repeat this gesture and what would such repetition signify? Why should or would it remain outside of the text, above the title or below the "normal" boundary of the page? What of all the relations involved in the legal and political context of the "copyright," including the complexity of its system and of its history? Why are copyright utterences making a serious claim at truth? Had I asserted a copyright, "for saying things that are obviously false," there could have been no doubt as to its appropriateness. But that John R. Searle should be so concerned with his copyright, for saying things that are obviously true, gives one pause to reflect upon the truth of the copyright and the copyright of the truth.

Might it not be sufficient to repeat *this*

" "*Copyright* © *1977 by John R. Searle*" "

in order to reconstitute, slowly but ineluctably, all the pieces of this "improbable" debate?

What is the infelicity of this—I mean, of Searle's seal? It resides in the fact that if Searle speaks the truth when he claims to be speaking the truth, the obviously true, then the copyright is irrelevant and devoid of interest: everyone will be able, will in advance *have been able*, to reproduce what he says. Searle's seal is stolen in advance. Hence, the anxiety and compulsion to stamp and to seal the truth. On the other hand, however, if Searle had the vague feeling that what he was saying was not obviously true, and that it was not obvious to everyone, then he would attempt passionately, but no less superfluously, to preserve this originality, to the point of provoking the suspicion, by virtue of his repeated and thus divided seal, that his confidence in the truth he claims to possess is a poor front for considerable uneasiness. Divided seal—is, as you can verify, a citation from *Signature Event Context* ("it . . . divides its seal," p. 194), from the section that plays with signatures and proper names.

Would it not be sufficient to repeat *this*

" " "*Copyright* © *1977 by John R. Searle*" " "

in order to reconstitute, gradually but inexorably, all the pieces of this most improbable debate?

I have just said *this* in order to avoid the imprudence and haste that would be implied in calling an event such as this seal a speech act. Is it a signature? If it were a speech act, what would be its structure, its illo- or perlocutionary force, etc.? And, of course, how can I be absolutely sure that John R. Searle himself (who is it?) is in fact the author? Perhaps it is a member of his family, his secretary, his lawyer, his financial advisor, the "managing editor" of the journal, a joker or a namesake?

Or even D. Searle (who is it?), to whom John R. Searle acknowledges his indebtedness: "I am indebted to H. Dreyfus and D. Searle for discussion of these matters." This is the first note of the *Reply.* Its acknowledgement of indebtedness does not simply fit into the series of four footnotes since its appeal is located not in the text but in the title,

on the boundary, and is directed, curiously enough, at my name—
"*Reply to Derrida*[1]"—

If John R. Searle owes a debt to D. Searle concerning this discussion, then the "true" copyright ought to belong (as is indeed suggested along the frame of this *tableau vivant*) to a Searle who is divided, multiplied, conjugated, shared. What a complicated signature! And one that becomes even more complex when the debt includes my old friend, H. Dreyfus, with whom I myself have worked, discussed, exchanged ideas, so that if it is indeed through him that the Searles have "read" me, "understood" me, and "replied" to me, then I, too, can claim a stake in the "action" or "obligation," the stocks and bonds, of this holding company, the Copyright Trust. And it is true that I have occasionally had the feeling—to which I shall return—of having almost "*dictated*" this reply. "I" therefore feel obliged to claim my share of the copyright of the *Reply*.

But who, me?

e

Who, me?

Among the many elements (and they are too numerous to count) neglected by the "authors" (three + n) of the "Reply to Derrida[1]", there is at the very least this one: the "signature" of *Signature Event Context*. Or rather, the *signatures*, since it can hardly have escaped the attention of anyone that there are a great number of them and that they are curiously situated on the lower edge (within? without?) of a section entitled, precisely, *Signatures*. A great number, of varying types, which seem to cite themselves (can a signature be cited, and if so, what are the consequences?) and to constitute the *objects* of the study, the themes and examples of an analysis, no less than the seal of the analyst. Who signed *Signature Event Context*? And what if the plural subtitle, "Signatures," were to signal not only the multiplication of the signature, which takes place at the end of the text, but also that, situated *within* the text as its "object," the signature no longer simply signs, even though it does still sign, being neither entirely in the text nor entirely outside, but rather *on the edge*? Who shall decide? And if one takes into account that the end of *Signature Event Context* is also the end of the book—the book entitled *Marges*, I mean to say—the entire context of this question necessarily expands beyond the article *which* our three + n authors have extracted [*prélevé*] and *from which* they have extracted. This context is further expanded and complicated by the fact that the *same* operation is repeated *elsewhere* in *other* books that I have pretended to sign, for instance *L'écriture et la différence*, or *Glas*.

Who signed *Signature Event Context*? And who *counterfeited* the signature in a *Remark* between parentheses and in the margin (". . . That dispatch should thus have been signed. Which I do, and counterfeit, here. Where? There. J.D.")? Furthermore: can signatory and author be identified? And even if they can (pure hypothesis), is the signature identical with the writing, that is the *mention*, of a proper name at the bottom of a text? Where is the boundary, in this case, between *mention* and *use*? And is the proper name to be identified with the patronym (including first names or initials) registered in the official records? I abandon here these questions which, let it be mentioned in passing, I have attempted to treat elsewhere, in another fashion. To remain with the "signature" of *Signature Event Context*, the "*Reply to Derrida¹*" seems to take it for granted, as though it were as clear and as certain as a copyright guaranteed by international *conventions* (up to a certain point, that is, and of relatively recent date). If, on the contrary, I recall and insist on the fact that none of this is either simple or certain, it is because these questions are not extraneous to our debate. Indeed, both common sense and traditional philosophy would say that they comprise the "central" "object" of the "apparent" "debate" between "Searle" and "me."

As the effect of an operation that can be considered *more or less* deliberate, intentional, conscious, fictional, ironic; between *use* and *mention*, undecided between citation and non-citation, *Signature Event Context* seems to conclude—apart from a *Remark* between parentheses, about which it would be difficult to know if it is in the text or outside of it—with "my" signature, handwritten (and hence, one might say, authentic), reauthenticated on several occasions by my initials in the margin (called paraph in the contractual code), and by "my" "proper name," in its official, that is conventional, form.

But: 1. The remark says that "I" (who?) "counterfeit" what I say that "I did," and this implies that I re-do (citing my signature: but can a signature be cited?) and "imitate" with a view towards deceiving (which in French, as in English, is the predominant meaning of "counterfeit" [*contrefaire*]). Naturally, the J.D. that claims to guarantee the identity of the "I" and of the signatory is itself guaranteed by nothing but the *presumed* authenticity of the handwritten signature. The latter, however, is explicitly designated as being "counterfeit" and it is reproduced, typo-photographically, in thousands of copies. Searle *himself* could easily imitate it.

2. The author of *Speech Acts* needs no lessons from me concerning the difference between mentioning one's name and using it in a signature. To write one's proper name is not the same as signing (although the American use of the signature makes it difficult to differentiate

graphically between it and the writing of one's name. If I write my name at the bottom of a check, it will not have the value qua mention that it will have on the card that I fill out in an airplane or a hotel).

3. I shall not, here at least, enter into the many supplementary complications arising from the publication of *Signature Event Context* in a book, multiplying the reproduction of my signature, then in translations: can a proper name be translated? Or a signature? And how do the "common," "generic" elements, which always exist even in a proper name, withstand contamination in and by foreign languages? In order to account for all sorts of necessities which I cannot go into here, I have, in other texts, devised countless games, playing with "my name," with the letters and syllables *Ja, Der, Da.* Is my name still "proper," or my signature, when, in proximity to "There. J.D." (pronounced, in French, approximately Der. J.D.), in proximity to "Wo? Da." in German, to "Her. J.D." in Danish, they begin to function as integral or fragmented entities [*corps*], or as whole segments of common nouns or even of things? Thus, without getting into such supplementary cases of parasitism (when and where did they begin?), which repeat and deport an allegedly original "event" that is itself divided and multiple (as with an oral communication preceded by a written text, dealing with the theme of communication, chosen for a colloquium said to be philosophical—a context that the three + n authors entirely ignore), I will settle for posing a question concerning the signature, "properly" handwritten, and which, in *Signature Event Context*, is called "improbable": *improbable*, i.e. having little chance of coming to pass *and* in any case impossible to prove. This word, "improbable," which the reader has already encountered above ("improbable debate") was therefore a clandestine citation. Now, this is my question: what happens, what will happen as far as the three + n authors of the *Reply* are concerned, if I tell them (where? "here") this: I am prepared to swear that this signature is not from *my hand.* I am not speaking here of its multiplication in thousands of printed "copies," nor of the capitalized proper name that supports it, rendering it legible and capable of being authenticated, nor of the infinitely complex relations in which they are involved, but rather of the "first," handwritten instance of the form " $\mathcal{J}.$ *Derrida.* ," the reproduction of which can be read "here." Will one contend that in this case, "my" signature will have been "imitated"? But by whom? For I imitate and reproduce my "own" signature incessantly. This signature is imitable in its essence. And always has been. In French one would say that *elle s'imite*, a syntactical equivocation that seems to me difficult to reproduce: it can *be* imitated, and it imitates *itself.* This is all that I ask my inter-

locutors to acknowledge. And yet, as we shall see shortly, the consequences of this very simple fact are *unlimited* and *unlimitable*.

I should have to dwell on this question at length to do it justice, but among the many contextual constraints weighing upon us there is that—economical in nature—which concerns the spatial limits (despite the generous hospitality of *Glyph*, which nonetheless has its own interest in inviting such parasites to its table) as well as the temporal ones (the time that I can devote to this long, transcontinental correspondence, and above all that which we can decently demand from the readers). What I wished to mark with this allegedly false-start was, first of all, that this *other hand*, perhaps, and none other, dictated the *Reply* to the three + n authors. I will return to this. Second, that the question of the "copyright," despite or because of its marginal or extra-textual place (but one which is never simply anywhere, since, were the © absolutely detached, it would lose all value), should no longer be evaded, in any of its aspects, be they legal, economical, political, ethical, phantasmatic, or libidinal [*pulsionnel*], etc. Third, that the word "improbable," in the first (French) version of the text, which was published *without* the handwritten signature in the Proceedings of the Colloquium (*La communication*, Montréal, 1973), is the next to the last word of the text. The last one, which is not my signature, is "signature": "the most improbable signature." And finally, that confronted by a *Reply* which exudes such confidence in the possibility of distinguishing "standard" from "non-standard," "serious" from "non-serious," "normal" from "abnormal," "citation" from "non-citation," "void" from "non-void," "literal" from "metaphoric," "parasitical" from "non-parasitical" etc.,—faced with a *Reply* so serenely dogmatic in regard to the intention and the origin of an utterance or of a signature, I wanted, before all "serious" argument, to suggest that the terrain is slippery and shifting, mined and undermined. And that this ground is, by essence, an underground.

f

Let's be serious.

Faced with this speech act ("let's be serious"), readers may perhaps feel authorized in believing that the presumed signatory of this text is only now beginning to be serious, only now committing himself to a philosophical discussion worthy of the name, and is thus admitting that what he has previously been engaged in was something entirely different.

But let's be serious. Why am I having such difficulty being serious in this debate, in which I have been invited, in turn, to take part? Why did I take such pleasure in accepting this invitation? Nothing compelled me to accept, and I could have yielded to the temptation of suggesting to interested readers that they simply reread *Signature Event Context* instead of obliging myself to comment or to repeat myself more than once. Where does the pleasure I take in this repetition, in prolonging the debate, or rather the "confrontation" come from? I have just cited the *Reply*. The word "confrontation" appears twice in the first paragraph, once in each sentence, the second stating that—*at (and in the) present* [*au présent*]—"the confrontation" between Austin and myself "never quite takes place." Is it because the confrontation never quite takes place that I take such lasting pleasure in it? Because I, too, think as much, almost that is, almost but not quite? Or is it, on the contrary, because I am very excited, I confess, by this scene? By the speech acts of the *Reply*, by their structure composed of denial, seduction, coquettishly fascinating underneath the viril candor, initiating a "confrontation" by saying that it has not taken place and, moreover, that *at (and in the) present*, between the late Austin and myself, *it does not take place*, or at least not entirely, *not quite*, both because I have missed the point, missed him, and because he was already dead ("a theory that Austin did not live long enough to develop himself"!) when I missed him, so that in fact I did not have much of a chance. The speech acts of the *Reply* do their utmost, apparently, to insure that this confrontation will not have taken place and moreover, that it shall not (ever) take place, or at least not quite; and yet they produce it, this confrontation that they sought to avoid, that they declare to be non-existent without being able to stop themselves from participating in it, from confirming and developing the event through the very gesture of withdrawing from it. But, it might be enjoined, it is the confrontation Austin-Derrida that is meant when the *Reply* states that it "never quite takes place." And if there is a confrontation, is it not provoked by the three + n authors of the *Reply*, who present themselves in the guise of Austin's legitimate heirs, bearing their heritage to fruition in the "general theory of speech acts" promised by the Oxford professor of moral philosophy, but which fate left to his American progeny, in the promised land, to fulfill. But would they have provoked this confrontation had it not already, in some manner, taken place? Yet, what does it mean for a "confrontation" of this type to take place (where? when? up to what point?)? And whoever claimed to be looking for a "confrontation" in the first place, in the sense of a face-to-face clash, declared, involving two identifiable interlocutors or adversaries, two "discourses" that would be identical with themselves and localizable?

This "never quite takes place," deported a bit beyond its initial, head-over-heels aggressivity (Derrida never encountered Austin and would not have encountered him even had Austin been still alive!) is one of the gayest things I have ever read in a text that presents itself as being, if not philosophical, at least theoretical, and in any event as serious: seriously supposing itself to know all about the difference between the serious and the non-serious, to know what it means for events taking the form of apparently written speech acts to take place or not to take place (where do writings take place?), writings whose presumed authors have never met each other but which circulate sufficiently to put us in the position we are in today, rereading them (how is this possible?), commenting on them, citing, questioning, translating, interpreting, while one of the participants, who died too young even to know of the debate, is represented, without his knowledge and without ever having given his consent (in a serious and "strict" sense), by a more or less anonymous company or corporation [*par une société plus ou moins anonyme*] (three + n authors) asserting the legitimacy of their lineage and sure of knowing what those "prominent philosophical traditions" are, and where they are.

Why did I say "société plus ou moins anonyme," "a more or less anonymous company or corporation"? The expression "three + n authors" seems to me to be more rigorous for the reasons I have already stated, involving the difficulty I encounter in naming the definite origin, the true person responsible for the *Reply*: not only because of the debts acknowledged by John R. Searle *before even* beginning to reply, but because of the entire, more or less anonymous tradition of a code, a heritage, a reservoir of arguments to which both he and I are indebted. How is this more or less anonymous company to be named? In order to avoid the ponderousness of the scientific expression "three + n authors," I decide here and from this moment on to give the presumed and collective author of the *Reply* the French name "Société à responsabilité limitée"—literally, "Society with Limited Responsibility" (or Limited Liability)—which is normally abbreviated to *Sarl*. I ask that the translator leave this conventional expression in French and if necessary, that he explain things in a note. If this expression does not simply translate "Limited," "Incorporated," or "Limited Inc," it is not unrelated to those terms, for it pertains to the same legal-commercial context. I hope that the bearers of proper names will not be wounded by this technical or scientific device. For it will have the supplementary advantage of enabling me to avoid offending individuals or proper names in the course of an argument that they might now and then consider, wrongly, to be polemical. And should they, perchance, see this transformation as an injurious or ironic alteration, they can at least join me in acknowledging the importance of the desires and fantasms that are at stake in a proper name, a copyright, or a signature. And, after all, isn't this the very question which, posed by *Signature Event Context*, will have involved us in this improbable confrontation? It is as a reminder of this, and not to draw the body of his name into my language by subtracting one *r* and two *e*'s, that I thus break Searle's seal (itself already fragmented or divided).

The gayest thing that Sarl has written, in the "never quite takes place," is "never quite." For this slightly too scrupulous nuance, if I haven't misunderstood it, opens a space for the very thing that should not, should never have taken place; thus, I get my foot in the door. Indeed, it has long since slipped in, and at bottom Sarl may not quite want me to pull it back, at least not too quickly. Or rather, Sarl's wishes in this regard seem rather paradoxical, caught in a kind of double bind, impelled to do everything to keep my foot there, to prolong the scene. To make it last, or at least, take place. What the *Reply* never takes into account is that the most insistent question in *Sec* (I suggest this as an abbreviation for *Signature Event Context*)[1] seeks to discover what an event—which, in the case of a speech act, is supposed to take place— might be, and whether or not the structure of such an event leaves room for certitude or for evidence. But we will have ample occasion to return to this point.

g

For Sarl—or the self-made, auto-authorized heirs of Austin—the confrontation "never quite takes place." How can they tell? Is it because the "central theses in Austin's theory of language" have been miscon- strued? Or because Sec has "misunderstood and misstated Austin's posi- tion at several crucial points"? Let us suppose, for a moment, that this is true, simply true. I would like to pose, then, the following question: if a misunderstanding (for example, of Austin's theses) is possible, if a *mis*- in general ("mistake," "misunderstanding," "misinterpretation," "mis- statement," to mention only those included in Sarl's list of accusations, from the first paragraph on) is possible, what does that imply concern- ing the structure of speech acts in general? And in particular, what does this possibility imply for Austin's, Sarl's or for "my own" speech acts, since, for an instant at least, in a passing phrase, this latter case is apparently not excluded entirely ("it is possible that I may have misin- terpreted him as profoundly as I believe he has misinterpreted Austin")? And if the supposed misunderstanding were of such a nature (if not of such a design [*destination*]) so as to leave the auto-authorized heirs of Austin no choice but to involve themselves—passionately, precipitately —in a "confrontation" that they claim "never quite takes place," what would all that imply? What is taking place at this very moment, right here? "Where? There." Let us not exclude the possibility that the "confrontation" that so fascinates Sarl may indeed not have taken place and that it may be destined never to take place: but what, then, of this destiny and of this destination? And what is going on "here and now"? I shall not answer this question, but there can be no doubt that it is the event of this question that interests me and makes me (but why?) so light-hearted and gay.

What I like about this "confrontation" is that I don't know if it is quite taking place, if it ever will be able, or will have been able, quite, to take place; or if it does, between whom or what. Evidently, John R. Searle and "myself" do not sign here, or speak for ourselves. We are nothing more than "prête-noms," "borrowed names," straw men. In this simulated confrontation, we are "fronts": I like this word, which I encountered in the film of Woody Allen[2] dealing with events dating from the era of McCarthyism, and where I learned that it signified "prête-nom," mask, substitute for a clandestine subject. But these "fronts" do not, as Sarl suggests, represent "two prominent philosophical traditions." Because, if there is only one sentence of the *Reply* to which I can subscribe, it is the first ("It would be a mistake, I think, to regard Derrida's discussion of Austin as a confrontation between two prominent philosophical traditions"), although for reasons other than those of Sarl. I know of no one, aside from Sarl, who could have formed such an hypothesis. Nor do I know why it was formed. For I, too, consider it quite false, though for different reasons. Among the many reasons that make me unqualified to represent a "prominent philosophical tradition," there is this one: I consider myself to be in many respects quite close to Austin, both interested in and indebted to his problematic. This is said in *Sec*, very clearly; Sarl forgets to mention it. Above all, however, when I do raise questions or objections, it is always at points where I recognize in Austin's theory presuppositions which are the most tenacious and the most central presuppositions of the *continental* metaphysical tradition. I will return to this in an instant. Moreover, what these "fronts" represent, what weighs upon them both, transcending this curious chiasmus, are forces of a non-philosophical nature. They will have to be analyzed one day. Here, within the limits of this discussion, such an analysis is impossible, but the forces that exceed those limits are already implicated, even here.

I like this improbable confrontation just as others like voyages and diplomacy. There are interpreters everywhere. Each speaking his language, even if he has some knowledge of the language of the other. The interpreter's ruses have an open field and he does not forget his own interests. Most of the authors of the *Reply*, if they have read *Sec* in their fashion, do not know me either personally or, obviously, through any of the other texts that form the context of *Sec* and endow it with a certain meaning. To a certain degree, the inverse is also true. *Sec* has apparently been read, and is generally cited in English (we shall mention certain consequences of this) within a *Reply* written in English. I have read it in English but I am trying to respond in French, although my French will be marked in advance by English and destined in advance for a translation that will doubtless present certain difficulties. These problems (re-production, iterability, citation, translation, interpretation, multiplicity of codes and of parasitisms) constitute the most apparent aspect of what is at stake in this so-called "confrontation." And it will have taken place (yes or no?) on a terrain whose neutrality is far from certain, in a publication and at the initiative of professors who for the most part are Americans (more or less), but who, in their work and in their projects are second to none in their knowledge of migrations and wanderings [*déplacements*]. Their position, in terms of the political significance of the university, is highly original and their rôle in this debate, whether it takes place or not, decisive. This, for me, comprises the most interesting and most important aspect of the situation. Since I will not be able, here, even to outline an analysis of all this, let me say the following: that which is not quite taking place, seems to be occurring—to take geographical bearings in an area that disrupts all cartography—mid-way between California and Europe, a bit like the Channel, mid-way between Oxford and Paris. But the topology of these "fronts" and the logic of its places will have more than one surprise in store for us. For example: isn't Sarl ultimately more continental and Parisian than I am? I shall try to show why. Sarl's premises and method are derived from continental philosophy, and in one form or another they are very present in France. If I may cite myself, for the last time referring to a text other than *Sec* (hereafter I will restrict myself to the latter essay), this is what I wrote in "Avoir l'oreille de la philosophie" [To Have the Ear of Philosophy] (see footnote 1): "*Signature Event Context* analyses the metaphysical premises of the Anglo-Saxon—and fundamentally moralistic—theory of the performative, of speech acts or discursive events. In France, it seems to me that these premises underlie the hermeneutics of Ricoeur and the archaeology of Foucault."

h

Let's be serious. I am going to try to engage myself in this confrontation without excessively prolonging the pleasure of the threshold [*limen*]. But for the sake of the record, I would still like to hazard two hypotheses. Two *types* of hypothesis. For reasons of economy, I will limit myself to underscoring the type. The interested reader can, if he wishes, multiply hypotheses of the same type.

The first type I shall baptize *set*. In French, *ensemble*, as in *théorie des ensembles*, set theory. And I say this: if this "particular debate" should develop further, the set of texts that will have been part of it (for example, *Sec*, Sarl's *Reply*, *Limited Inc*—but the list is not limitable either in the past or in the future) will have been not so much theoretical discourses ("constative" or "descriptive") dealing with the question of speech acts, of the performative, of illocutionary or perlocutionary acts, of iterability, of citation, of writing, speech or signature, etc.; nor will they have been discourses dominating the *ensemble* of this field and stating the truth about it. Rather, they will have constituted elements of that *ensemble*, parts of an open corpus, *examples* of events, to which all the questions and categories accredited by the theory of speech acts will still be applicable and reapplicable: whether or not they are performatives, in what measure and aspect they depend upon the per- or illocutionary, whether they are serious or not, normal or not, void or not, parasitic or not, fictional or not, citational or not, literary, philosophical, theatrical, oratorical, prophetical or not, etc. But my hypothesis does not concern all the pleasure (or pain) that one can wish to anyone who wants to attempt such analyses. Rather it concerns the essentially *interminable* character of such an analysis. For the latter will still form a part of the ensemble and will therefore raise the same questions. It will necessarily be what I will here call—parodying a French expression and challenging the translator-interpreter not to abandon at once [*aussi sec*] a copyright—a *prise de partie*, that is: *partial*. It will always be lacking the completeness of a set.

i

The second type I shall call *mis*, mistype if you like. The *Reply* teems with evaluative decrees involving *mis*. They are situated beyond, around, beneath utterances that are apparently constative, but which through their gesture of "this is so and so" tend to produce determinate effects, often quite different from those apparently intended. I shall take only one example, the first paragraph of the *Reply*. In the citation I am about to make, I shall underline all the decrees in *mis* (or related meanings). They deliver the conclusions before the demonstration has taken place, putting the reader in the proper state of mind, setting the tone or the stage, and generally aiming to produce certain effects. I shall therefore underline certain words or word-fragments (what happens when, in a citation, certain word-fragments are underlined? Does it still constitute a case of "citing," of "using," or "mentioning"?): "It would be a *mis*take, I think, to regard Derrida's discussion of Austin as a confrontation between two prominent philosophical traditions. This is not so much because Derrida has *failed* to discuss the central theses in Austin's theory of language, but rather because he has *mis*understood and *mis*stated Austin's position at several *crucial* points, as I shall attempt to show, and thus the confrontation *never* quite takes place."

I have cited at length and shall continue to, so the reader is now forewarned. I shall do so, first of all, because it gives me pleasure that I would not like to miss, even though it may be deemed perverse: a certain practice of citation, and also of iteration (which, despite what Sarl asserts, was never confused with citation, as we shall verify) is at work, constantly *altering*, at once and without delay—*aussi sec*, including *Sec*—whatever it seems to reproduce. This is one of the theses of *Sec*. Iteration alters, something new takes place. For example, here the *mis* takes place; and to account for the possibility of such *mis*ses in general is, to put it still in Sarl's code, the *crux*, the *crucial* difficulty of the theory of speech acts. Furthermore, I shall cite at length in order to limit the confusion, the denials or the selective simplifications which it seems to me the *Reply* has introduced into the debate. This may help to increase the rigor of the discussion. Finally, the citational and (more generally) iterative corpus that constitutes the object of discussion will thereby be augmented and enriched.

The overture in *mis* will have set the tone. This is then incessantly replayed throughout the *Reply*, with an insistence and a compulsive force that can hardly be simply external to the contents of the argumentation. It is as though it were imperative to recall all the *mis*takes, *mis*understandings, *mis*statements, etc. all the more loudly, nervously, regularly, to denounce and to *name* them all the more frequently, because at bottom they are not quite as evident as all that: there is always the danger of their being forgotten. It is to remind us of this less-than-evident evidence that the word *obvious, obviously* (as in "obviously false," p. 203) is so often invoked, as though to nip any doubt in the bud. But the effect produced is the reverse. For my part, wherever and whenever I hear the words "it's true," "it's false," "it's evident," "evidently this or that," or "in a fairly obvious way" (p. 204), I become suspicious. This is especially so when an adverb, apparently redundant, is used to reinforce the declaration. Like a warning light, it signals an uneasiness that demands to be followed up. Even without taking into account the fact that, given the great serenity which marks his understanding of the value of evidence, Sarl should have been able to remark that the notion of evidence, together with its entire system of associated

Jacques Derrida

values (presence, truth, immediate intuition, assured certitude, etc.), is precisely what *Sec* is calling into question, and that this is exemplified in the element of writing, in the narrow, if not "strict" sense of the word.

For those who may have forgotten, here are some of the reverberations, echoing interminably, of the peremptory evaluations of the first paragraph: ". . . *what is wrong* with these arguments . . ." (p. 199); "Derrida has a *distressing* penchant for saying things that are *obviously false*" (p. 203); . . . "he has *mis*understood Austin in several *crucial* ways [crucial *ways* this time, after "crucial *points*"] and the internal weaknesses in his arguments are closely tied to these *mis*understandings. In this section therefore I will *very briefly summarize* his critique and then simply list the *major mis*understandings and *mis*takes" (p. 203); . . . "Derrida's Austin is *un*recognizable. He bears *almost* [!] no relation to the original" (p. 204); "Related to the first *mis*understanding . . . is a *mis*understanding . . ." (p. 205); ". . . what is *more than simply a mis*reading . . ." (p. 206).

I would have liked to quiet my suspicions in order to enjoy such candor unreservedly. Loyalty and the absence of simulation are so rare in French-language polemics, which are characterized by the use of elision, ellipsis, self-censorship and a strategy that is both artful and indirect. Why did I not succeed? This is just what I shall endeavor to explain.

Among all the adverbial locutions that I have just underlined, whose curious functions may be analyzed at one's leisure, one in particular deserves to become proverbial and I shall indulge myself by citing it once again: ". . . *more than simply a mis*reading . . ."! More than simply a mis-; what might that involve? Where will it lead us? Let us be patient a little while longer.

j

And among all the effects produced, if not intended, I shall for the moment retain only this one, abbreviated for the sake of time, to the hypothesis in [the key of] *mis* (and in more than simply a mis-). This is only one of the effects produced on me.

Listening, with a certain ear, to this percussion in *mis-major*, I have the impression that, despite all appearances to the contrary which I will deal with later on, Sarl has, in fact, very well understood the *Sec*-effect. How else can his passionate and exacerbated struggle to combat arguments that are "obviously false," "major misunderstandings," etc. be explained? How was he capable of replying so seriously to such unserious aberrations? Or even of recognizing an Austin so unrecognizable as to bear *almost* no relation to the original, i.e. an Austin who is never *quite* himself. And how, in view of all this, was he able to find his bearings and himself [*s'y reconnaître*].

Thus, Sarl did indeed understand. No question here of the essentials being misunderstood. Or rather, if "understanding" is still a notion dominated by the allegedly constative regime of theory or of philosophy, let us not use the word "understood," let us say instead that Sarl was touched. That is, Sarl has not been missed by the set, the ensemble of these misunderstandings, of these misstating missiles. In the family of Latin languages, a speech act, whether written or spoken, is only said to be *pertinent* when it touches: the object to which it seems to refer, but also—why not?—someone, its addressee, upon whom it produces certain effects, let us say of a perlocutionary sort. Thus, in analyzing the violence and the type of evaluative reactions, I had the impression that *Sec* had touched the mark, right in the middle, as it were. If I said that Searle himself had been touched, I would be going out on a limb. For it may very well be not Searle himself, as a whole, or even in part, but in the final analysis a "front," something making its way beneath Searle's more or less indebted or mortgaged signature; something identifying itself so much with Austin that it can only read *Sec* feverishly, unable to support the fact that questions might be posed serenely concerning the limits or the presuppositions of Austin's theory. Or at least unable to tolerate this when it is done by *others*. It is this last feature that I find most interesting: what characterizes a self-proclaimed heir (especially when the father has died too young, at the age of 48!) is the fact that, doubting his own legitimacy, he wishes to be the only one to inherit and even the only one, in a *tête à tête*, to break, now and then, the filial bond of identification, in what is here the height of identification; he alone shall have the right of criticizing or correcting his teacher, defending him before the others at the very moment of murderous identification, of parricide. All this is familiar in philosophy and, mutatis mutandis, has been ever since the *Sophist*; also, ever since the Sophists, and no one will be astonished when I observe that they haunt our present debate, as more than one sign shall indicate. Thus, Sarl would like to be Austin's sole legitimate heir *and* his sole critic: "I should point out that I hold no brief for the details of Austin's theory of speech acts, I have criticized it elsewhere and will not repeat those criticisms here" (p. 204). And forgetting what is demonstrated in *Sec*, namely, that the question of detail is not always a question of detail, Sarl refers several times to articles of J. R. Searle, which, dating from 1975, could not have been taken into account by *Sec* (1971). And yet, knowing me as I do, I would not have escaped a certain sense of guilt here, especially had I been able to anticipate clearly that this trajectory would end by touching Sarl and by impeding the procedure of inheritance and of legitimation. This is why shortly, indeed as soon as possible, I shall incorporate these most recent publications of J. R. Searle into the dossier of this discussion.

How, therefore, will it be possible, from now on, to know just exactly *which* Searle *Sec* has failed to miss? I therefore prefer, out of prudence but also out of courtesy, to endeavor to respond—not reply— to Sarl. Who knows whether J. R. Searle is more dogmatic than Austin in handling with such assurance the obviousness of the true and the false or the wrong? Sarl, however, *is*. *Sec* begins by insisting on those aspects of Austin's analysis that it describes as "patient," "open," in "constant transformation"; and also, by insisting, among other claims to our inter- est, upon the fact that "Austin was obliged to free the analysis of the performative from the authority of the truth *value*, from the true/false opposition,[5] at least in its classical form, and to substitute for it at times the value of force, of difference of force (*illocutionary* or *perlocutionary force*). (In this line of thought, which is nothing less than Nietzschean, this in particular strikes me as moving in the direction of Nietzsche himself, who often acknowledged a certain affinity for a vein of English thought.)" "5. '. . . two fetishes which I admit to an inclination to play Old Harry with, viz. (1) the true/false fetish, (2) the value/fact fetish.' "

Things are, of course, more complicated. *Sec* takes this supplemen- tary complication into account, in differentiating remarks that seem to have escaped Sarl's attention; one such is the observation, at the bottom of the same page, which might have served as the sign of a prudent and discriminating reading: "As a result, performative communication be- comes once more the communication of an intentional meaning."[7]

"7. Which occasionally requires Austin to reintroduce the criterion of truth in his description of performatives. Cf. for example, pp. 50–52 and pp. 89–90."

k

Instead of precipitously, in the name of truth, hurrying on to sen- tences (in the French—but also English—sense of the word: to the verdicts, the decrees of justice, even to the condemnations) on the wrong or false, or the "obviously false," a theoretican of speech acts who was even moderately consistent with his theory ought to have spent some time patiently considering questions of this type: Does the prin- cipal purpose of *Sec* consist in being *true*? In appearing true? In stating the truth?

And what if *Sec* were *doing something else*?

What? All right, some examples: 1. Saying something apparently "false" (the economical and limited hypothesis of Sarl, designed to incorporate the thing), or something dubious, but presenting it in a manner, form, and shape which (full of traps and parasitical in nature) would increase the chances of the debate getting started; and rendering it inevitable that the auto-authorized descendants of "prominent" philosophical traditions could not but reply, would be obliged to reply (a case anticipated by Austin), even if they did not; or, growing angry, would say whatever came to mind, or else very determinate things which would then set the stage for the confrontation they would have always hoped "never quite takes place." Or else, 2. Proposing a text, as is again here the case, a writing and signatures, whose *performance* (structure, event, context, etc.) defines at every moment the oppositions of concepts or of values, the rigor of those oppositional limits that speech act theory endorses by virtue of its very axiomatics; offering the performance of a text which, by raising in passing the question of truth (beyond Austin's intermittent impulses in this direction) does not *simply* succumb to its jurisdiction and remains, at this point, qua textual performance, irreducible to "verdictive" (as Austin might say) sentences of the type: this is true, this is false, "completely mistaken" or "obviously false." "More than simply a misreading," an expression of which I am particularly fond, would be a better description of the operation of *Sec*, on the condition, however—but isn't this always possible? and this is precisely my question—that it is made into a misreading of sorts, or into "more than simply a misreading" with regard to what can be presumed to be the true intention of Sarl. Can one deny what I have just said in 2? How is it possible to miss the point that *Sec*, from one end to the other, is concerned with the question of truth, with the system of values associated with it, repeating *and* altering that system, dividing and displacing it in accordance with the logical force of the *iter*, which "ties repetition to alterity" (*Sec*).

One could continue in this vein for quite some time. Here, however, I shall interrupt, decisively, these two series of preliminary [*protocolaires*] hypotheses, *set* and *mis*. For if *Sec* caused a more or less anonymous company of readers, of whom I was not then thinking, to lose their patience, I would not want to become a cause of impatience to those readers of whom I am thinking today, nor to the translator, who is a friend. I shall endeavor, therefore, to address myself now to what is at stake in this debate, and to do this in a manner as normal and serious, as strict, brief, and direct as possible, while reducing the parasitism as much as I can. You can take my word for it.

However, precisely in order to clarify the discussion, I shall have to adopt certain technical procedures and propose several conventions.

Jacques Derrida

Naturally, the reader or interlocutor, whom I have neither the means nor the desire to consult on this matter, can always decide not to subscribe and even to interrupt his reading at this point. But in proposing conventions that I deem to be *reasonable*, haven't I already consulted and involved him a bit, inasmuch as I impute a certain degree of reason to him, and even a certain amount of good faith? All this remains forever in doubt.

My first technical convention: concerned to spare Sarl and possible readers the trouble of having to read or reread other texts of mine, I shall make reference only to *Sec*, the sole essay which, according to the implications of the convention, has been read and discussed by Sarl, and the sole, as we now know, to carry, among other signatures, "my own," and that more than once, in an authentic *facsimile*. But naturally, armed with this same convention (Sarl is understood to have read this text), I shall take the liberty of referring to the quasi-totality of this essay, *Sec*, and not, as Sarl has done, only to those passages that are deemed to be "the most important" ("I will concentrate on those [points] that seem to me to [be] the most important and especially on those where I disagree with his conclusion"). As we shall see, these "important" points are hardly separable from a good many others, with which they form a systematic chain of a singular type. On the other hand, as one will have already noticed, I do not "concentrate," in my reading (for instance, of the *Reply*), either exclusively or primarily on those points that appear to be the most "important," "central," "crucial." Rather, I deconcentrate, and it is the secondary, eccentric, lateral, marginal, parasitic, borderline cases which are "important" to me and are a source of many things, such as pleasure, but also insight into the general functioning of a textual system. And were there to be a center to this debate, we would have reached it already, in the form of this difference in styles of reading. But what is involved is more than a difference in style.

Another technical convention: since the readers cannot be expected to remember the two texts verbatim, and yet no resumé will be adequate, I shall quote at length, as I already said, from *Sec* and from the *Reply*, in order, as far as possible, to avoid confusion, distortion, displacement, or biased selection.

But I will have to limit my arguments in number to eighteen. One of the conventions of this debate (and, says *Sec*, not the least determining, in the final analysis) is that it should take place, if it takes place, in a graphic element of a type that is phonetic, and more precisely, alphabetical. This is not without a certain arbitrariness. Its effect: henceforth I will have at my disposal only 18 letters or 18 blows and I will have to make the best of them. But, one will protest, is not this limit utterly contingent, artificial and external? Are we now going to integrate such fringes into the text, and take account of such frames? Are all these parasites to be incorporated into the *economy* of discourse? Must the surface of the paper, the contents of the time at our disposal, etc. all be integrated into our calculations? If so, what about the ink[3] remaining in my typewriter ribbon? And yet: why not? That is the question.

Finally, I give my word of honor that I shall be of good faith in my argument. I promise this in all sincerity and in all seriousness, literally, raising my hand above the typewriter.

I begin.

1

How is it possible to accept the procedure adopted by Sarl, from the paragraph beginning, "His paper [that is, *Sec*] divides naturally into two parts" (!?). With this (!?) I resort to a device that Austin wrongly (?) calls "very jejune;" but, after all, I am writing and I am more or less sure that these mute signs, these "rather crude" artifices will be understood.[4] And if Sarl's statement is difficult to accept, is it not because in each of its words it is "obviously false"? Even at the level of academic, external signs, *Sec* consists of *three* sections, not two, plus a preamble, an epilogue, a title, and signatures that are difficult to place; and none of all that is either superfluous or entirely fortuitous. Within each section—and each element—the "division," to say the least, can hardly be considered very "natural," and this holds no less for "his paper." Yet if I cannot endorse the statement, it is above all because the comfortable resumé that follows supports the convenient distinction between the "most important" and the rest. Even if we assume *Sec* to be a theoretical text claiming to speak the truth in a serious and systematic form, it would not constitute a juxtaposition of "points," of which some could be singled out at the expense of others. This is not merely a formal or procedural remark concerning the systemic or contextual implications of *Sec*. I shall try, shortly, to show that by ignoring this or that moment of the text he claims to be discussing, Sarl creates for himself a version of *Sec* which is easily domesticated since it is, after all, nothing but Sarl's own autistic representation. Would the reader care to have an initial, general, and massive idea of this? In this case, he can verify without difficulty that among the "points" totally omitted by Sarl are included all those involving

1. Signature
2. Event
3. Context

I don't know if this was because they were judged to be devoid of importance or whether it was because they were not the object of any disagreement ("I . . . will concentrate on those that seem to me to [be] the most important and especially on those where I disagree with his conclusion."), but in both cases, this monumentotal omission can hardly be without its consequences. No? Since Sarl does not devote a single word to signature, event, context, I ask the reader interested in this debate to consult *Signature Event Context*, which I do not want to cite or to mention in its entirety, so that he can judge for himself the effects of such serious negligence.

m

Having proposed a conveniently domesticated résumé of the opening pages of *Sec*, Sarl prepares, under the title *Writing, Permanence and Iterability*, "to get at what is wrong with these arguments." Imputing to *Sec* the intention of distinguishing between writing and speech, or even of opposing the two, he poses the question: "what is it exactly that distinguishes written from spoken language?" (p. 199). And, by evoking two hypotheses ("Is it iterability . . . ?" "Is it absence . . . ?") Sarl turns their respective rejection into an objection to *Sec*, or rather, to a certain reading of it. To appreciate fully the strangeness of this operation, it will suffice to reread it. For the moment, it is not yet necessary to reread *Sec* in its entirety. The easily digestible "Reader's Digest" which precedes it will do. This "digest" *itself* recalls that *Sec* generalized certain predicates usually attributed to writing in order to show that they are *also* valid for spoken language, and even beyond it. It is strange that, after having recalled that *Sec* analyzed the characteristics *common* both to writing and speech, the *objection* is made that, from the standpoint of iterability, there is no difference: precisely the thesis of *Sec*, if there is one! And it is no less strange when Sarl asks what it is that distinguishes written from oral language, as though such a distinction were required by *Sec*, and then answers: "Is it iterability, the repeatability of the linguistic elements? Clearly not. As Derrida is aware, any linguistic element written or spoken, indeed any rule-governed element in any system of representation at all must be repeatable . . ." (ibid.). Indeed, it is so "clear" and I am so "aware" of it, that this proposition is one of indispensable levers in the demonstration of *Sec*. This lever is explicitly posed as such from the very beginning. The demonstration of *Sec* moves in an area where the distinction between writing and speech loses all pertinence and where "every mark, including those which are oral," can be seen as being "a grapheme in general" (*Sec*, p. 183). How Sarl, citing this phrase on the very next page, can turn it into an objection to *Sec*, is a *mis*tery. If the simple argumentation of *Sec* is made into an *objection* to *Sec*, isn't it because, as I said earlier, that *other* hand, the one that signed *Sec* also dictated the *Reply* behind its back? But we are not yet done with this curious programmation of what, in French, I would call the *objection à-Sec*, and which, in English, might be rendered as *Sec dry up!* or also as the *Dried-out-objection*. However, for reasons of economy and of formalization, I shall refer to this simply as *from/to-Sec*, thus designating a gesture which recurs regularly in the *reply* and consists in taking arguments borrowed *from Sec* [*à Sec*], as though there were nowhere else to turn, and changing them into objections *to Sec* [*à Sec*]. With the other hand. Whence my perplexity at finding myself in this discussion often obliged to argue with a discourse moving *from/to Sec*, seeking to repeat against *Sec* what it has taken from *Sec*, or, in terms of the venerable fantasm of the *copyright*, what "belongs" *to* or stems *from Sec*. Would I have been spared this mistake or this mishap had I stamped each argument in advance with a ©? Concerning iterability, for instance: in reiterating what can be read on each page of *Sec*, re-plying or reapplying it, it is difficult to see how the *Reply* can object to it. Which does not, however, amount to saying that the consequences drawn from this iterability are, to be sure, the same here and there. In brief, since this scene seems destined to reproduce itself incessantly, you shall henceforth understand what I mean to say when I write: "discourse from/to-*Sec*" or "it reapplies" [*ça rapplique*]. The translator has my sympathy, but the difficulty of translation constitutes part of the demonstrandum.

n

And now, absence ("Is it iterability? Is it absence . . . ?").

"It reapplies" again, to and towards the "discourse from/to-*Sec*" although this time things are a bit more complicated. In order to treat this second point, Sarl begins *again* with the question disqualified by *Sec*, determining what distinguishes "written from spoken language." "Is it absence," asks the *Reply*, "the absence of the receiver from the sender? Again, clearly not. Writing makes it *possible* to communicate with an absent receiver, *but* it is not *necessary* for the receiver to be absent. Written communication can exist *in the presence* of the receiver, as for example, when I compose a shopping list for myself or pass notes to my companion during a concert or lecture" (ibid.). I have underlined the words "possible," "but," "necessary," "in the presence." The response is easy and clear. *Sec never said* that this absence is *necessary*, but only that it is *possible* (Sarl agrees) and that this possibility must therefore be taken into account: it pertains, *qua possibility*, to the structure of the mark as such, i.e., to the structure precisely of its iterability. And hence must not be excluded from the analysis of this structure. We need only reread *Sec*. We will find the words "possible," "possibility" innumerable times, but not even once the word "necessary." Even Sarl recalls this in the short initial resumé which, as convenient as it is, still cannot help but contradict itself by confusing possibility and necessity. Sarl writes that "the argument [that of *Sec*] is that since writing *can and must be able* to function in the radical absence of the sender, the receiver and the context of production. . . ." Again I have underlined. *Must be able*: to function in the absence of. . . . But this does not mean that it does, *in fact*, necessarily function in the absence of. . . . "Does one really have to point this out?" If I insist here, it is because this is indispensable to the demonstration and even to the minimal intelligibility of *Sec*. I repeat, therefore, since it can never be repeated too often: if one admits that writing (and the mark in general) *must be able* to function in the absence of the sender, the receiver, the context of production etc., that implies that this power, this *being able*, this *possibility* is *always* inscribed, hence *necessarily* inscribed *as possibility* in the functioning or the functional structure of the mark. Once the mark *is able* to function, once it is possible for it to function, once it is possible for it to function in case of an absence etc., it follows that this possibility is a *necessary* part of its structure, that the latter must *necessarily be such that* this functioning is possible; and hence, that this must be taken into account in any attempt to analyze or to describe, in terms of necessary laws, such a structure. Even if it is sometimes the case that the mark, in fact,· functions *in-the-presence-of*, this does not change the structural law in the slightest, one which above all implies that iterability admitted by Sarl. Such iterability is inseparable from the structural possibility in which it is necessarily inscribed. To object by citing cases where absence *appears in fact* not to be observable is like objecting that a mark is not essentially *iterable* because *here and there* it has not *in fact* been repeated.

But let's go a bit further. Does this kind of *fact* really exist? Where can we find it? How can we recognize it? Here we reach another type of analysis and of necessity. Isn't the (apparent) *fact* of the sender's or receiver's presence complicated, divided, contaminated, parasited by the *possibility of an absence* inasmuch as this possibility is necessarily inscribed in the functioning of the mark? This is the "logic," or rather, the "graphics" to which *Sec* seeks to do justice: As soon as [*aussi sec*] a possibility is essential and necessary, *qua possibility* (and even if it is the possibility of what is named, *negatively*, absence, "infelicity," parasitism, the non-serious, non-"standard," fictional, citational, ironical, etc.), it can no longer, either de facto or de jure, be bracketed, excluded, shunted aside, even temporarily, on allegedly methodological grounds. Inasmuch as it is essential and structural, this possibility is always at work marking *all the facts*, all the events, even those which appear to disguise it. Just as itera*bility*, which is not iteration, can be recognized even in a mark which *in fact* seems to have occurred only once. I say *seems*, because this one time is in itself divided or multiplied in advance by its structure of repeatability. This obtains *in fact*, at once [*aussi sec*], from its inception on; and it is here that the graphics of iterability undercuts the classical opposition of fact and principle [*le droit*], the factual and the possible (or the virtual), necessity and possibility. In undercutting these classical oppositions, however, it introduces a more powerful "logic." Yet in order to accede to this transformation, one must follow the trajectory that I have just reconstituted and not simply confuse, as Sarl does, the necessary with the possible, or construct an entire line of argument upon two "facts" that *appear* to be exceptions. For if they seem to be exceptional and artificial constructs, the two phenomena introduced by Sarl do not contradict, even as exceptions, the rigorous universality of the law. The "shopping list for myself" would be neither producible nor utilizable, it would not be what it is nor could it even exist, were it not possible for it to function, from the very beginning, in the absence of sender and of receiver: that is, of *determinate, actually present* senders and receivers. And *in fact* the list cannot function unless these conditions are met. *At the very moment* "I" make a shopping list, I know (I use 'knowing' here as a convenient term to designate the relations that I necessarily entertain with the object being constructed) that it will only be a list if it implies my absence, if it already detaches itself from me in order to function beyond my "present" act and if it is utilizable at another time, in the absence of my-being-present-now, even if this absence is the simple "absence of memory" that the list is meant to make up for, shortly, in a moment, but one which is already the following moment, the absence of the now of writing, of the writer maintaining [*du maintenant-écrivant*], grasping with one hand his ballpoint pen. Yet no matter how fine this point may be, it is like the *stigmè* of every mark, already split.[5] The sender of the shopping list is not the same as the receiver, even if they bear the same name and are endowed with the identity of a single ego. Indeed, were this self-identity or self-presence as certain as all that, the very idea of a shopping list would be rather superfluous or at least the product of a curious compulsion. Why would I bother about a shopping list if the presence of sender to receiver were so certain? And why, above all, this example of the reminder, of the memorandum [*pense-bête*]? Why not some other example? It would have been no less pertinent, or no more: even in the extreme case of my writing something in order to be able to read (reread) it *in a moment*, this moment is constituted—i.e. divided—by the very iterability of what produces itself *momentarily*. The sender and the receiver, even if they were the self-same *subject*, each relate to a mark they experience as made to do without them, from the instant of its production or of its reception on; and they experience this not as the mark's negative limit but rather as the positive condition of its possibility. Barring this, the mark would not function and there would be no shopping list, for the list would be impossible. Either I wouldn't need one or it would be unusable as such. This necessitates, obviously, a rigorous and renewed analysis of the value of presence, of presence to self or to others, of difference and of *différance* [differing and deferring—Tr.].⁶ To affirm, as does Sarl, that the receiver is *present* at the moment when I *write* a shopping list *for myself*, and, moreover, to turn this into an argument against the essential possibility of the receiver's absence from every mark, is to settle for the shortest, most facile analysis. If both sender and receiver were entirely present when the mark was inscribed, and if they were thereby present to themselves—since, by hypothesis here, being present and being present-to-oneself are considered to be equivalent— how could they even be distinguished from one another? How could the message of the shopping list circulate among them? And the same holds force, *a fortiori*, for the other example, in which sender and receiver are hypothetically considered to be neighbors, it is true, but still as two separate persons occupying different places, or seats. I thus pass from the example of shopping lists to that of my companion in a concert or a lecture. The sender and the receiver certainly seem to be present here, present to each other, present to themselves and to whatever they write or read. But these notes are only legible or writable to the extent that my neighbor can do without my being present in order to read whatever I could write without his being present, and hence, also to the extent that these two possible absences construct the possibility of the message itself, at the very instant of my writing it or of his reading it. Thus, these possible absences, which the note is precisely designed to make up for and which it therefore implies, leave their mark in the mark. They *remark* the mark in advance. *Curiously*, this *re*-mark constitutes *part* of the mark itself. And this remark is inseparable from the structure of iterability: it is and should be capable of being reiterated as though it were the first time, in the absence of the first time, or the second in the absence of the second, in the supplement, mark, or trace of presence-absence. And this holds *for all cases*, whether I am "alone" or in company, whether I pass my time sending myself shopping lists during concerts and lectures, or even if I wink at someone while listening to my favorite music or my favorite ad in a supermarket.

o

Let us pursue our reading of the *Reply*. Thus, Sarl continues to act as though *Sec* sought to oppose "written and spoken language." This point is brought forward with such insistence that I am forced to ask myself whether Sarl did not really believe, in all good faith, that *Sec* sought to oppose "written and spoken language," even though the most cursory reading should have sufficed to demonstrate the contrary.

Attempting, therefore, to show that such an opposition would be erroneous, Sarl is not satisfied with imputing the intention of opposing "written and spoken language" gratuitously to *Sec* (gratuitously, but not disinterestedly). In addition, the following argument is also attributed to *Sec*, no less mistakenly: what supposedly distinguishes writing from speech is the "permanence" of the "text." Then, *Sec* is accused of confounding iterability and permanence. But were the two ever confused? Before responding to this question, I prefer to cite the *Reply*:

> . . . for the purposes of this discussion the most important [*the most important* definitely belongs to Sarl's idiom: there is a constant fear of missing the most important] distinguishing feature is the (relative) permanence of the written text over the spoken word . . . Now the first confusion that Derrida makes, and it is important [again!] for the argument that follows, is that he confuses iterability with the permanence of the text. He thinks the reason that I can read dead authors is because their works are repeatable or iterable. Well, no doubt the fact that different copies are made of their books makes it a lot easier, but the phenomenon of repeatability: the type-token distinction is logically independent of the fact of the permanence of certain tokens . . . This confusion of permanence with iterability lies at the heart of his argument . . . (P. 200)

Once again, *it-reapplies* in the *discourse from/to-Sec. Sec* furnishes Sarl with an argument that the latter attempts to oppose to it.

Let us recall, to begin with, what is most striking. *At no time, either* in *Sec or* in any of the writings that led to it, was the "permanence" (even relative) of writing, or of anything else for that matter, *either* used *or* even mentioned as an argument. Neither the word nor the concept of permanence. Moreover, both have been *criticized explicitly* elsewhere (but that matters little, here), in the preparatory writings to which I have just alluded. Even without going to the point of actually reading these texts, Sarl might have posed the question of why the word "permanence," which is used and attributed to *Sec, never appears in that essay.* And even if it had appeared there, what matters here is that it would never have been used to oppose writing to speech. Sarl might have considered why it is that *Sec* speaks of "restance" [remainder], and even of "*restance* non-présente" [non-present *remainder*] rather than of "permanence." Had Sarl been sufficiently present to what it was writing or rewriting, the passage in question might have cleared up the misunderstanding: in it, what is discussed, with an insistence that should have prevented all haste and confusion, concerns not permanence, but remainders or remains, *non-present* remains. How, then, can a non-presence be assimilated to permanence, and especially to the substantial presence implied by the temporality of permanence? I shall cite once again, re-citing what was cited by Sarl although without much presence-of-mind to what was being read and being written (had we both been together in Montreal while I was reading *Sec*, I would surely have sent off a note to help Sarl's wandering attention, so that despite this slight tendency to *absent*mindedness, what is "most important" might still not be missed; had *Sec*, now, been a shopping list, we would have to conclude that Sarl had forgotten to buy the necessary items for what in French is called the "plat de résistance"; but doesn't this prove that the *written* list is made to supplement an absence that is always possible, and someone, either Sarl at one moment, or, at another, a part of Sarl— let us say, for instance, D. Searle—can send Sarl back to the list, or even to the supermarket to get what is missing). Thus, I cite Sarl citing *Sec*. Sarl writes: "He writes, 'This structural possibility of being weaned from the referent or from the signified (hence from communication and from its context) seems to me to make every mark, including those which are oral, a grapheme in general; which is to say, as we have seen, the non-present remainder [*restance*] of a differential mark cut off from its putative "production" or origin' " (p. 183). I don't know if this phrase is more difficult to read than a shopping list. It does, however, contain numerous signals designed to prevent one from confusing the *remains* of a grapheme in general with the *permanence* or survival of a "written language" in the standard sense. What are these signals? 1. The fact that *restance*, in French a neologism that clearly has the function of replacing a standard and traditional concept, is set in italics. Without even referring to other writings dealing with remains and remainders (I have not forgotten my rule proscribing such references), I would have thought that a neologism in italics would be sufficiently clear to an attentive reader, and especially to a specialist in matters of language, to preclude any rapid retranslation into a standard and trivial idiom. 2. Jeffrey Mehlman and Sam Weber, for their part, did well to translate *restance* by *remainder* and not by permanence. I cannot say whether or not *remainder*, by itself, adequately translates *restance*, but it matters little since no single word, out of context, can by itself ever translate another word perfectly. The fact, in any case, that Mehlman and Weber found it necessary to add *restance* in brackets signals a difficulty in translation. That should have sufficed to avoid a careless reading or a trivial interpretation and to indicate the need for a certain labor of thought. Even in French, the neologism, *restance*, is designed to serve as a warning—although one word alone can never suffice—that work will be necessary in order to avoid equivalents such as "permanence" or "substance," which are, by essence, "presences." The confusion is also possible in French and all this supposes that one deconstruct a certain discourse on presence. I cannot elaborate this any further here. Except to note that the graphics of *restance* comprises an indispensable part of any such elaboration. 3. This is why the word *restance* is not only in italics, as a kind of warning light. It is also associated with "*non-present.*" This is, I admit, paradoxical, but *Sec* never promised to be orthodox. This "non-present" adds a spectacular blinking-effect to the warning light. How could a specialist in speech acts have missed it? Would it not have escaped him even had we limited ourselves, out of simplicity, to an *oral* utterance? Blinking is a rhythm essential to the mark whose functioning I would like to analyze. I shall return to it. 4. Finally, if *Sec* had indeed been even remotely interested in the "permanence of the written text over the spoken word" (*Reply*, p. 200), why does the phrase cited by Sarl speak not of the "written text" but of the "grapheme in general. And why should it include under that heading "oral" marks as well ("seems to me to make every mark, *including those which are oral*, a grapheme in general; which is to say, as we have seen, the non-present *remainder* [*restance*] of a differential mark cut off from its putative 'production' or origin" [p. 183]). How could "permanence" be attributed to an "oral mark"? Once the necessity of passing from writing (in the standard sense) to the grapheme in general, an essential movement of *Sec*, had been neglected, Sarl could only go from one confusion to another.

If *Sec* does not, therefore, write what Sarl can or wants to read there, what does it write? First, among other things, precisely what the *Reply* claims to oppose to it and could have found in it, namely, that "the survival of the text is not the same as the phenomenon of repeatability" (p. 200), although the latter is indeed the condition of the former. The remainder is not that of the signifier any more than it is that of the signified, of the "token" or of the "type," of a form or of a content. Without recalling what has been brought forward elsewhere concerning *remains* [du *reste*] and the *remainder* and limiting myself to the restricted context of this debate, it can be asserted that even in *Sec* the remainder, which has nothing in common with "*scripta manent*," is bound up with the minimal possibility of the re-mark (see above) and with the structure of iterability. This iterability, as Sarl concedes, is indispensable to the functioning of all language, written or spoken (in the standard sense), and I would add, to that of every mark. Iterability supposes a minimal remainder (as well as a minimum of idealization) in order that the identity of the *selfsame* be repeatable and identifiable *in*, *through*, and even *in view of* its alteration. For the structure of iteration—and this is another of its decisive traits—implies *both* identity *and* difference. Iteration in its "purest" form—and it is always impure—contains *in itself* the discrepancy of a difference that constitutes it as iteration. The iterability of an element divides its own identity *a priori*, even without taking into account the fact that this identity can only *determine* or delimit itself through differential relations to other elements and that it hence bears the mark of this difference. It is because this iterability is differential, within each individual "element" as well as between the "elements," because it splits each element while constituting it, because it marks it with an articulatory break, that the remainder, although indispensable, is never that of a full or fulfilling presence: it is a differential structure escaping the logic of presence or the (simple or dialectical) opposition of presence and absence, upon which opposition the idea of permanence depends. This is why the mark qua "non-present remainder" is not the contrary of the mark as effacement. Like the trace it is, the mark is neither present nor absent. This is what is *remarkable* about it, even if it not remarked. This is why the phrase of *Sec* speaks of "the non-present *remainder* of a differential mark cut off from its putative 'production' or origin." Where does this break [*coupure*] take place? To situate it, it is not necessary (cf. *Sec*, p. 180) to imagine the death of the sender or of the receiver, to put the shopping list in one's pocket, or even to raise the pen above the paper in order to interrupt oneself for a moment. The break intervenes from the moment that there is a mark, at once [*aussi sec*]. And it is not negative, but rather the positive condition of the emergence of the mark. It is iterability itself, that which is remarkable in the mark, passing between the *re-* of the repeated and the *re-* of the repeating, traversing and transforming repetition. Condition or effect—take your pick—of iterability. As I have done elsewhere, I will say that it cuts across [*recoupe*] iterability at once, recovering it as though it were merging with it, cutting the cut or break once again in the remark.

The remainder does not amount [*ne revient pas*] to the repose of permanence, and the "concept" of remainder is not, I confess, a sure thing [*de tout repos*]. I put "concept" between quotation marks because if the concept of "concept" depends upon the logic deconstructed by the graphics of remainder, the remainder is not a concept in the strict sense. To remain, in this sense, is not to rest on one's laurels or to take it easy, as Sarl does, for instance, relaxing with a confident and convenient

reading of *Sec*. Especially when, after having found repose in the confusion of remainder and permanence, Sarl concludes with imperturbable
assurance: "I conclude that Derrida's argument to show that all elements of language (much less experience) are really graphemes is without any force. *It rests* [My emphasis—J.D.] on a simple confusion of
iterability with permanence" (p. 201).

There is no doubt that the "permanence" or the "survival" of the
document (*scripta manent*), when and to the degree (always relative)
that they take place, imply iterability or remaining in general. But the
inverse is not true. Permanence is not a necessary effect of remaining. I
will go even further: the structure of the remainder, implying alteration,
renders all absolute permanence impossible. Ultimately, remaining and
permanence are incompatible. And this is why *Sec* is in fact far removed
from implying any kind of permanence to support its argumentation. It
clearly distinguishes iterability from permanence. Sarl opposes to it an
argumentation that in fact has been borrowed from it. To the extent of
this borrowing, at least, Sarl can be said to have understood *Sec* quite
well, even if everything is done to create the contrary impression, one
which, it must be admitted, often seems very convincing.

p

Is it out of line to recall that *Sec* is a difficult text? I shall attempt
later on to indicate certain of the (typical) reasons that render it foreign, in its functioning and in its structure, to the predilections and
selections of the theoreticians of speech acts and to the types of acts that
can be identified with the categories or categorical oppositions they have
fashioned for themselves. For the moment, at this point in the discussion, the difficulty does not simply involve the blinking quasi-concept of
"remainder." The latter is the effect not of a conceptual deficiency or
theoretical laxity on the part of a particular philosophical discourse, but
rather of the iterability to which it is bound and which, it should be
realized, allows for no other kind of "concept" (identity *"and"* difference, iteration-alteration, repetition *"as" différance*, etc.). The difficulty
also involves what has been called the grapheme in general as well as
the strategic reasons that have motivated the choice of this word to
designate "something" which is no longer tied to writing in the traditional sense any more than it is to speech or to any other type of mark.
But the entire essay explicates this strategy, although Sarl has preferred
to ignore it completely. And this, although *Sec* treats the strategy explicitly, in its initial as well as in its concluding pages. I take the liberty,
therefore, of referring the reader to these pages. Paying no attention to
this strategic movement, Sarl clings stubbornly to the traditional con-

cept of "written language," although what is at stake is precisely the attempt to put this concept into question and to transform it. For Sarl it is this traditional concept that is "genuinely graphematic." Sarl writes, for example: "The principle according to which we can wean a written text from its origin is simply that the text has a permanence that enables it to survive the death of its author, receiver, and context of production. This principle is genuinely 'graphematic.'" (p. 200–1). But from the standpoint of *Sec's* logic and strategy, this particular graphematic instance (which I do not consider to be "genuine," just as I do not seek to establish any kind of authenticity) is nothing more or less than a very determinate form derived from iterability or graphematicity in general. Consequently when, a bit further on, Sarl writes: "But again this possibility of separating the sign from the signified is a feature of any system of representation whatever; and there is nothing especially graphematic about it at all. It is furthermore quite independent of those special features of the "classical concept" of writing which are supposed to form the basis of the argument," I not only agree fully, but have already argued as much (since the argument was developed in *Sec*); if, that is, by "especially graphematic" is meant, as is the case, what already has been called "genuinely graphematic": the standard and traditional concept, in its most "classical" form, which *Sec* is precisely proposing to reelaborate by extracting certain predicates that can be extended to every mark. This "classical concept" comprises the "basis" of Sarl's argument, no doubt, but also the *target* of *Sec*. This target, however, is not one object among others. The structure of the area in which we are operating here calls for a strategy that is complex and tortuous, involuted and full of artifice: for example, exploiting the target against itself by discovering it at times to be the "basis" of an operation directed against it; or even discovering "in it" the cryptic reserve of something utterly different.

q

In the same section (p. 201), Sarl then arrives at the problem of intention and of intentionality. This is what is called, once again, "the most important issue" ("I have left the most important issue in this section until last"). Since this occurs, indeed, at the end of the section, there is unfortunately a considerable risk that the premises of Sarl's reading, with all of the confusions that we have just encountered, will bar the way to everything in *Sec* that concerns intention and intentionality. And in fact, Sarl continues to think within a traditional opposition of speech and writing. But what is worse is that Sarl continues to act as if *Sec*, too, were operating within those terms, concluding with blissful tranquility that intentionality "plays exactly the same role in written as in spoken language."

That reapplies, again, the discourse-from/to-*Sec*. I agree, of course, that the role is "the same": *Sec* says it and Sarl, infallibly, reiterates it, but once more in the inverted form of an objection!

But what, after all, is this "role"? On several occasions, passing moreover too quickly from intention to intentionality (but let's skip that), Sarl attributes to *Sec* the following affirmation: intentionality is (supposedly) purely and simply "absent" from writing; writing is supposedly purely and simply cut off, separated, by the effect of a radical interruption ("some break," "radical break"). Having thus translated and simplified *Sec*, Sarl has an easy time objecting that intentionality is not "absent from written communication." For example, still under the heading, "quite plain": "It seems to me quite plain that the argument that the author and intended receiver may be dead and the context unknown or forgotten does not in the least show that intentionality is absent from written communication; on the contrary, intentionality plays exactly the same role in written as in spoken communication." I know this argument well. It, like the entire substratum of Sarl's discourse, is phenomenological in character (cf. Husserl's *Origin of Geometry*, for instance).[7] I have never opposed this position head on, and *Sec* doesn't either. Without returning to what is said in *Sec* about the value of communication (Sarl says, "in written as in spoken *communication*"), I must first recall that *at no time* does *Sec* invoke the *absence*, pure and simple, of intentionality. Nor is there any break, simple or radical, with intentionality. What the text questions is not intention or intentionality but their *telos*, which orients and organizes the movement and the possibility of a fulfillment, realization, and *actualization* in a plenitude that would be *present* to and identical with itself. This is why, as any reader with even the slightest vigilance will have remarked, the words "actual" and "present" are those that bear the brunt of the argumentation each time that it is radicalized. Sarl should have been able to note the insistence and the regularity with which these words accompanied that of "intention." He should have been able to read this, for example, without it being necessary to underline certain words, which I shall do now (as though for a companion, listening to a lecture): "For a writing to be a writing it must continue to 'act' and to be readable even when what is called the author of the writing no longer answers for what he has written, for what he seems to have signed, be it because of a temporary absence, because he is dead or, *more generally, because he has not employed his absolutely actual and present intention or attention, the plenitude of his desire to say what he means*, in order to sustain what seems to be written *'in his name'* " (p.181). The value of a law, here of an eidetic law, resides not in the indicative and variable examples (an absence that is real or factual, provisional or definitive, such as death for instance), but rather in a condition that may be defined *in general* and that, moreover and once again, is nothing but a consequence of iterability: namely in the fact that intention or attention, directed towards something iterable which in turn determines it as being iterable, will strive or tend in vain to actualize or fulfill itself, for it cannot, by virtue of its very structure, ever achieve this goal. In no case will it be fulfilled, actualized, totally present to its object and to itself. It is divided and deported in advance, by its iterability, towards others, removed [*écartée*] in advance from itself. This re-move makes its movement possible. Which is another way of saying that if this remove is its condition of possibility, it is not an eventuality, something that befalls it here and there, by accident. Intention is a priori (at once) *différante*: differing and deferring, in its inception.

This is what Sarl should have been able to read without its having been necessary to underline certain words, which I am obliged to do once again. Sarl will remark that the words *determinate, actual,* and *present* are, to me, *the most important*: "Why is this identity paradoxically the division or dissociation of itself, which will make of this phonic sign a grapheme? Because this unity of the signifying form only constitutes itself by virtue of its iterability, by the possibility of its being repeated in the absence not only of its "referent," which is self-evident, but in the absence of a *determinate* signified or of the intention of *actual* signification, as well as of all intention of *present* communication" (p. 183). This is immediately followed by the phrase already commented, on the "non-present remainder of a differential mark . . ."

(Perhaps it should be said in passing that the *différance*, as we have just seen, removes from itself what "seems to have been written *'in its name.'*" Namely, the proper name, which suddenly finds itself removed. It can thus transform itself, at once, and change itself into a more or less anonymous multiplicity. This is what happens to the "subject" in the scene of writing. That Searle's seal should become, at once and without waiting for me, Sarl's seal, is therefore anything but accidental. It is a little like the multitude of stockholders and managers in a company or corporation with limited liability, or in a limited, incorporated system; or, like that limit which is supposed to distinguish stockholders from managers. Even here, the signatory is no exception.)

Once again, to be precise: what is at stake here is an analysis that can account for *structural possibilities*. Once it is *possible* for X to function under certain conditions (for instance, a mark in the absence or partial absence of intention), the possibility of a certain non-presence or of a certain non-actuality pertains to the structure of the functioning under consideration, and pertains to it *necessarily*. But I want to be even more precise on this point since it seems to have troubled Sarl's reading of *Sec* considerably. The possibility of which I have just been speaking seems to be understandable in two senses, both of which reinforce the argument of *Sec*. First of all, there is possibility as what in French is called *éventualité*, eventuality (I shall come back to this word and to its translation): it can happen that a mark functions without the sender's intention being actualized, fulfilled, and present, and which *to this extent* must be *presumed*. Even if this (eventual) possibility only occurred once, and never again, we would still have to account for that one time and analyse whatever it is in the structural functioning of the mark that renders such an event possible. The condition will have obtained, and be it only in this unique case, that a fulfilled, actualized, and present intention was not indispensable. The possibility of a *certain* absence (even a relative one) must then be conceded and the consequences must be drawn. That is possibility qua eventuality. It might, however, also be said: *in fact* that doesn't *always* happen like that. But at this point, we must pass to possibility qua necessity (see above), and moreover, we must recognize an irreducible contamination or parasitism between the two possibilities and say: "to one degree or another that always happens, necessarily, like that": by virtue of the iterability which, in every case, forms the structure of the mark, which always divides or removes intention, preventing it from being fully present to itself in the actuality of its aim, or of its meaning (i.e. what it means-to-say [*vouloir-dire*]). What makes the (eventual) possibility possible is what makes it happen even before it happens as an actual event (in the standard sense) or what prevents such an event from ever entirely, fully taking place (in the standard sense). I have already recalled the role played in all this by another kind of graphics of the event in general. What is here in question, then, is the value of the kind of event that supports the entire theory of speech acts.

What is valid for intention, always differing, deferring, and without plenitude, is also valid, correlatively, for the object (qua signified or referent) thus aimed at. However, this limit, I repeat (*"without"* plenitude), is also the ("positive") condition of possibility of what is thus limited.

This is why if, on the one hand, I am more or less in agreement with Sarl's statement, ". . . there is no getting away from intentionality, because a *meaningful sentence is just a standing possibility of the corresponding* (intentional) *speech act*" (p. 202), I would, on the other hand, add, placing undue and artificial emphasis on *-ful*, that for reasons just stated, there cannot be a "sentence" that is fully and actually meaning*ful* and hence (or because) there can be no "corresponding (intentional) speech act" that would be fulfilled, fully present, *active* and *actual*. Thus, the value of the *act* (used so generally and analyzed so little in the theory of speech acts), like that of the event, should be submitted to systematic questioning. As in the entire philosophical tradition that supports it, this value implies that of presence which I have proposed to defer to questions of differential [*différantielle*] iterability. But we cannot unfold this analysis here.

What is in question here, for the moment, through the analysis ventured by *Sec* (and elsewhere)—one whose point of departure is in Husserl, but whose consequences work against him—is precisely the plenitude of intentional meaning [*vouloir-dire*], and all of the other values—of consciousness, presence, and originary intuition—which organize phenomenology. But by saying that the graphematic mark (in general) implies the possibility of functioning without the full and actual presence of the intentional act (that of the conscious ego fully present to itself, to what it says, and to the other), *Sec* has not simply effaced or denied intentionality, as Sarl claims. On the contrary, Sec insists on the fact that "the category of intention will not disappear, it will have its place . . ." (p. 192). (Let it be said in passing that this differential-deferring [*différantielle*] structure of intentionality alone can enable us to account for the differentiation between "locutionary," "illocutionary," and "perlocutionary" values of the "same" marks or utterances. With a more active, attentive, and present intention, Sarl would have been able to remark a passage like the one I am now compelled to cite, for reasons of clarity. I trust that the length of this citation will not be held against me, since it contains, with regard to iteration and citation, certain important details that Sarl has omitted and which will be useful a little further on. I cite, therefore, and underline in passing:

> Could a performative utterance succeed if its formulation did not repeat a "coded" or iterable utterance, or in other words, if the formula I pronounce in order to open a meeting, launch a ship or a marriage were not identifiable as *conforming* with an iterable model, if it were not then identifiable *in some way as a "citation"*? [I also underline the quotation marks.] *Not that citationality in this case is of the same sort* as in a theatrical play, a philosophical reference, or the recitation of a poem. That is why there is a relative specificity, as Austin says, a "relative purity" of performatives. But this relative purity does not emerge *in opposition to* citationality or iterability, but in oppositon to other kinds of iteration within a general iterability which constitutes a violation of the allegedly rigorous purity of every event

of discourse or every *speech act*. Rather than oppose citation or iteration to the non-iteration of an event, one ought to construct a differential typology of forms of iteration, assuming that such a project is tenable and can result in an exhaustive program, a question I hold in abeyance here. In such a typology, *the category of intention will not disappear; it will have its place*, but from that place it will no longer be able to govern the entire scene and system of utterance [*l'énonciation*]. Above all, at that point, we will be dealing with different kinds of marks or chains of iterable marks and not with an opposition between citational utterances, on the one hand, and singular and original event-utterances, on the other. The first consequence of this will be the following: given that structure of iteration, the intention animating the utterance *will never be through and through present to itself and to its content*. The iteration structuring it a priori introduces into it a *dehiscence* and a cleft [*brisure*] which are essential. . . . Above all, this essential absence of intending the actuality of utterance, this *structural unconsciousness*, if you like, prohibits any saturation of the context. In order for a context to be exhaustively determinable, in the sense required by Austin, conscious intention would at the very least have to be totally present and immediately transparent to itself and to others, since it is a determining center [*foyer*] of context. The concept of—or the search for—the context thus seems to suffer at this point from the same theoretical and "interested" uncertainty as the concept of the "ordinary," from the same metaphysical origins: the ethical and teleological discourse of consciousness. . . . By no means do I draw the conclusion that there is no relative specificity of effects of consciousness, or of effects of speech (as opposed to writing in the traditional sense), that there is no performative effect, no effect of ordinary language, no effect of presence or of discursive event (*speech act*). It is simply that those effects do not exclude what is generally opposed to them, term by term; on the contrary, they presuppose it, in an asymmetrical way, as the general space of their possibility. (*Sec*, pp. 191–3)

Among other words, I have underlined *dehiscence*. As in the realm of botany, from which it draws its metaphorical value, this word marks emphatically that the divided opening, in the growth of a plant, is also what, in a *positive* sense, makes production, reproduction, development possible. Dehiscence (like iterability) limits what it makes possible, while rendering its rigor and purity impossible. What is at work here is something like a law of undecidable contamination, which has interested me for some time.

After the long passage that I have had to cite, *Sec* addresses itself necessarily to the question of signatures. Sarl has totally ignored this question, although it develops, precisely by reading Austin, the consequences of what has just been said. Since Sarl has not made the slightest allusion to this, I shall leave it out of the debate or at least will not treat it directly, leaving it to the reader to reread the pages in question. If he does, he will be in a position to measure the enormity of the exclusion that has taken place: the section on signatures concerns the putative "origin" of oral or written utterances, and thus, the constant and indispensable recourse of all speech act theory.

r

Let us follow, then, the *Reply* as closely as possible. Still occupied with "the most important issue in this section," Sarl thus purports to oppose to *Sec* what could have been had from reading it, namely that "intentionality plays exactly the same role in written as in spoken communication." And he continues: "What differs in the two cases is not the intentions of the speaker but the role of the context of the utterance in the success of the communication" (p. 201).

Here, two remarks. 1. Since the role of context is determinant, and the horizon of the "total context" is indispensable to the analysis, the contextual difference here may be fundamental and cannot be shunted aside, even provisionally, in order to analyse intention. Isn't the assertion that the difference involves *only* the context a surprising proposition to make, even from the standpoint of speech act theory? 2. Intention, itself marked by the context, is not foreign to the formation of the "total" context. For Austin it is even an essential element of that formation. And yet, Sarl feels authorized in excluding temporarily the consideration of context. Yet even if it were only temporary and methodological, useful for the clarity of the demonstration, such an exclusion would, it seems to me, be both impossible and illegitimate. To treat context as a factor from which one can abstract for the sake of refining one's analysis, is to commit oneself to a description that cannot but miss the very contents and object it claims to isolate, for they are intrinsically determined by context. The method itself, as well as considerations of clarity should have excluded such an abstraction. Context is always, and always has been, at work *within* the place, and not only *around* it.

But let's follow Sarl. For a while, in an initial phase of the argument, context is ostensibly left aside.

1. *Initial phase*: The hypothesis of intention (or of text) without context being considered. To support this hypothesis with a didactic example, Sarl proposes a rich and wondrous fiction. If I ever have the time, I would be tempted to devote one or more works to it. But, interrupting all the fantastic reveries towards which this evocation had begun to draw me, I shall confine myself to a discussion of its logical structure and its demonstrative function. Here it is: ". . . ask yourself what happens when you read the text of a dead author. Suppose you read the sentence, 'On the twentieth of September 1793 I set out on a journey from London to Oxford.' Now how do you understand the sentence?"

Having posed this question, Sarl believes it necessary—and possible —to distinguish rigorously between two possibilities.

a. First possibility: "The author said what he meant and you understand what he said." To grant such a possibility, even as a hypothesis, is to grant a myriad of problematic presuppositions. But, for the moment, that is not important; we will return to it later. What does Sarl hope to conclude from this possibility? As always it is better to cite, but I shall permit myself to underline: *"To the extent* that the author said what he meant and you understand what he said you will know that the author intended to make a statement to the effect that on the twentieth of September 1793, he set out on a journey from London to Oxford, and the fact that the *author is dead and all his intentions died with him is irrelevant to this feature of your understanding of his surviving written utterances."*

This last argument, which I have just underlined, should not be opposed to *Sec.* It derives from *Sec*: namely, from the first of its three sections, which places much emphasis on the fact that "death," and in general the non-presence of a vital, actualized, determinate intention, does not prevent the mark from functioning; it also stresses that the *possibility* of this "death" (and of everything implied by this word, in particular the hypothesis formed by Sarl) is inscribed in the functional structure of the mark. This argument even provides indispensable leverage for the demonstration undertaken in *Sec.* It is inseparable from the iterability to which I incessantly return, as constituting the minimal consensus of this discussion. I have used the phrase "functioning of the mark" rather than "understanding" the "written utterance." In the absence of the presumed author this function, which depends upon iterability, operates *a fortiori* within the hypothesis that I fully understand what the author meant to say, providing he said what he meant. But the function also operates independently of such an hypothesis and without in itself implying either that I *fully* understand what the other says, writes, meant to say or write, or even that he intended to say or write *in full* what remains to be read, or above all that any adequation need obtain between what he consciously intended, what he did, and what I do while "reading." Sarl will retort: such an adequation is for the moment our hypothesis ("to the extent . . ." etc.). Surely. But this ideal hypothesis seems to me untenable. Not so much because of the possibility of a factual accident, which can always (as Sarl will later admit) "corrupt," contaminate parasitically a situation held to be ideal and in some sense essential [*juridique*]. Rather, the very structure of the mark (for example, the minimum of iterability it requires) excludes the hypothesis of idealization, that is, the adequation of a meaning to itself, of a saying to itself, of understanding to a sentence, whether written or oral, or to a mark in general. Once again, iterability makes possible idealization—and thus, a certain identity in repetition that is independent of the multiplicity of factual events—while at the same time limiting the idealization it makes possible: *broaching* and *breaching* it at once [elle l'*entame*]. To put it more simply and more concretely: at the very moment (assuming that this moment itself might be full and self-identical, identifiable—for the problem of idealization and iterability is already posed here, in the structure of temporalization), at the very moment when someone would like to say or to write, "On the twentieth . . . etc.," the very factor that will permit the mark (be it psychic, oral, graphic) to function beyond this moment—namely the possibility of its being repeated *another* time—breaches, divides, expropriates the "ideal" plenitude or self-presence of intention, of meaning (to say) and, *a fortiori*, of all adequation between meaning and saying. Iterability alters, contaminating parasitically what it identifies and enables to repeat "itself"; it leaves us no choice but to mean (to say) something that is (already, always, also) other than what we mean (to say), to say something other than what we say *and* would have wanted to say, to understand something other than . . . etc. In classical terms, the accident is never an accident. And the *mis* of those misunderstandings to which we have succumbed, or which each of us here accuses the other of having succumbed to, must have its essential condition of possibility in the structure of marks, of remarkable marks or, if Sarl prefers to circumscribe the object, of oral or written utterances. Limiting the very thing it authorizes, transgressing the code or the law it constitutes, the graphics of iterability inscribes alteration irreducibly in repetition (or in identification): *a priori*, always and already, without delay, *at once, aussi sec*: "Such iterability—(*iter*, again, probably comes from *itara*, *other* in Sanskrit, and everything that follows can be read as the working out of the logic that ties repetition to alterity) structures the mark of writing itself, no matter what particular type of writing is involved" (*Sec*, p. 180). This etymology, of course, has no value qua proof and were it to be false, the very shift in meaning would confirm the law here indicated: the time and place of the *other time* already at work, altering from the start the start itself, the *first time*, the *at once*. Such are the *vices* that interest me: the other time in(stead of) the first, at once.

This holds for every mark and in particular, since Sarl is only interested in this type, for every speech act, however simple or complex. What sets the times, the *vices*, is a strange law which prescribes that the simpler, poorer, and more univocal an utterance may seem, the more difficult its comprehension, more elusive its meaning, and more indeterminate its context will be. And yet the more complex an utterance becomes, the more the same tendency will prevail. Thus, the example given by Sarl seems to be simple: "On the twentieth . . . ." It seems simple, that is, if we leave aside, as I must do here, the enormous problem (broached by *Sec* in the section, "Signatures," ignored by the *Reply*, but also in other works) raised by the fact that the example chosen is an utterance made in the first person. Is this indispensable for the demonstration? Did Sarl consider this trait as pertinent? Or would an utterance in the third person have been as much (or as little) use in this context? The choice of the first person would *seem* to make things easier to the extent to which one might generally be tempted to expect that someone who says *I* and who speaks of himself would best satisfy the idealizing hypothesis of "saying what he means": the intention of the speaker, one might think, is closest to, if not absolutely present in what is said. Yet nothing is less certain: the functioning of the *I*, as is well known, is no less iterable or replaceable than any other word. And in any case, whatever singularity its functioning might possess is not of a kind to guarantee any adequation between saying and meaning. Since I cannot, here, develop this problem any further, I shall leave aside everything in this example relating to "myself saying I." I will make do by remarking the following: the functioning of the mark, a certain iterability, here a certain legibility that is operative beyond the disappearance or demise of the presumed author, the recognition of a certain semantic and syntactic code at work in this phrase—none of all this either constitutes or requires a full understanding of the meaning*fulness* of this phrase, in the sense of the complete and original intentionality of its meaning (-to-say), any more than for the phrase, "I forgot my umbrella," abandoned like an island among the unpublished writings of Nietzsche.[8] A thousand possibilities will always remain open even if one understands something in this phrase that makes sense (as a citation? the beginning of a novel? a proverb? someone else's secretarial archives? an exercise in learning a language? the narration of a dream? an alibi? a cryptic code—conscious or not? the example of a linguist or of a speech act theoretician letting his imagination wander for short distances, etc?), all possibilities that Sarl would no doubt subsume under those contextual elements excluded from phase 1 by hypothesis, or under the "corruptions" excluded by possibility 1. Nevertheless, I must repeat that iterability prohibits *a priori* (and in principle) the full and rigorous attainment of the ideal plenitude such exclusions purport to isolate. These hypothetical exclusions cannot be formed. They are illegitimate and impossible inasmuch as they suppose the self-identity of an isolated element which iterability—i.e. an element constitutive of the hypothesis

Jacques Derrida

—divides at once. And this holds *a fortiori* for cases of utterances that are more complex than those proposed by the *Reply*.

Since *possibility 1* is only evoked by Sarl as part of what is designated as a "strategy," and since a similar strategic gesture will reproduce itself shortly, I shall reserve until later a general discussion of the law or the rule of this strategy as well as of the problem of strategy in general.

Still within the scope of possibility 1 ("the author said what he meant and you understand what he said"), Sarl admits another supposition. As though by concession. I quote:

> But suppose you decide to make a radical break—as one always can— with the strategy of understanding the sentence as an utterance of a man who once lived and had intentions like yourself and just think of it as a sentence of English, weaned from all production or origin, putative or otherwise. Even then there is no getting away from intentionality, because a *meaningful sentence is just a standing possibility of the corresponding (intentional) speech act.* To understand it, it is necessary to know that anyone who said it and meant it would be performing that speech act determined by the rules of the languages that give the sentence its meaning in the first place. (Pp. 201–2)

The principle of my response to this sub-hypothesis should now be clear and predictable. In order to limit misunderstandings as much as possible, I shall confine myself to the following three points:

a. The fact that a "break" with "the strategy of understanding the sentence as an utterance of a man who once . . ." etc., is always possible ("as one always can") and that the mark still does not cease functioning, that a minimum of legibility or intelligibility remains, constitutes the point of departure of *Sec's* argumentation and hence, it can hardly be held up as an objection to it. But it is no less necessary to draw the consequences, as *Sec* does, from this fact, namely that up to a certain point this "break" remains *always possible* without its preventing the mark from functioning. This implies, however, that even in the ideal case considered by the strategy, there must already be a certain element of play, a certain remove, a certain degree of independence with regard to the origin, to production, or to intention in all of its "vital," "simple" "actuality" or "determinateness," etc. For if this were not so, the "break" (with all its consequences, variables, etc.) would be impossible. And if a certain "break" is always possible, that with which it breaks must necessarily bear the mark of this possibility inscribed in its structure. This is the thesis of *Sec*.

b. I repeat that *Sec never* adduced, from the possibility of this "break," the pure and simple absence of all intentionality in the functioning of the mark that remains; rather, what it calls into question is the presence of a fulfilled and actualized intentionality, adequate to itself and to its contents. I cannot see, therefore, to what or to whom such an objection might be addressed since it is one that *Sec*, too, could endorse.

c. As I have already noted, the equivalence between "to understand it," in the sense of grasping its "meaning*fulness*," and the minimum it is indeed "necessary to know" in order to attain such understanding, seems to me problematical. One of the things *Sec* is driving at is that the minimal making-sense of something (its conformity to the code, grammaticality, etc.) is incommensurate with the adequate understanding of intended meaning. I am aware that the English expression "meaningful" can also be understood in terms of this minimum of making-sense. Perhaps even the entire equivocation of this discussion is situated here. In any case, the incommensurability is irreducible: it "inheres" in intention itself and it is riven [*creusé*] with iterability.

But the equivocation is exacerbated by the fact that the very basis of our consensus is endangered. What is this consensus? What convention will have insured up to now the contract of a minimal agreement? Iterability: here Sarl and I seemed to be in agreement, both concerning iterability itself and concerning the systematic link between iterability and code, or to put it differently, between iterability and a kind of conventionality. The conventional consensus thus concerned ultimately the possibility of conventionality. Our common and minimal code has been the existence and the effects of the code itself. But this basis, as I just said, seems to me to be fragile, limited, and in danger. Why?

The questioning initiated by the logic and the graphics of *Sec* does not stop at the security of the code, nor at its concept. I cannot pursue this problem too far, since that would only add new complications to a discussion that is already too slow, overdetermined, and over-coded in all respects. I shall simply observe that this line of questioning is opened in the first of *Sec's* three parts, and to be exact by the following phrase: "The perhaps paradoxical consequence of my here having recourse to iteration and to code: the disruption, in the last analysis, of the authority of the code as a finite system of rules; at the same time, the radical destruction of any context as the protocol of code" (p. 180). The same direction, that of an iterability that can only be what it is in the *impurity* of its self-identity (repetition altering and alteration identifying), is charted by the following propositions: "As far as the internal semiotic context is concerned, the force of the rupture is no less important: by virtue of its essential iterability, a written syntagma can always be detached from the chain in which it is inserted or given without causing it to lose all possibility of functioning, if not all possibility of "communicating," precisely. One can perhaps come to recognize other possibilities in it by inscribing it or *grafting* it onto other chains. No context can entirely enclose it. Nor any code, the code here being both the possibility and impossibility of writing, of its essential iterability (repetition/alterity)" (p. 182). And: ". . . in so doing [i.e. by the iterability *or* the citationality that it permits] it [the sign] can break with every given context, engendering an infinity of new contexts in a manner which is absolutely illimitable. This does not imply that the mark is valid outside of a context, but on the contrary that there are only contexts without any center or absolute anchoring [*ancrage*]" (pp. 185–6).

We are still within the hypothesis of possibility 1. Still very certain that this "rather obvious point" has not been understood, Sarl mulls over the causes of this lack of understanding. The resulting diagnosis is acute and far-reaching: reaching, that is, the obstacles deemed to have prevented this "rather obvious point" from being understood, blinding *Sec* to the evidence.

Let's be serious. Although I have endeavored to demonstrate that this point was so obvious precisely because it had previously been explicitly taken into account and analyzed in *Sec*, I am still ready to examine what those obstacles to understanding *might have been*, had there in fact been misunderstanding or incomprehension. After all, I have promised to be both exceedingly scrupulous and exceedingly serious in my argumentation. These obstacles, then, are supposedly of two kinds: "There are two obstacles to understanding this rather obvious point, one implicit in Derrida, the other explicit."

The diagnosis does not remain at the surface: it delves into the phenomenon in order to seek out the causes lurking behind it, or rather, it penetrates the non-phenomenon in order to search out the obstacles that lie behind and have prevented the natural, normal phenomenon which we have every right to expect, from emerging; moving beyond blindness towards its cause, the diagnosis seeks to uncover the implicit cause hidden behind the explicit one. What is this implicit cause which, behind everything that is already behind, explains this blindness to the "rather obvious"? What is the hindrance here to sight? It is nothing more or less than: an illusion. Which illusion? The illusion that there is something lurking *behind*. Let's see, or rather, cite:

There are two obstacles to understanding this rather obvious point, one implicit in Derrida, the other explicit. The first is the illusion that somehow illocutionary intentions if they really existed or mattered would have to be something that *lay behind* the utterances, some inner pictures animating the visible signs. But of course in serious literal speech the sentences are precisely the realizations of the intentions: there need be no *gulf* at all between the illocutionary intention and its expression. The sentences are, so to speak, fungible intentions. Often, especially in writing, one forms one's intentions (or meanings) in the process of forming the sentences: there need not be two separate processes. (P. 202)

This first illusion must indeed be unfathomably "implicit." I have looked in vain for the slightest apparent sign of it in *Sec*. And this perhaps explains why Sarl, not being able to mention a single example, is forced to take refuge here in the implicit, i.e. in something that, this time, could only be located precisely "*behind* the utterances." The illusion thus unmasked *behind* [*derrière*] the text of *Sec*, namely that someone named Derrida supposedly believes in "something *behind* the utterances, some inner pictures animating the visible signs," this illusion belongs—and hence the terrifying severity of the accusation—to the repertoire of a psychology of language (mechanistic, associationist, substantialist, expressionist, representationalist, pre-Saussurian, pre-phenomenological, etc.), more exactly to a pre-critical psychologism; one can only wonder by means of what perverse or baroque regression *Sec* might have succumbed to such psychologism, especially since such doctrine has long since disappeared from the curriculum, and the works which stand "behind" *Sec* not only presuppose its critique but graphically accentuate it. However, I recognize that this argument alone is not sufficient. What should suffice, by comparison, is the *explicit* criticism, from the initial pages of *Sec* on, of the concepts of "representation," "communication," and "expression" (pp. 177 ff.). All such concepts appeal to a notion of intention as something separable, intrinsic, and "behind" the "expression." What should also suffice is the suspicion concerning the *sign* and even concerning the opposition signifier/signified: this suspicion, legible in every line, bears on the entire system that supports this opposition, and consequently, among others, on that of an intention hidden behind the "visible sign" (the signifier). Hence, the substitution of "mark" for "sign," of intentional effect for intention, etc.

Nevertheless: to assert, against this purported "illusion," that "the sentences are precisely the realizations of the intentions" is to employ a language that seems to me to stem from that good old representationalist and expressionist psychology (Sarl speaks, moreover, continually of "representations," and always designates language as a set of "expressions"), for which the distinctions between "intention" and "realization," "intention" and "expression" are still intact. They are intact both as purely conceptual (non-real) oppositions in the ideal case to which we shall return in a moment ("in serious literal speech"), in which utterances "are precisely the realizations of intentions, and as simply real oppositions in the other cases, or at least in almost all other cases." Just such a psychology (disarmingly enough today, I must confess) seems to me to permeate this short, rather improvised description of the process of writing: "Often [?], especially [?] in writing, one forms one's intentions (or meanings) in the process of forming the sentences. . . ." Even if it were not simplistic, empiricist, and vague, this kind of descriptive psychology could not teach us anything about the object in which we are interested precisely because it is a psychology whereas that object is not essentially psychological. Unless, that is, Sarl considers it to be psychological, or deems the theory of those objects designated as speech acts to be a psychology, an interior domain of psychic life. In this case, however, the illusion that Sarl denounces would be explicitly Sarl's own. This would not be the first such case, nor the last.

We are not quite done with this "first" "illusion," which is "implicit." Will my snail's pace ever be forgiven? If I am abusing everyone's patience (including my own), it is in the hope of leaving as little as possible—above all, of those illusions—implicit. That was my "promise." To be sure, in the examination of this objection, I have saved the most important point for last: "serious literal speech." Everything, of course, begins here: "But of course in serious literal speech the sentences are precisely the realizations of the intentions: there need be no *gulf* at all between the illocutionary intention and its expression."

Let us anticipate a bit the discussion that will develop about the second section of the *Reply*, that which concerns Austin and what is called "serious" discourse. Sarl has just opposed the case of "serious literal speech" to *Sec*, speech in which intention is presumed to be "realized." *Sec*, however, proposes, even if Sarl fails to make the slightest allusion to it, an *explicit* deconstructive critique of the oppositions "serious/non-serious," "literal/non-literal" and of the entire system of related oppositions. One need only consult, for instance, what is said there concerning "the suspicious status of the 'non-serious' " (p. 197) and everything that forms its context. Involved are not merely the extreme difficulties which, *in fact*, can arise in the attempt to isolate the ideal purity of what is "serious" and "literal." Such difficulties are familiar enough to John R. Searle. The embarrassed, even endless precautions that he feels constrained to take, in *Speech Acts* for instance, bear sufficient witness to this fact. Rather, what is at stake above all is the structural impossibility and illegitimacy of such an "idealization," even one which is methodological and provisional. The word "idealization" here is a citation from *Speech Acts*. In imposing the convention upon my readers, I have agreed not to cite anything but *Sec* among the writings which carry, among other things, "my" own signatures, but I never said that I would not cite John R. Searle, co-signatory, director, and, within the limits of his liability responsible [*responsable limité*] for the *Reply*.

In a gesture that appears thoroughly classical in its rigor and logic, dictated by those exigencies to which philosophy, from Plato to Rousseau, from Kant to Husserl, has always sought to respond, Searle acknowledges the necessity of an "idealization of the concept analyzed" at the very moment when he undertakes to define the "structure of illocutionary acts."[9] In face of "the looseness of our concepts," which could "lead us into a rejection of the very enterprise of philosophical analysis," he reacts much as, in appearance at least, the great philosophers of the tradition have always done (Austin being in this respect a partial exception). He considers this "looseness" as something extrinsic, essentially accidental, and reducible. And he writes (I underline):

. . . rather the conclusion to be drawn is that certain forms of analysis, especially analysis into necessary and sufficient conditions, are likely to involve (in varying degrees) *idealization of the concept analyzed*. In the present case, our analysis will be directed at the *center* of the concept of promising. *I am ignoring marginal, fringe, and partially defective promises*. . . . Furthermore, in the analysis I confine my discussion to *full blown explicit promises and ignore promises made by elliptical turns of phrase, hints, metaphors, etc*. . . . In short, I am going to deal only with a *simple and idealized* case. This method, one of constructing idealized models, is *analogous* to the sort of theory construction that goes on in *most* sciences, e.g. the construction of economic models, or accounts of the solar system which treat planets as points. *Without abstraction and idealization* there is no systematization. . . . I want to give a list of conditions for the performance of a certain illocutionary act, which do not themselves mention the performance of any illocutionary acts. . . .

And, a little further on, in a subsection entitled:

1. *Normal input and output conditions obtain*. I use the terms "input" and "output" to cover the large and indefinite range of conditions under which any kind of *serious and literal*[1] linguistic communication is possible. . . . Together they [the two terms] include such things as that the speaker and hearer both know how to speak the language; both are conscious of what they are doing; they have no physical impediments to communication, such as deafness, aphasia, or laryngitis; *and they are not acting in a play or telling jokes*, etc. It should be noted that this condition excludes *both* impediments to communication such as deafness and also *parasitic* forms of communication such as *telling jokes or acting in a play*.
1. I contrast "serious" utterances with play acting, teaching a language, reciting poems, practicing pronunciation, etc., and *I contrast "literal" with metaphorical, sarcastic, etc*.

This long quotation will not have been excessive if it has clarified the logic of the *Reply*, and above all of the phrase: "But of course in serous literal speech the sentences are precisely the realizations of the intentions." And if, at the same time, it has clarified my reading of it. In this passage I find confirmation not only of the fact that the criterion of intention (responsible, deliberate, self-conscious) is a necessary recourse in order that the "serious" and the "literal" be defined—something which is self-evident and which Searle would probably not deny—but also and above all of the fact that this intention must indeed, according to his own arguments, be situated "behind" the phenomenal utterance (in the sense of the "visible" or "audible" signs, and of the phono-linguistic manifestation as a whole): no criterion that is simply *inherent* in the manifest utterance is capable of distinguishing an utterance when it is serious from the same utterance when it is not. Solely intention can decide this and it is not identical with "realization." Nothing can distinguish a serious or sincere promise from the same "promise" that is nonserious or insincere except for the intention which informs and animates it. And the same holds for the other oppositions. But I have already broached this above and if we shall meet it again, this is not what interests me most at the moment. What does is the "center" of this sweeping theoretical perspective. As we have just seen, the isolation of "serious literal speech" presupposes an entire system of theoretical-methodological idealizations and exclusions. I shall not object to such an undertaking, the classical and profoundly philosophical necessity of which I do not ignore, either by referring to the factual difficulties it poses, to the labyrinths of empiricity or to the interminability of the analysis. For the empirical difficulties involved in isolating this ideal residue do not, in fact, exclude the possibility of a theoretical process [*le procès juridico-théorique*] leading to an essential definition. And if one wishes to know what conditions are necessary for a promise, for instance, to be a promise, it ultimately matters little whether or not *in fact* a promise has ever existed, or whether one has ever been actually discovered which would fully and rigorously satisfy the requisite conditions. In any case, inasmuch as classically fact has been opposed to essence (or to principle), matters would become more complicated if the object named "speech act" (as well as the very enterprise of a theory of speech acts, in Austin's version) were to render such oppositions invalid. Nor will I object to the fact that certain concepts, which intervene under the names of "non-strict," or "metaphorical," "sarcastic" etc., are treated as though they were self-evident. Instead, I shall go directly to the "center" (since, as Searle has once again made perfectly clear, it is always the "center" that holds his interest), to the center of the question of essence or principle [*de droit*]. And I will confine myself for the moment to two arguments.

Firstly, it is in the name of *analogy*, underlined in my citation, that Searle justifies the idealizing method within the theory of *speech acts* when he speaks of the structure of illocutionary acts. He authorizes this procedure by drawing an analogy with the construction of models in "most" sciences. Let us pass over the fact that this fundamental theoretical preamble [*protocole*], which defines and delimits the entire enterprise, that this metalanguage on the different theoretical languages already involves a lax (or non-strict, if you prefer) recourse to a resemblance, indeed to a non-literal figure. Let us also pass over the enormous problem of the construction of "models" in the sciences, in *different* sciences at different moments of their history. To speak simply of "most" sciences is in this regard to resort to woolly approximations that are most surprising, especially in this particular place. But all this would hold us up too long. Let us consider solely a limit *of principle* that obtains in this analogy: namely, that by contrast with *all* the other sciences, the theory of speech acts has as its object—lest we forget—speech acts said to be ordinary in languages said to be natural. This fact, far from facilitating the process of abstraction and of idealization, which in turn is always a process of objectification, on the contrary limits it. The language of theory always leaves a residue that is neither formalizable nor idealizable in terms of that theory of language. Theoretical utterances are speech acts. Whether this fact is regarded as a privilege or as a limit of speech act theory, it ruins the analogical value (in the strict sense) between speech act theory and other theories. Not only is analogy between essentially heterogeneous theories not strictly legitimate, but the very utterance which poses, proposes, supposes, alleges such an analogy ultimately *refers* to an analogical or metaphorical utterance even if it is not in itself metaphorical. In Searle's terms, it is based *ultimately* on the metaphorical, the sarcastic, on the non-literal. And this is rather disturbing for an utterance that purports *to found the entire methodology* (abstraction, idealization, systematization, etc.) of the theory of speech acts.

This argument of principle concerns a structural *limit.* (In passing I note with astonishment that Searle chooses to ignore "marginal, fringe" cases. For these always constitute the most certain and most decisive indices wherever essential conditions are to be grasped. On this point at least, Searle does not follow the tradition, but in view of the fact that he does not call the overall logic of the traditional procedure into question, I view this merely as a slight inconsistency of an empiricist type). This argument concerning the structural limit is of the same kind as the set-argument a while back. Here, now, is an argument of another kind.

Secondly: the iterability of the mark does not leave any of the philosophical oppositions which govern the idealizing abstraction intact (for instance, serious/non-serious, literal/metaphorical or sarcastic, ordinary/parasitical, strict/non-strict, etc.). Iterability blurs *a priori* the dividing-line that passes between these opposed terms, "corrupting" it if you like, contaminating it parasitically, qua limit. What is re-markable about the mark includes the margin within the mark. The line delineating the margin can therefore never be determined rigorously, it is never pure and simple. The mark is re-markable in that it "is" also its margin. (This structure is analyzed in *Sec* and in its context; for instance—but not only—in the essays collected under the title, *Marges* [Margins], and which operate "marginally" from their very opening [*Tympan, La double séance, Glas*, etc]. Even if it only threatens with a perpetually possible parasitism, this menace is inscribed *a priori* in the limit. It divides the dividing-line and its unity at once. Moreover, why (for whom) should this possibility appear as a menace, as a purely "negative" risk, as an "infelicity"? Once it is iterable, to be sure, a mark marked with a supposedly "positive" value ("serious," "literal," etc.) can be mimed, cited, transformed into an "exercise" or into "literature," even into a "lie"—that is, it can be made to carry its other, its "negative" double. But iterability is also, by the same token, the condition of the values said to be "positive." The simple fact is that this condition of possibility is structurally divided or "differing-deferring" [*différante*].

But in this case, one will say, in view of the irreducibility and generality of this structure of iterability ("iterability looms large in both of these arguments," Sarl observes with apparent regret: but so it is with structures that are universal and necessary), will it not be susceptible of idealization, abstraction, simplification, purification? Does it not authorize an *overall* systematization [systématisation d'*ensemble*] which in turn will be vulnerable to the preceding objection? I would say that this is not the case: the unique character of this structure of iterability, or rather of this chain, since iterability can be supplemented by a variety of terms (such as *différance*, grapheme, trace, etc.), lies in the fact that, comprising identity *and* difference, repetition *and* alteration, etc., it renders the *project* of idealization possible without lending "*itself*" to any pure, simple, and idealizable conceptualization. No process [*procès*] or project of idealization is possible without iterability, and yet iterability "itself" cannot be idealized. For it comports an internal and impure limit that prevents it from being identified, synthesized, or reappropriated, just as it excludes the reappropriation of that whose iteration it nonetheless broaches and breaches [*entame*].

But under such circumstances, one will reply, no scientific or philosophical theory of speech acts in the rigorous, serious, and pure sense would be possible. That is, indeed, the question. Or rather, it is what I am suggesting, at least as long as we continue to invoke the traditional model of theory as our reference. And it is because of this that I agree with Sarl that the "confrontation" here is not between two "prominent philosophical traditions" but between *the* tradition and its other, an other that is not even "its" other any longer. But this does not imply that all "theorization" is impossible. It merely de-limits a theorization that would seek to incorporate its object totally but can accomplish this only to a limited degree. This object, for example, would have to include the hierarchy of oppositional values. For it can hardly be denied that these value-oppositions constitute hierarchies, that they are posed and re-peated as such by the very theory which claims to analyze, in all neutral-ity, their mere possibility. I am well aware of the fact that the speech acts theoretician does not, on moral grounds, advise us to prefer the serious to the non-serious, for instance, or the normal to the parasitic. Not, that is, in the sense of non-theoretical, ordinary language. But even prior to the hypothesis of such neutrality, the opposition serious/non-serious (sarcastic, etc.—but there are also other species of the non-serious), literal/metaphorical, ironic etc., cannot become the object of an analysis in the classical sense of the term: strict, rigorous, "serious," without one of the two terms, the serious or the literal, or even the strict, proceeding to determine the *value* of the theoretical discourse itself. This discourse thus finds itself an integral part—part and parcel, but also *partial*—of the object it claims to be analyzing. It can no longer be impartial or neutral, having been determined by the hierarchy even before the latter could be determined by it. A theoretical discourse of this (classical, traditional) type must indeed tend, in accordance with its intrinsic ethics and teleology, to produce speech acts that are in prin-ciple serious, literal, strict etc. The only way that speech act theory might escape this traditional definition would be for it to assert (the-oretically and practically) the right of its own speech acts not to be serious, etc., or rather not *simply* serious, strict, literal. Has it done this up to now? Might it have escaped me? In all seriousness, I cannot exclude this possibility. But am I serious here?

Thus, it does not suffice merely to say that such oppositions are inherited, pre-critical philosophemes, dogmatically employed; or that the hierarchical trait governing the relation of one value to another has, from its inception, been blurred, lacking purity and rigor from the start. We must add this: the necessity, assumed by classical theory, of submit-ting itself to the very normativity and hierarchy that it purports to analyze, deprives such theory of precisely what it claims for itself: seri-ousness, scientificity, truth, philosophical value, etc. Because the model speech act of current speech act theory claims to be serious, it is normed by a part of its object and is therefore not impartial. It is not scientific

Jacques Derrida

and cannot be taken seriously. Which is what constitutes the drama of this family of theoreticians: the more they seek to produce serious utterances, the less they can be taken seriously. It is up to them whether they will take advantage of this opportunity to transform infelicity into delight [*jouissance*]. For example, by proclaiming: everything that we have said-written-done up to now wasn't really serious or strict; it was all a joke: sarcastic, even a bit ironic, parasitical, metaphorical, citational, cryptic, fictional, literary, insincere, etc. What force they would gain by doing this!! But will they take the risk? Will we have to take it for them? Why not?

Hasn't *Sec* indeed already done it? At the very moment of invoking "serious literal speech" to support the objection being advanced, Sarl might have forseen that none of these values could be considered as self-evident in such a discussion. He might have foreseen this had he considered *Sec* as constituting part of the context of the discussion of *Sec*. He might have foreseen it had he read what is said there concerning the "suspicious states of the "non-serious"" (already cited), but also point 1 of the introduction: ". . . the value of the notion of *literal meaning* [*sens propre*] appears more problematical than ever." It is not, of course, necessary to know or to adopt the conclusions of other writings on this subject, but it is necessary to take into account the fact that in this context, in *Sec*, the notion of "literality" or of the "serious" is posed as being problematical. Since this problematic character of the serious constitutes part of *Sec's* premises, can one legitimately, "seriously" oppose to it, qua dogma, what it seeks to call into question?

Let us return to our point of departure. It is, we see, no accident if Sarl has so laboriously sought out the "implicit"—having found nothing explicit to support the strange allegation that *Sec* was referring to "something *behind* the utterances," to "some inner pictures animating the visible signs." To reject the belief in "intentions" or "inner pictures" *behind* the utterances, however, does not amount to endorsing the belief in any simple adequation of the utterance to itself, or, in terms that are strictly those of Sarl, in an adequation between "the intention and its expression" in an ideal utterance which would be the "realization" of the intention. Even were I to accept this expressionist or representationalist description of language; even were I to consider the utterance as the "realization" of an "intention," I would at the very least have to recall that the dehiscence already discussed does not intervene, primarily, between an "intention" and an "expression," but already, from the start, as an effect of iterability within each of these putative instances. And although I am convinced that this problem is even more complex than described, I shall limit myself to what has been said in order not to stray too far from the *Reply* and its code.

This leads me to the second "illusion" diagnosed by Sarl, the "explicit" one this time. According to *Sec*—so Sarl—"intentions must all be conscious." Confronted with this assertion I must confess that I had to rub my eyes. Was I dreaming? Had I misread? Mistranslated? Was the text suddenly becoming sarcastic? Or even, as I had just wished, ironic? Was it all a joke? Was the patented theoretician—or theoreticians—of speech acts calling us to task for forgetting the existence of the unconscious? What a fake-out, leaving me flat-footed in the camp of those insufficiently aware of the unconscious! I always love to watch a good fake-out, even if it's at my expense. But my delight, unfortunately, is short-lived. I cannot imagine how Sam Weber is going to translate "fake-out." For his benefit let me specify that, ever since my adolescence, I have understood the word above all as a soccer term, denoting an active ruse designed to surprise one's opponent by catching him offbalance. Littré, however, lists the following, which can be used as necessary: "CONTRE-PIED 1. Hunting term. The trail followed by the prey and which the dogs, led astray, take instead of the new trail upon which the animal continues. To follow the *contre-pied* is to follow tracks in the wrong direction. 2. Fig. The contrary of something. 'People have taken precisely the *contre-pied* of the will.' La Fontaine."

To claim that for *Sec* all intentions are conscious is to read *à contre-pied*, fake(d) out, in the sense of Littré. For not only does *Sec* say that all intentions are *not* conscious: it says that *no* intention can *ever* be fully conscious, or actually present to itself. Nor is this so different from Austin, who in "Three Ways of Spilling Ink" asserted "the only general rule is that the illumination [shed by intention] is always *limited*, and that in several ways."

More systematically, *Sec*'s enterprise is in principle designed to demonstrate a type of "structural unconscious" (p. 192) which seems alien, if not incompatible with speech act theory given its current axiomatics. The latter seem constructed in order to keep the hypothesis of such an Unconscious at a safe distance, as though it were a giant Parasite. I am speaking here, briefly, summarily, but in a direct and unequivocal manner of the Unconscious—of what is still designated by this name in psychoanalysis—and of its relation to graphematics in general and to speech in particular. I am not speaking of unconsciousness in the sense that Sarl seems to envisage, as a kind of lateral, virtual potential of consciousness. What is at stake in the debate initiated by *Sec* situates itself in this area as well, and it involves ethical and political consequences to which we shall doubtless have occasion to return. Each time that the question of the "ethical and teleological discourse of consciousness" (ibid.) arises, it is in an effort to uncover and to break the security-lock which, from *within the system*—inside of the prevailing

Jacques Derrida

model of speech acts that governs the current theory in its most coherent and even most productive operation—condemns the unconscious as one bars access to a forbidden place. By placing under lock and key, or by sealing off; here, by prohibiting that the Unconscious—what may still be called the Unconscious—*be taken seriously*; be taken seriously, that is, *in (as) a manner of speaking*, up to and including its capacity for making jokes. The Unconscious not only as the great Parasite of every ideal model of a speech act (simple, serious, literal, strict, etc.), but the Unconscious as that parasite which subverts and dis-plays [*déjoue*], parasitically, even the concept of parasite itself as it is used in the theoretical strategy envisaged by Austin or by Searle. This is what *Sec* was aiming at. If the question of a bond between intention and consciousness is indeed raised there, it is solely insofar as Austin deems that bond indispensable in order to maintain precisely what *Sec* criticizes. Who will be persuaded that Austin took *this Unconscious* into account in his analysis of speech acts? And who will be persuaded that Searle is here doing what Austin failed to? Confining myself to the analysis of the ideal structure of illocutionary acts and to the passage from *Speech Acts* that has already been cited, I wish only to recall that the conditions of a "strict and literal" speech act, here a promise, included the following: the exclusion of all "parasites," and the necessity that speaker and hearer be "conscious of what they are doing." And in the *Reply* itself this condition is reiterated at the very moment that Sarl, without convincing anyone, claims to be taking a certain unconsciousness into account. In fact what is thereby evoked is only a potential, limited consciousness that has not yet become thematically self-conscious; and above all Sarl reminds us that we must not "separate" (but had anyone done this?) "conscious states" on the one hand, from operations of writing and of speaking on the other. I underline: "This illusion [the implicit one] is related to the second, which is that intentions must all be conscious. But in fact rather few of one's intentions are ever brought to consciousness as intentions. *Speaking and writing are indeed conscious* intentional activities, but the intentional aspect of illocutionary acts does not imply that there is a separate set of conscious states apart from simply writing and speaking" (p. 202). It could not be more clearly stated that writing and speaking are considered to be conscious activities through and through and structurally. As for the "structural unconscious" proposed by *Sec*, it was at least supposed *to situate* the possibility of articulating a general graphematics based not on an axiomatics confined to the "psychology" or the "phenomenology" of consciousness, but on what for instance and for the instant can be called the Unconscious. This Unconscious is absolutely excluded by the axiomatics (which is also an axiology) of current speech act theory, in particular as formulated by Searle. To give only one example: suppose that I seriously promise to criticize implacably each of Sarl's theses. If I consult *Speech Acts* (ch. 3, p. 58), I discover that such a promise has no meaning. It is a *threat or warning,* and there is a "crucial distinction between promises on the one hand and threats on the other." Wherein does the crucial, and hence insurmountable distinction consist? In the fact "that a promise is a pledge to do something for you, not to you; but a threat is a pledge to do something to you, not for you. A promise is defective if the thing promised is something the promisee does not want done; and it is further defective if the promisor does not believe the promisee wants it done, since a non-defective promise must be intended as a promise and not as a threat or warning. . . . The promisee wishes (needs, desires, etc.) that something be done, and the promisor *is aware* of this wish (need, desire, etc.)" (my emphasis). And after an examination of apparent counter-examples, defined as "derivative from genuine promises," sometimes qua "emphatic denial," Searle then concludes: ". . . if a purported promise is to be non-defective, the thing promised must be something the hearer wants done, or considers to be in his interest, or would prefer being done to not being done, etc; and the speaker *must be aware of or believe or know,* etc., that this is the case" (my emphasis). This description ultimately excludes every criterion other than the distinct, determining, and determinable consciousness of the intentions, desires, or needs involved. The rigorous distinction between promise and warning or threat, for instance, is established only by this expedient. Yet what would happen if in promising to be critical I should then provide everything that Sarl's Unconscious desires, for reasons which remain to be analyzed, and that it does its best to provoke? Would my "promise," in such a case, be a promise, a warning or even a threat? Searle might respond that it would constitute a threat to Sarl's consciousness, and a promise for the unconscious. There would thus be two speech acts in a single utterance. How is this possible? And what if Sarl *desired* to be threatened? And what if everything that is given to please or in response to a desire, as well as everything that one promises to give, were structurally ambivalent? What if the gift were always poisoned (gift/*Gift*) in a manner so as to prevent any *simple* logic (desire/non-desire, for example) from being able to decide, i.e. to distinguish between the two or to determine their meaning univocally? And if, now, I were unable *to know* (to "be aware of or believe or know" as *Speech Acts* puts it) what it is that Sarl as speaker consciously or unconsciously desires, would I not be incapable as speaker either of promising or of threatening to criticize? What is the unity or identity of the speaker? Is he responsible for speech acts dic-

Jacques Derrida

tated by his unconscious? Mine, for instance, might well wish to please
Sarl by gratifying the wish to be criticized; or it might want to cause
Sarl unhappiness by refusing to be critical; or to please Sarl by being
uncritical and cause pain by being critical; or to promise Sarl a threat or
to threaten with a promise; also to offer myself as a target for criticism
by taking pleasure in saying things that are "obviously false," inviting
Sarl to delight in my weakness or to enjoy the exhibition from above,
etc. All that simply to suggest, briefly, that it is sufficient merely to
introduce, into the manger of speech acts, a few wolves of the type
"indecidability" (of the *pharmakon*, of the *gift*, of the supplement, of
the hymen) or of the type "unconscious" (an unconscious pleasure may
be experienced as pain, according to *Beyond the Pleasure Principle*), of
the type "primary masochism," etc., for the shepherd to lose track of this
flock: one is no longer certain where to find the identity of the "speaker"
or the "hearer" (visibly identified with the conscious ego), where to find
the identity of an intention (desire or non-desire, love or hate, pleasure
or suffering) or of an effect (pleasure or non-pleasure, advantage or
disadvantage, etc.). This is only another reason why, at the "origin" of
every speech act, there can only be Societies which are (more or less)
anonymous, with limited responsibility or liability—Sarl—a multitude
of instances, if not of "subjects," of meanings highly vulnerable to
parasitism—all phenomena that the "conscious ego" of the speaker and
the hearer (the ultimate instances of speech act theory) is incapable of
incorporating as such and which, to tell the truth, it does everything to
exclude. Without ever fully succeeding, since incorporation, in "psychoanalytical" terms, requires that the defending body of the subject make
place "inside" for that which it excludes. And yet, how can the theory of
speech acts in its current state account for this kind of incorporation,
which nevertheless registers essential effects on all language? Especially
in view of the highly simplistic and univocal manner in which the theory
deals with distinction and exclusion! At the end of the passage quoted a
moment ago on the conditions of *genuine* promises, we read the following: "I think a more elegant and exact formulation of this condition
would probably require the introduction of technical terminology of the
welfare economics sort." Perhaps. But economics—even "welfare"
economics—is not one domain among others or a domain whose laws
have already been recognized. An economics taking account of effects of
iterability, inasmuch as they are inseparable from the economy of (what
must still be called) the Unconscious as well as from a graphematics of
undecidables, an economics calling into question the entire traditional
philosophy of the *oikos*—of the *propre*: the "own," "ownership,"
"property,"—as well as the laws that have governed it would not only be

very different from "welfare economics": it would also be far removed from furnishing speech acts theory with "more elegant" formulations or a "technical terminology." Rather, it would provoke its general trans-formation.

Sarl will probably assert that I have examined all sorts of contextual variables or possible corruptions of the promise. None of all that, Sarl will then say, contradicts the following proposition: if a promise (genuine, serious, univocal, strict) were to take place (even if there never was such a thing), it would have to involve a speaker who is conscious with regard to a hearer who is equally conscious and desirous of what is promised to him. Such a proposition, Sarl might then conclude, in the very poverty of its logical armature, is unassailable; it constitutes part of the semantic-axiomatic analysis of the concept of promise. Let us grant this. It would then, however, also have to be granted that this entire machinery of idealization firstly implies ("logically," Sarl would say) and concerns speakers and hearers only inasmuch as they are "conscious egos," and secondly presupposes the univocity of ethical-teleological values in language. To this extent, within the very *limited* and apparently well-founded scope of such phenomena, would not the coherence of this proposition be unassailable? It would seem to fit into the great tradition of Kant and of Husserl. Its only "defect," however, is that these "phenomena" are not phenomena: they never appear as such. The same holds for the effect, "conscious ego," which, however limited it may be, can never be isolated ideally in its pure identity; the reasons for this I have already discussed above: they involve that iterability which ruins (even ideally) the very identity it renders possible. (I refer here to the end of the second section of *Sec*, dealing with the "ethical and teleological discourse of consciousness" and with speech acts qua "effects.") All this amounts to the following: the hypothesis of possibility 1, with which we are still concerned ("the author says what he means"), cannot even be formulated ideally. Except, that is, under the heading of "fiction," about which I could not say whether or not it would be serious, or external to the field of other types of fiction (in particular, to that of literature), but which would certainly lead to the following question: in what way, or to what extent does traditional philosophical discourse, and that of speech act theory in particular, derive from fiction? Is it capable of assuming full responsibility for such fictional discourse, or of positing itself as such, and if so, how? etc. But I do not believe that this latter concept of fiction would be very compatible with Searle's thematics of fiction.

Let us now proceed to possibility 2, still situated within the *initial phase*.

Jacques Derrida

S

Second Possibility. What hitherto has been excluded, as though it were an accident: "corruption," a word that does not imply, as Sarl will emphasize a bit farther on with regard to "parasitical," "non-serious," "empty," etc., *any* pejorative connotation, or even any value judgment, be it ethical or axiological in general. Let us grant, therefore (*concesso non dato*, for such an admission is not easy, given a word such as "corruption"), that the qualification of "corrupt" does not imply any evaluation of this type, and let us read the following: "To the extent that the author says what he means the text is the expression of his intentions. It is always possible that he may not have said what he meant or that the text may have become corrupt in some way; but exactly parallel considerations apply to spoken discourse. The situation as regards intentionality is exactly the same for the written word as it is for the spoken..." (p. 202).

I shall not return to this "parallel" or identity ("exactly parallel," "exactly the same"). Once more, "it reapplies" as an argument from/to-*Sec*. It is the nerve of the demonstration in *Sec* and it takes nerve to raise it as an objection to *Sec*. As for the inadequation between meaning and saying, as well as the alleged "corruption" of the text, once they have been acknowledged to be "always possible," their exclusion, whether on provisional-methodological, or on theoretical grounds, constitutes the very object of the critique proposed by *Sec*. A corruption that is "always possible" cannot be a mere extrinsic accident supervening on a structure that is original and pure, one that can be purged of what thus happens to it. The purportedly "ideal" structure must necessarily be such that this corruption will be "always possible." This *possibility* constitutes part of the *necessary* traits of the purportedly ideal structure. The ("ideal") description of this structure should thus include, and not exclude, this possibility, whereby "include" here does not simply mean "to incorporate" it (in the psychoanalytical sense, i.e. retaining the object within itself but as something excluded, as a foreign body which is impossible to assimilate and must be rejected: this is what happens with Austin and Searle when they speak of all the "negative" effects: corruption, infelicities, parasites, etc.). What must be included in the description, i.e. in *what* is described, but also in the practical discourse, in the *writing that describes*, is not merely the factual reality of corruption and of alteration [*de l'écart*], but corrupt*ability* (to which it would be better henceforth not to give this name, which implies generally a pathological disfunction, a degeneration or an ethical-political defect) and dissocia*bility*, traits tied to itera*bility*, which Sec proposes to account for. That can only be done if the "-bility" (and not the lability) is recognized from the *inception* on [dès l'*entame*] as broached and breached [*entamée*] in its "origin" by iter*ability*.

2. *Second Phase*. Just as only a few lines are devoted to what Sarl feels justified in excluding under the rubric of corruption and of alteration, so only seven or eight lines are consecrated to contextual variations ("When we come to the question of context . . ." p. 202) after they have been excluded from the long examination of possibilities 1 and 2. Shall we say that such a lack of interest in the effects of context marks a corruption or degeneration of the Austinian heritage, or an alteration of Austin's intentions, of what he meant to say? No, because what Austin said and did was sufficiently ambiguous, in its iterability, to authorize such an exclusion *as well*. If one were fond of this word, and of the evaluation it carries with it, one would have to say that corruptability, too, is part of the heritage and of its legitimation.

Thus, when Sarl arrives at context, it is to say things that would be simply trivial were they not above all dubious. One might even, in fact, depending on the context, assert precisely the contrary of what is stated in the lines that I will begin by citing, underlining certain of the words: "When we come to the question of *context*, as Derrida is aware, the situation really is quite different for writing than it is for speech. In speech one can invoke all sorts of *features of the context* which are not possible to use in writing intended for absent receivers, without explicitly *representing these features in the text*. That is why verbatim *transcripts* of conversations are so hard to interpret. In conversation a great deal can be *communicated* without being made explicit in the sentence uttered" (pp. 202–3).

Considering that I have already essentially addressed this question, I shall simply add several remarks dealing specifically with this paragraph.

1. How can a theoretician of speech acts treat a contextual criterion as though it were of secondary importance, or at least as a criterion that can be excluded or deferred from consideration without impairing the latter? *Either* the contextual difference changes everything, because it determines what it determines *from within*: in this case, it can hardly be bracketed, even provisionally. *Or* it leaves certain aspects intact, and this signifies that these aspects can always separate themselves from the allegedly "original" context in order to export or to graft themselves elsewhere while continuing to function in one way or another, thus confirming the "graphematic" thesis of *Sec*. In order that this either/or not be an alternative or an insurmountable logical contradiction, the value of context must be reelaborated by means of a new logic, of a graphematics of iterability. Such a reelaboration, however, does not ap-

pear to me to be possible in accordance with the theoretical axiomatics of Austin and of Searle. It is this reelaboration that *Sec* endeavors to initiate. In passages such as the following, which I re-cite: "Every sign, linguistic or non-linguistic, spoken or written (in the current sense of this opposition), in a small or large unit, can . . . break with every given context, engendering an infinity of new contexts in a manner which is absolutely illimitable. This does not imply that the mark is valid outside of a context, but on the contrary that there are only contexts without any center or absolute anchoring [*ancrage*]." (pp. 185–86). I shall take advantage of this citation to acknowledge that the word "engendering" is not sufficiently rigorous. It might, in an insufficiently explicit context, falsify or "corrupt" (!) the dominant argument of *Sec*. It would have been better and more precise to have said "engendering *and* inscribing itself," or being inscribed *in*, new contexts. For a context never creates itself *ex nihilo*; no mark can create or engender a context on its own, much less dominate it. This limit, this finitude is the condition under which contextual transformation remains an always open possibility.

2. Sarl adheres to a narrow definition of writing as the *transcription* or *representation* of speech. He thereby adheres to a certain interpretation of phonetic writing, indeed to the alphabetic model, to the *a b c*'s of logo-phonocentrism. Hence, his *discriminating* example: "verbatim transcripts of conversations. . . ." This model of writing is precisely called into question in *Sec* (and elsewhere).

3. Sarl adheres to a definition of language as *communication*, in the sense of the communication of a *content* ("a great deal can be communicated . . ."). This definition is precisely called into question in *Sec* (and elsewhere).

4. Sarl adheres to a definition of the text as the contents of an oral utterance, whether it is directly "present" or merely transcribed (". . . representing these features in the text"). This definition of the text is precisely called into question in *Sec* (and elsewhere).

t

That the import of context can never be dissociated from the analysis of a text, and that despite or because of this a context is always transformative-transformable, exportative-exportable—all this is exemplified in the following paragraph of the *Reply*, one that will permit me to cite once again, without the slightest modesty: "Derrida has a distressing penchant for saying things that are obviously false." In the example and demonstration given to support this assertion, Sarl *cuts, avoids, omits*: cutting one of the examples of *Sec* out of its dominant or most determining context; avoiding to cite more than three words; omitting the most "important" word, Sarl then hastens to apply the scheme prefabricated in *Speech Acts* around the distinction—itself rather laborious and problematical—of *mention* and *use*. This procedure may not correspond to a conscious, deliberate intention, or even to any intention at all. Austin would surely ask: "Intentionally?" "Deliberately?" "On purpose?" But the fact remains and it can be analyzed. As might be expected, I choose to cite at length. Because of my oath to act in good faith and with all seriousness, to be sure, but also, as some will doubtless suspect, to endow the promised criticism with a stronger pertinence. I shall begin, once again, with the *Reply*.

Derrida has a distressing [why distressing? for whom?] penchant for saying things that are obviously false. I will discuss several instances in the next section but one deserves special mention at this point. He says the meaning-less example of ungrammatical French, "le vert est ou," means (*signifie*) one thing anyhow, it means an example of ungrammaticality. But this is a simple confusion. The sequence "le vert est ou" does not MEAN an example of ungrammaticality, rather it IS an example of ungrammaticality. The relation of meaning is not to be confused with instantiation. This mistake is important because it is part of his generally mistaken account of the nature of quotation, and his failure to understand the distinction between use and mention. The sequence "le vert est ou" can indeed be *mentioned* as an example of ungrammaticality, but to mention it is not the same as to *use* it. In this example it is not used to mean anything; indeed it is not used at all. (P. 203)

I now cite the passage from *Sec* which is thus incriminated after having been precipitously abstracted and furiously truncated:

Thus, it is solely in a context determined by a will to know, by an epistemic intention, by a conscious relation to the object as cognitive object within a horizon of truth, solely in this oriented contextual field is "the green is either" unacceptable. But as "the green is either" or "abracadabra" do not constitute their context by themselves, nothing prevents them from function-ing in another context as signifying marks (or indices, as Husserl would say). Not only in contingent cases such as a translation from German into French, which would endow "the green is either" with grammaticality, since "either" (*oder*) becomes for the ear "where" [*où*] (a spatial mark). "Where has the green gone (of the lawn: the green is where)," "Where has the glass gone in which I wanted to give you something to drink?" [*Où est passé le verre dans lequel je voulais vous donner à boire?*] But even "the green is either" itself still signifies an *example of agrammaticality*. And this is the possibility on which I want to insist: the possibility of disengage-ment and citational graft which belongs to the structure of every mark, spoken or written, and which constitutes every mark in writing before and outside of every horizon of semio-linguistic communication; in writing, which is to say in the possibility of its functioning being cut off, at a certain point, from its "original" desire-to-say-what-one-means [*vouloir-dire*] and from its participation in a saturable and constraining context." (P. 185)

Jacques Derrida

The "confrontation" of the two citations ought to be clear enough. As clear as the operation undertaken by Sarl. And yet, I shall insist. In what way is the "confusion" "mentioned" by Sarl most of all the one into which Sarl cannot avoid rushing? What are the first signs of this?

To begin with, instead of quoting even a single sentence of the paragraph without interruption, the citation has been cut precisely before the one little word that suffices to ruin the point Sarl is trying to make. Where in *Sec* we can read, and I underline, "But even 'the green is either' *still* signifies *an example of agrammaticality*," [. . . signifie *encore exemple d'agrammaticalité*], Sarl cuts out the *encore*, which I have just underlined and which transforms the utterance entirely. "*Signifie encore*" still signifies that yet another, supplementary meaning can be added, grafted onto the first, even onto a non-meaning. It is this possibility of the graft that is manifestly and principally in question throughout this paragraph. The "encore" that Sarl blissfully forgets also marks the fact that the supplementary graft has been added to another mark which itself, of course, does not "originally" [*primitivement*] signify an "example of agrammaticality," but which also does not constitute an authentic, elementary, initial, normal state of the mark existing *before* the graft.

To avoid a confusion in which distinct interests play their part—a confusion that I was naive enough to believe would have been excluded by a context as clear and as insistent as this one—I should perhaps have taken a supplementary precaution for Sarl's sake. I should have followed an indication given by Searle in *Speech Acts*, precisely in the chapter on *Use and Mention*.[9] I should perhaps have multiplied the quotation-marks and written: "the green is either" indeed signifies nothing (to the extent, at least, to which signification or meaning is bound to discursive grammaticality, something that is by no means obligatory), but the citation of the (mentioning) phrase ". . . "the green is either" . . ." can also, as a citational reference, signify *in addition* (*encore*): "this is an example of agrammaticality," this example of agrammaticality " " "the green is either" " " proving unmistakably, by virtue of its functioning, that a graft is always possible; just as every phrase endowed with grammaticality that is cited in a certain context, for example in a grammar book, can *also* signify (*encore*): I am an example of grammar. Yet even had I done all this, would I have thus prevented (and why, after all, should one even try?) a phrase from being cut, or a graft from being torn out of context? Would I have appeased Sarl's anger at the confusion of "use" and "mention," treated as a radical evil, which I agree it may very well be, although I don't have the time here to elaborate why (beyond noting that if, in fact, good and evil are involved, it is because

use and mention are always susceptible of being confused). Thus, even if I had been able to calm Sarl down, I would certainly have had no luck with Searle, who, in the same chapter of *Speech Acts*, mounts a crusade against that "philosophy of language" which leads to the interminable multiplication of quotation marks upon quotation marks. He finds this point of view "absurd" and he adds (but why?) that "it is not harmlessly so," having "infected other areas of the philosophy of language."[10] What is there in a theory that can be harmful and infectious? I can only advise all those interested in such matters of public health and welfare, and in particular in distinctions such as "use" and "mention" or any of the others, no less fraught with concern and passion, to read the entire chapter attentively. The recourse, there, to what is called "normal use" (are these quotation marks necessary or superfluous?) in order to distinguish between what "has its normal use" and what "does not have its normal use" (p. 74) is as stubborn and insistent as the criterion between normal and not-normal is essentially elusive. To say, for instance, that an expression which has become an object of discourse or a citation "is not being used normally" (p. 75), is to make an assertion that requires justifications not to be found in the demonstration of Searle. And if, as he says, "we already have perfectly adequate use-mention conventions" (p. 76), it is hard to see how such harmful and infectious absurdities might arise, harmful or dangerous in the sense that masturbation or writing seemed so to Rousseau (I want to suggest that this analogy is not entirely artificial, or at least no more so than quotation marks around quotation marks, or masturbation "itself").

If conventions are, in fact, never entirely adequate; if the opposition of "normal" and "abnormal" will always be lacking in rigor and purity; if language can always "normally" become its own "abnormal" object, does this not derive from the structural iterability of the mark? The graft, by definition, and herein no different from the parasite, is never *simply* alien to and separable from the body to which it has been transplanted or which it already haunts [*hante*]. This graft, which is discussed in the paragraph butchered by Sarl, also defines (for instance) the relation between "use" and "mention." This possibility must be taken into account. Its mode is defined as the obsession [*la hantise*] of the graft.

I shall not dwell on this for fear of further trying the reader's patience. I will restrict myself to a single example, in order to test the distinction between "use" and "mention," and will pose a single question. "*Iter*," in the subtitle of *Sec*, and hence everywhere else, is *also* (*encore*) a citation. The word appears for the "first time" in the title of the section devoted to Austin, which we shall discuss in a moment. I recall this title: "*Parasites. Iter, Of Writing: That It Perhaps Does Not Exist.*" I cannot here give an exhaustive commentary of this subtitle. Whether Sarl (or any other reader) may have recognized it or not—and this double possibility already poses all kinds of problems—there is also a citation there, more or less cryptic ("perhaps" cryptic), more or less parodic, ironic, altered, lateral and literal, but at the same time very serious (as serious as the question concerning the proof of the existence of God): a citation of the fifth of Descartes' *Metaphysical Meditations*. But is it a citation in the strict sense? There are no quotation marks. And yet, if the word "iter" is itself here an iteration without quotation marks, it is difficult, given the context—that of a text addressed to a distinguished gathering of specialists of "Philosophy in the French Language" (the Congress in Montreal)—not to speak here of a citation. But for the moment this is of little matter, for the question lies elsewhere. I cite the title of Descartes: *De essentiâ rerum materialum; et iterum de Deo, quod existat*, which is translated in French as: *De l'essence des choses matérielles; et derechef de Dieu, qu'il existe* [*On the Essence of Material Things; And Likewise of God, That He Exists*]. The latter part of the title, beginning with *iterum*, is, as is well known, a subsequent addition of Descartes, who thus returned to his original title, repeating and changing it in this way, augmenting and completing it with a supplementary *iterum*. I cannot here take up again the classical debate and pursue the question—this time referring to our discussion of the structure of iterability—of why Descartes deemed it necessary to demonstrate the existence of God for a second time, after the proof had already seemed established according to the order of reasons in the third *Meditation*. Had I room for it here, I would endeavor to shift the question out of the necessary and rigorous debate held some twenty years ago and involving certain great Descartes scholars (Guéroult, Gouhier, Brunschwig), and draw it toward the regions in which we have been navigating. What of *use* and *mention* in the case (unique or not?) of the Divine name? What, in such a case, of reference and of citation? What shall we think of the possibility or even of the necessity of repeating the same demonstration several times, or rather of multiplying the demonstrations in view of the same conclusion, concerning the same object? And this precisely where the object concerned (God) is held to be beyond all doubt and the ultimate guarantee (being unique, irreplaceable, beyond all substitution, both *absolutely repeatable* and *unrepeatable*) of all certitude, all proof, all truth? What is repetition—or the iteration of "iterum"—in this exemplary case, if this exemplariness is both that of the unique and that of the repeatable? What does its possibility or its necessity imply, in particular concerning the event of language and, in the narrow sense or not, that of writing? In substituting "of writing" for "of God," *Sec* has not merely replaced one word by another, one meaning or finite being by another which would be its equivalent (or not): *Sec* names writing in this place where the iterability of the proof (of God's existence) *produces writing*, drawing the name of God (of the infinite Being) into a graphematic drift [*dérive*] that excludes (for instance) any decision as to whether God is more than the name of God, whether the "name of God" refers to God or to the name of God, whether it signifies "normally" or "cites," etc., God being here, *qua* writing, what at the same time renders possible and impossible, probable and improbable oppositions such as that of the "normal" and the citational or the parasitical, the serious and the non-serious, the strict and the non-strict or less strict (it all amounting, as I have tried to show elsewhere, to a *différance* of *stricture*). But let's leave all that. The "perhaps" of the "that it perhaps does not exist" does not oppose the status of writing to that of God, who, Himself, should certainly exist. It draws the consequences from what has just been said about God himself and about existence in general, in its relation to the name and to the reference. In leaving the existence of writing undecidable, the "perhaps" marks the fact that the "possibility" of graphematics places writing (and the rest) outside the authority of ontological discourse, outside the alternative of existence and non-existence, which in turn always supposes a simple discourse capable of deciding between presence and/or absence. The rest of the trace, its remains [*restance*] are neither present nor absent. They escape the jurisdiction of all onto-theological discourse even if they render the latter at times possible.

As for the function of the word "parasites" (in the plural), as in the other title, "Signatures," it designates *both* (thus already functioning parasitically) parasites in general (phenomena of language treated in this section of *Sec* and in the works of Austin) *and* what immediately follows in the title, namely an example, an event of parasitism, that of one title by another (which hence is no longer quite a title), the parasitism of the famous title borrowed from [*prêté à*] *René Descartes*, a title that had already parasited itself as we just saw. In view of this parasitism, effected *in* and *by* a discourse on parasitism, are we not justified in considering the entire chapter, the entire discussion of Austin, as only an exercise in parody designed to cause serious philosophical discourse to skid towards literary play? Unless, that is, this seriousness were already the para-site of such play, a situation which could have the most serious consequences for the serious. But—one may enjoin—if he has discussed Austin solely in order to play games with Descartes' titles, it's not serious and there is no theoretical issue worthy of discussion: he is evading the discussion. This might be true: I detest discussions, their subtleties and ratiocinations. But I still have to ask myself how it can be explained that such a frivolous game, doing its best to avoid all discussion, could have involved and fascinated other "philosophers" (from the very first day on), responsible theoreticians aware of being very serious and assuming their discourse? How could such thinkers have been moved to argue so seriously, even nervously, against a kind of game which they were the first, if not the only ones, to take so seriously, while at the same time being unable to take into account (but *that* can't be serious) the structure of utterances such as titles and subtitles, unable to recognize the parasitism that they are so intent on flushing out wherever it may be? Who, or what, is responsible?

But let's leave all that. What is a title anyway? Is it a normal speech act? Can one imagine a sequence without a title, etc.? Such sophisticated considerations could occupy us for some time. But here is the promised question: Does "*Parasites. Iter, Of Writing: That It Perhaps Does Not Exist*" involve *use* or *mention*? This question can no longer be confined to this sequence. It concerns everything that surrounds the sequence, and that it, in turn, involves, frames, determines, contaminates. And if one responds that this is a case where we have both at once (*use* and *mention*), intermingled or interwoven, I can only reiterate: where is the dividing-line between the two? Can it be rigorously located? I shall wait patiently for an answer. And if this title is judged (but on what grounds?) to be too complex, perverse, or singular; if it is considered not entitled to be a title because it is both the object and the definition of the text that follows it, producer and product, seminal and fertilized, then I shall settle for an answer to the same question, bearing this time on a title that is apparently simpler, for instance *Speech Acts*. Or *Limited Inc*, which aside from its use-value in the legal-commercial code that marks the common bond linking England and the United States (Oxford and Berkeley), also *mentions* in translation a seal related to the French code (s.a.r.l.);[11] *condenses* allusions to the internal regulation through which the capitalist system seeks to limit concentration and decision-making power in order to protect itself against its own "crisis"; *entails* everything said by psychoanalysis about incorporation, about the *limit* between incorporation and non-incorporation, incorporation and introjection in the work of mourning (and in work generally), a limit in which I have been much interested during these last years, with the result that texts such as *Glas* and *Fors* (two untranslatable titles) become, in principle, inseparable from our debate and indispensable for a minimal reading of the title *Limited Inc*. And hence, of all the rest: et coetera.

u

"Derrida's Austin" is the title of the second section of the *Reply*. The way in which Sarl's "Derrida's Austin" presents itself is familiar enough by now: "I believe he [Derrida] has misunderstood Austin in several crucial ways and the internal weaknesses in his argument are closely tied to these misunderstandings. In this section therefore I will very briefly summarize his critique and then simply list the major misunderstandings and mistakes" (p. 203).

Although it is overloaded, because or despite of its reduced dimensions, Sarl's "Derrida's Austin" races ahead. This is always a risky business on roads that aren't straight, but I won't belabor this word of warning. If the summary is "very brief," whose fault is it? Concerning this very brief summary I shall have only two things to say, neither of which bear on its brevity.

1. Before proposing a more gradual and more patient analysis, I recall, for the sake of better determining a context that Sarl has done everything to obliterate, that the relation of *Sec* to Austin is far from being simple or simply critical as Sarl would like to suggest. I have already pointed out that at the beginning of section III four reasons are mentioned to explain why Austin's undertaking can be regarded as being new, necessary, and fecund, both in itself and in the developments that it has provoked. The arguments of *Sec* were meant less to criticize individual analyses of Austin than to show in what respects the "general doctrine" he says he "is not going into" could not be a simple *extension*, a development that might be postponed for strategic or methodological reasons, but that on the contrary it would have to entail a reelaboration of the axiomatics or of the premises themselves. Sarl's accusation notwithstanding, *Sec* indicates with all clarity that the exclusions practiced by Austin *present themselves as* procedures of strategic or methodological suspension, even though, as I shall endeavor to show later, such a strategy is fraught with metaphysical presuppositions. But concerning the strategic or methodological *intention* there is no misunderstanding in *Sec*. In this regard Sarl's charge does not bear the slightest examination, such as, for instance, the citation of this passage (one among others):

> Now it is highly significant that Austin rejects and defers that "general theory" on at least two occasions, specifically in the Second Lecture. I leave aside the first exclusion ["I am not going into the general doctrine here: in many such cases we may even say the act was 'void' (or voidable for duress or undue influence) and so forth. Now I suppose some very general high-level doctrine might embrace both what we have called infelicities *and* these other 'unhappy' features of the doing of actions—in our case actions containing a performative utterance—in a single doctrine: but we are not including this kind of unhappiness—we must just remember, though, that features of

this sort can *and do constantly obtrude* into any particular case we are discussing. Features of this sort would normally come under the heading of 'extenuating circumstances' or of 'factors reducing or abrogating the agent's responsibility', and so on" (p. 21, my emphasis).] The second case of this exclusion concerns our subject more directly. (*Sec*, p. 189).

How could anything be clearer as to what is here "highly significant," namely: a. the purportedly methodological character of an exclusion (referring to a "general doctrine" of action or acts while failing to submit this value of the *act* in general to those fundamental deconstructive questions necessitated, in my view, by the graphematics of iterability. Austin argues as though he knew what an act is). b. the difficulty (here only suggested, but rendered explicit by the entire context) in following Austin when he undertakes to exclude provisionally "these other 'unhappy' features in the doing of actions" which not only "can" always occur, but which, as he too must admit, "*do constantly obtrude into any particular case we are discussing.*" I have discussed this matter above and I shall return to it.

2. It is in dealing with the "second exclusion," still within that "very brief" initial summary of *Sec*, that Sarl gravely *falsifies* matters. I note here that I seem to have become infected by Sarl's style: this is the first time, I believe, that I have ever accused anyone of deception, or of being deceived. Since the entire discussion rests upon this massive falsification, it should suffice to re-cite *Sec* to make short shrift of the problem. First, I shall cite the *Reply*: "More to the point [! I would specify that the exclamation-point were mine, were there not, among other difficulties involved in signing for an exclamation-point, that requiring me to mention here, cryptically, [*sous crypte*], another text apparently "signed" by me on the exclamation-point ("!"), for instance in Mallarmé, which should serve as an extenuating circumstance reducing or abrogating my responsibility; and Sarl will henceforth scarcely be able to deny Austin's recourse, in the above citation, to responsible intentionality and to ethical-juridical value-judgments!], according to Derrida, Austin excludes the possibility that performative utterances (and *a priori* every other utterance) can be quoted. Derrida makes this extraordinary charge on the grounds that Austin has excluded fictional discourses. . . ." (p. 203).

More to the point! Naturally, I defy anyone to find anything in *Sec* that would sustain this "extraordinary charge," which Sarl charges me with charging Austin. But not only does *Sec* never do anything of the sort: it *begins*, on the contrary, by recalling that Austin evokes the possibility of a performative being cited (and *a fortiori* of other utterances as well), and that he is hence aware, in a certain way, of this as a

constant possibility. This is indisputable—it is the *abc*'s of our reading—
and the only question at stake concerns the manner in which Austin
takes this into account and the treatment he reserves for it. In this
respect, *Sec* distinguishes clearly between *possibility* and *eventuality*;
the possibility or fact that performatives can always be cited ("can be
quoted" as Sarl puts it; and *Sec* never said that Austin excluded the fact
"that performative utterances *can be quoted*") is not the same as the
eventuality, that is the fact that such possible events—citations, "unhap-
pinesses"—do indeed happen, occur, something which Austin, no less
indisputably, excludes from his analysis, at the very least *de facto* and
for the moment ("we are deliberately at present excluding"). Evidently it
is regrettable that the distinction made in *Sec* between *possibility* and
eventuality was not rendered in the English translation. This might have
constituted an extenuating circumstance for Sarl, whose reading refers
primarily to the translation, were it not for the fact that the entire
paragraph plainly dissipates the difficulty. How, within an interval of
two lines, could one possibly assert both that Austin excludes this possibility and that he insists upon defining it as the ever-present possibility
of parasitism or abnormality? In any event, Sarl's charge against *Sec*—
that is, against its supposed charge against Austin—is so grave that one
would be justified in expecting a somewhat closer attention to detail and
to the strict literality of the text. In order to elucidate graphically the
"falsification" involved in the *Reply*, I will have to cite again from *Sec*,
at length and adding emphasis:

The second case of this exclusion concerns our subject more directly. It
involves [*il s'agit de*] precisely the *possibility* for every performative utterance
(and a priori every other utterance) to be quoted [the text says *il s'agit de*,
literally: "what is involved or concerned"—and not, "what is excluded"—is
the possibility . . . ; moreover how, given the hypothesis of such an exclusion,
could Austin be suspected of excluding the possibility of "every other
utterance" being quoted?!] Now Austin excludes this *eventuality* [*éventualité*,
initially translated as "possibility"] (and the general theory which would
account for it) with a kind of lateral insistence, all the more significant in its
off-handedness [*latéralisant*]. He insists on the fact that this possibility remains *abnormal, parasitic*, that it constitutes a kind of extenuation or
agonized succumbing of language that we should strenuously distance ourselves from and resolutely ignore. And the concept of the "ordinary," thus of
"ordinary language," to which he has recourse is clearly marked by this
exclusion. As a result, the concept becomes all the more problematical, and
before demonstrating as much, it would no doubt be best for me simply to
read a paragraph from the Second Lecture: "(ii) Secondly, as *utterances*
our performances are *also* heir to certain other kinds of ill, which infect
all utterances. And these likewise though they might be brought into a more
general account, we are deliberately at present excluding. I mean, for example, the following: a performative utterance will, for example, be *in a*

peculiar way hollow or void if said by an actor on the stage, or if introduced in a poem, or spoken in soliloquy. This applies in a similar manner to any and every utterance—a sea-change in special circumstances. Language in such circumstances is in special ways—intelligibly—used not *seriously* [my emphasis, J.D.] but many ways *parasitic* upon its normal use—ways which fall under the doctrine of the *etiolations* of language. All this we are *excluding* from consideration. Our performative utterances, felicitous or not, are to be understood as issued in ordinary circumstances" (Pp. 21–22). Austin thus excludes, along with what he calls a "sea-change," the "non-serious," "parasitism," "etiolation," "the non-ordinary" (along with the whole general theory which, if it succeeded in accounting for them, would no longer be governed by those oppositions), *all of which he nevertheless recognizes as the possibility available to every act of utterance*. It is as just such a "parasite" that writing has always been treated by the philosophical tradition, and the connection in this case is by no means coincidental. (P. 190)

This is surely very clear: nowhere does *Sec* say or even suggest that Austin excludes the fact "that performative utterances can be quoted." How could *Sec* have possibly asserted as much while at the same time citing at length passages from Austin in which this very possibility is not only admitted, but described as being *ever-present*? What is no less clear, however, is that once this possibility ("can be quoted") has been recognized everywhere and by everyone, Austin nevertheless excludes from his considerations "at present"—we have just verified this literally —the *fact* or *facts* that transform this ever-present possibility into an event, making the possible come to pass: precisely what *Sec* designates as eventuality. Austin thus proposes a theoretical fiction that excludes this eventuality in order to purify his analysis.

I have just recalled what *can always* happen when Sarl writes "I will very briefly summarize his critique and then simply list. . . ." This summary is so summary, so "void" and "false" that I would be tempted to repeat, with the very words of the *Reply*: "The problem is rather that Derrida's Austin is unrecognizable. He bears almost no relation to the original." This is true. But what is unrecognizable, bearing no relation to the original, is not simply Austin, but indeed "Derrida's Austin." I fully subscribe to what Sarl says: reading it there, "Derrida's Austin *is* unrecognizable."

It will therefore not come as too great a shock to find that the five criticisms directed at "Derrida's Austin" are, from their very inception, trapped in the most resistant autism. I could have made do with having quoted, but I don't want to abuse this advantage. I shall cite Sarl again, copiously, and I shall make every effort not to leave the slightest detail obscure.

V

First objection. We read in the *Reply*:

1. Derrida has completely mistaken the status of Austin's exclusion of parasitic forms of discourse from his preliminary investigations of speech acts. Austin's idea is simply this: If we want to know what it is to make a promise or make a statement we had better not *start* our investigation with promises made by actors on stage in the course of a play or statements made in a novel by novelists about characters in the novel, because in a fairly obvious way such utterances are not standard cases of promises and statements. We do not, for example, hold the actor responsible today for the promise he made on stage last night in the way we normally hold people responsible for their promises, and we do not demand of the author how he knows that his characters have such and such traits in a way that we normally expect the maker of a statement to be able to justify his claims. Austin describes this feature by saying that such utterances are "hollow" or "void" and "nonserious."[1] Furthermore, in a perfectly straightforward sense such utterances are "parasitical" on the standard cases: there could not, for example, be promises made by actors in a play if there were not the possibility of promises made in real life. The existence of the pretended form of the speech act is logically dependent on the possibility of the nonpretended speech act in the same way that any pretended form of behavior is dependent on nonpretended forms of behavior, and in that sense the pretended forms are *parasitical* on the nonpretended forms. (Pp. 204–5)

Here is my response to this objection. *Sec never* suggested that the "investigation" "start" with promises made by actors on stage. (Moreover, I want to stress that according to the logic of this hypothesis, it would not be the actor who should be held responsible but rather the speaker committed by the promise *in the scene*, that is, the character. And indeed, he is held responsible in the play and in the *ideal*—i.e. in a certain way *fictional*—analysis of a promise, the choice between the two being a matter of indifference here. But let's leave that for the moment.) Thus, although *Sec* never suggested beginning with theatrical or literary fiction, I do believe that *one neither can nor should begin by excluding* the possibility of these eventualities: first of all, because this *possibility* is part of the structure called "standard." What would a so-called "standard" promise or a statement be if it could not be repeated or reproduced? If, for example (an *example* of iteration in general), it could not be mimed, reproduced on the stage or, *another* example (my emphasis, a *different* example), in a citation? This *possibility* is part of the so-called "standard case." It is an essential, internal, and permanent part, and to exclude what Austin himself admitted is a *constant* possibility from one's description is to describe something other than the so-called standard case.

Translated into the code of Austin or Searle, *Sec*'s question is, in a word, the following: if what they call the "standard," "fulfilled," "normal," "serious," "literal," etc. is *always capable* of being affected by the non-standard, the "void," the "abnormal," the "nonserious," the "parasitical" etc., what does that tell us about the former? Parasitism does not need the theater or literature to appear. Tied to iterability, this possibility obtains constantly as we can verify at every moment, including this one. A promise that could not be reiterated (was not reiterable) a moment afterwards would not be a promise, and therein resides the possibility of parasitism, even in what Sarl calls "real life," that "real life" about which Sarl is so certain, so inimitably (almost, not quite) confident of knowing what it is, where it begins and where it ends; as though the meaning of these words ("real life") could immediately be a subject of unanimity, without the slightest risk of parasitism; as though literature, theater, deceit, infidelity, hypocrisy, infelicity, parasitism, and the simulation of real life were not part of real life!

It should also be remembered that the parasite is by definition never simply *external*, never simply something that can be excluded from or kept outside of the body "proper," shut out from the "familial" table or house. Parasitism takes place when the parasite (called thus by the owner, jealously defending his own, his *oikos*) comes to live *off the life* of the body in which it resides—and when, reciprocally, the host incorporates the parasite to an extent, willy nilly offering it hospitality: providing it with a place. The parasite then "takes place." And at bottom, whatever violently "takes place" or occupies a site is always *something* of a parasite. *Never quite* taking place is thus part of its performance, of its success as an event, of its taking-place.

The "standard" case of promises or of statements would never occur as such, with its "normal" effects, were it not, from its very inception on, parasited, harboring and haunted by the possibility of being repeated in *all kinds of ways*, of which the theater, poetry, or soliloquy are only examples, albeit examples that are more revelatory or congenial for the demonstration. From this iterability—recognized in principle by Austin and Sarl—*Sec* seeks to draw the consequences: the first and most general of which being that one neither can nor ought to exclude, even "strategically," the very roots of what one purports to analyze. For these roots are two-fold: you cannot root-out the "parasite" without rooting-out the "standard" [*le "propre"*] at the same time. What is at work here is a *different* logic of mimesis. Nor can the "pretended forms" of promise, on the stage or in a novel for instance, be "pretended" except to the extent that the so-called "standard cases" are reproduced, mimed, simulated, parasited, etc. *as* being in themselves reproducible, already *parasiticable*, as already impure. *Sec*: "For, ultimately, isn't it true that what Austin excludes as anomaly, exception, 'non-serious,' *citation* (on stage, in a poem, or a soliloquy) is the determined modification of a general citationality—or rather, a general iterability—without which there would not even be a 'successful' performative? So that—a paradoxical but unavoidable conclusion—a successful performative is necessarily. an 'impure' performative, to adopt the word advanced later on by Austin when he acknowledges that there is no 'pure' performative" (p. 191).

It will not have escaped notice that the notion of "logical dependence" or of "logical priority" plays a decisive role in Sarl's argumentation no less than in Searle's *Speech Acts*. We are constantly told: to respect the order of logical dependency we must begin with the "standard," the "serious," the "normal," etc., and we must *begin by excluding* the "non-standard," the "non-serious," the " abnormal," the parasitical. Temporary and strategical, such an exclusion thus supposedly submits its *ordo inveniendi* to a *logical* and onto-logical order. In the passage quoted Sarl writes: "The existence of the pretended form of the speech act is *logically dependent* on the possibility of the nonpretended speech act in the same way that any pretended form of behavior is *dependent* on nonpretended forms of behavior, and in that sense the pretended forms are *parasitical* on the nonpretended forms" (my emphasis). This argument of "logical dependence" constructs the axiomatics and the methodology of speech act theory as well as of the book that bears this title. It underlies the first of the five criticisms addressed at *Sec* on the subject of Austin. It is because of the confidence placed in this kind of "logical dependence" that Sarl feels able to make the distinction between "research strategy" or "temporary exclusion" on the one hand and "metaphysical exclusion" on the other. Before multiplying counterobjections of various types, I shall cite and underline yet another paragraph from the *Reply*:

Austin's exclusion of these parasitic forms from consideration in his preliminary discussion is a matter of research strategy; he is, in his words, excluding them "at present"; but it is not a metaphysical exclusion: he is not casting them into a ditch or perdition, to use Derrida's words. Derrida seems to think that Austin's exclusion is a matter of great moment, a source of deep metaphysical difficulties, and that the analysis of parasitic discourse might create some insuperable difficulties for the theory of speech acts. But the history of the subject has proved otherwise. Once one has a general theory of speech acts—a theory which Austin did not live long enough to develop himself—it is one of the relatively simpler problems to analyze the status of parasitic discourse, that is, to meet the challenge contained in Derrida's question, "what is the status of this parasitism?" Writings subsequent to Austin's have answered this question. But the terms in which this question can be intelligibly posed and answered already presuppose a general theory of speech acts. Austin correctly saw that it was necessary to hold in abeyance one set of questions, about parasitic discourse, until one has answered a logically prior set of questions about "serious" discourse. But the temporary exclusion of these questions within the development of the theory of speech acts, proved to be just that—temporary. (P. 205)

I am *not* in agreement with *any* of these assertions. For the following reasons:

a. The determination of "positive" values ("standard," serious, normal, literal, non-parasitic, etc.) is dogmatic. It does not even derive from common sense, but merely from a restrictive interpretation of common sense which is implicit and never submitted to discussion. More disturbingly: nothing allows one to say that the relation of the positive values to those which are opposed to them ("non-standard," nonserious, abnormal, parasitical, etc.), or that of the "nonpretended forms" to the "pretended forms," should be described as one of *logical dependence*. And even if this were the case, nothing proves that it would entail *this* relation of *irreversible* anteriority or of *simple* consequence. If a form of speech act that was "serious," or in general "nonpretended," did not, in its initial possibility and its very structure, include the power of giving rise to a "pretended form," it would simply not arise itself, it would be impossible. It would either not be what it is, or not have the value of a speech act.

And *vice-versa*, for I do not mean simply to *inverse* the order of logical dependence. A standard act depends as much upon the possibility of being repeated, and thus potentially [*éventuellement*] of being mimed, feigned, cited, played, simulated, parasited, etc., as the latter possibility depends upon the possibility said to be opposed to it. And both of them "depend" upon the structure of iterability which, once again, undermines the simplicity of the oppositions and alternative distinctions. It blurs the simplicity of the line dividing inside from outside, undermines the order of succession or of dependence among the terms, *prohibits* (prevents and renders illegitimate) the procedure of exclusion. Such is the *law* of iterability. Which does not amount to saying that this law has the simplicity of a logical or transcendental principle. One cannot even speak of it being fundamental or radical in the traditional philosophical sense. This is why I spoke of "two-fold roots" a while ago: two-fold roots cannot play the role of philosophical radicality. All problems arise from this non-simplicity which makes possible *and* limits at one and the same time.

b. If, as Sarl claims, the question here were simply one of "logical dependence," of logical priority ("logically prior"), it would be impossible to comprehend all the value-judgments (valorisation/devalorisation) that obtrude so massively in Austin no less than in Searle. For in the last analysis, seriously, who ever said that a dependent (logically dependent) element, a secondary element, a *logical* or even chronological consequence, could be qualified, without any further ado or justification, as "parasitical," "abnormal," "infelicitous," "void," etc.? How is it possible to ignore that this axiology, in all of its systematic and dogmatic insistence, determines an object, the analysis of which is in essence not "logical," objective, or impartial? The axiology involved in this analysis is not intrinsically determined by considerations that are merely logical. What logician, what theoretician in general, would have dared to say: B depends logically on A, therefore B is parasitic, nonserious, abnormal, etc.? One can assert of anything whatsoever that it is "logically dependent" without immediately qualifying it (as though the judgment were analytical, or even tautological) with all those attributes, the lowest common denominator of which is evidently a pejorative value-judgment. All of them mark a *decline* [*déchéance*] or a *pathology*, an ethical-ontological deterioration [*dégradation*]: i.e. more or less than a mere logical derivation. This axiological "more or less" cannot be denied. Or at least not without constituting, as far as Searle is concerned, the object of what is known [psychoanalytically] as a denial [*dénégation*].

c. The effect of this denial: the purported recourse to logical considerations is only one of "the pretended forms" of this discourse, i.e. of speech act theory. That the determining instance is not logical in character, that another kind of decision (non- or alogical) is at work here, can be discerned in another feature. Which? The analysis must now go further (higher or lower, whichever one prefers). Logic, the logical, the *logos* of logic cannot be the decisive instance here: rather, it constitutes the object of the debate, the phenomenon that must first be explained before it can be accepted as the deciding instance. The matter we are discussing here concerns the value, possibility, and system of what is called logic in general. The law and the effects with which we have been dealing, those of iterability for example, govern the possibility of every logical proposition, whether considered as a speech act or not. No constituted logic nor any rule of a logical order can, therefore, provide a decision or impose its norms upon these prelogical possibilities of logic. Such possibilities are not "logically" primary or secondary with regard to other possibilities, nor logically primary or secondary with regard to logic itself. They are (topologically?) alien to it, but not as its principle, condition of possibility, or "radical" foundation; for the structure of iterability divides and guts such radicality. It opens up the *topos* of this singular topology to the un-founded, removing language, and the rest, from its philosophical jurisdiction.

d. I therefore cannot accept the distinction between *strategical* decision and *metaphysical* presupposition. Every strategical operation, or more classically, every methodological aspect of discourse, involves a decision, one which can be more or less explicit, concerning metaphysics. And in the case with which we are dealing, this is quite spectacularly so. For it to be spectacular, however, it is not indispensable that a philosopher manifest his anxiety before "a matter of great moment" or before "a source of deep metaphysical difficulties." Such pathos is indeed alien to Austin (at least in appearance) and I find him considerably more serene and less nervous than his heirs. But the question of metaphysics lies elsewhere. The more confident, implicit, buried the metaphysical decision is, the more its order, and calm, reigns over methodological technicity.

Metaphysics in its most traditional form reigns over the Austinian heritage: over his legacy and over those who have taken charge of it as his heirs apparent. Two indications bear witness to this: 1. The hierarchical axiology, the ethical-ontological distinctions which do not merely set up value-oppositions clustered around an ideal and unfindable limit, but moreover *subordinate* these values to each other (normal/abnormal, standard/parasite, fulfilled/void, serious/non-serious, literal/non-literal, briefly: positive/negative and ideal/non-ideal); and in this, whether Sarl likes it or not, there is metaphysical pathos (infelicity, nonserious, etc. . . .). 2. The enterprise of returning "strategically," ideally, to an origin or to a "priority" held to be simple, intact, normal, pure, standard, self-identical, in order *then* to think in terms of derivation, complication, deterioration, accident, etc. All metaphysicians, from Plato to Rousseau, Descartes to Husserl, have proceeded in this way, conceiving good to be before evil, the positive before the negative, the pure before the impure, the simple before the complex, the essential before the accidental, the imitated before the imitation, etc. And this is not just *one* metaphysical gesture among others, it is *the* metaphysical exigency, that which has been the most constant, most profound and most potent. In *Sec* (as in its entire context) this force is not ignored but rather put into question, traced back to that which deploys it while at the same time limiting it. Although this "exigency" [*"requête"*] is here essentially "idealistic" I do not criticize it as such, but rather ask myself what this idealism is, what its force and its necessity are, and where its intrinsic limit is to be found. Nor is this idealism the exclusive property of those systems commonly designated as "idealistic." It can be found at times in philosophies that proclaim themselves to be anti-idealistic, in "materialisms." Or in discourses that declare themselves alien to philosophy. All discourse involves this effect of idealism in a certain manner. This particular one, for example, in a different manner.

e. Hence, the exclusion under discussion could not be "temporary." To avoid it, a different strategy would have been required. This is precisely what *Sec* sought to point out. The exclusion could not be temporary and in fact, contrary to what Sarl asserts, it has not been. Neither in Austin, nor to my knowledge in the self-proclaimed heirs of his problematic. This holds in particular for Searle, whose *Speech Acts* seem to me to reproduce Austin's strategy of idealizing exclusions, or even, I would say, to systematize and to rigidify it (with the ensuing losses and gains), using essentially the same conceptual instruments, hierarchical oppositions, and axiology. As to the "general theory," Sarl would like Austin both to have had one (which would put him beyond the pale of empiricism) and also, having died too young, not to have really had (or "developed") one, so that the copyright of the "general theory" in the proper, literal sense, as an adult and fully developed speech act, could be the rightful property only of the more or less anonymous company of his sons, here represented by the footnoted reference to John R. Searle. This is why—as we shall see in an instant—the paragraph beginning with "Once one has a general theory of speech acts . . ." constitutes a true wonder, a masterpiece of metaphysical-oedipal rhetoric. Imagine the scene: Austin's will is about to be unsealed. Although the envelope has not yet been entirely opened, the lawyer of one of the sons begins to speak: "Once one has a general theory of speech acts. . . ." Once? We still don't know if Austin had one or was going to have one. This "once," from a rhetorical point of view and floating as it does between the logical and the chronological, organizes the suspense among all the presumptive heirs. Did Austin have it? In which case the heritage would be more certain? Did he not quite have it, in which case it would still have to be developed? If so, by whom, with what justification, in what direction? Sarl has said "Once one has. . . ." Ah! That "one": it is the moment of anonymity, oscillating between Austin and Searle, who, at the end of this paragraph, is going to take things in hand, or rather, in a footnote. I re-cite and underline: *"Once one has* a general theory of speech acts—a theory which Austin did not live long enough *to develop himself*—it is one of the relatively simpler problems to analyze the status of parasitic discourse, that is, to meet the challenge contained in Derrida's question, "What is the status of this parasitism?" Writings subsequent to Austin's have answered this question.[4]" And has footnote to this "subsequence": "4. For a detailed answer to the question, see J. R. Searle, 'The Logical Status of Fictional Discourse,' *New Literary History* 5 (1975)."

I sincerely regret that "Austin did not live long enough," and my regret is as sincere as anyone else's is, for there are surely many of us who mourn his loss. It is unfortunate, even infelicitous. But through my tears I still smile at the argument of a "development" (a word sufficiently ambiguous to mean both produce, formulate, *as well as* continue, so as to reach those "detailed answers"), that a longer life might have led to a successful conclusion. Searle might thus be considered to have "developed" the theory: to have produced it, elaborated, and formulated it, *and* at the same time to have merely extended it in detail, guided it to adulthood by unfolding its potential.

Like Sarl I also believe that Austin had, in an implicit state, a general theory. It was presupposed (Sarl says "presuppose" in the following line) and it cannot be the effect of an extension or accumulation of results or analyses of details. But this general theory did not permit him—and has never permitted anyone—to integrate what it started out by excluding, even strategically, in the name of those metaphysical concepts, values, and axioms upon which this theory was constructed qua general theory.

And after Austin? What happened *once* ("Once one has . . ."), using the general theory, detailed answers will have been given to the questions left in suspense by the will?

After Austin? I don't know if the signatory of *Sec* should have apologized, in 1971, for having not yet read or anticipated the article of Searle which, in 1975, is supposed to have "answered the question." For my part, I have just read it. With considerable interest and attention. With the desire to reread it and to discuss it elsewhere in detail. But I have yet to find the slightest answer, in principle or in detail, to the questions that concern us here. Notably involving the "status" of parasitism. This notion is still operational in the recent article (see especially p. 326), where it is used to explain the "break" with or "suspension" of the "vertical rules" that govern the "normal operation" of illocutionary acts and the world, by means of horizontal conventions (of an extralinguistic, nonsemantic character) which render "fiction" possible. But concerning the structure and the possibility of parasitism itself, or the value-judgment normal/abnormal, nothing further is said. All the distinctions proposed (the two meanings of *to pretend*, the interaction of the so-called vertical rules with the horizontal conventions, the difference between "work of fiction" and "fictional discourse"), however interesting they may be, seem to me to reproduce the logical apparatus that I am calling into question here: they re-pose the same questions instead of, as Sarl claims, providing an answer, whether in principle or in detail. Leaving the discussion of each of these distinctions, and even of each of these examples, until a later date, I will have to make do here with an indication. But it will be general and sweeping. Here it is. I was surprised to see this article cited as a "detailed answer" to the questions (and above all to the decisive question of parasitism) that Austin, allegedly for lack of time, left unresolved: either unresolved in detail or insufficiently "developed." In 1977 Sarl recalls that Searle's article "answered this question." But in 1975 Searle didn't seem to think this at all. His conclusion was clear: "The preceding analysis leaves one crucial [again!] question unanswered: why bother? That is, why do we attach such importance and effort to texts which contain largely pretended speech acts?" If this excellent question indeed imposes itself and remains unresolved, it is because all the previous distinctions are not rigorous, either in fact or in principle. Had they been so, there would have been no contamination possible between our (serious) interest for the one and our disinterest for the other. The problem, in a word, is that the logic of parasitism is not a logic of distinction or of opposition, and that Searle constantly seeks to analyze parasitism *in* a logic that it has rendered possible and impossible at once. A parasite is neither the same as nor different from that which it parasites. The possibility of fiction cannot be derived.

I said that the Searle of 1975, by contrast with the Sarl of 1977, did not claim to have furnished an answer either to the "crucial" question or to that of the "general theory" which would have resolved it. Instead, there is, first of all, a disappointing reference to the mystery of "imagination" in "human life," as though the mention of this "faculty" would be of the slightest help. Here it is: "The preceding analysis leaves one crucial question unanswered: why bother? That is, why do we attach such importance and efforts to texts which contain largely pretended speech acts? The reader who has followed my argument this far will not be surprised to hear that I do not think there is any simple or even single answer to that question. Part of the answer would have to do with the crucial [again!] role, usually underestimated, that imagination plays in human life, and the equally crucial [!] role that shared products of the imagination play in human social life." A big help. And concerning the "imagination" (why should this name, which traditionally covers an entire field of problems of interest to us here, be refused?) there is not even an allusion to the extraordinary richness of a traditional philosophical discourse that would never have deigned to accept the little that is offered us here. But the conclusion of the article is close at hand. And nine lines further down, we discover indeed that the general theory of how "pretended illocutions" can "convey" such "serious illocutionary intentions," that this "general theory" (which itself comprises only a part of the overall general theory) does not yet exist. And if one believes, as I do, that this particular part—on parasitism—is parasitic of the whole, certain consequences become inescapable. Here are the final words of this "detailed answer to the question": "Literary critics have explained on an ad hoc and particularistic basis how the author conveys a serious

Jacques Derrida

speech act through the performance of the pretended speech acts which constitute the work of fiction, but there is as yet no general theory of the mechanisms by which such serious illocutionary intentions are conveyed by pretended illocutions." The End.

w

Sarl's *second objection* is practically redundant with regard to the first. It consists in recalling that Austin's concept of "parasitism" involves a relation of "logical dependence": "It does not imply any moral judgment and certainly not that the parasite is somehow immorally sponging off the host." I have already answered this objection in principle. I will simply add that it is not necessary to point to a flesh-and-blood example, or to write moralizing pamphlets demanding the exclusion of wicked parasites (those of language or of the *polis*, the effects of the unconscious, the *pharmakoi*, people on welfare, nonconformists or spies) in order to speak an ethical-political language or—and, in the case of Austin at least, this is all that I wished to indicate—to reproduce in a discourse said to be theoretical the founding categories of all ethical-political statements. I am convinced that speech act theory is fundamentally and in its most fecund, most rigorous, and most interesting aspects (need I recall that it interests me considerably?) a theory of right or law, of convention, of political ethics or of politics as ethics. It describes (in the best Kantian tradition, as Austin acknowledges at one point) the pure conditions of an ethical-political discourse insofar as this discourse involves the relation of intentionality to conventionality or to rules. What I wanted to emphasize above, however, in this regard was simply the following: this "theory" is compelled to reproduce, to reduplicate in itself the law of its object or its object as law; it must submit to the norm it purports to analyze. Hence, both its fundamental, intrinsic moralism and its irreducible empiricism. And Hegel knew how to demonstrate how compatible both are with a certain kind of formalism.

As for the second part of this second objection ("it is simply a mistake to say that Austin thought parasitic discourse was not part of ordinary language," p. 206), I remind you that *Sec* never said anything of the sort. Merely this: according to Austin, the parasite *is part* of so-called ordinary language, and it is part of it *as* parasite. That's all. I also recalled, just a little while ago, that the parasite *is part*, in its way (neither the same nor other), of what it parasites and is not simply external or alien to it. But if Austin recognized this "being-part-of," it didn't prevent him from proposing to "exclude" (see above) this part. That's all. "All this [i.e. *"parasitic"* as opposed to *"normal* use"—my emphasis] we are *excluding* from consideration." Isn't that clear enough? Did or did not Austin propose to exclude, under the rubric of parasitism, something which *is part* of ordinary language but which, he claimed, is not *normally* a part of *normal* ordinary language? This is why *Sec* never argued that for Austin the parasite is not part of ordinary language but rather, that "the concept of the 'ordinary,' thus of 'ordinary language' to which he has recourse is clearly marked by this exclusion." *"Marked by* this exclusion"—can this be denied?

x

We now come to the *third objection*. It is aimed at what is so admirably entitled *"more than simply a misreading of Austin."* This objection repeats—or makes slightly more explicit—the preceding ones. The response has already been given twice: in *Sec* and here. But I am certainly ready to try patiently to adapt these responses to the precise literality of this third objection. I shall cite it, responding to it point by point. I am referring to the first three paragraphs of point 3 of the *Reply* (Section II, p. 206). The fourth paragraph begins with "On a sympathetic reading of Derrida's text we can construe. . . ." Although it hardly satisfies me, this remorse is an interesting signal. It deserves to be treated separately. Here, now, are my responses:

a. It was *never* said or suggested in *Sec* that "Austin somehow denied the very possibility that expressions can be quoted." It was said rather that by the exclusion of which we have just spoken, he deprived himself of the means that would have enabled him to take into account both the *possibility* of citation within that allegedly normal structure, and certain other things as well. He deprives himself of the means with which to account for a possibility inscribed in the use he himself calls "normal."

b. It was *never* said or suggested in *Sec* that the "phenomenon of citationality" is "the same as the phenomenon of parasitic discourse." It was never said in *Sec* that the novelist, poet and actor are "in general quoting," although they can also do that. What *Sec* was driving at, without confusing citationality with parasitism (or fiction, literature, or theater), was the possibility they have in common: the iterability which renders possible *both* the "normal" rule or convention *and* its transgression, transformation, simulation, or imitation. From this, *Sec* drew consequences different from those drawn by Austin; above all, the illegitimate and unfeasible character of the exclusions proposed either on strategic grounds or on methodological (idealizing) ones. I will add here (and is this only a matter of detail?) that parasitism (in the strict sense, if one can still speak of this) is always susceptible to the parasitism of citation, just as citationality can always be parasited by the parasite. The parasite parasites the limits that guarantee the purity of rules and of intentions, and this is not devoid of import for law, politics, economic, ethics, etc.

I have already stated my reservations concerning the ultimate rigor of the distinction between *use* and *mention*. But even to the extent that such a distinction is accepted as being trivially evident, as the initial manifestation of a rigidified effect, even at this level there is still no confusion ever in *Sec* of citation (in the sense considered strict by Sarl: that which is indicated by quotation-marks) with that other effect of iterability, the "parasite" excluded by Austin. Nor was citationality ever confused with iterability in general, but simply traced back to it, as in the case of a more spectacular or more pedagogical example or illustration. *Sec* even warned of the confusion Sarl charges it with having committed. The proof? Here it is. Of course it's a quotation, taken from the very statement cited and hence presumably read by Sarl, but which evidently requires rereading. The "or rather" in this passage marks, as might be expected, a distinction, as does the series enumerating the different types of excluded phenomena: "For, ultimately, isn't it true that what Austin excludes as anomaly, exceptions, 'non-serious' *citation* (on stage, in a poem, or a soliloquy) is the determined modification of a general citationality—*or rather, a general iterability*—without which there would not even be a 'successful' performative?" (p. 191). (This time I have underlined what might not have performed "successfully" or sufficiently so for certain readers.)

By virtue—here as always—of a certain interest, Sarl has paid insufficient attention to the *very* letter of the *very* phrase that was cited; Sarl was inattentive to what this citation said about what should not be confused with citation. But if this is so, how can one expect Sarl to have paid attention to all the other statements he didn't cite? To all those utterances (perhaps he'll begin looking for them now) where the *or* which articulates the relation between citation and iteration (citation "or" iteration), between citationality and iterability (citationality "or" iterability) evidently signifies *neither* equivalence, dissociation, nor opposition? This "or" marks another relationship. The "confusion" that Sarl denounces precipitously in *Sec* ("Derrida in this argument confuses no less than three separate and distinct phenomena: iterability, citationality, and parasitism"), this "confusion" is precisely that of which *Sec* warns: explicitly, insistently, *literally*. For example, and I underline here:

We should first be clear on what constitutes the status of "occurrence" or the eventhood of an event that entails in its allegedly present and singular emergence the intervention of an utterance [*énoncé*] that in itself can be only repetitive or citational in its structure, *or rather, since those two words may lead to confusion: iterable.* (P. 191)

Is this clear enough? No? Then let us continue:

I return then to a point that strikes me as fundamental and that now concerns the status of events in general, of events of speech or by speech, of the strange logic they entail and that often passes unseen.

Could a performative utterance succeed if its formulation did not repeat a "coded" or iterable utterance, or in other words, if the formula I pronounce in order to open a meeting, launch a ship or a marriage were not identifiable as *conforming* with an iterable model, if it were not then identifiable *in some way as a "citation"*?

Is this clear enough, with quotation-marks around " "citation" " and "in some way"? No? Then let us continue:

Not that citationality in this case is of the same sort as in a theatrical play, a philosophical reference, or the recitation of a poem. That is why there is a relative specificity, as Austin says, a "relative purity" of performatives. But this relative purity does not emerge *in opposition to* citationality *or* iterability, but in opposition to *other kinds of iteration* within a general iterability which constitutes a violation of the allegedly rigorous purity of every event of discourse or every *speech act.* Rather than oppose citation or iteration to the non-iteration of an event, one ought to construct a differential typology of forms of iteration, assuming that such a project is tenable and can result in an exhaustive program, a question I hold in abeyance here. (P. 192)

Is this finally clear? The reasons for my reservation at the end will perhaps be more evident now: once iterability has established the possibility of parasitism, of a certain fictionality altering at once—*Sec* too [*aussi sec*]—the system of (il- or perlocutionary) intentions and the systems of ("vertical") rules or of ("horizontal") conventions, inasmuch as they are included within the scope of iterability; once this parasitism or fictionality can always add *another* parasitic or fictional structure to whatever has preceded it—what I elsewhere designate as a "supplementary code" ["*supplément de code*"]—everything becomes possible against the language-police; for example "literatures" or "revolutions" that as yet have no model. Everything is possible except for an exhaustive typology that would claim to limit the powers of graft or of fiction by and within an analytical logic of distinction, opposition, and classification in genus and species. The theoretician of speech acts will have to get used to the idea that, knowingly or not, willingly or not, both his treatment of things and the things themselves are marked in advance by the possibility of fiction, either as the iterability of acts or as the system of conventionality. He will therefore never be able to *de-limit* the object-fiction or the object-parasite except by another counter-fiction.

Sec has not, therefore, confused iterability, citationality, or parasitism. If all the same it did not simply set them in opposition to one another in an alternative distinction; if it, on the contrary, associated them without confusing them, namely, by means of an *or, or rather*, it is because the logic of iterability demands such an opposition. Iterability cannot be simply the genus, of which citation or other phenomena (the parasite in the "strict" sense, for instance) would be the species. Fiction (parasite) can always re-work [*re-traverser*], remark *every* other type of iteration. But iterability is, however, not a transcendental condition of possibility making citation and other phenomena (parasites, for example) into conditioned effects: it is neither an essence nor a substance to be distinguished from phenomena, attributes, or accidents. This kind of (classical) logic is fractured in its code by iterability. Parasitic contamination, once again, broaches and breaches all these relations. If *Sec* had confused citation with iteration, how would it be possible to explain that each of these words would have to be regularly qualified or supplemented by the other (precisely to guard against such confusion)? We have seen how the *or*, and *or rather* function between the two terms. Here, now, is the device of the parenthesis: "The graphematic root of citationality (iterability) is what creates this embarrassment and makes it impossible, as Austin says, 'to lay down even a list of all possible criteria' " (*Sec*, note 10). The parentheses do not mark synonyms or an identification but rather the *possibility* referred to by citationality, which here, a traditional philosopher might say, serves as the guiding thread of the analysis. No citation without iteration. Who could doubt that citation implies iteration? Placed in parentheses, "iterability" can define citationality *in its possibility*, and its "graphematic root" as well.

I have just evoked the figure of the traditional philosopher. This figure is still necessary, if only to remind Sarl that the word "modification," in the phrase cited, refers to *mode* and not merely, as it often implies (parasitically enough) in an all too ordinary language, to *transformation*. *Sec* uses/mentions the code of traditional philosophy (among others); one of its conventions which, like all others, cannot be fully and rigorously justified, supposes the knowledge of certain *a b c*s of classical philosophy, so that when it uses or mentions the word "modification," it is also to signify modal determination: the contraction of a substance or an attribute into a mode or a modality. "Modification" is therefore not opposed to exemplification ("instantiation") as Sarl seems to think in objecting: "Like all utterances, parasitic forms of utterances are instances of, *though not modifications of*, iterability, for—to repeat—without iterability there is no language at all" (p. 206, my emphasis). Sarl here misconstrues the classical sense of the word "modification," except, that is—to repeat—without iterability there is no language at all, nor many other things either. But the latter is precisely the argument of *Sec*, from beginning to end; and I repeat it here. Once again: it-reapplies.

The mechanism of the "it-reapplies," which consists in not wanting to read in *Sec* the arguments one tries to use against it, is kept in motion by a sort of fascinated allergy which all of a sudden, presumably due to exhaustion, turns (recognizing itself?) into a movement of sympathy hitherto strictly forbidden. It is the final paragraph of the third objection, which, as I said, I shall treat separately. It recalls that precisely this general iterability cannot be made into an objection to Austin. As if anyone had ever done this! I cite this paragraph of "sympathy." The latter, as you will see, is rather limited:

> On a sympathetic reading of Derrida's text we can construe him as pointing out, quite correctly, that the possibility of parasitic discourse is internal to the notion of language, and that performatives can succeed only if the utterances are iterable, repetitions of conventional—or as he calls them, "coded"—forms. But neither of these points is in any way an objection to Austin. Indeed, Austin's insistence on the conventional character of the performative utterance in particular and the illocutionary act in general commits him precisely to the view that performatives must be iterable, in the sense that any conventional act involves the notion of the repetition of the same. (P. 207)

(I have again quoted a paragraph *in extenso*. Adding up all the quotes, I believe that I will have cited the *Reply* from beginning to end, or almost. Did I have the right(s)? I have, so to speak, incorporated (with or without quotation-marks) it into this "Limited Inc," without even being certain, at the moment of writing this—while Sam Weber is translating and the Johns Hopkins Press is harrying the two of us—who exactly will be entitled to its copyright ©, or who is going to share it with whom, both the "original" and/or the so-called translation. (I might add that the writing of the so-called "original," in return, has continually been transformed by the translation: a case of parasitic feedback, including this very parenthesis. I cannot even say if the lawyer representing the Company holding the copyright of the *Reply* is going to bring suit against the Company of "Limited Inc" for having reproduced and incorporated (I didn't say destroyed) all or almost all of the *Reply*? Perhaps then at least I may get to explain to the court all the implications (psychoanalytic, political, juridical, censorial [*policières*], economic, etc.) of this debate, something that I have not been able to do here, the incorporation of the *Reply* having taken up too much time and space.)

In view of the fact that the paragraph of sympathy is one of the

Jacques Derrida

briefest, I can only ask: had something of this sort, i.e. a sympathetic reading of *Sec*, been able to take place and to last, wouldn't it have endowed the *Reply* with a kind of absolute brevity?

But as feeble and intermittent as it may be, this sympathy does not suffice. Look at this paragraph of "sympathetic reading": it still contains the charge that *Sec* accuses Austin of forgetting iterability. Nonsense. *Sec* endeavors to account otherwise for this iterability and to draw rigorous consequences from this account, something that Austin, for reasons already discussed, did not do in a systematic manner.

This iterability (about which there seems to be general agreement) is immediately associated, in the same paragraph, with conventionality and "the repetition of the same." But despite all the sympathy between us, I cannot follow Sarl here: neither concerning the "repetition of the same" (I have already said why the other and alteration works parasitically within the very inner core of the iter qua repetition of the identical), nor concerning conventionality. I do not believe that iterability is necessarily tied to convention, and even less, that it is limited by it. Iterability is precisely that which—once its consequences have been unfolded—can no longer be dominated by the opposition nature/convention. It dislocates, subverts, and constantly displaces the dividing-line between the two terms. It has an essential rapport with the force (theoretical and practical, "effective," "historical," "psychic," "political," etc.) deconstructing these oppositional limits. This is indeed a very important ("crucial"!) motif for our discussion, although I cannot go into it any farther here. I have done so elsewhere, and very often.

y

I will now cite Sarl's fourth objection, underlining several words here and there to be taken up in my response.

4. Derrida *assimilates* the sense in which writing can be said to be *parasitic* on spoken language with the sense in which fiction, etc., are parasitic on nonfiction or standard discourse. But these are quite different. In the case of the distinction between fiction and nonfiction, the relation is one of *logical dependency*. One could not have the concept of fiction without the concept of serious discourse. But the dependency of writing on spoken language is a *contingent fact* about the history of human languages and not logical truth about the nature of language. Indeed, in mathematical and logical symbolism, the relation of dependence *goes the other way*. The spoken, oral version of the symbols is simply an orally communicable way of representing the primary written forms. (P. 207)

Responses. a. It is imprudent to assimilate too quickly, more quickly than one can, what is not easily assimilable. Otherwise, what is liable to result is what certain psychoanalysts call incorporation without introjection: a sort of indigestion more or less desired by the unconscious and provoked by the other or alien body which cannot yet be assimilated.

Sec never, nowhere, "assimilated" what Sarl would like it to have assimilated so that it in turn could then be assimilated by Sarl to something else. It never assimilated the parasitism of writing in regard to speech to that of fiction in regard to "standard" discourse. Had Sarl taken the trouble, as I have been doing, to cite the incriminated phrase, the confusion could have been easily avoided: "It is *as just such* [*Aussi comme un*] a 'parasite' that writing has always been treated by the philosophical tradition, and the connection in this case is by no means coincidental" (p. 190). If the translation here is ambiguous, the French is not: "*Aussi comme un* 'parasite' . . ." that is, "*as another such* parasite . . ."! It is not a question of assimilating these parasites to each other but of remarking that *also* [*aussi*], in the case of writing, one speaks of a parasite *as well* [*encore*], and that it is neither fortuitous nor insignificant that this is done in all these cases. The symptom has interested me for a long time. The parasitic structure is what I have tried to analyze everywhere, under the names of writing, mark, step [*marche*], margin, *différance*, graft, undecidable, supplement, *pharmakon*, hymen, *parergon*, etc. Just as the phrase of *Sec* that we have just read is itself a kind of citation, in a hidden, fictitious, or parasitic way, I am *also* quoting *Sec* (thus conforming to the rule that I adopted or imposed upon myself by force: not to cite any other text signed by me) in citing this: "It is in the course of this second demonstration that the literally Saussurian formulas reappear within the question of the relationships between speech and writing; the order of writing is the order . . . of the *"parasitic"* (*Of Grammatology* [Baltimore: Johns Hopkins Univ. Press, 1976], p. 54). This citation, sub-cited by *Sec*, includes a citation from Jakobson and Halle, who write in *Phonology and Phonetics*: "There is no such thing in human society as the supplantation of the speech code by its visual replicas, but only a supplementation of this code by parasitic auxiliaries."[12] As though an auxiliary could not supplant! As though a parasite should not supplant! As though "supplanting" were a simple operation, the object of a simple cognition! As though "to add" something like a "parasite" constituted a simple addition! As though an addition were ever simple! As though that to which a parasite is "added" could possibly remain as it is, unaltered! As though an addition or repetition did not alter! Finally, still developing the sub-citation of *Sec*, the following—and I will have then finished with this point—which *directly* concerns our debate:

The purity of the within can henceforth only be restored by *accusing* exteriority of being a supplement, something inessential and yet detrimental to that essence, an excess that *should not have been* added to the unadulterated plenitude of the within. The restoration of inner purity must therefore reconstitute, *recite*—and this is myth itself, the *mythology*, for example, of a *logos* recounting its origin and returning to the eve of a pharmacographical assault—that to which the *pharmakon* should not have been added, thereby intruding and becoming a *literal parasite*: a letter invading the interior of a living organism, *nourishing* itself there and disturbing the pure audibility of a voice. Such are the relations between the supplement of writing and the *logos-zoôn*. To heal the latter of the *pharmakon* and to banish the parasite, the outside must be put back in its place. The outside must be kept out. This is the gesture inaugurating "logic" itself, that good "sense" in accord with the self-identity of *that which is*: the entity is what it is, the outside is out and the inside in. Writing should thus become once more what it should never have ceased being: accessory, accidental, excessive.[13]

b. I have already said why relations of a logical order have seemed to me devoid of all pertinence. When Sarl writes: "One could not have the concept of fiction without the concept of serious discourse," one could with equal legitimacy reverse the order of dependence. This order is not a one-way street [*à sens unique*] (how can the serious be defined or postulated without reference to the nonserious, even if the latter is held to be simply external to it?) and everything that claims to base itself upon such a conception disqualifies itself immediately. This is the case of speech act theory and all its "strategic" exclusions: they must always invoke the authority of this one-way movement.

c. This does not, however, imply that the asserted "dependence" of writing in regard to spoken language is "a contingent fact about the history of human language." This dependence is not, of course, "a logical truth about the nature of human language." I agree, and I have sought elsewhere to draw all sorts of consequences from this. But to reduce it to a "contingent fact" seems to me very simplistic. Structural and historical laws have constructed this "dependence" everywhere where it has manifested itself, with everything it has produced, above all in the way of symptoms and of lures. The length and nature of the analyses that I have endeavored to devote to this question cannot be summarized here. It's not a serious problem, but it is unfortunate, infelicitous, inasmuch as these analyses form part of the implicit context of *Sec*, and hence of its conventional premises, its rules. To this extent at least the speech acts of *Sec* remain unintelligible, illegible and in any case inoperative for anyone who is not also interested in the questions that gave rise to such analyses. This is also an extenuating circumstance for anyone who does not understand them. In saying "infelicitous" and "extenuating circumstance" I am, of course, citing *Sec* citing Austin (p. 189).

d. As for the argument according to which the dependency-relation of writing to speech is different "in mathematical and logical symbolism," I can hardly take it as an objection since it can be retraced to *Sec* even more quickly than usual. It is one of the essential arguments in the deconstruction of phono-logocentrism. And it can even be found in the forefront. Ten years ago it opened the first chapter of the book cited a few pages back, and it dealt with the question of parasitism. Neither Sarl nor anyone else can, of course, be expected to know something which, although outside of *Sec*, still forms part of its context. But whoever accepts the convention that consists in saying that one is going to read and criticize *Sec* is required to read what, within its limited corpus, points towards this context: for example, the *three conclusions* concerning "the exposure [*mis en cause*] of this effect that I have called elsewhere logocentrism." These three conclusions open with the formula, "To conclude this *very dry* [sec] discussion:" (pp. 194–6).

And, for the second time, I am going to conclude a bit abruptly, since I see that all I have left is the letter

z

Nor, finally, can I accept as an argument against *Sec* what Sarl claims to oppose to it in the fifth and last *objection*: "Indeed, I shall conclude this discussion by arguing for precisely the converse thesis: the iterability of linguistic forms facilitates and is a necessary condition of the particular forms of intentionality that are characteristic of speech acts" (pp. 207–8). This "necessary condition" is one of *Sec*'s most insistent themes. How can one seriously claim to raise this as an objection to it, much less assert it to be "the converse thesis," when in fact one is saying the very same thing? Naturally, in the effort to reach this point, Sarl must act as though *Sec* had postulated the pure and simple disappearance of intention in speech acts. I have already recalled that this is not the case. What is limited by iterability is not intentionality in general, but its character of being conscious or present to itself (actualized, fulfilled, and adequate), the simplicity of its features, its *undividedness*. To cite once again: "In such a typology, *the category of intention will not disappear*; it will have its place, but from that place it will no longer be able to govern the entire scene and system of utterance [*l'énonciation*]. Above all, at that point we will be dealing with different kinds of marks or chains of iterable marks and not with an opposition between citational utterances, on the one hand, and singular and original event-utterances, on the other. The first consequence of this will be the following: given that structure of iteration, the intention animating the utterance will never be through and through present to itself and to its content. *The iteration structuring it a priori* introduces into it a dehiscence and a cleft [*brisure*] which are essential" (p. 192, my emphasis). How, after this, can one seriously assert that, for *Sec*, iterability is "in conflict with the intentionality of linguistic acts" (p. 208)?

The *fifth objection* thus develops one of *Sec*'s arguments while at the same time pretending to pose it as an objection—all this by means of a feint or pose which could either be a sort of infelicitous ruse (the first sense of *to pretend*) or a successful fiction (or at least for the duration of a good show, in the second sense of *to pretend*). (I shall leave this question open and not claim the copyright, in the name of the signatories of *Sec*, to the arguments borrowed from it and reproduced, almost literally and with regularity by Sarl, while pretending to pose them as objections. I will not claim the copyright because ultimately [*en dernière instance*] there is always a police and a tribunal ready to intervene each time that a rule (constitutive or regulative, vertical or not) is invoked in a case involving signatures, events, or contexts. This is what I meant to say. If the police is always waiting in the wings, it is because conventions are by essence violable and precarious, *in themselves* and by the fictionality that constitutes them, even before there has been any overt transgression, in the "first sense" of *to pretend*.) Here, parenthetically, I shall give Searle some advice, if he permits, while awaiting a later date to renew this debate more patiently and to use another *a b c*. In his article in *New Literary History*, Searle gives us the following explanation of the two meanings of *to pretend*: "If I pretend to be Nixon in order to fool the Secret Service into letting me into the White House, I am pretending in the first sense; if I pretend to be Nixon as part of a game of charades, it is pretending in the second sense. Now in the fictional use of words, it is pretending in the second sense which is in question" (pp. 324–25). All that is true, and yet I am not entirely satisfied, as I shall explain elsewhere. In what sense and to what extent is the example itself ("If I . . .") a fiction? For the moment, here is my advice: it applies to the day when the person who says *I* (Searle) will no longer, as in 1975, be in *New Literary History*, Virginia, but instead will be dreaming of being taken (I don't say mistaking himself) for Jimmy Carter and demanding to be finally admitted to the White House. Upon encountering certain difficulties, as one can anticipate, he will, if he takes my advice, tell the Secret Service: it was all a fiction, I was pretending in the second sense; I was pretending (in the second sense) to pretend (in the first sense). They, of course, will ask for proof, for witnesses, not being satisfied with declarations of intention; they will ask which of the "horizontal conventions" were involved in this game. My advice to Searle, at this point, is to say that he is playing all by himself, that he alone forms a company, just like certain chess players who play by themselves or with fictitious opponents; or he can also say that he was experimenting with a fiction ("to pretend" in the second sense) in view of writing a novel or a philosophical demonstration for

Glyph. Let's not worry about details. If he insists upon entering the White House with such declarations, he will be arrested. If he continues to insist, the official psychiatrist will not be long in coming. What will he say to this expert? I leave that to the imagination; and although my advice stops here, my foresight doesn't: at one moment or another he will notice that between the notion of responsibility manipulated by the psychiatric expert (the representative of law and of political-linguistic conventions, in the service of the State and of its police) and the exclusion of parasitism, there is something like a relation. My last bit of advice, then, is for Searle to try to move the psychiatric expertise in the direction of the questions posed by *Sec*. That will also leave us enough time to take up this discussion again. Apropos: in what sense did Nixon pretend to be Nixon, President of the United States up to a certain date? Who will ever know this, in all rigor? He himself?

I shall therefore not claim a copyright because this entire matter of the police must be reconsidered, and not merely in a theoretical manner if one does not want the police to be omnipotent; and also because the copyright is the object of *Sec*, its issue [*chose*] and its business, its cause (*Sache, Ursache*) and its trial, process, proceeding, [*procès*], albeit one that is impossible to appropriate. I close the parenthesis.)

It is clear that, despite all its borrowing from *Sec*, I am far from subscribing to all the statements made in the *Reply*. For instance, each time it is a question of "communication" (almost all the time), of "mastery" and of identity (". . . the speaker and hearers are masters of the sets of rules we call the rules of language, and these rules are recursive," p. 208). Iterability is at once the condition and the limit of mastery: it broaches and breaches it. And this cannot be devoid of consequences for the concepts of "application," of "rules," of "performance," etc.

I promised (very) sincerely to be serious. Have I kept my promise? Have I taken Sarl seriously? I do not know if I was supposed to. Should I have? Were they themselves serious in their speech acts? Shall I say that I am afraid they were? Would that mean that I do not take their seriousness very seriously?

What am I saying? What am I doing when I say that?

I ask myself if we will ever be quits with this confrontation.

Will it have taken place, this time?

Quite?

Jacques Derrida

Translated by Samuel Weber

NOTES

1. What is a title, according to the general theory of speech acts? And for example, from this point of view, the title *Speech Acts*? And *Signature Event Context*, these three nouns juxtaposed without either copula or apparent attribution? And what I am deciding here and from this instant on to designate with the conventional sign (but conventional to what point?), *Sec*? And is it only due to brevity? The translator can, if he likes, say *Dry*. He has already done so (in the text) and will find his authorization (a supplementary one, since he has every right) in the fact that the presumed author of *Sec* deliberately programmed the thing. Three pages before the end of *Sec* you can read this: "In order to function, that is, to be readable, a signature must have a repeatable, iterable, imitable form; it must be able to be detached from the present and singular intention of its production. It is its sameness which, by corrupting its identity and its singularity, divides its seal [*sceau*]. I have already indicated above the principle of this analysis.

To conclude this very *dry* discussion [*Pour conclure ce propos très sec*] . . ."

Sec is set there—in a manner which, you may take my word for it, was hardly fortuitous—in italics. Three points follow, which lead to the apparent simulacrum of "my" signatures, of my seal in bits and pieces, divided, multiplied. All that isn't very serious, Sarl will perhaps say. Serious? Not serious? That is the question: why does that absorb and irritate Sarl to such a degree? And were Sarl to object that in each one of these examples (titles, names, abbreviations, etc.) there are several *functions* at the same time, cohabiting parasitically with each other, how is that possible? And all that within the appearance of one and the same body, one and the same utterance? And how could this lack of seriousness have been taken so seriously?

The "very dry discussion" conducting *continuously* to the multiple signature of *Sec*, *Sec* will henceforth designate the whole of *Sec* plus (including) its multiple, presumed, divided, and associated signatories. Which signals—to arrive at a temporary conclusion concerning the question of titles, under the title of "perhaps more serious than one thinks,"—that *Signature Event Context* might also lend credence to the parasite of a "true" dependent proposition: "signature event that one texts" [*signature événement qu'on texte*]. Concerning the calculated necessity of this neological usage of the verb *to text* [*texter*], cf. "Having the Ear of Philosophy," [*Avoir l'oreille de la philosophie*], Conversation with Lucette Finas, reprinted in *Ecarts, Quatre essais à propos de jacques Derrida* (Paris, 1973). In particular, one can read there the following: "'That which for the discursive consciousness is impossible to anticipate [*l'inanticipable*] calls for a new logic of the repressed [*re-foulé*]. Concerning the effects of timbre (*tympanon*) and of signature, *Qual Quelle* situates a "paradoxical logic of the event": this should account for the irreplacable, which only produces itself in losing itself *aussi sec* [a French idiom meaning immediately, on the spot, without delay—*at once*], textually, in the process of iteration: signature, event that one texts [*signature, événement qu'on texte.*] The *sur-number* [*surnombre*] of *La dissémination* already marked this pluralization that fractures the event, even of the unique, while at the same time causing it *to occur* [*arriver*].

The system of presence, of the origin, of archeology, or of production must be deconstructed so that the event can occur, and not simply be thought or uttered. One could even say that the event (is what) deconstructs. Blanchot: 'Does that happen'—'No, that doesn't happen.'—'Something, nevertheless, is coming.' "

Does that ever quite take place?

2. The film, "The Front," starring Woody Allen, was shown in France under the title, "Le Prête-nom." (Translator's note)

3. A propos, the dossier of this debate should include Austin's article, "Three Ways of Spilling Ink" (in his *Philosophical Papers* [London: Oxford University Press, 1976], pp. 272–287). In it Austin analyzes the differences between "'intentionally," "deliberately," "on purpose (purposely)." I refer to it here in a kind of *oratio obliqua*. After a paragraph explaining why it "would be wholly untrue . . . to suggest that 'unintentionally' is the word that 'wears that trousers,' " Austin underlines the word *limited* in the passage that follows (where "my idea of what I'm doing" is compared to "a miner's lamp on our forehead"): "The only general rule is that the illumination is always *limited*, and that in several ways. It will never extend indefinitely far ahead . . . Moreover, it does not illuminate *all* of my surroundings. Whatever I am doing is being done and to be done amidst a background of *circumstances* (including of course activities by other agents). . . . Furthermore, the doing of it will involve *incidentally* all kinds of minutiae of, at the least, bodily movements, and often many other things besides" (p. 284). I am indebted to Sam Weber for bringing this text, which is highly illuminating in more ways than one, to my attention.

4. J. L. Austin, *How to Do Things with Words* (London: Oxford University Press, 1976), p. 74.

5. For a more detailed discussion of the divided *stigmè*, in regard to philosophical conceptions of temporality (in Aristotle, Hegel and Heidegger), see: J. Derrida, *"Ousia* AND *Grammé*: A Note to a Footnote in *Being and Time*," translated by Edward S. Casey, in F.J. Smith (ed.), *Phenomenology in Perspective* (The Hague: Martinus Nijhoff, 1970), pp. 54–93. The French text may be found in: J. Derrida, *Marges de la philosophie* (Paris: Editions de Minuit, 1972). An English translation of *Marges* is in preparation at the Harvard University Press. (Translator's note)

6. See "La différance," in *Marges*, op. cit. An English translation of this essay (by David B. Allison) is included in: J. Derrida, *Speech and Phenomena* (Evanston: Northwestern University Press, 1973). (Translator's note)

7. Derrida has translated and introduced this text, an English translation of which is being prepared by John Leavey for publication by Nicholas Hays Ltd. in 1977. See Edmund Husserl, *L'origine de la géométrie*, tr. Jacques Derrida (Paris: Presses Universitaires de France, 1962). (Translator's note)

8. Nietzsche's phrase is discussed at the conclusion of Derrida's essay on Nietzsche, "Eperons. Les styles de Nietzsche." The French text, as well as translations in English, Italian, and German, may be found in: J. Derrida, *Eperons/Sproni/Spurs/Sporen* (Venice: Corbo e Fiore Editori, 1976). (Translator's note)

9. John R. Searle, *Speech Acts: An Essay in the Philosophy of Language* (London: Cambridge University Press, 1970), p. 55.

10. Ibid., p. 74.

11. *Société à responsabilité limitée* and not, as the French often misinterpret it, *société anonyme à responsabilité limitée*, which would yield, once again, one *a* more or less. As though one would translate S.a.r.l. by Speech Acts *à responsabilité limitée* [i.e. with limited liability]. My friends know that I have composed an entire book with *ça* (the sign of the Saussurian signifier, of Hegel's Absolute Knowing, in French: savior absolu, of Freud's Id [the Ça], the feminine possessive pronoun [sa]). I did not, however, think at the time of the s.a. of speech acts, nor of the problems (formalizable?) of their relation to the signifier, absolute knowing, the Unconscious or even: to the feminine possessive pronoun. If that didn't interest me, perhaps I wouldn't have had enough desire to respond. All of this [*ça*] in order to pose the question: *ça*, is it *used* or *mentioned*?

12. Roman Jakobson, Morris Halle, "Phonology and Phonetics," in Jakobson/Halle, *Fundamentals of Language* (The Hague: Mouton, 1956), p. 117.

13. J. Derrida, *La dissémination* (Paris: Editions du Seuil, 1972), p. 147.

NOTES ON CONTRIBUTORS

ALICIA BORINSKY teaches Spanish American literature at The Johns Hopkins University. She is the author of *La ventrílocua y otras canciones* (poems), *Macedonio y sus otros* (to appear in Buenos Aires), and articles on Spanish American fiction. She is the editor of the correspondence of Macedonio Fernández and is currently working on a book about Spanish American poetry.

JACQUES DERRIDA teaches philosophy at the Ecole Normale Supérieure in Paris. He is best known for his theory and practice of "deconstruction," which he elaborates in such texts as *La voix et le phénomène, De la grammatologie, L'écriture et la différence, La dissémination,* and *Marges.* His more recent work has dealt with writers such as Genet and Hegel (*Glas*), Kant, Maurice Blanchot, and Francis Ponge.

EUGENIO DONATO is Director of the Program of Comparative Literature at the State University of New York at Buffalo. His numerous essays have dealt with critical theory and with French and Italian literatures. He is currently preparing a monograph entitled "The Script of Decadence: Essays on the Fictions of Flaubert."

PHILIPPE LACOUE-LABARTHE and JEAN-LUC NANCY are two of the most distinguished members of the younger generation of philosophers in France. In addition to teaching philosophy at the University of Strasbourg, they are founders and active members of the *Groupe de recherches sur les théories du signe et du texte.* They have collaborated on a work on Jacques Lacan, *Le titre de la lettre*. M. Lacoue-Labarthe has also written on Friedrich Schegel, German Romanticism, Nietzsche, and Heidegger; M. Nancy has written on Kant (*Logodaedalus*), Hegel (*La remarque speculative*), Plato, and Nietzsche.

JEFFREY MEHLMAN is the author of *A Structural Study of Autobiography* and *Revolution and Repetition*. He teaches French at The Johns Hopkins University and is currently completing a book on the contemporaneity of Diderot.

TIMOTHY C. MURRAY is a teaching fellow in comparative literature at The Johns Hopkins University. His essays have appeared in *Renaissance Drama* and *MLN*.

JOHN CARLOS ROWE is assistant professor of English at the University of California, Irvine. The author of *Henry Adams and Henry James: The Emergence of a Modern Consciousness*, he is currently completing a study of nineteenth-century American fiction, *Marginalia: Nineteenth-Century Pretexts for American Modernism*.

MICHAEL RYAN teaches English and comparative literature at the University of Virginia. He is writing a novel with Gayatri Spivak based on life of Antonio Gramsci.